ACID
CONNECTIONS
PART 2

A Novel By

Deanne T. Smith

Deanne T. Smith
FB, IG, Twitter- Deanne T. Smith
deannetsmith@gmail.com
https://www.deannetsmith.com

Cover Designed By: Devon Guillery
Editors: Val Pugh & Charlee Redman

Dedication

Acid Connections 2 is dedicated to my sons, Dylan and Ehsan. Thank you for continuously being my motivation. Thank you for being the ONE reason I will never give up. Thank you for being the driving force behind my striving for success. I love you boys with all my heart and am blessed to be your mom!

Acknowledgements

I would like to express my sincere gratitude to those have continued on this author journey with me. Thank you for your continuous support, believing in me, and your kind words of motivation. I thanked everyone in Book 1, so this time I'm going to keep it short, but remember, dreams do come true, so dare to dream and DREAM BIG!!

I want to thank GOD above all for making this dream become my reality. Only GOD could turn my MESS into a MESSAGE, my TEST into a TESTIMONY, and my TRIAL into a TRIUMPH! God is so super awesome.

NaNa, you are one of a kind. You are the guardian angel that GOD gave me to protect me and always love me. Words will never express my gratitude and appreciation for all that you have done for me. Thank you for your unconditional love. I LOVE YOU!!

Daddy, I used to think that you were hard on me. But today I am grateful for a father like you. You have made me the

1

hard-working go-getter that I am today. I LOVE YOU, DADDY!!

Mommy, thank you for the continuous building and supporting. We can do ALL things through Christ, who strengthens us! I LOVE YOU!!

Sisters: Sydney, Adrianne, Diamond, Raya, and Ashley, THANK YOU for being you and making me be a big sister that you have always held to a standard. I AM MY SISTERS' KEEPER!

Uncle Chris: EVERY child needs someone to believe in them and to hear the words "you can do anything that you can put your mind to." THANK YOU for always being the one who embedded that in me because now I am doing just that.

Gerty, Candy, Bia, Donniece, and Ciarra: Thank yawl for being yawl. God makes no mistakes with those he places in your life. We laugh, live, love, encourage, share, support, and I enjoy every moment. God showed out when he brought yawl in my life.

Tia: You saw this dream at ground zero. Thanks for being my #1 fan and always supporting me, love you, boo!!!

Kimmy: Thank you for knowing how to be a FRIEND. 27 years and I can always count on you to call and say "what do you need, how can I help, and let's get it done!"

Latoya Smith: I love you. You are my cousin but my first friend, and we are bonded for life.

Aisha: Thank you for having ESP and always knowing when I am going through it, because everything is a crisis - and knowing that I need a text or to hear you love me. I love you to the moon and back.

Tonya: Thank you for always being there for me no matter what, no questions asked. 20 years and our friendship hasn't changed a bit - that's a BLESSING

Chanae: Thank you for ALWAYS being there no matter what time the wee hours of the morning I call or text. You are something sweet and special and I love me some you.
Waldina and Tanya: Yawl are everything!! So many days I thought I would quit and give up but yawl voices haunted me. Thank you for being my biggest supporters and believers.

Leon: My brother from another mother, thank you for ALWAYS having my back and being there for your nephews. I am a pain, I know, but you NEVER let me down and I appreciate you more then words can express.

To my **READERS**: I can't thank you enough for all your support. If it wasn't for all the continuous support, my writing would just be a hobby, so I can't thank you enough! I hope you enjoy and are ready for what's to come!

~Chapter 1~

Umma G, Don't Watch Me, Watch TV

It was Christmas evening, and Dhara's house in Montclair, New Jersey was rocking. People were on the first floor spread all throughout the spacious open floor plan. The living room, dining room, and oversized kitchen were filled with family and friends. More people were in the basement with dice and blackjack games going. The second floor was maxed to capacity with children and teenagers listening to music and playing video and board games while the other kids were on their cell phones, on Facebook, on Instagram, and just chillin watching the 72-inch flat screen in the den.

Abdora and his immediate circle were on the first floor in the kitchen. They had the giant space to themselves. Some were playing bid whist for $50 a hand and talking shit. Others were stuffing their faces with a variety of food, while the niggaz to the left of them were watching the football game and blowing down the best weed in Jersey.

"Y'all should've seen this nigga in da Bean a few weeks ago. He was soft as pie," Bryce said with a look that made his words seem funnier than they were.

"Oh nigga, you got jokes?" Dora asked.

He was the only nigga who could get away with jokes.

"Yeah, nigga, I got jokes. Babygirl had you damn near singing 'I'm Sprung,'" Bryce laughed.

Everyone else started laughing, too.

"Oh, so y'all just going to sit in my momma's house and laugh at me, huh?" Dora asked with a slight chuckle that let everyone know that he really wasn't finding anything funny. "I'm a gangster, my nigga, so don't disrespect me. It ain't in me to be soft."

"Let me find out you're in denial," Bryce said, cracking up in tears.

Everyone knew Dora had it bad for Tavares, including Abdora himself. With all the time that he'd been spending with Tavares, it wasn't hard to tell that he was into her hardbody. Everyone was laughing but Abdora. He pulled out his chrome .38, and niggaz stopped laughing real fast - everyone except Bryce, of course.

"Why we gotta bring guns and shit into this?" Bryce asked, still laughing so hard that he was in tears.

Abdora couldn't even be mad at his best friend for pulling his card about being open for shorty. He just didn't like other niggaz thinking they could laugh about it, because they couldn't. Abdora's cell phone interrupted the laughter. *Speaking of the devil,* he thought.

"Merry Christmas, Beautiful," Dora answered.

"Merry Christmas," Tavares said, sounding like there was nothing merry about her Christmas.

"Damn, where's the cheer and Christmas spirit, Miss Bubbly? Why you sound all sad and shit?" Abdora asked, concerned.

Tavares was always happy and bubbly, so he knew something was wrong. Dora could feel all eyes on him as his niggaz carried on doing what they had been doing before Bryce put him on blast.

"I just had a very long day, not so great day."

"What happened? It's Christmas, so how bad could your day have been?"

5

Tavares just laughed, and replied, "If you only knew. It's a long story that I don't want to talk about, at least not right now. My day is about to turn around, so I don't even want to ruin it and get mad all over again. I'm on my way to the airport to catch a flight."

"You're on the way to see me," Abdora joked like that was what she had really said.

"No, I'm not," Tavares laughed. "But nice try, though. I really must give it to you. You caught me off guard with that one. You just be too fucking forreal for me."

Tavares was happy to crack a smile for the first time all day.

"So, if you're not going to the airport to come see me, then where you going?"

"Good question. I have no clue. Just need to get away, so I'm about to get on a flight and go somewhere to get some me time in. I need a vacation like yesterday," Tavares sighed.

"Damn, Ma. What's wrong?" Abdora asked because he could hear the pain in her voice. "If something got you feeling like that, then I need a vacation, too. Let's do the damn thing."

Abdora had all eyes on him like he was plotting a murder or something.

"Where we going?" Dora asked.

"*We?*" Tavares said, stressing the word hard. "I didn't say WE were going anywhere."

Tavares laughed because he never failed with trying to get his way.

"I said I was going away for some me time. Not some *we* or *me and you* time. I said *me time,*" Tavares emphasized, trying to help him comprehend. "I was just calling to tell you,

6

because I'm turning my phone off for the next week, and I didn't want you to be worried. Next week, I have to meet the girls in Atlanta for Leslie's birthday, so I may turn it back on then. But, for now, I need some serious down time for the next week."

"Ok, so where are WE going for some down time? I want to turn my phone off for a whole week straight, too. I can let these extra nosey ass niggaz staring me in my face hold shit down."

"Dora, how did you get *we* out of *me*?"

"You didn't have to say *we* or some *you and me* time, because I said it," Abdora said, checking Tavares.

"Ok, who heard that?" Tavares asked, hearing him loud and clear and recognizing that she'd just been checked. "You kill me with the bully power, always trying to tell people what to do. Since you feel the need to bully yourself on my trip, I'm going to just catch a flight there. Then, tomorrow morning, we can get up and catch a flight some place."

"See, now we're on the same page. Now you're with the program. A few minutes ago you were acting like you needed Hooked on Phonics or some shit," Dora said.

"Go to hell," Tavares said as she laughed at his smart mouth.

"Say what you want, but before you board your flight, call me. I don't want you at the airport waiting, so that'll give me time to get there."

"I know y'all have a house full of people, so I'll just grab a taxi at the airport. Leave your truck unlocked so I can put my suitcases in it. I'll see you in a few hours," Tavares said.

When Abdora hung up, everyone set into him.

7

"Where are you going?"

"You're taking a vacation?"

"Who was that? Boston?"

The only one who didn't say or ask anything was Bryce because he knew already.

"Damn, you niggaz are nosey as some old gossiping ass grandmothers. Don't watch me. Watch TV," Dora said, popping his collar.

Two and a half hours later, Tavares pulled up to Abdora's mother's house to see no available parking. There were cars in the long driveway, on the sidewalk, in front of the house, and all the way down the block on both sides. Dhara's house was packed. Tavares walked in and felt like she was experiencing déjà vu. It felt like what Doll's house would have been like on Christmas. It was just a different house and different people. *This is real crazy,* Tavares thought to herself. The house was packed and people were everywhere having a good time. Weed was in the air. Kids were running happily back and forth. The scent of food lingered in the air from the various plates people had. Tavares felt right at home.

Tavares went to say hello to Miss Dhara. Dhara's eyes lit up as she hopped off her chair. Tavares had been to Miss Dhara's house every time she'd come to visit Dora. They were cool in the game with each other. Tavares loved Miss Dhara because she was so pretty, smart, and hood all in one. It was hard to believe that she'd come from being a homeless crackhead to a successful businesswoman. Tavares loved that Dora's mother was so real. Everything about her was real, and she gave it to you straight-laced with no chaser. She was always spitting knowledge on life, men, the game, the streets, God, struggles of addiction, historical facts, and anything else that you could think of. She was a wise woman without a doubt. That's why you had to love her.

Dhara had slung dope, run hoes, numbers, and anything else that got dough in her day. In her prime, she dated only drug cartels, no low-level drug dealers for her. Dhara had shot, stabbed, and beat both men and women senseless in her wild days. Now she was a Christian woman who had been clean for fourteen years with the exception of weed. Dora definitely got his gangster from his mother no matter how saved she was now.

"Miss Thing, what are you doing here? My son didn't tell me that you were coming. Luckily, I got a present for you under the tree, so I'm glad you made it."

"Yeah, me too," Tavares said, feeling the love in the air. "I got a present for you, too. Your son put it upstairs in your room. It's a very private gift," Tavares laughed, thinking about the vibrator that she'd gotten Miss Dhara.

Dhara was a born freak and still was a freak in her older age. She was reserved but not hidden about it. One of the weekends Tavares had visited, she and Abdora attended a toy party at her house. It was a party for real. People were everywhere drinking, eating, and watching the toys being presented. The lady hired to do the party was fun and raunchy with it, so the older ladies were on the edge of their seats. The men were just sitting around waiting to catch them one slippin. Tavares was in pure laughter watching the old ass freaks. The funny thing was that everyone at the party, with the exception of Dora, Tavares, and Dora's friends, was over the age of forty. Dhara was off the chain.

"Oh shoot, my fault," she said to her company. "Everyone, this is Tavares, hopefully my soon-to-be daughter-in-law," Dhara announced to everyone in her dining room.

"Yeah, she got my nephew running around all love-sick," Dora's Aunt Red joked.

"Ms. Red, I keep telling you that's not the case, so you better stop saying that," Tavares said, blushing.

"Girl, please. Red don't tell no lies," Dhara said, sticking up for her sister.

Tavares was ok in Dhara's book, because she brought a smile and a look to her son's face that she'd never seen before.

"Miss D, I can't believe you be doing it way big like this."

"Like what?"

"You got all these people over here like it's a huge party for real."

"Yeah, girl. I gots to. I have to enjoy this big ole house, so you go enjoy yourself. Go in there and get you some food. I'll see you before you go."

Tavares said her goodbyes to the dining room full of ladies, and found her way to the kitchen where Abdora and his friends definitely had it on lock down. Tavares walked in and said *Merry Christmas*, and all eyes were on her. Everyone greeted her with *What's up* and *Merry Christmas*. The fellas and their girlfriends were sizing her up because Dora had fallen for the Boston native hard. Tavares could feel them on her indirectly, but she didn't care. She was used to all eyes being on her.

"Come with me," Dora said, grabbing Tavares by the waist.

"Where we going?"

"I told you that you ask too many questions. Sometimes you should just do as you're told," Dora said, screwing his face up at the only person who ever put up a question with him.

"Damn, I can't ask where we going? Fine, lead the way with your bully ass," Tavares said, rolling her eyes.

Everyone watched Dora and Tavares make their exit without saying anything else. Tavares followed Dora up the tall spiral staircase into a bedroom. Once they were inside, Dora closed the door behind Tavares.

"So what's up, punk?" Tavares asked with her hands on her waist and her head slightly tilted in a seductive manner.

"Nah, don't try to play nice wit a nigga now. You didn't even want to come with me. I just wanted to give your punk ass your Christmas gifts."

Dora went into the top drawer of the tall blue marble dresser and came out with two small boxes wrapped in pretty, shiny cherry-red wrapping paper.

"Ooooh, they're little! You know what that means," Tavares joked as she jingled the boxes and her big blue eyes bulged out of her face.

Tavares took the wrapping paper off both boxes. When she opened the bigger of the jewelry boxes, she found a thick, heavy diamond-encrusted gold chain that had a long diamond-encrusted key on it. The second box contained a beautiful charm bracelet that had diamonds all the way around it and on the links of the charms. Huge charms swung from the bracelet. There was a heart, a shoe, a T, a purse, a sun, a moon, a scroll, a diamond ring, and an eternity symbol. Each charm was made of nothing but diamonds, making the bracelet sparkle a little too much. Tavares looked from the jewelry to Dora and from Dora to the jewelry. After doing that three times, Tavares came back to reality.

"Yo, I can NOT accept these. Don't get it fucked up, I want to. Really I want to, but I can't. You had to jack a small fortune on them, and I just can't do it."

"Yo, Tav, I told you it ain't tricking if you got it. I don't buy anything I can't afford. Plus, I had that bracelet and chain made especially for you. They weren't picked up out a bootleg jewelry exchange type store. My jeweler custom-made them. So, throw your shit on and rock it with pride. I don't like you rocking that ring, but Im'ma let you do you for now. Just know when I come, I'm coming correct, so you can keep that one for now."

"Dora, I can't walk around with this jewelry on. Someone will take my goddamn neck off for that chain and key and my wrist off for this iced out bracelet."

"I wish a nigga might fucking wish to," Dora said, dismissing her foolish thoughts.

"Dora, I didn't spend $30,000 like I'm willing to bet you did, but I did get you some presents," Tavares said, feeling bad.

Had Dora gone to the store he might have spent that, but his jeweler was good to him as always. He'd only spent $21,000 on both pieces.

"Ma, I don't care what you got me. I'd be happy if you gave me some socks."

Tavares laughed, because if he meant that shit, that was some real sweet shit.

"Damn, I didn't do you that cold."

"Well, what did you get me?"

"Dang, I ain't going to tell you. That takes the fun out of it."

"Fun out of what? I ain't no fucking kid. Christmas is for the kids and for all the greedy money-hungry whores thinking a nigga owe them something."

"Damn, that's how you feel about Christmas, you goddamn scrooge?"

"Yeah, because we never had shit for Christmas growing up. It was only once I started making Christmas happen that it became a big tradition. So, when you're the one doing all the spending, you ain't too pressed about Christmas. So now, what did you get me?"

"Nope, not telling you, you big ass scrooge. If you want to know, go downstairs to your truck and get the larger of the two suitcases."

"Damn, you got a suitcase full of shit?" Dora said, surprised.

"Yeah, I wasn't supposed to, but the more that I was shopping, I just kept picking shit up. So, you go get the suitcase and Im'ma make my way to the kitchen to get a shot."

Ten minutes later, Tavares returned with a double shot of chilled Patrón Silver and Dora had made his way upstairs with the large LV suitcase.

"What the fuck you got in here, a fucking body? If so, that ain't a Christmas present," Abdora laughed.

"No, smart ass. Open it and find out."

13

"Well the wrapping paper is sure pretty," Dora joked, referring to the silver paper with huge pink polka dots.

"I love pink, and my tree at home is pink and white, so shut up."

Tavares got comfortable and took a seat on the bed as she watched Abdora open present after present, not even realizing that he was smiling like a big ass kid. By the time Abdora unwrapped thirty days' worth of new socks, tees, and boxers, all of which were Polo, he was like very satisfied. He moved on and unwrapped two pairs each of wheat and black Timberlands, Dolce & Gabbana shades, a red plush robe that had "The King" monogrammed on the back with matching slippers, and a charcoal gray pea coat.

Abdora couldn't stop smiling from ear to ear when he got to the last of his presents. After smelling the Happy for Men, Issey Miyake, Burberry Touch, and Versace Dreamer, he was definitely about to make her a keeper. Not because of what she bought, but because of the thought she put into each gift. Dora was totally happy and didn't even know how to express it.

"Yo, you bought me shit like a woman who knows how to shop for her man. Let me find out," Dora laughed lightly, impressed at how well the gifts suited him. "You knew what to buy like you know me and shit. I would have truly went in the store and picked out the same shit for myself. How did you do that without asking my sizes?"

"Awww, get off me. I got my ways," Tavares laughed.

Shopping for him wasn't hard and Tavares didn't even realize that she'd actually grown to know Abdora and his style so well.

After exchanging thank yous and conversation for another half hour, Tavares said, "We been gone long enough. Let's get back. I don't want people thinking I'm up here taking advantage of you," she said, poking Dora in his chest.

"Girl, please. They ain't worried about us. You know you wanna take advantage of a nigga. It's ok because if I was you, I would want to take advantage of me, too," Dora said, laughing before he could even get the last word fully out.

As they made their way back downstairs to mingle, Tavares was happy that she'd actually gotten on the plane and did what her heart was telling her, because her mind was saying to stay with Dame's trifling ass in Boston. By the time Tavares and Dora returned to the kitchen, all eyes were on them.

"Goddamn, is everyone gonna keep looking at them all crazy and whatnot?" Bella asked with her outspoken self.

Bella was Maniac's girlfriend. Tavares didn't know Bella but was digging her style and her outspokenness.

"Shut up," Maniac said.

Bella just sucked her teeth because she didn't understand why everyone was making such a big deal about Abdora and his lady friend. The fellas were in awe that he was feeling her so hard, and the other girlfriends were slightly hating on her. Tavares could feel all the other girlfriend's looking at her like they had no intention of letting her into their inner circle, but what they didn't know was that Tavares didn't give a fuck.

All activities in the kitchen resumed. Bella had removed herself from the other ladies and was talking to Tavares to make her more comfortable. Bella was 5'9" and all legs. She had a nice thickness to her height. She had smooth, toffee-colored skin and she was wearing bold, bright makeup. Her funky sense of style and short haircut let it be known that she marched to her own beat, and Tavares could dig that. Tavares and Bella were kickin' it about Bella's over the top wedding that she was planning.

"Girl, we have a wedding party of fifty and a guest list of two hundred-fifty and not my doing. Maniac gave me a budget of 300k and said make it memorable."

"Damnnnn," Tavares said. "Y'all are doing it way big."

"Don't worry, I'm sure you'll be Abdora's date," Bella said, winking her eye.

Abdora was gambling and saw that all the chicks were smoking but not swinging his shorty a blunt. He didn't get mad or say nothing, he simply said *Babygirl*, and when Tavares turned around, he threw her a seven of some blueberry haze and some cigarillos. Tavares winked her eye because she caught the cold shoulder the other chicks were giving her, and now they could kick rocks. After rolling four blunts, Tavares smoked two with Bella and excused herself outside for some fresh air.

Bella said, "You mind if I join you?"

"Not at all," Tavares said, and together they made their way outside to the back porch.

Tavares lit the third blunt and was enjoying the fresh air and the quiet after the long day she had.

"So tell me. What's up with you and Dora?" Bella asked.

Tavares laughed because she loved the boldness and the lack of beating around the bush.

"Dora and I are friends even though it seems like a whole lot more."

16

"Hmmm, is that right?" Bella asked, only half buying it.

"Yeah, that's right, Miss Bella. Maybe in the near future we'll be more, but as of this moment, we're just friends. Dora's my dude, though. That I can't deny. I got a soft spot for him."

"You and every other woman, so you better pay attention and act like you know. Why you think all them other huzzies are in there hating on you?" Bella laughed. "Either one of them, or one of their girls were digging him. He wasn't beat, so they got stuck with one of his boys. Dora's a hot and rare commodity, so I don't suggest you let him pass you by."

"I hear you, Bella, but it's a lot more complicated than that."

"Well, how complicated can it be? You're a beautiful girl with a real catch of a man after you."

"I'll save the crazy story for another time," Tavares chuckled before inquiring, "So you weren't a Dora fan?"

"Nope, never! Dora and I have been tight since elementary school, and he introduced me to Maniac in high school. That's the love of my life, the king of my castle, and the only man for me! We just got engaged," Bella said, proudly extending her ring to show off her flawless five-carat princess cut pink diamond.

"That's what's up," Tavares said.

They chatted for another half hour before Dora appeared looking for them.

"Bella Mafia," as Dora had nicknamed Bella, "you better not be out here telling my shorty no bullshit about me."

17

"Oh, nigga please. I ain't telling her nothing that she don't already know," Bella laughed. "I told her how much of a dog and womanizer you are. I told her you're cheap and to run for the hills."

"Bull motherfucking shit. You know goddamn well I ain't none of that."

"I know," Bella laughed.

"Actually, Bella was telling me how much of a great catch you are, so you better thank her for putting in a good word for you."

"Babygirl, I ain't gotta thank Bella because her long-legged ass is like the sister I never wanted, so she just did what she was supposed to."

The trio kicked the shit and blew the last blunt before returning to the kitchen.

Eating, gambling, talking, and partying the night away actually lifted Tavares's Christmas spirits. It was 2:00 a.m. by the time everyone started to clean up and head out. Tavares and Dora were the last to leave at 2:45 a.m. They were kicking it as they cruised the highway, but Tavares had a question that had been in the back of her mind since early that morning.

"Dora, I need to ask you a question," Tavares said with a serious but hesitant tone.

"Anything, what's up, Babygirl?" Tavares didn't want to beat around the bush.

"I know what transpired with Damien and your boy, and he got shot today. Did you have anything to do with Damien getting shot?"

Abdora knew this question would eventually be coming after he approved the hit.

Dora looked Tavares straight in the eyes and said, "I told you I wasn't going to touch son or get at him."

He knew who had popped Damien, and it wasn't his orchestrating, although he did give the ok. However, he wasn't going to tell Tavares that. Furthermore, Dora couldn't have cared less if Damien lived or died.

Rather than express his true feelings, he just said nonchalantly, "Ma, you do dirt, you get dirt."

What he really wanted to tell her was that Damien was a no good, grimy bitchass nigga who deserved what he got.

Tavares didn't know if she believed Dora. She wanted to, and he was real convincing, but after Damien had shot his friend, she couldn't think of who else would have shot him. Damien had enemies, but it was way too coincidental to think that he'd gotten shot right after Dora's boy did. Tavares couldn't prove it, but she felt like Dora knew more than he was letting on.

"Abdora, so you're going to sit here and look me in the face and tell me that you honestly had nothing to do with Damien getting shot?"

"That's exactly what I'm going to tell you. Right now you're angry and looking for someone to blame, but momma, I am not the person."

Dora felt bad lying to Tavares for the first time, but some things he just couldn't tell her, and this was one of those things. Of course she didn't blame him and knew that he was right karma, but it didn't feel right if she was fucking with the nigga who shot or had Damien shot. Tavares let it go and lay back to enjoy the ride.

She dozed off for a quick second but awoke in New York. She knew where she was just by the sound of the city.

19

New York always sounded and felt like it was moving fast to Tavares. She looked around to see that they were stopped in front of a tall skyscraper building that looked across the Hudson River in New Jersey.

"Where are we?" Tavares asked, half-awake, because it wasn't one of the fancy hotels they usually stayed at.

"We're at my house."

"Your house? I didn't even know you had a house."

"Yeah, this is where I rest my head, call home, and come when it's all said and done," Dora said like it was no big deal.

"Hmmm... and I'm just now coming here?" Tavares said, fully awake now and feeling some kind of way. "All the times I've come to visit, we've stayed in hotels. I'm not really feeling the funny shit," Tavares said with a half of an attitude. "I wasn't good enough to come to your house or something?" Tavares questioned.

"Listen momma, it's nothing personal. I don't bring no one here. No one. To be honest, you're the first past Bryce, my mother, and brother to come here. So, you need to shut up and feel special," Abdora said, playfully poking Tavares's forehead.

"I feel special alright," Tavares said sarcastically, not caring that she was the only woman to ever step foot in his house in the whole five years he lived there.

When they finally made it to the fiftieth floor and entered Abdora's duplex condo, Tavares knew why he stayed in such elaborate hotel rooms. Abdora showed Tavares around, and she was awed by each room that had a different color scheme. The red room was sexy. He replaced the panel in the ceiling with stained red glass to make the room have a red tint. There was a movie screen-sized TV built inside the wall. An aquarium-sized fish tank was built in on the other wall. In front of the tall oversized window was a bar that had any and every drink that you could think of. There was a huge red sectional that consumed quite a bit of the interior.

The white room was the showroom. It wasn't to be touched or sat in. It was furnished with all white. There was a leather sofa, couch, and chair, with white marble coffee and end tables. There was a beautiful white chandelier draped in the center. On the back wall of the white room were beautiful white antique vases with fresh sunflowers in them. The plush white carpet made you want to sink your feet into what looked soft as cotton. The green room had large money-green walls. It was Dora's smoke room. Dora maxed out in his green room and blew it down. It was the only room in his house that he smoked in. He kept smoke supplied in round bowls with a cover to keep it fresh on each end table and the coffee table. There was a huge stereo system with eight speakers and a drop-down flat screen TV. The black and white checkered-themed kitchen had red appliances everywhere. The black and white marble table with tall red leather chairs was hot and set the kitchen off.

"So what woman decorated your house, because I know you didn't do all this on your own?"

"Well, I guess you know wrong then. Ain't no bitch pick out a goddamn thing in here. I picked out and paid for everything."

"So your mouth says," Tavares said, getting the last word before moving the conversation on. "So where would you like to go?"

"I don't know, Ma. It don't matter because wherever we go, I'm going to have a good time."

Tavares and Dora grabbed some shot glasses to go with the bottle of silver Patrón in Dora's hands. While making their way upstairs to the bedroom, they talked and laughed about how Tavares ended up in Jersey on Christmas after she said nothing would get her there.

"Tavares, I don't know..."

"What's up, homeboy?"

"It's not in me to belittle the next man, but I want you to do what you said about some soul-searching. You can have all the time you need to yourself on this trip, because I want you to really dig deep."

Tavares could tell that he was serious and not trying to be an asshole.

"I know, Dora. My shit is fucked up. Trust me, I know. I just need a long hot shower, because today has been way too long for me."

"Yeah, you do that. I'll go refill our shot glasses."

Tavares made her way to the shower and when she got out she could hear Abdora talking, so she left the water running. Tavares listened to Abdora talk to someone about business. She turned the water off as she heard the conversation wrap up.

When she exited the bathroom, Tavares asked, "Who were you talking to?"

"I was talking to my secretary Talia. She's booking the flights and the hotel arrangements. Im'ma go take a shower and get right. Make yourself comfortable," Dora said as he slid into his new robe and headed toward the shower.

Tavares called her friends and woke them up. They had all clicked each other in on three-way. Tavares informed them that she was going away with Dora, and she got different reactions from everyone.

Mona-Lisa said, "Tavares, no matter what you do, you better be there for Leslie's birthday."

Jazz asked, "Well, what about Dame? Are you really going to go away with that nigga lying up in the hospital? You're buggin'."

"Excuse me, Jazz? I'm buggin'? No, he's buggin'. I've never turned on him, and after the last two weeks alone, he doesn't deserve to have me by his by bed. If it's that heartbreaking to you, how about you go sit next to his fucking bedside."

"I heard that, Boo," Randee said, rooting for Tavares.

Leslie said, "Can I just go wherever you and the community boyfriend are going?"

"I wish, boo. That would have been the best birthday ever," Tavares said.

After saying *I love you*, Tavares and her friends hung up with plans to meet in six days.

"Damn, it's 6:30," Abdora said, looking at the clock by his bedside. "We might as well go down to the green room, twist up a few blunts, and watch a movie for about an hour. Our flight is at 10:45 a.m. I packed and showered while you and your girls were on the horn, so all we have to do is head to the airport."

"Sounds like a plan to me," Tavares said, heading downstairs to the green room that definitely smelled like *green.*

23

Tavares and Dora watched a movie, snuggled up, and blew two blunts before they got up from the comfortable position they were lying in.

~Chapter 2~
A Drunk Mind Speaks a Sober Tongue

By 8:30 a.m., Tavares and Dora were at JFK Airport ready to board their flight to peace for the next five days. They stepped off the plane in Cancún, Mexico, happy to feel the heat. When they exited through customs and got their luggage, they were bombarded with tourist booths and reps. Reps were in their faces with tour packages trying to convince them that they had the better deal.

"Ma, let's get to the hotel first. We can do this at the hotel, trust me."

"Alright," Tavares said, not caring one way or another.

They flagged down a way too cool ass Mexican cab driver. Louie was short with olive-colored skin and a short dark crew cut. He had on some snug jean shorts with a white t-shirt and an orange Hawaiian print vest over it. He thought he was fresh with tall black socks and white high-top converse sneakers with his dollar store sunglasses on.

The conversation started with, "Hola, mamacita. Tu es muy bonita. Tu esposo?"

"No mi amigo."

The next thing Dora knew, they were holding a full conversation in Spanish.

"Hmmm ok ok. So what y'all like to do? I from here and know everything."

Abdora was looking confused. *This girl can speak fluent Spanish,* he thought to himself, awed.

"Check you out, ma."

Tavares didn't like Spanish. It was the one thing her mother made her learn as a kid, and there was no reason when they lived like Americans. It came second nature because Tavares starting speaking it as a baby and carried all the way through school.

"What did he just say?" Abdora asked.

"He said he got whatever we need, and he does mean *whatever*. Coke, weed, crack, whatever you need he can get it," Tavares said, laughing at the cab driver who was doubling as a pusher.

"Damn, Louie. That's how you doing it, my nigga? Well leave me your card, and I'll holler at you."

"I don't got no card, Papa, but you call me. I got one of them cell phones. So just call me from the hotel. I take you and mami where you need to go. Just call me."

Tavares and Abdora arrived at the hotel and checked into the Omni Parker House.

"Damn, this is nice," Tavares said as she stood on the terrace area and looked at their private deck that overlooked the ocean and the beach. There was a Jacuzzi that could fit ten people and an Olympic-sized swimming pool. The water was glistening beautifully under the warm sun.

"I have no bathing suit," Tavares said, looking at Abdora as if there was no chance of them getting in any water together.

"Oh no, you ain't slick. You're getting a bathing suit. How are you even going to be saying you hopping on a plane for a vacation and you don't have a bathing suit? That's crazy. So, before you get comfortable here's $500. Go get you some bathing suits, and I'll be here waiting when you get back."

Tavares didn't know if she should be offended or grateful, but she took the money.

"Damn, I'm not sure if I like your smart ass mouth."

"You don't have to like it, Ma. You just have to respect it," Abdora said, joking but meaning it.

Tavares went shopping. Abdora was gone when she came back. She wondered where he could have gone. She decided to take a shower and get ready to head out for whatever they were going to do for the evening. Tavares had just finished getting dressed when Abdora walked in excited with a thick book of packets.

"Where have you been?" she asked, rolling her eyes.

"I was downstairs. And, is something wrong with your eyes?"

"No, there isn't anything wrong with my eyes," Tavares said, rolling her eyes again.

"I was downstairs booking our activities for the next five days, 'Ms. My Eyes are Fine rolling in my head.' You know those activities that they were talking about at the airport. So how about you calm your ass down."

Looking at everything he had planned, Tavares felt bad. Their next five days were going to be activity-filled and spent in or by the water for Tavares to catch some airtime in her new two-piece bathing suits. They called Louie to find out where they should have dinner. When they arrived at the outdoor restaurant, Tavares and Abdora enjoyed the scenery of the busy crowded streets that were filled with hustling natives and tourists. The strip was full of hotels, clubs, restaurants, and bars. They were amazed at the difference of the freshly made tortilla chips versus the tortilla chips in the bag.

"This is what you call real salsa," Tavares said, tasting the true blend of onions, peppers, and tomatoes.

27

"I could make a killing on these chips," Abdora said, filling his mouth with them.

They enjoyed the sunset and the luxury of free margaritas while stuffing themselves on the best red snapper fish in the world with a side of Spanish rice and vegetables. Free drinks was one of the many offers at the restaurants as a marketing tool to attract customers. Tavares and Abdora spent the evening bar-hopping. Every bar had a bottomless drink special for a flat fee. They decided to chill at the XXX outside bar that faced the street. They were drinking, relaxing, and enjoying the moment.

"Yo, what is that lady selling?" Tavares asked as she looked at the little Mexican running around the bar selling shots.

The lady was wearing a beret-style hat on her head and a whistle around her neck. She was charging $3.00 American money for each shot, and she was kissing the person and blowing the whistle after they took the shot she sold to them. It wasn't clear if people were paying for the shot or the kiss.

"She has a lot going on," Tavares said. "She's way too excited about her job."

Together they laughed and drank till the wee hours before stumbling back to the hotel. Tavares hadn't expected the night to end the way it did, but she wasn't complaining one bit.

She woke up the next morning to the strong sunshine, the birds chirping, and an empty spot next to her. She wanted to go back to sleep, but she knew she was up for the day. She got out of bed and put a robe over her nude body before she went to the bathroom to wash her face and brush her teeth. Feeling so fresh and so clean, Tavares walked through the suite looking for Abdora. He was nowhere to be found. She stepped outside on the deck where Abdora was eating breakfast poolside. Tavares sat down to mounds of food.

"What did you do, order the whole menu? I'm not a big girl all like this. I got some meat to me, but goddamn."

"You was sleeping and just looked too good for me to wake you. So I just ordered a little bit of everything. I figured you would wake up sooner or later and would be starving after the night we had. At least I hoped you were," Abdora said, chuckling, causing his dimples in each cheek to jump out. "And stop always talking shit. Ain't no one call you a big girl or tell you to eat everything. Just eat and go get dressed. Wear sneakers today, too."

"Yes sir," Tavares said sarcastically as she piled her plate with grapes, strawberries, eggs, and toast.

After breakfast, they got dressed and looked like twins unintentionally. Abdora had on a red Jordan sweatsuit with a black tee and some red and black 11s. Tavares had on some cute red form-fitting Banana Republic shorts that hugged her butt perfectly with the matching white tee shirt with Banana Republic in red and some red and gray Airmax 95s.

"Can you tell me how we always tend to go in different rooms and come out in the same shit?" Abdora asked as he looked Tavares up and down in disbelief.

"Tell me about it," Tavares said, playfully rolling her eyes. "I want you to stay out of my luggage," Tavares said, eyeing Dora up and down like they had beef. "How are we looking like a corny couple and we aren't even a couple?"

29

"Not yet, and I'm too gangster to ever look corny, so watch your mouth."

"Where are we going?" Tavares asked as they headed out the door.

"Don't worry about it. Just follow my lead, Little Momma."

Tavares and Abdora boarded a huge tour bus and rode for forty-five minutes before they pulled into a ranch in the middle of nowhere. They stepped off the bus near a bar area with picnic tables. The area to the left was roped off with fifty chairs lined up in the dirt. Tour guides were directing people to the chairs of their activity for either horseback riding or ATV riding so they could be given instructions.

"So, what are we doing?" Tavares asked, curious to see what Dora had chosen for them.

"Both," Abdora said, smiling at Tavares, knowing she wasn't expecting that to be the answer.

"We're riding ATVs first, and then we'll get all lovey dovey and ride the horses."

Tavares suited up in a helmet and learned how to operate a four-wheeler. The group that had five other people set out on their ATV course. They ripped through the paths, the bushes, the dirt roads, and over large sand banks. Tavares was having a ball till she lost control, went off the road, and flipped over head first. *Oh fuck!* was all that could be heard as the ATV flipped over on Tavares. Everyone rushed to Tavares, who was ok but more embarrassed.

"I'm ok," Tavares said, getting up with a deep cut on her ankle that truly was shaped like a weed plant from the bushes.

Other than that and being a little embarrassed, Tavares was truly ok.

"You're ok, Babygirl. Get up and dust that shit off and get your ass back on."

Tavares did what she was told and ended up having a great time. Tavares and Abdora ended the ATV course, went back to where they got off the bus, and ate the dinner that came as a part of the package. After dinner, they set out on two horses with a guide leading them on a third horse. They walked the trails and the same sands they'd just gone over with the ATVs, and it was a really different feeling. Instead of a rush of adrenalin, they were smiling, laughing, and blushing as they strolled under the sunset. It was the most romantic moment Tavares had ever experienced. *Damn, six years with Dame and Dora just topped him in six months.*

"Are you having a good time?" Abdora asked like he was reading her mind.

"Definitely am. I couldn't be having a better time."

"I'm glad, because I like seeing you smile and those big bright eyes lighting up."

The guide led the horses into the water where they got soaking wet and didn't even care because they were in the beautiful water on horses under the sunset. They splashed each other and laughed till they were soaking wet.

"See what you done did?" Tavares whined.

"Yeah, I know," Dora said. "Blame it on me that you look like you were in a wet tee shirt contest."

After getting off the horses and playing in the water for a little while, they saddled back up and headed back. So happy to be back on the bus headed to the hotel, Tavares and Abdora curled up together and drifted off to sleep. They arrived back at the hotel, made their way to their villa, and stripped immediately out of their wet clothes. Looking at Tavares made Abdora's manhood stand straight up in the air. Tavares couldn't help but laugh.

"Oh my God. I want him to not be doing that, just popping his whole ten inches out there."

"He didn't do it. You did it. I gotta take a shower," Abdora said, upset that he wasn't about to take his manhood down the way he wanted.

He went into the bathroom, climbed into the shower, and stroked his manhood as he thought about Tavares naked. After ten minutes and a bit of satisfaction, Abdora took a long hot shower.

Things were hot as fire in Boston. It was shooting after shooting once Damien got shot. Damien felt fucked up that the streets were a blazing fire, but what could he do as he lay in a hospital bed and listened to people call him day after day to tell him of all the people who'd been shot.

Damien had laid in his hospital bed calling and calling Tavares but he was unsuccessful and getting angrier with each call. He needed someone to talk to, so he called his mother, who had gone home to shower and change her clothes. Damien dialed her number and knew he wasn't going to like what his mother had to say, but he called her anyway. Doll saw Boston Medical Center come across her caller I.D. and answered in a hurry, thinking that something may be wrong with her son.

"What you doing?" Damien asked with a saddened tone.

"I just got dressed. Is everything ok?"

"Yeah, everything's fine. I just wanted to talk to you."

"Boy, you scared me because I was just there and then saw the hospital number."

"Naw, I was just lying here thinking about Tavares and decided to call you."

"Have you spoken to her?" Doll asked sadly, knowing the answer to her own question.

"Naw. I been calling her, but her phone's off. Ma, I think me and Tavares are really over this time."

"Well, Damien, how long did you think that you could mistreat that girl before she'd walk out on you?"

"Ma, I know I did her wrong, but I really don't think I thought Tavares would really pack up and leave. Now she's gone."

"Well boo, you gotta pray on it and leave it in God's hands. That girl loved you more than she loved herself at times and you took advantage of her and her love. I can't lie to you and tell you that she's coming back because I don't know and doubt it."

"Ma, I love her and I just want her back."

"Well, baby, pray on it. Mommy's going to finish getting dressed. I'll be back there in an hour, and we can finish this conversation."

Damien said ok and hung up knowing that his mother was right. He put the phone back on the cradle and tried to figure out what he was going to do to get his girl back. For six years Tavares had Damien's back through thick and thin. She tolerated his bullshit, lying, cheating, and being in the streets. She took care of house and home, and she hustled as hard as he did in the streets while balancing being a college student. She catered to his every need and want, and

33

Damien repaid her with expensive gifts, nice cars, a beautiful home, and taking her for granted. Damien himself wasn't sure he had a chance, now that Tavares had finally opened her eyes to recognize her worth.

Tavares exited the cab, looked at the sign that read Fat Tuesdays, and asked, "Are you sure the boat is leaving from here?"

"Yo, this is the address, so it gotta be it. Let's just go inside."

There were multiple rooms with different genres of music. The waitresses were wearing skimpy outfits and selling Jell-O shots and shooters. Cooling steam was blowing on the pub tables and booths. For people who were standing up, there were tables next to the windows that overlooked the water. In each section of the club was a different bar that sold the same twenty different flavors of frozen drinks. Each drink contained different liquors and grain alcohol. They also sold regular alcohol and mixed drinks. A kitchen with a long list of American and Mexican dishes was deep in the corner.

"Hmm, that sounds good," Tavares said, reading the menu.

"Damn, for someone who ain't a big girl, you're always looking at a food menu."

"Whatever, yo," Tavares laughed, knowing that she'd set herself up for that one. "I was just looking at what they have."

"The boat leaves from outside," Abdora said.

They saw another bar outside with a huge courtyard deck over the water. People were everywhere with frozen drinks. Abdora and Tavares both got a drink while they waited for the boat to leave the pier behind Fat Tuesdays.

As they were walking down toward the boat, they saw a row of women who each had a small child under five standing in front of them. They all looked poor, dirty, and hungry. Tavares's heart broke for the women using their children as a means to get money from the tourists. Abdora, who was soft when it came to children, dropped a $50 bill in each child's bucket that they were holding. Tavares just shook her head and said nothing.

When they boarded the boat, they were welcomed to the Booze Cruise, where they'd party on the boat and drink all of the signature punch or alcohol they wanted till they got to the Isla de Amor. The boat crew partied with the tourists as they headed to the Mexican fiesta. Abdora was networking while Tavares was on the floor doing the Spanish cha cha. Dora loved her for being so carefree and outgoing as she worked her dance moves. She was on the floor getting it in with the Mexicans and enjoying herself like she was one of them.

"'Pardon," a man with a thick Spanish accent tapped Abdora on the back.

"Mi ma, she said you gave her something back."

"Oh yeah, the little sweet Spanish lady. She dropped her money and I gave it back to her. Why? What's up?" Abdora said, getting defensive.

"Oh no, mi friend. I just wanted to say thank you. Mi ma was thankful," the suave but thugged out Spanish man said.

"I would buy you a drink, but all the alcohol is free," he joked.

"Oh no problem," Abdora said, giving the man dap.

From there they engaged in conversation, hit it off, and parted on a friendly note with the intention to talk more in the states.

The boat finally made it to the island and both Tavares and Abdora were excited about the evening ahead. There was going to be dinner, a show, games, and more all you could drink alcohol on the island. They sat at a candlelit table under palm trees and ate steak and shrimp with vegetables and Mexican rice. Before the show started, they passed time playing drinking games with some of the other outgoing tourists, took pictures, drank, bought souvenirs, and drank some more. At show time, Tavares and Abdora were both intoxicated and still had another hour and a half before they headed back. Before the show ended they had a ball taking part in the contests and each winning a separate contest and then winning a couples contest. When they won massage oil as the couple contest, they locked eyes with a look that read: *it's going to be a hell of a night.*

"Ok, everyone, we had a very good time tonight. I hope everyone enjoyed their evening on the Isla de Amor. The myth is that anyone who comes here is blessed with love from whoever they came with, so good luck. In thirty minutes, we will be boarding the boat. Goodnight," the man on the stage said over the microphone.

They were lost in conversation as they strolled along the sand, hand in hand. Abdora needed to tell Tavares how he felt about her, so he stopped walking but continued to hold her hands. He was fucked up, so as the saying goes, "a drunk mind spoke a sober tongue."

He looked into Tavares's eyes and said, "I want to love you."

Her blue eyes popped out of her head because he blindsided her.

"You make me want to give you the world. You make a nigga feel good. I love and enjoy everything about you. I want to protect you and be with you every night. I don't know what you did to me, but Ma, you got me. And, I'm hot off the press so you better get me," Dora laughed. "You aren't like these other women who have a motive behind wanting to be with me. They want money, status, perks, and a whole bunch of other dumb frivolous shit.

"I need someone who just likes me and wants me for who I am at the end of the day, when the street shit is over. But, I also need someone like you who can hold me down on a hood level," Abdora said, licking that oh so sexy bottom lip. "I don't feel like you'll set me up or do some grimy shit to me. If anything, I feel like you want to help elevate me to a higher level. Whatever I got is yours, Ma. And, if I don't have it, which I probably will, I'll go out there and get it for you by any means necessary.

"I'm not trying to compare myself to the next nigga, I just want to love you better than you been loved and treat you like the queen that you are. I want to spend my life with you. I been looking for your little sexy fine ass my whole damn life."

Tavares was speechless. She knew that Dora was feeling her, but not how he'd just expressed. Tears started to stream down Tavares's face rather than words coming out her mouth.

"What's wrong, Babygirl?" Abdora asked.

Tavares was crying because her heart was telling her one thing and her mind was telling her another thing. Her heart said be with Abdora and live the life she so deserved. Then her head said be loyal to the one who was there when you had no one.

"You don't know how pretty you look in that dress," Abdora said, referring to Tavares's chocolate brown linen halter-top sundress that went to her feet and flowed when she walked.

"You have no business crying. Wipe those pretty eyes."

"You caught me off guard, Abdora. I didn't see that coming. I'm flattered. I'm going to tell you the truth. I'm so at a loss for words, so you're going have to give me some time to come back at you. I can't lie. I've fallen for you, too. Word, I have. I want to be with you and do it way big, but you know I have a situation at home that I have to take care of before there could ever be any us. I don't want to give you half of me or part of me - I want you to have all of me. You DESERVE all of me. So, before I can do that, I need to close the open chapter and leave the baggage behind."

"I can respect that, Ma," Dora said, not liking her answer but respecting it.

Tavares grabbed his hand and they quietly went to board the boat. They arrived back at Fat Tuesdays and decided to have a drink before turning in.

"My little buzz wore off after you said what you said," Tavares joked.

"How about we take some shots of tequila?" Abdora said, thinking that it would be fun to watch Tavares lick and suck without even getting in the bed.

Tequila always led to bad behavior with Tavares so she was afraid to drink with good reason. After one shot, Tavares was reeled in. Five shots later, Tavares was feeling way too sexy for herself. They headed out of Fat Tuesdays and flagged a cab back to the hotel. Tavares's limit had been hit at three shots, and she was past ready to get back to the hotel as she stretched out across Abdora in the cab. As they exited the cab, Tavares was clearly more intoxicated than Abdora. Abdora was feeling good and loving what he saw as Tavares was sashaying in front of him.

"Tavares, you sure you don't need me to carry you?" Dora volunteered, wanting to hold her ass in his hands.

"I'm fine. I can walk," Tavares slurred.

"Let me carry you for the hell of it then," Abdora said, sweeping her off her feet before she could say no.

"You just don't take no for an answer, do you?"

"Never, Babygirl."

Dora took Tavares over his shoulder like it was nothing, carried her inside, laid her across the bed flat on her back, and kissed her soft lips. Tavares let him take the lead with no rejection. Abdora was turned on as hell seeing that she had on no panties as he slid her out of her dress. He kissed Tavares from head to toe, missing no place in between. Using his tongue as a weapon of mass destruction, he attacked and conquered. There was no way Tavares could contain her squirming and squirting that had him thinking he'd scored him a porn star forreal. Dora had teased and tasted every place before he gave Tavares a real serious dick down. After they both climaxed, they lay naked, cuddled tight, and got lost in the moment.

Tavares had been in Mexico for three days and hadn't called her friends, so she picked up the hotel phone and called home.

"Hey, Bitch. What's going on?" Tavares said, all excited.

"Yo, Ms. Cuddles and Bubbles. Shit is hectic around these parts."

"What do you mean shit is hectic? I was home a few days ago and Winky passing was the only thing hectic. Oh and of course Damien's ass being shot up in the process," Tavares said, mad that she'd even said his name.

"Yo! I don't know what the fuck is going on, but niggaz are dropping dead left and right. And you got the nerve to be on that island all in love and shit."

"Shut up."

"No, you shut up. You're the one laid up like shit is a game or something. The streets have been on fire since you left," Leslie said with pure disgust in her voice for her lost generation. "Since Dame got shot, it's been some crazy domino effect with niggaz wanting to come out and shoot their guns. Niggaz are shooting to kill. Tavares, no bullshit there's going to be three funerals of niggaz who came up with us. They said Holly Hood got at niggaz real hard for the stunt they pulled shooting him. Got at them niggaz hard-body from the bricks, and he laid two niggaz from their hood down. Stix got caught in the middle of one of the shootings."

"Three funerals back to back, are you kidding?" Tavares asked, knowing that she wasn't, but she still wished that her best friend was.

"Girl, I wish I were. Burying our niggaz is real as real gets. Not to mention our other close friends we've buried in

40

various hood wars over the last year. R.I.P. Chee Bey, Jim-Black, Yorky, Leon, Dre, Damian, Scooter, Cheese, Shizzy, Baha and Lefty," Leslie said, already knowing how going to all those funerals had affected them.

It was one thing to read about the shootings in the *Boston Herald* but to read about them, know the people firsthand, and be real friends of theirs was a whole other playing field. It was more heartbreaking than the people on the outside looking in could fathom for a young black woman watching her friends drop like flies.

"Tavares, the funerals are all two days apart. Starting on the third with Winky's. What a way to end the goddamn year, right? Please tell me that you're still meeting us in Atlanta."

Silence captivated the line.

"Are you fucking kidding, Tavares?! You can NOT be having that much fun to not want to come party with us for my birthday."

"But I don't want to leave," Tavares pleaded. "I'm having a ball! Bitch, do you know what it's like to have a nigga be good to you with no catches, no bullshit, no nothing? It's crazy and orgasmic. Plus, he doesn't want me to leave him either."

Tavares had to make clear to her friend.

"Mr. Man has a way better idea than me leaving him. How about you guys fly here? He'll pay for everything. All you need is the spending money that you were already taking to Atlanta with you," Tavares said, resting her case.

Leslie said, "Hell yeah. I'm with it. Say no more. We can go to Atlanta anytime. I'll break the news to the other three bad news bears. I'm glad you called home, though. We know you're ok with Dora, but we just need to hear your voice and confirm it."

"I'm good, really good. So good that I want to go to Jersey and never come back," Tavares joked, but really meaning it. "Alright, Babygirl. I'm not going to hold you up. I'll call you back when Dora has everything confirmed."

Everyone said *I love you* before they hung up.

~Chapter 3~
When Passion Explodes

Damien was lying in the hospital two days before New Year's beating himself up for his bullshit. He was overlooking the Mass Ave exit of the highway that took you in every different direction of Boston. He couldn't help but think to himself over and over, *Wow, I'm shot and the one person who is supposed to be here isn't and it's really all my fault.* As Damien looked around his room at all the flowers, balloons, and teddy bears that people had brought, he realized that none of it was lightening his mood. None of the chicks who sent the gifts even mattered, because they hadn't been worth going through the bullshit and possibly losing the one female that he knew loved him for him, regardless of all his faults and bullshit.

Tavares never wanted anything from Damien, nothing but for him to love her. That made him gravitate toward her and spoil the hell out of her. She was always willing to go out and get her own so he respected her for that. She was that chick in his eyes. He'd tried calling her day after day since she left the hospital, but he got her voicemail each time he tried. He just hoped that she would forgive him and come back to him.

While Damien was in deep thought about his relationship with Tavares, there was a knock at the door.

"Hey, Damien."

Jazz had been to the hospital every single day since Tavares had gone missing in action. Damien didn't know why Jazz had kept coming to see him, but it was obvious

43

that her purpose was more than just checking on him as she said Tavares asked her to do. She was trying to make herself feel like she was his girl by trying to run his errands and do everything for him when his mother wasn't around. She knew better than to pull the bullshit in front of Doll.

"Jazz, what's up?"

"I was just coming to make sure that you're alright and didn't need anything. I hear that you'll be going home tonight. Would you like for me to go to the house and get you some clothes? Tavares left her keys with Randee."

"Nah, I'm straight. My mother will take care of it." Damien was aggravated at the no-good chick in front of him.

"Listen, you already know how I get down. So, tell me really, why is it that you keep coming to check on me? You already know what's good. I'm not leaving Tavares and she's not leaving me. So are you really willing to fuck your friendship up to taste my dick?" Jazz was shocked like she didn't know what it was.

"Look, you don't have to get snappy with me. Shit, at least I give a fuck to be here while you're laid up in that bed. Tavares is way in Mexico, so I was just trying to look out for you."

"What the fuck did you just say?"

Oh fuck, Jazz thought to herself, knowing that she'd just fucked up and not really on accident. Damien sat up straight, looked Jazz in the face, and asked, "Who the fuck is Tavares in Mexico with?"

Silence came between them.

"Please, let's not get quiet now."

Jazz knew she could have told Dame some bullshit, but she spilled it all from how Tavares had met Dora and

44

had been kickin it with him for months to how she was in Mexico and that instead of going to Atlanta for Leslie's birthday, they were going to meet Tavares in Mexico on Dora's dime.

"He's paying to fly us and his homeboys out there for Leslie's birthday."

Damien felt his body go from normal to flaming in a matter of seconds.

"That's how my bitch is doing it? She's playing out of teezy with niggaz? Rendezvousing with niggaz OT and shit, huh?"

Damien was furious. He felt fucked up from the pain he was in, but he felt like his heart had just stopped. Listening to the fact that Tavares was in Mexico and with some nigga she'd been fucking with for months had Damien past pissed. *Payback is a bitch* crossed Damien's mind, but he wasn't going to let Jazz know that she'd just struck a major chord.

"Jazz, I think you should go."

Jazz thought that telling Damien everything was going to draw him closer, but little did she know her plan backfired in her face.

"I don't wanna be bothered and especially not with no rat ass bitch. You thought throwing your girl under the bus was gonna get you some points but definitely not. Im'ma deal with my bitch when she gets home, but you ain't shit for throwing your girl under the bus. Apple has been your girl through thick and thin, and you just sat here and ran it down like she was a bitch in the street that you just met. Let yourself out and shut my fucking door in the process,"

Damien said, turning his TV on and acting like Jazz wasn't even there.

Jazz held her head down in shame and exited Damien's hospital room. She beat herself up all the way to the elevator. She'd just betrayed and crossed her best friend - her best friend who was her A-1 since day one, who always had her back no matter what, and for what? Jazz didn't know how this would play out, but she was hoping that hadn't just written a check her ass couldn't cover.

Jazz, Randee, Mona-Lisa, and Leslie entered the Cancún Airport and couldn't help but be excited to be in the sun in Cancún, Mexico on New Year's Eve.

"Tavares held us down with this one," Randee said.

"Hell to the yeah she did! I think this is going to be the best birthday ever. Shit, how can it not be? We're on an island balling out for free! You know we love anything about the f-r-e-e," Leslie joked.

Seeing the cab driver holding a sign that read "Secret Squirrel Club," they fell out laughing and knew that the Mexican cab driver was looking for them.

"Tavares ain't shit," Leslie said as she shook her head at the sign that referenced their code name.

"She definitely been talking to her boy toy a little too much," Mona-Lisa said.

"Hola, Chica Ritas. You're some fine, sexy, hot mommas. Welcome to Cancún, Mexico," Louie said in his slick, thick Spanish accent. "I was told to take good care of you and get you to the Omni in one piece."

The ladies just laughed at how cool Louie was. They got into the cab while he loaded up the trunk with their

luggage. The ladies were in awe as they approached the hotel that was purely beautiful with blooming bright
flowers and waterfalls everywhere. They got their luggage and said their goodbyes to their new homeboy Louie as they walked to the double sliding doors.

"Welcome to the Omni Cancún, ladies," the bellman said as he took their bags.

The ladies checked into their room and headed to the fortieth floor to get settled into their five-bedroom ocean view suite. Upon entering the hotel suite, the girls couldn't help but be ecstatic about their weekend living quarters. They were high off excitement as they stood looking around at the surround sound system, flat screen TV, fully stocked bar, leather furniture, full kitchen with a dining room table, two pool tables, two Jacuzzis, and swimming pool. Dora had even gotten them some weed and rolling utensils. By the time Tavares came in the door smiling bright as she wanted to be, everyone was on her.

"Uhhh huh," Mona-Lisa said. "Why you looking all happy and grinning and shit? Looking like a damn goofy fool."

"Yeah, I want you to not be smiling that hard," Leslie said.

"Leave Apple alone," Randee said.

"I know, my gosh," Tavares said.

"Shut your white girl ass up," Jazz joked.

"What's wrong with smiling and having a good time?" Tavares said, turning red from blushing so hard.

"Yo, I was trying to not be the one to ask, but who gave you the chain and bracelet?" Leslie asked, looking out the side of her eyes.

47

"I was thinking the same shit," said Randee. "That chain and bracelet is iced the fuck out. You better only rock them on special occasions."

"Yeah, they're beautiful pieces," Mona said.

Jazz already knew and changed the subject to hide her jealousy.

"How about you twist up?" Jazz asked, definitely trying to rack Tavares's nerves.

"How about I don't," Tavares answered. "I supplied everything through Dora, so I'm on a pass for the weekend. Sorry, Babygirl," Tavares laughed.

Jazz was mad, but not because Tavares didn't want to twist up. She was mad because Tavares had the two niggas that she ever really wanted head over heels in love with her.

"You get on my motherfucking nerves never wanting to roll," Jazz said real nastily. "I don't get how you want to fucking smoke, but think that you're too good to roll."

"Are you kidding me, Jazz?" Tavares asked, getting upset that her friend was ruining the moment. "You need to be, because this nitpicking that you're doing is real fucking stupid. Out of everyone in the room, why the fuck you want me to roll so badly? Get the fuck over yourself and kiss my ass."

"No, fuck you and your spoiled ass, Tavares. If you don't roll, you ain't gonna be smoking."

"Says who, Jazz? Who the fuck died and made you the fucking rolling police? Real talk, you sound fucking stupid and fucking petty. I don't have time for this petty bullshit! I ain't rolling a motherfucking thing. I got plenty of weed downstairs in my villa that Dora will gladly roll for me. I'm out, y'all," Tavares said, getting up steamy mad. "Jazz, get that stick out your ass before the New Year comes, because if not you can keep it shoved up your ass and get out my life."

Tavares was heated because she was on to Jazz. She knew Jazz too well. After she told Jazz how she felt, Tavares got up, stormed out, and slammed the door as she headed to her villa to smoke and calm down. As soon as Tavares left, everyone gave it to Jazz. She tried to defend herself by saying that Tavares was spoiled and needed to get over thinking she was the queen of the castle. No one was going for it, though.

"Jazz, was that really that serious?" Mona asked. "She got niggaz in Cancún for Leslie's birthday and you want to complain about her fucking rolling. Come on, yo."

"Get real," Randee said.

"Yeah. Jazz, that was some real bullshit you just pulled with Tavares and all for nothing. All three of us can roll, so why you just didn't ask one of us?" Leslie asked.

Jazz didn't mean to fuck up the mood, but her jealous feelings got the best of her. She loved Tavares. She just hated that Tavares was that chick that she yearned to be. She hated to admit it, but she was jealous of her friend who had never done anything but been there for her and loved her. Jazz tried hard to stand out. Tavares fell back but somehow always managed to steal the show. Jazz threw herself at niggaz, but niggaz always looked past her to Tavares. Just like Abdora had done and now Tavares was living it up.

New Year's Eve was just another night of major partying for them. Tavares and her friends along with Dora and his friends drank the evening away at an all-night beach party. Leslie was in her glory on the beach in Cancún,

49

Mexico for her birthday free of charge because of Tavares's new boo. Shots of tequila were being taken as the punishment when you messed up in a game called Questions. The object of the game was for a group of people to ask absolutely ANY question to a person in the group, whether it was nasty, crazy, funny, or even absolutely stupid. The person wasn't allowed to not answer, laugh, or stutter. If they did anything other than fire another question to a person in the group, they had to take a shot. It was funny to listen to the questions.

Bryce looked at Mona-Lisa and asked, "Do you like mops up your butt?"

Mona-Lisa asked Kollar Dollar, "Do you scratch your ass and grit your teeth while digging in your nose in your sleep?"

Kollar Dollar asked Leslie, "Do you wipe from front to back or back to front when you shit?"

Leslie busted out laughing and said, "No you fucking didn't."

She broke the flow, so she had to take a shot. It was funny because something that sounded so easy to play was actually hard to do because of not knowing if the nature of the question was going to catch you so off guard that you laughed or answered rather than keep going.

Leslie threw back her shot then asked Jazz, "Do you like red licorice up your ass during sex?"

Jazz asked Tavares, "When is the last time you got freaky with a dick on your forehead?"

"Last night. Fuck you, bitch," Tavares said and took her shot.

Tavares looked to Abdora and asked, "Do you play dress up in pink dresses at night?"

He quickly said, "Fucks no and pass me a shot," with no problem. "You ain't shit," he said, knowing that she purposely got him.

Everyone took a shot to that one. They played Questions along with every other drinking game that they could come up with. It was crazy because when the ball dropped everyone was already drunk and totally forgot that it was New Year's Eve. They were more interested in who was going to go get the next round. By 4:00 a.m., everyone was past stumbling and holding each other up to make it to their rooms.

Tavares came into the room and kicked off her wedge heel slide-on sandals and dropped her snug-fitting one-piece romper, ready to hit the shower.

"Damn, are you really going to do that to me?" Abdora said, looking down at this dick that truly had a mind of its own. "You cannot just strip like that and walk away."

Tavares needed some water on her body to try and sober up.

She said, "Well what do you want me to do? How else can I take a shower?"

"Whatever, Ma. Just get your little thick, big booty ass in the shower before it be some problems that you aren't even ready for."

Tavares just tossed her hair over her shoulder with a look that said *I'm ready for whatever problems you want.* She shook her head and made her way to the bathroom. Abdora was about to murder her pussy in the shower. He stripped and was in the bathroom in record time. Tavares was fully lathered from head to toe when he opened the glass shower door and knew that he was about to have a ball. Dora pulled Tavares close and pushed her underneath the showerhead to rinse her off as he sucked her bottom lip slow and steady. When she tried to pull away, he slipped his warm wet tongue into her mouth. He placed his right hand on the tip of her clit while his left hand slowly caressed her fully erect nipples.

"Your nipples are so large," Abdora whispered as he nibbled on Tavares's ear.

He went from her ear to her shoulder blade and made his way down to put both nipples in his mouth. Tavares stepped out of the way of the water that was slapping her back and her hair so that she and Abdora could trade places. Tavares lathered Abdora from head to toe and he thought he was going to melt at the touch of her soft hands all over his body. While bathing each other, kissing, and touching, they got lost in time. Abdora dropped to his knees and took one of Tavares's legs over his shoulder and made music with his tongue. Staring in Tavares's eyes with every stroke, he worked the middle more and more as her eyes rolled further in the back of her head. Tavares was trying to hold on for dear life, but her orgasm was trying to take over her body. She started to caress her own erect nipples.

"Awww!" Tavares screamed as she splashed her orgasm everywhere like the water that was coming down from the shower.

Abdora was in awe that shorty could squirt like a professional X-rated movie star. Tavares and Abdora showered again, rinsed off, and got out. Before Tavares could grab a terry cloth towel, she was swept off her feet.

52

"Oh my God, I'm fucking dripping wet. Can you please put me down so that I can dry off?"

"Nope, I got you just how I want you."

Abdora laid Tavares on the king-size bed, and went to work kissing Tavares dry on every part of her body. He started at her eyelids and kissed down the center to her nose and made a pit stop at her mouth. He slid his tongue in her mouth and savored the sweet taste. As Abdora kissed Tavares with passion that could be felt in her soul, she started to melt between the legs. *Awww* and *oh my god* was all that she could moan from the pure pleasure of his mouth all over her body.

When Abdora went from sucking one breast at a time to sucking both nipples at the same time real slow and enticingly, Tavares screamed and came like she'd never experienced in her life. The real bliss was Abdora knowing how to touch her without her needing to say a word. When he was done sucking her sweet, firm nipples, he kissed his way down her belly without missing a spot. Abdora slid his long, thick tongue real slow like molasses across Tavares's dripping wet clit. Tears started to fall from her eyes as she climaxed without control. Tavares came in his mouth and he sucked it down like it was a power drink.

After Abdora had his appetizer, dinner, and dessert between Tavares's legs, he got up and kissed Tavares and let her taste her own fruits. She obliged with no hesitation. He thought he was going to bust off the sexiness he found in that alone. After five minutes of kissing intimately, Abdora took Tavares's legs and lifted them all the way back behind her head and slid his thick, ten-inch-long dick inside her little by little, seeing the pain in her face. When Abdora got all the way inside Tavares's pussy, it felt like his dick had found its final resting place. Her snug pussy wrapped around his dick so perfectly. What started slow and steady ended with Tavares screaming from the mean dick down. Dora flipped Tavares over on her stomach and teased her by rubbing his dick on her clit followed by a little more teasing before he gave a slow, steady back shot. Tavares came endlessly, leaving a puddle beneath them.

After laying the dick face down ass up, he knew she officially had the best pussy he'd ever had - and he'd had a lot. Tavares was throwing it back like she was meant to be riding his dick. Abdora tried to hold his nut back, but Tavares was squeezing her pussy muscles around his dick that fit so perfectly and got the best of him. Abdora pulled out and saw that he didn't get to her ass fully in time, but he was good that it didn't catch her inside.

"I'm going to fuck you up," Tavares screamed at what felt like the inside of a Boston cream pie donut oozing on her butt.

"Damn. My bad, Apple. That shit was crazy. That was the first time, and I wasn't about to control my nut. You caught me, Ma, but I pulled out, so you're good."

"Are you done?" Tavares asked with sly eyes.

"Only if you are," he said, knowing that he had another three rounds in him.

Tavares got up without a word and left Abdora lying in the bed wiping his dick. When Tavares returned, the sun was just starting to peek out. Abdora knew that the morning was just getting started by looking at Tavares.

"Damn, are your hands full enough?" he said, laughing at the sexual picnic.

She had chocolate, whipped cream, strawberries, and bananas, all on a tray. By the time the sexual match made in heaven made love two more times, the sheets were ruined and not ever coming back. It was time to take a shower and lay it down. They decided to go outside to lie on the full-size hammock where they slept under the morning sunshine. When Dora woke up, he kissed Tavares till she awakened.

"Damn, Ma. It's two in the afternoon. I couldn't have asked for a better New Year, but it's time to rise and shine," Abdora said as he and Tavares were snuggled outside naked under clean crisp sheets on the hammock.

"Me neither, but now I have to go home and face the music with Dame and go to these funerals," Tavares said sadly.

"Ma, listen. I don't know what's good with you and son, but that nigga is no good for you. The real nigga in me won't allow me to bad-mouth son, as I always tell you. So I'm just going to tell you this, open your eyes. I would love to off son, but I gotta let you handle that."

"I know, Abdora."

"Listen, Tavares. I'm not trying to cut you off, but let me tell you something. I need you in my life bad. You do it all for a nigga. You make me laugh, smile, and make me feel a way I've never felt before. I just feel so at ease with you, and I want it full time, not part time. I want to give you the world, but I can't be the side nigga. I need all of you. I need you to decide if you want to love or be loved. So, I'm going to let you do what you need to, even if it's staying with homeboy. But, know that when you're ready, I'm here. I'm a real ass nigga as you've seen, so I'm not gonna front to you. I'm going to be doing me, but know that I'm trying to do it for real with you, Babygirl."

Tavares didn't respond out loud, but in her mind she told herself it was time to do some serious thinking because Dora made her happy. He genuinely made her happy, and being happy was what life was all about. Maybe it was time to live her life and stop feeling like she owed Damien. Abdora kissed Tavares's cheek, her lips, and eyes, and she sighed. Then, she drifted back off to sleep in Dora's arms. They awoke to someone banging at their door.

"You go get it," Tavares said, nudging Dora as she lay tightly wrapped in his strong, muscular tattooed arms. Sliding off the hammock, Dora grabbed a towel for his lower body from the bedroom and went to the door.

"Who is it?" Dora said loud and letting it be known that he was mad as hell that he'd been interrupted.

"It's us. Open up," Randee said.

"Y'all been shacked the hell up all damn day. Open up," said Mona-Lisa as Dora opened the door.

The ladies looked at his body up close and personal and lost their thoughts. Seeing the inked body from head to toe that was all muscle was too much.

"Uhhh, weee uhhh," Mona said.

"Where the hell is Tavares?" Jazz said, not even fazed by what she wanted and couldn't have.

"Come in, ladies. Have a seat in the living room. I'll go get Tav."

As they waited for Tavares, the ladies passed time talking about how he was just too fucking fine to be a human specimen.

"Man, listen. Tavares needs to send Dame packing and get her mind right," laughed Leslie.

Everyone was laughing when Tavares walked in wrapped in a white sheet. They all just stopped laughing and looked at Tavares from head to toe.

"Uhhh, did we come at a bad time?" Jazz asked.

"Naw, we were sleep. Y'all did me a favor. It's time to get dressed and get it in for our last night here."

"Tavares, you just came in from outside, so please tell me that you weren't sleeping outside naked," Randee said, looking at her friend real puzzled.

"Alright, I won't tell you then. So what are we going to do for the night?" Tavares asked, switching the topic.

"KJ, Bryce, Hawk, and Nas are all in the casino," Leslie said. "They said when you two get up, to come find them."

"We just been lying on the beach drinking. We're bored, so you two need to get up."

"Alright," Tavares agreed. "Give us thirty minutes, and we'll meet in the lobby."

Tavares and Abdora got a quickie in while they took a shower. The quickie gave them the boost of energy they needed. Forty-five minutes later they were headed to the lobby hand in hand for their last night in Cancún, Mexico.

After a week of having a ball in the sun jet-skiing, scuba-diving, horseback riding, ATVing, parasailing, drinking, lying on the beach, and shopping, Tavares was crushed that she had to go home to three funerals. They enjoyed their last night with their friends, and packed all of their things early the next morning before they headed to the airport.

"Tavares, are you ready?" Abdora asked as he pulled her close.

"Yeah, I'm ready even though I don't want to leave."

"Don't tell me that because you know I'll say let's stay."

"That sounds good, babe, but I got to go home to get shit together so I can go to these funerals and take my ass back to school for this last semester."

After kissing for ten minutes and trying to fight the urge for another quickie, they headed downstairs to meet their friends. Tavares and her girls got into their limo and Abdora and his friends got into theirs and headed to the airport to fly back to the east coast to the reality of their lives.

Tavares and her girls boarded the plane, took their seats in first class, and started getting tore down on the complimentary drinks.

"Tavares, what are you going to do about Abdora and Dame?" Mona-Lisa asked.

"I have no clue."

Jazz was quiet because no one knew that she'd slipped up and told Dame about Tavares and her secret affair.

"Dame got a lot of shit going on," Jazz said. "Just let the chips fall where they may."

"I agree," Leslie said.

"Forget letting the chips fall where they may," said Mona-Lisa. "I say pack your shit and tell Dame to kick rocks. After all his bullshit since you been home, then the shit at the hospital, I say fuck him."

"Dittooo," Randee sung.

"Ladies, y'all know I wish it was that easy, but as fucked up as Dame is, I do love him. That's just the bottom line. I'm totally head over heels for Abdora, who makes me happy beyond words, but me and Damien been together a long time. I'm gonna work it out, though. That's my word," Tavares said.

Nobody commented. Instead, the ladies talked and reminisced about their trip all the way to Boston.

Six hours later, everyone was hopping in separate cabs and heading to their homes. Tavares got home, looked at the steps to her house, and knew that climbing them was the last thing she wanted to do. As she entered the first floor, the whole house was completely pitch-black. Tavares didn't touch anything. She dragged her bags upstairs and got ready for bed. She'd deal with Damien tomorrow. It was clear that he hadn't been home, so Tavares was glad that she'd have another night to get her mind right.

~Chapter 4~
One Man's Trash Is Another Man's Treasure

Damien had been at his mother's house since he left the hospital. He was tired of being in the house. He'd been in the hospital bed since Christmas and in the house for New Year's Eve. It was time to hit the streets. He had to bury his best friend the following day, so he wanted a breath of fresh air before he did. Damien got off his mother's couch and got dressed. Doll was in the kitchen cooking when he grabbed his mink coat out the closet.

"Nigga, you know you ain't healed. You better not get back into them streets ripping and running," Doll said with her focus never leaving her food.

"Ma, I'm not about to rip and run. I'm going to get up with this bitch. Tavares is out of town smutting off, so I'm going to snatch this breezy and do the same."

"So you know Tavares is out of town with some nigga, huh?"

"I sure do," Dame said, getting mad all over again.

"And just how did you obtain this information?" Doll asked, not too convinced her son knew what he was talking about.

Dame just chuckled and said, "A little birdie told me."

"So you have to get your payback? Damien, grow up."

"Ma, you stay taking her side on some real bullshit."

"It's far from bullshit. All I'm saying is that two wrongs don't make a right. Furthermore, you were running around slinging your black ass dick with all these two-dollar bitches

60

before Tavares was out of town. Don't be mad, because what's good for the gander is good for the gangster."

"Ma, I'm out of here," Damien said, mad that his mother had politely given him the business when it was Tavares who was in the wrong.

Damien pulled up on Fort Hill and looked at the view of the whole city while he waited for his thick juicy jump-off to come downstairs. Talesha was bad. She was small on the top with huge natural watermelons and a lower body that consisted of nothing but baby-bearing hips and ass for miles and miles. She was a thick thickems for sure. Her face was easy on the eyes without a doubt with her high round tight cheekbones, long curvy lashes, and chinky eyes. Looking at her walk out the house, Damien knew that he was going to fuck the shit out of her tonight. He was still a little banged up, but his dick was working just fine.

After taking Talesha to the movies and Dave and Buster's where they played video games, ate, and had drinks, Damien was ready to do what he do, so they headed back to his house. Damien had never disrespected Tavares and brought another woman into their house, but seeing that she was on vacation with another man, he lied to himself and said it was ok. He knew it was wrong and disrespectful, but Tavares would never know, and he wasn't going to waste money on a hotel. He was taking Talesha to one of the spare bedrooms in his house.

When they got in the room, Damien dropped his jeans and Talesha went in like she was the headmaster of dick schooling. She opened her whole mouth and took all of him in. Her mouth was so warm that he was ready to bust in her mouth and get the first nut over with. *Damn, this is too good to bust*, he thought, controlling his nut.

Talesha opened her mouth and took him fully in and out her wet, warm mouth and gargled with his dick. She was going hard, thinking that being pretty and giving good head was the way to lock Damien down. Talesha was squatting flat on her feet froggy-style before she dropped to her knees and went to town on the dick. She massaged Damien's long, thick manhood while she slowly sucked around the head with a slow, steady rotation.

Damien was moaning so loud that he didn't even realize how lost he was in this mind-blowing head job. After ten minutes of sucking Damien's dick, Talesha stood up and took off all her clothes and made Damien do the same. He never hit bitches raw unless it was his wifey, and she wasn't about to be an exception to the rule. He slid the magnum condom on and lay down on the pillow-top king-size bed. Talesha got on top of Damien, squatted, and rocked the tip of her pussy across Damien's dick that was standing straight up in the air.

Tavares hated when she had to wake up in the middle night to go to the bathroom. That shit ruined her sleep like nothing else. She dragged herself out of the bed and walked to the bathroom in the dark with her eyes still closed. She knew the route to the bathroom inside-out, so she never had to turn on the lights or open her eyes. Tavares pissed, sighed, and opened her eyes out of relief. As she stood at the bathroom sink washing her hands, she thought about Damien and how tomorrow wasn't going to be nothing but some bullshit when she saw him. She still wasn't ready to face him and said fuck it, "Let me take my ass back to bed."

As Tavares got back into bed, she heard a vague thump. She got up scared because she could hear something downstairs and Damien wasn't home. *Oh my God*, Tavares thought as she went to safe and entered 4-2-3-1 on the digital keypad. She grabbed her Glock 9, shut the safe, and slowly crept out of her bedroom. The noise was loud, but unclear as Tavares exited down the stairs. When Tavares got closer to the bottom of the stairs, the noises started to become clearer. Tavares crept off the stairs toward the left side of the hall where the corner spare bedroom was located. She pushed the door open and didn't know whether to watch, shoot, or yell since they never heard the door open. Pain washed her heart and tears came rushing down her face. Tavares had hurt enough and this was it. Damien had for sure just crossed the final line and any future for them. He didn't have the wrong one, he had the right one because Tavares was done.

"You dirty dick no good motherfucker!!" Tavares screamed with her gun pointed straight at Damien and the bitch he had bent over doggy-style.

Damien hopped out the pussy in utter shock. He got up with his well-hung dick straight up in the air, brick hard.

"Tavares! Wait! Tavares, please!" Damien pleaded with his eyes never leaving her licensed gun.

He was caught way past redemption and didn't know if Tavares would have the compassion not to shoot him. He knew her all too well. Tavares wanted to shoot Damien, but if she did she probably wouldn't stop.

"Damien, you know I should shoot you right now, right?"

The look in her eyes said she would, if his mind didn't tell him. Damien knew better than to answer. Tavares was hurt past words and the inner pain was shining right now.

"Since you just got out the hospital for some bullet wounds, Im'ma let you live. I ain't even gonna do it to you, even though you fucking deserve it," Tavares said, feeling the tears that wanted to run down her face.

Damien got up and said, "Yo, Tav, please let's talk about this. Put the fucking gun down. This bitch is not this serious for you to have a gun pointed at me."

"Fuck her scuzzbucket ass! You were fucking her in my house!" Tavares said, looking at him sideways like he was truly crazy.

Talesha rolled her eyes but didn't say nothing.

"Please put your gun down before you get trigger-happy," Damien pleaded.

He was dismissing the woman like she wasn't there because he knew what she didn't know, that Tavares would shoot both of them. Tavares's eyes were on the bitch lying ass-naked like she lived there. Talesha locked eyes with Tavares and chuckled smugly like she found something funny or a joke.

"Bitch, you find something funny?" Tavares asked, knowing that she was going to be mopping this bitch's ass all up and down her brownstone before she kicked her down every stair and onto the street.

"Come on, Yo. You got a gun pointed at us like you got the heart to shoot us."

As soon as Talesha said that, she felt the bullet ricochet off the bed to the wall, and she regretted her words.

"Oh my God! Damien, this bitch is crazy!"

"Bitch, shut the fuck up, because you ain't seen crazy yet!" Tavares snapped with her blue eyes on fire forreal. "I could have just shot you, so know you only got one more time to say a motherfucking thing before I shoot you," Tavares said with murder in her eyes. "Put your clothes on and get the fuck out my house!" Tavares shouted with the gun still pointed at her and Damien.

Tavares stood strong, refusing to shed a tear in front of this bitch who had helped Damien just break up what they had forever. Dame had officially abused Tavares for the last time. The sight of him fucking a bitch in her house wouldn't get out of Tavares's mind.

Talesha rushed to the corner to put her clothes on and in a hushed tone said, "I have no money to get home."

"Walk, you dog bitch," Tavares said, not giving two fucks.

Talesha was ready to walk with no problem after hearing Tavares's words and the tone in her voice. Talesha thought she was home scot-free, but as she went to walk out the door, Tavares gave her a backhand slap with her gun still in her hand. As Tavares dropped the gun that was on safety, she gave Talesha enough time to prepare for the ass whoopin' of her life. Damien just fell back knowing that he would definitely get shot if he dare tried to save Talesha.

Talesha and Tavares were going hard for a minute. Talesha was trying her best to hang on, but Tavares was slamming her head up and down off the dresser, and she knew she'd lost. Tavares threw Talesha to the floor and literally kicked her out of the room, all the way down the hall, down the twenty stairs to the first floor, and out the door onto the street. Tavares didn't give a fuck that it wasn't her fault. That bitch laughed like it was joke and got the ass whoopin' she so deserved.

Tavares went into the kitchen, laid her back on the double-door stainless steel refrigerator, slid down, and dropped her head into her hands. She was stuck in the moment of watching Damien fuck the shit out of another bitch in her house. She let all her pain run out through her tears. The hurt was too much, and if he wanted her gone he had for sure pushed her away once and for all. Long, hard sobbing was all that Damien could hear from the top of the second floor stairs. Each minute that passed, he told himself he was going down to console her. As he listened for an hour, he never found the courage because he could hear the pain he'd caused her in every sob and with every teardrop. Tavares cried for what felt like forever until she just didn't have the energy to hurt anymore.

Tavares got up and dried her eyes that always turned from blue to gray when she cried. She washed her hands and found the strength to climb the two flights of stairs to her bedroom.

When Tavares got to the second floor, she could hear Damien on the phone with his mom saying, "I lost her. I lost her forever, Mommy."

Damien was sobbing, but his pain meant nothing to Tavares. He did this, not her. Tavares walked past the room where Damien had committed his final act of betrayal. She kept going toward her bedroom on the third floor. She was packing her Louis Vuitton custom-made pink and brown signature luggage when Damien came upstairs.

"Tavares, please don't go. I know I fucked up, baby. You got me begging, though. Please, don't go. You got my word that I'll never cheat again. Never and that is on everything I love. I'll do whatever you want. Please just give me another chance. I promise shit will be different, Tavares."

Tavares thought he was losing his mind. Surely he had to be. If not, he truly had Tavares twisted. Not because of what he was saying but because they both knew it was a lie.

"Damien, not even you believe that shit would be different. We can't come back from this. How can we when you saw nothing wrong with what you just did? Had you not been caught, you wouldn't even feel no kind of way. So, no, I don't believe that you deserve another chance or that shit will be different!"

Tavares let her emotions get the best of her and the pain started to run out through her tears again.

Tavares stopped and screamed, "You were fucking a bitch in our house! Like, who does that?! We've lived here and rested our heads here! That was a major violation!"

As she gained her composure, Tavares stopped trying to talk some sense into the dummy before her. She went back to giving her undivided attention to her walk-in closet. When she was finished packing five bags, she exited her closet.

"I don't know when, but I'll be back for the rest of my stuff," Tavares said to Damien, who was sitting on the bed looking real sad and stupid.

"Tavares, I'm fucking sorry, yo! I give you my word shit will be different. Please don't leave like this. We can fix this."

"Damien, what do you want from me? Like, what the fuck? Really, what more can I have done or how much more of a better girlfriend did you need me to be in order for you to have respected me more than you did tonight?"

"Tavares, respect? Was you respecting me, when you was running around with your sidekick the last few months? My man wasn't lying when he said he saw you in the A. I was mad at you when I was lying in the hospital, but I'm over it. I know about Mexico and yet still I'm begging you not to go."

Oh shit, how the fuck does he know about Abdora? Tavares thought but wasn't falling into that trap.

"Damien, you just don't get it. I done did this too long, too hard, and gave too much of me to just keep letting you hurt me. I'm not some bum, broke-down, ugly, low self-esteem ass bitch. I loved the fuck out of you all these years and you just treated it like it was a game. There are too many niggaz who would love to have me because of how real I am, fuck my looks!" Tavares spat. "I'm fucking beautiful, down to earth, smart, and get money. So you tell me why the fuck would I want to stay in this fucked up situation? Oh and don't me wrong, I know ain't no nigga in the street perfect and in this life you pick your battles, but now my battles are getting bigger than me, so I can't do this. Oh, and I'm taking your car," Tavares said, daring Dame to challenge her.

Damien didn't even bother saying anything. Tavares would have let loose, and he was trying to stay clear of her hands and her gun. With pain in her heart and on her mind, Tavares left before she broke down crying again. She loaded the 745 and pulled off with no clue as to whose house she was about to go crash at at 5:00 a.m. Tavares went to looking for her cell phone and realized she'd left her phone and purse. She busted a U-turn on Mass Ave and headed back to her house. When she got into the house, all she could hear was Damien yelling.

The next thing she heard was, "Nigga, that's my bitch. I made that bitch and bred that bitch, so nigga she's my bitch and here to stay. I don't give a fuck how many places you take her and how much fucking bullshit quality time you put in!"

Oh my God, he's fucking talking to Dora, Tavares thought and took off up the stairs to the second floor. She walked into the room where she should have shot Damien.

"Damien, what the fuck? Are you kidding me? Like no, are you really kidding me? I bust you and then you have the nerve to start going through my purse and my phone?"

"Bitch, fuck you and your two-dollar smut ass. Yeah, your purse that I bought and your phone that I pay for, so fucking spare me. You're tainted goods, bitch. You been running round town, outta town, and in other countries with a 'real nigga,' huh? You weren't smutting or creeping, you were being a whore. A two-dollar ass whore. You talked all that fucking shit like you were little Miss Fucking Angel, and you wasn't nothing but a blue-eyed whore in disguise. You nasty bitch, you been sucking and fucking us both, huh? Take your phone and your purse and get the fuck out, you trick bitch."

Tavares just listened and let his words sting her soul like hot grease on her skin.

"Damien, you got a lot of fucking nerve," Tavares said, crushed because she wasn't any of the things he was calling her. "I'm not a fucking whore, Bitch, and you know it. I slept with him and had a ball with him, but guess what? I'm not a jump off, the nigga digs me...digs me deep in my soul. Yeah, I fucked the nigga, but guess what? Payback is a bitch, Motherfucker. He wants to wife me, be loyal to me, and love all of me in a way that I couldn't pay your stupid fucking ass to do if your life depended on it. How are you mad that the next nigga did what you weren't willing to do and appreciates what you had? So, truly, whose fucking fault is this? Ask yourself that.

"You're supposed to always take care of home - something you don't know how to do. Dog me out. Say what you want, but in all the years we've been together, he's the first person I've ever cheated on you with. I slept with one person in six years, so you can save that guilt trip. One person. Can you honestly say that? Just answer that. All these years, it was your baby's mother, the bitches, the drama, word in the streets of you being a dog, and all I EVER did was take it! So you really have no leg to stand on.

"I just caught you in my motherfucking house giving it to another bitch like she was me, and you want to tell me about a nigga trying to love me through all your damage. How about I'll leave and you can keep everything that I don't already have. I don't need shit from you. You want to dog me like I'm a trashcan! Bitch, be my guest. I'll go with the little bit I got, but just remember you're nothing without me because I'm the only wholesome thing in your life after your family. All I did was love you and be loyal after all you've ever done to me, so fuck you, Dame. You don't fucking deserve a good bitch like me!"

Damien listened and as mad as he was, he knew that Apple was telling the truth.

"I was fucking good to you, Apple. You're buggin'."

"Am I really, Damien? It's not even what you did. It's the fact that you did it where I live and you see no problem with it. Then, you want to flip the shit on me. Hell fucking no! Take responsibility for your actions, because I am. I'm done with this and done with you. I'll never come back here unless you're dead. We can switch cars in a few days."

Tavares left knowing that she would never be coming back to the place she called home for years. Damien was lost because he felt in his soul that if she could help it, she would never again talk to him. Tavares got into Damien's car and headed toward Mattapan to Leslie's house. Dora was calling over and over but she couldn't bring herself to answer. Tavares was in deep thought as she headed up Seaver Street to Blue Hill Avenue. She couldn't believe that after so long, she was back at square one with nothing. She had plenty of money stacked from hustling and Damien, but as of the moment she had nothing and not even a place to call home.

How did I get here? Tavares asked herself. Damien had taught her well, but she never imagined leaving, so she didn't foresee ever being homeless as she now was. Tavares pulled onto Mattapan Street, parked, and laid on the doorbell.

"Who the fuck is it!?" Leslie yelled, looking over her second floor porch, heated because the doorbell woke her up.

"It's Apple, Bitch. Let me in."

"Apple, you're so lucky it's you, because I was about to go off. Im'ma buzz you in."

71

Tavares brought all her stuff upstairs as Leslie helped her in the house.

"What the hell is all of this? Come in my room and let's roll a blunt because something tells me that this is deep."

"Bitch, deep is an understatement," Tavares said and instantly burst into tears.

"Oh my god, Apple! It's going to be okay," Leslie said while wrapping her arms around her friend as she tried to soothe her.

Tavares and Leslie smoked two blunts while Tavares brought her to speed and called their friends. When the crew got there, they twisted three more blunts while they talked. They went through another four blunts while Tavares cried and they just consoled her.

"Tavares, I get it, but it's not like you don't have a nigga in the winds waiting to love you," Randee said. "And that nigga wants to love you forreal with no games, no bullshit, or nothing involved."

"I get that, Ran. Really I do, but Damien and I have a history. He's all the family that I have past y'all. I love him and his family like my own past him being my man. So how do I just wipe them all away and not love them?"

"Tavares, you have to do what you have to do for you, momma," Mona-Lisa said so genuinely that Tavares could feel her words.

"What are you going to do about school?" Jazz asked.

"I can pay for school," Tavares said.

"How can you pay for school?" Jazz asked, shocked that Tavares was banking.

"What the fuck do you mean how can I pay for school?" Tavares asked, confused by the line of questioning.

"How do you think I can pay for school? The money that I have fucking saved."

"Nah, Tavares, relax. I'm just saying it costs you good dough to go to school and pay for your apartment and shit, so I was just wondering," Jazz said, trying to clean up her shade comments.

"I got it, Jazz. I haven't been hustling and being with Damien for nothing. I actually have enough money to open a business and still go to school, if you want me to be honest," Tavares said, mad at Jazz's line of questioning for some reason.

Tavares had no problem with covering all her school expenses that Damien would have usually taken care of for her. After paying her tuition, fees, rent for the semester, and buying books, she'd probably end up spending $20,000. She was proud that she'd accumulated enough money to be set if she and Damien ever split. So, she had no problem with the fact that she was going to be dishing out that kind of money.

"Alright, well I've heard enough sad talk and smoked too many blunts. We have to get something to eat before we get ready for Winky's funeral," Mona-Lisa said, feeling the steam.

Attending the last of the three funerals was the hardest because everyone was tore down from Winky's and Squizzy's funerals over the past few days. They were past drained. Tavares and her girls couldn't believe all the traffic that had shown up for Stix's funeral. Gunfire erupted in Mattapan while he was talking to Squizzy. Stix ran under a bus for cover and got crushed. The streets were packed on the day of his funeral because out of all the deaths that had taken place, he was the innocent one. Stix had simply been at the wrong place at the wrong time. Cars were triple-parked everywhere. If a person's character could be determined by the amount of people in attendance at his funeral, then he was truly a good man. Stix was someone who had problems with no one and was loved by everyone, so it was no surprise to see so many people there to pay their respects.

The ladies entered Morning Star Baptist Church. The church was full of chickenheads crying all over the place and being way too overly dramatic. Hood niggaz sat with their respective hood wearing their mean mugs on their faces and terror in their eyes. Family members filled in a little bit of everywhere. They were scattered in the front, the back, the middle, and the overflow. The ladies spotted Damien as they were walking straight to the front to give their condolences to Mrs. Mims, who they knew very well. He had his eyes locked on them. It had been almost a week, and Tavares still had his car and hadn't talked to him. She didn't even acknowledge him at his best friend Winky's funeral. Giving Mrs. Mims kisses and hugs, the ladies chatted briefly and then strutted back down the middle of the aisle. They took a seat in the rear right corner of the church, listened to the eulogy, and cried at the different people speaking of how loving, caring, and kind Stix was and how he'd lost his life too soon.

"Now we'll have a few short words from a close and dear friend of Stanly 'Stix' Mims," the preacher announced.

Tavares thought about Abdora and the fact that she hadn't called him back since she walked in on Damien speaking with him on the phone. She closed her eyes for a brief moment. When she opened them, she couldn't believe what she saw in front of her. She thought she was trippin'.

"Hello, my name is Abdora Santacosa."

From that point on, every word from his mouth was breathtaking and moving to the large crowd. He'd brought everyone to their feet in tears and clapping as he talked about losing a friend such as Stix to a world of havoc in the streets that no longer played by the rules of the streets. He brought Stix back to life with his kind and so true words about him. He moved the females with his poise, sexy demeanor, and fine presence. He gained respect from the older people by being honest about who he was but marching to a different set of rules that maintained order. He moved the hood niggaz with his being real about the fact that life was real, and the reality was that some people were in the streets and it wasn't a life that was easy, but a life to some nonetheless. He stressed to the street players that it wasn't what you do, but how you do it.

"Play by the rules, and don't let jealousy and envy make you result to evil. You reap what you sow," were his final words.

Tavares and her girls were floored at his captivating words. Abdora could have been a preacher if he were a Christian man and not a gangster. He didn't even know it, but he had a higher calling. He had the swagger to lure and move the crowd wherever he was. When the funeral was over, everyone was teary-eyed as they took their last view of Stix before they headed to the cemetery to lay him to rest.

Abdora headed straight for Tavares when he saw her and her girls huddled in the back of the church. Abdora looked at Tavares in her all black, fitted knee-length dress with a double-breasted matching blazer over it and couldn't help but think that she was sexy. She was even sexier from the knees down in sheer black stockings around her firm legs and black stilettos that said *come fuck me* in a conservative way. *Damn, she's sexy even in distress*, Abdora thought as he approached Tavares and her friends.

"Hello, ladies. Sorry to see you under these circumstances, but it's still nice to see y'all nonetheless," Abdora said, giving them each a hug.

Damien was in the background watching how he gave a longer, tighter hug to Tavares. He recognized the familiar face from Holton's Christmas party. *That's the flashy nigga who was acting like he had a personal with me*, Dame thought. He chuckled to himself, thinking, *this is the nigga that got her open because she wouldn't be openly hugging him so long in public with me in the building if it wasn't.* Damien walked straight toward them.

"Yo Apple, let me talk to you for a minute," Damien said, grabbing Tavares's arm.

Everyone including Abdora looked at Damien like he'd lost his cotton-picking mind. Abdora looked from Tavares to Damien, then from Damien to Tavares. Tavares started to wild out but didn't want to cause a chain reaction, so she caught herself. To avoid a scene, she said ok and followed Damien's lead.

"What the fuck are you doing, Tavares?"

"What are you talking about? And furthermore, you need to watch your mouth in the house of the Lord," Tavares said, rolling her eyes.

"So that's your boo?"

"What?" Tavares asked him like he was truly buggin'.

"Don't what me. Is that the nigga that you was in Mexico with?"

Tavares gave a blank expression and still didn't answer.

"Wasn't dude at Lilly's party? So you was there fronting like you didn't know him? I remember him, so don't tell me he wasn't there."

"I'm not about to tell you nothing, so you ain't gotta worry about what's the truth and what's a lie."

"I can dig it, Tavares. Do what you do. Get yours. I'm no hater. Just don't disrespect me in the process of doing it. We're over, so you say, but as long as you're pushing my car, people don't know that. You're representing me in my car, and my niggaz won't see you hollering at the next nigga. So don't fucking disrespect me, and I'm not gonna say it again."

Tavares cracked up laughing, calmed back down, and then said, "Damien, just think about the last thing you did to me the last time we were face to face and then you give a lecture on disrespect. Tell your friends all about you disrespecting me in my house, and then let's see if they agree that I can do damn well what I please."

Tavares walked past Damien through the crowd toward her friends with a look that said *fuck you* since she couldn't say it out loud in the house of the lord. Abdora was the first one to break the silence.

"Tavares, what's good?" Abdora asked calmly because he was really steaming inside.

If it hadn't been Stix's funeral, he would have forreal shot Damien. Damien didn't know it, but Stix being laid to rest had just saved his life. Dora didn't tolerate disrespect from anyone and especially not from niggaz who wasn't on

77

his level. As far as he was concerned, Damien was nowhere near being on his level. Damien had just infuriated him, but he was trying to contain it on the strength of where they were and the occasion. Damien didn't know that his passes were getting shorter and shorter, though. Not even Tavares was gonna be able to save him in a minute.

I'm good, Abdora," Tavares said, blatantly lying in the church. "Let's go to the cemetery and I'll call you later. That's my word."

Tavares knew that a person's word meant everything to Abdora, so she had no choice but to deal with him on top of what she was going through with Damien.

Listening to "Amazing Grace" being sung by Danielle was heartbreaking and brought everyone to tears on the cold winter day that had the sun shining brightly on Stix. Danielle had been messing with Stix from way back, but no one ever knew because they had kept it on the down low. This was because Stix was the best friend of her baby's father, who had passed away years ago. She'd come by the house often with Stix when Damien had card parties with his exclusive poker players. Danielle was cool especially because she always encouraged Stix to live a different life and use his drawing talents.

When she was done singing, the soil beneath everyone was soaked with tears. Danielle was crying the hardest because she'd just lost the second man that she ever loved to murder. She didn't know what her life would be like without Stix and she wasn't ready to find out. His sideline hoes were whaling from the top of their lungs. You would have thought that he was married to some of them the way they were carrying on and making a spectacle of themselves. Stix's boys were fighting to contain their tears. Some succeeded while others weren't so strong.

Dora wanted to cry, but he hadn't cried since he was seven years old, so he didn't know if he even knew how to cry. Mrs. Mims was the strongest of everyone with not a tear coming down. She was from the old school and believed that when it was your time to go, it was your time to go and that God made no mistake in calling her son home. She was just grateful and at peace that her son was being laid to rest in such a beautiful manner. Damien laid a dozen white roses on the casket before they lowered it down. One by one Abdora's crew released a white dove in the air. Damien watched and was mad that he was outdone by the nigga that was trying to move in on his territory.

Stix's funeral hurt everyone because he was so loved. Being the good dude he was, he was gone but never would be forgotten. Everyone said their goodbyes and headed to the Carver Lodge, where Stix's repast party was being held. When Tavares and her girls arrived at the Carver Lodge on Talbot Avenue, they couldn't help but blow a kiss to Stix for all the people who loved him.

"This is crazy," Mona-Lisa said.

"Stix knows he's wrong for being loved by this many people," Randee said.

"It must be nice," Jazz added. "We can park around the corner in my Uncle Todd's garage."

As they headed toward Vesta Road, the ladies parked and made their way to the Carver Lodge. As they entered the overly spacious hall, there were people everywhere mixing and mingling. Everyone was smiling. Stix was a good dude who died bad, so you had to smile on the day you laid him to rest. Abdora was kicking it with Stix's mother. Her face was sad, but her strength kept her from breaking down. Stix had paid for and planned his own funeral in case anything happened to him. Mrs. Mims didn't have to do anything except buy a new dress. It was sad, but her son was prepared. All too often, he would remind her that she'd be straight if he died. That flashed across Mrs. Mims' mind as she talked to Abdora.

"Abdora, I want you to be safe in these streets," Mrs. Mims said in her thick Bajan accent.

"I have no idea what you and my son were doing in New York at age sixteen when y'all met, but he found a good and a true friend in you. I love you like a son. I never want to see anything happen to you. So you be safe in those streets. They'll tear you down and take all you have in a blink of an eye. When I came here from Barbados, I wanted a better life for my boy. He was everywhere, loved by many, and just moving fast. America gave my timid island boy a bad rush of too much fast and wild city life. He did things that I'm not proud of, but he was a good boy."

"Ma, I know he was, and that's why all these people are here. Should you need anything, and I do mean anything, even a ride to church, you call me and there will be a driver at your front door."

Mrs. Mims smiled because she knew Abdora was true to his word when he said call for anything, even a ride to church. Her son and Abdora had been close over the years, so she knew he said what he meant and meant what he said.

"You're a good boy just like my Stanley, so I can't stress it enough to you for you to please be safe, Abdora."

Abdora kissed Mrs. Mims goodbye because the hidden hurt in her was taking over him. He made his way to the cut because it appeared to be all eyes on him. Chicks were lurking trying to figure out who the gangster was in the perfectly tailored, obviously expensive black suit. He had on a crisply pressed white shirt with a red tie and red gators on his feet. He was by far the flyest dude in the building, and the ladies were definitely on him. The niggaz could feel a real gangster was in the building, so Abdora had them on their ps and qs. Abdora was chillin', though. He wasn't worried about anyone. He was just waiting for a nigga to act stupid at his man's repast so that he could really show niggaz in Boston how he got down.

Damien was in the corner with his niggaz just watching Abdora.

"I don't like that nigga," Damien said. "It's like the nigga is trying to be low-key, but he can't help but stand out."

"Nigga, you just don't like the nigga because you think him and Tavares are going hard-body," Rollo clowned. "That nigga is doing him."

"Nigga, please," Damien said, knowing what his brother had said was true. "I just ain't feeling dude!"

"It's whatever with the nigga," Rollo stated, having his brother's back, "but that nigga ain't thinking about you."

"He ain't thinking about me, my ass! He gotta be because he's trying to knock my bitch," Damien said with nothing but disgust and malice in his voice.

Abdora could feel Damien all over him, but he didn't give a fuck. He wasn't thinking about Damien because he left many niggaz staring when he stepped in a place, and few were bold enough to get at him, though. Abdora mixed and mingled with his niggaz. His main concern was making sure that no one acted up or disrespected the celebration of his man's life. Everyone had been able to get in with at least one gun, so they were ready for whoever and whatever.

Tavares was watching Abdora and was turned on by how he was working the crowd with his charismatic ways. You would have thought he was the mayor the way people were breaking their necks to talk to him.

"Your boy got a mean swagger," Jazz said as they looked at Abdora from a distance and sipped on their drinks.

"Tell me about it," Tavares said. "Everyone always gravitates to him likes he the man. What can I say?"

Tavares took off her jacket and was in a form-fitting black dress that zipped up her back and had a v-neck in the front. It was sexy but classy.

"I'll be back," Tavares said and off she went.

Tavares made her way through the crowd. Her hips and ass were all that you saw as she glided toward Abdora. When she approached Abdora, Tavares found him talking to Lilly and Holton.

"Hi," Tavares said, giving them each a hug.

"Nice to see you, Señorita," Lilly said.

She loved Tavares in an odd, motherly kind of way but contained her excitement of seeing her for the sake of not wanting to raise curiosity to Holton. Tavares never judged her, which was why they had grown close over the years. Tavares accepted Lilly for who she was, flawed and all, so Lilly had a genuine love for the girl.

Holton couldn't help but stare indirectly at Tavares. She was gorgeous and her eyes were so mesmerizing. It wasn't the color but the look in the eyes that gave him a feeling he experienced long ago in his past. Holton was digging the young bad bitch. He was older but never had a problem getting a woman old or young. He made a mental note to do a background check on Tavares. He had meant to do one a few weeks ago, but it truly slipped his mind. During the four-way conversation Tavares could feel Holton looking at her in a different kind of way and wondered if Abdora and Lilly noticed because she sure did. After making short talk, Holton and Lilly worked their way through the crowd.

"So what's up, Babygirl? Why ain't I heard from you?"

"I been going through a lot, Dora. It ain't got shit to do with you. I just been going through a whole lot since I got back."

"I take it your wack ass boyfriend calling me has a major part to play in what you been going through?"

"Yeah," Tavares said, totally embarrassed.

"You don't seem like you want to talk about it right now, so I'll wait 'til you're ready," Dora said.

He picked up on her change of body language when he brought Damien up.

"Just know, though, when you shut the world off, you don't have to shut me off," Dora snapped in his gangsterly, caring manner.

Tavares couldn't help but smile. Dora had that effect on her and she could appreciate it.

"Well, when are you leaving?" she asked, feeling bad for the dirty thoughts going through her head.

She was trying to get some of that serious dick before he went back home.

83

"I'll be here for a few days to make sure that Mrs. Mims is straight. I'm going to outright pay for her house. Stix left money to pay it off in case anything ever happened to him. She wouldn't let him do it when he was living, so that was the deal if anything ever happened to him. So, once that is a go, I'll be back home to business as usual."

"Well, I'll call you tomorrow early evening once you've taken care of your business. I got a few things to handle also, so it works out."

"Sounds good, Beautiful, and remember what I said. You can call me for anything. I'm trying to make you mine, so you better get me before all these hungry wolves try to sink their fangs into me," Abdora joked.

"Whatever," Tavares laughed, knowing that it was true. "I'll call you tomorrow."

Tavares made her way back to the table and couldn't help but feel uneasy with Abdora and Damien in the same room. It was like they were both watching her to see her interaction with the other.

~Chapter 5~
Real "Gs" Do Real Things

Damien was all on Tavares. She didn't care about him seeing her talk to Dora. So what if she was driving his car? Damien watched Tavares take a seat with a big smile on her face. Ready to rain on her parade, Damien got up and made his way across the large function hall.

"What's up, ladies?" Dame said, approaching Tavares and her home girls.

Everyone said *what's up, hello* and *hi*, except for Tavares.

"Yo, Tav, get off the funny shit before you get embarrassed in public."

Sucking her teeth and rolling her eyes, Tavares spat, "Here you go, ready to start some bullshit."

"Naw, not yet Tavares, but I need to talk to you because you got me totally fucked up."

Not trying to entertain the bullshit, Tavares simply said, "Damien, I'm NOT doing this. Now ain't the time nor the place. So how about you just go back to your table and keep whatever fucked up shit you want to come out your mouth in your mind."

"Nah, because you're on some brand new shit that's going to get you fucked up. So I'm trying to help you out."

"Dame, I'm not going nowhere with you, so you can forget it. If I get fucked up, I get fucked up. I really don't care to hear a motherfucking thing you gotta say to me, considering that you were fucking another bitch in my house."

"Tavares, your mouth is just real out of fucking pocket, yo!"

"What you think? They, of all people, don't know the truth?" Tavares giggled.

Damien wanted to reach across the table and slap the shit out of Tavares, but he wasn't going to disrespect Stix so he spun around with anger welled up in him and made his way outside to blow a blunt. Abdora watched the whole scene transpire and decided that it was time he and Damien had a chat. A chat that was long overdue. Damien was due for some real chin-checking and he was going to give it to him. Never a man to need an army, Abdora simply slipped away from the crowd and walked outside and found Damien.

"My man, let me holler at you for second."

"What the fuck you need to holler at me for?" Damien responded.

Abdora chuckled because it was his experience that niggaz that played the biggest gangsters had never encountered a real gangster such as himself.

"Yo, my man, we can save the tough shit because I ain't the one. A nigga like me will leave you lying on this pavement and walk the fuck back inside like nothing ever happened. Then, I'll send your mother a check to bury you."

Abdora was so cool, cold, and icy that Damien caught his drift.

"What's good? Say what you need to say," Damien said, knowing better than to get too smart.

"I just came out here to tell you that Tavares ain't your property no more, so you can stop tryna check her before I take that shit personal. You fucked up, son. You walked all over her, violated her and your relationship, and now she's moved on to bigger and better things. She deserves to be loved, and Im'ma love her since you wasn't capable. You was talking real greasy on the jack but that shit wasn't bout nothing to me. Know that you done had two ghetto passes, and you ain't getting a third one with me."

Damien knew that Abdora was trying to punk him and he wasn't that dude.

"Look here, I don't know who you THOUGHT you were checking, but you ain't sparing me a motherfucking thing. If you feel froggy, leap."

Dora just laughed because Damien didn't know the next encounter they had he would be more than leaping. He would be leaving his mother to bury him.

"You're such a bitch ass nigga that I can't do nothing but laugh. But, nigga, you've been warned about MY bitch."

He left Dame standing there and made his way back inside knowing that Damien had heard him loud and clear. Damien's dislike turned to pure hatred for Abdora. He did his homework on the ruthless killer and he was gonna stay in his lane and deal with Abdora. He would keep his hands clean and take care of Abdora with one phone call. He would have the last laugh and get his bitch back. Damien was going to play the game, but he wasn't going to play fair.

After drinking, eating, and partying the night away, the ladies left happy, drunk, and full of tears. Tavares got everyone home safely but as she and Leslie headed up Blue Hill Avenue, a milk delivery truck almost came through them as Tavares took a left turn on a red light while the oncoming traffic light had already turned green. Their lives flashed before their eyes in what seemed like a blink of an eye.

"Oh my God, Tavares! Get me fucking home. That delivery truck was about to demolish us, and had we lived Damien would have killed us for crashing his car."

"Fuck Damien!" Tavares started to yell and cry at the same time. "Fuck him! That nigga did me dirty! I hope he dies. I fucking hate him."

Tavares was clearly fired up from being drunk.

"I know, Boo, but you'll get through this. Just hang in there."

Tavares got to Leslie's, made her way upstairs, and cried herself to sleep.

Abdora handled his business with Mrs. Mims, saw his soldiers off, and headed back downtown to the Omni Parker House Hotel. Just as Abdora stepped out of the shower, he heard Tavares's ringtone, "Miss Independent," and smiled.

"Girl, what are you doing to me?" Abdora answered.

"Not a damn thing," Tavares said with a sassy attitude. "Where are you? I'll be there to get you in an hour."

"Downtown at the Omni. I'll be out front at 8:00 p.m., so be here on time slowpoke," Abdora teased.

"Surely will and with bells on," Apple shot back sarcastically.

Tavares left Leslie's cute from head to toe in a pair of tight-fitted black jeans, tall thigh-high black boots, and a black and white designer shirt with a red winter blazer on. She was matching with her black Gucci bag. Tavares hopped in the 745, threw on the heated seats, and made her way downtown. She pulled up two minutes early. Abdora came out of the hotel promptly at eight o'clock, and she couldn't help but get wet at the sight of him. He was so ruggedly gangsta but relaxed and sexy at the same time.

Abdora got in and said, "Nice car."

"Oh, you're trying be funny," Tavares chuckled. "Thanks, but it's not mine. It's borrowed."

"Borrowed from who?"

"Doesn't matter, just be the passenger."

"It does matter. I don't want to be in a stolen car," Abdora joked because he knew whose car it was.

"Relax and enjoy the passenger seat for the evening."

"Ok, since it's top-secret about whose car you have me in, where are we going?" Dora asked, liking that Tavares was taking charge of the evening.

"We're going to Legal Seafood for dinner. After that, I'll tell you the next stop of the evening."

"So you going to tell me what you been going through?" Dora asked as he looked at the pretty girl with heaviness in her eyes.

"More than I care to talk about right now. Let's just have a good night because I'm not trying to dampen the mood with all the bullshit going on in my life."

"Whatever you say, Ma. I'm falling back and rolling wit' you."

After chatting and having double stuffed lobster dinners and cocktails of Patrón margaritas, Tavares was ready to call it a night but knew it was too early. Tavares and Abdora waited for the valet to bring the car and saw a horse and carriage.

"Fuck that car, Ma. We gonna ride the horse and carriage. It's on me."

"Naw, we can ride the horse and carriage, but I got it," Tavares said, letting it be known that the night was on her.

Dora smiled and swept Tavares off her feet while giving her a kiss that melted her instantly between the legs.

"Hot boy, you can't be doing that," Tavares said and burst into laughter.

He had no clue what his lips on her mouth did to Tavares between the legs. Dora flagged the horse and carriage down, and told the driver to take them for a two-hour ride all over the city of Boston. Tavares and Abdora snuggled up under a blanket and were taken around the Boston Commons, up past the state house, down through Government Center where all the courthouses and city hall were located, and back around into the center of downtown Boston past Suffolk University and the other side of the Commons. The driver made his way to Faneuil Hall, where there were shops, restaurants, and clubs everywhere. Next, they headed down the way to the infamous Italian north end where they sold the best pastries and had the most authentic Italian food. When they looked up they were on the waterfront, looking at Boston Harbor.

"Damn, that shit is beautiful," Tavares said.

The sound of Tavares's voice said she was there but she was a million miles away in her thoughts, and she was. She was wondering how her life came to be and how men like Abdora really existed in real life.

"Ma, we can do this shit every day. It's nothing. As long as I got air in me, I wanna make it my mission to see you happy."

Tavares started to cry because she couldn't understand how the one nigga she thought would always love her hadn't, but now she had the most perfect nigga in front of her and she was scared to go hard with him.

"Why're you crying, Beautiful? Your eyes done changed colors and some more shit. Stop that shit. You ain't gotta cry." Abdora instructed the driver, "Take us back to where you picked us up."

Going through the financial district, down Tremont Street through the theater district, the horse and carriage made its way back toward the Luxury Park Plaza Hotel where the upscale seafood restaurant was.

"Hold up, Ma," Abdora stopped Tavares as she went to get out of the carriage. "We ain't done."

"Yes we are," Tavares said.

"Nah we ain't. I want to hear you say this shit is so beautiful again."

"A thug with a sensitive side," Tavares said, blowing him a kiss.

"Girl, you're the only thing that makes me sensitive, so don't get your boy twisted. It's not my fault that I'm a gangsta who can romance. So, fall back and let me take care of this shit."

Tavares just fell back and snuggled under the blanket as she waited for Abdora to return.

Abdora entered the hotel where the valet was and said, "Here's $300. Take care of the navy blue 745 and keep the change."

The young black man was happy to take the $200 tip. Abdora came back outside, slapped the driver a high five, and slipped him $600.

"Buddy, I'm sure that will take care of the rest of the evening."

91

"Abdora, I told you I had it," Tavares said defensively.

"Nah, Ma. Let me do this. I want to. Plus, I already broke him off."

Tavares just shook her head and snuggled back under Abdora as they took off down the street toward Newbury Street, where all the upscale shopping was. It was always busy, full of natives and tourist enjoying the scenery and the lively atmosphere. It was cold out, but their body heat was keeping them warm as they snuggled under the blanket.

Taking them down Newbury Street past tons of stores like the Chanel Boutique, Marc Jacobs, Nike Town, Gap, Condom World, and Urban Outfitters, they turned right to go up Mass Ave. They crossed the Mass Ave Bridge, which was surrounded by the Charles River.

"Isn't that shit just so peaceful and serene?" Tavares asked Dora like she was in another world.

"Take us around this whole river," Abdora said as he saw the look of serenity in Tavares's eyes.

The driver had no gripes taking them anywhere for the six crisp bills that he counted three red lights ago. After cruising the city, talking, laughing, and kissing the night away, they ended their ride at the historic landmark Wally's Jazz Club. It was as big as a narrow hallway in a house, but the live jazz was cool along with the strong drinks the friendly bartender was serving. After taking shot after shot trying to out-drink each other, they both ended up drunk.

"Yo, I'm fucked up," Tavares said, sweeping her fingers through her hair after her six double shots had snuck up on her.

"You ready to roll?" Dora asked, because he sure was.

He was feeling the liquor, too, and was trying to do more than stand close to Tavares. They flagged a cab, and Tavares and Abdora ended up at his hotel ready to make magic. After rolling around in the sheets until the sun rose, Tavares and Abdora passed out for the morning. When Tavares woke up, Dora was in the foyer at the desk on the phone making some sort of reservations. *Where the hell is he going now?* Tavares asked herself, but wasn't going to question him. When Dora heard Tavares in the bathroom, he got the last details for his last-minute trip and made his way to the bedroom.

"Good afternoon, Beautiful. Or, should I say Sleeping Beauty?"

"Please. We didn't go to sleep till seven, so are you kidding me?"

"Be quiet and relax with your feisty pretty ass. I was just joking. When do you start classes?"

"Why, are we going to be together till I go back to school?"

"You know what, Miss Tavares. With all that attitude you got and the speed that you ask a question with a question, we just might have to send your little feisty ass to law school."

"I'm going to go to law school. Believe that."

"Good, it will give you something to do with all that assertion and aggressiveness."

"Whatever," Tavares laughed as she stood naked in a bathrobe with her hair everywhere looking like she got the business all morning.

"I'm asking the questions, so like I asked the first time, when, Miss Tavares, do you start classes?"

"I start class one week from Monday."

"Good, clear your schedule and meet me at the airport in five hours."

"Excuse me?"

"You heard me."

"Yeah, I heard you, but who told you that you can just be clearing my schedule? Just because everyone else jumps to your word doesn't mean that I do. Who told you that I can just clear my week to slide to who knows where with you?"

Tavares rolled her eyes as if she meant what she'd said. Dora loved that she had to put up a fight about everything. It was humbling.

"Girl, would you stop talking and get dressed so you can make it?"

It was clear that he dismissed the foolish idea that she wouldn't be clearing her schedule to come with him. Tavares wasn't the fastest person, so she didn't think she'd make it.

"There's no way in hell I can shop, pack, get my hair and nails done, and make it to the airport in five hours. That's just totally unrealistic."

"Babygirl, it's very doable," Abdora said with a look that read *make it happen and shut up*. "Prioritize. Do what you think you really feel you need most. If you come with nothing, don't worry about it. We can get you whatever you need when we get to where we're going."

"Where are we going?"

"Damn, the questions never stop, do they? Naw, you gotta ask questions like you tryna piece a puzzle together!"

"I ask questions 'til I'm all out or all the pieces seem to fit."

"Well, guess what? I ain't answering no more questions, so don't ask. There's a car ready to take you to your car when you get dressed. Pack for warm weather is all that I'm telling you. Our flight leaves at eight o'clock, so you better be there. Meet me at the American Airlines ticket counter."

Abdora kissed Tavares's forehead and left her there dumbfounded as he went to handle some business. Tavares debated shopping or going to get her hair done because there was no way she was going to have time to do both. Shopping won. Tavares bought everything she needed from cute shorts and tee shirts to accessories, bras, panties, and flat pretty sandals. Her nails were done, so she was just going to wet her hair and wear it in its natural curly state. Tavares was rushing from the mall not even believing that she'd made it. She parked Dame's car at the house, left him a note on the counter that said thanks for everything, and even though she was being strong enough to walk away, she still loved him. Tavares called a cab and was on her way to the airport.

By the time they arrived in Miami, the night breeze was blowing perfectly and Tavares was ready to hit the streets. Miami wasn't the place to come and just sit around. There was too much to do. They arrived at the Marriott on Collins, showered, and headed out.

"Don't you look cute," Dora teased, referring to Tavares's black dress shorts, leopard print pumps, and red fitted blazer with a leopard bra.

"Always," Tavares replied.

"You're so stuck up that it's sad."

"I'm not stuck up, I'm confident. So get it correct, Mr. Man."

Dora was looking sexy in his tan linen shorts, brown and tan Gucci bowling sneakers, and a fitted white tee with his jewelry blinging from every angle. They headed out looking like the perfect couple, and they were about to get white girl wasted on South Beach.

Holton was in his home office sipping on cognac and working on building blue prints. There was a tap at his office door. In walked a tall, burly-sized man who was decent in looks, just too big in size.

"What's up, Holton?"

"Gillis, glad to see you."

"I got the information you asked for."

Holton was true to his word. The day following the repast, he'd contacted his private investigator to do a background check on Damien's girlfriend, who seemed to be more interested in Abdora.

"I wanted to bring it to you personally."

Gillis wasn't sure Holton was ready for what was inside the report. *What could be in there so serious that Gillis hand-delivered this package to me?* Holton thought, dropping his pen and extending his hand to give the man dap.

"Was there anything good to be learned about her pretty, sexy little ass?"

Gillis didn't even know where to begin about the young girl he made reference to wanting to bang, so he just said, "It's all in there."

Gillis slid the thick package over to Holton, collected his pay, and headed out the door. Holton wanted to examine everything when he had time to go through it all, so he threw it in his top drawer with the intentions of looking at it later that evening.

After a week of eating, drinking, and sex in Miami, Tavares had truly enjoyed herself. Jet-skiing on South Beach, riding mopeds, parasailing, going to the Bahamas, and shopping on Collins had Tavares not wanting to leave Dora's side. The more time she spent with Abdora, the more she anticipated waking up to him daily. The feeling of being with him was intoxicating. Tavares was boarding her plane back to school, sad that she was leaving Abdora. After telling him about everything she'd been through, he took her away to get her mind right before going back to school. Tavares was on the plane with a clear mind, ready to go back to school and to keep pushing toward her goal. She exited the Savannah International Airport, hopped in a cab, and headed toward Tybee Island, where her luxury apartment was located.

When she entered the duplex apartment, she found a note from her roommate saying: *Baby momma, I missed you over the break. I went to get us some dinner. Be back in an hour. Love you. P.S. That package on the bar came for you today.* Tavares smiled at her roommate's note and went to the bar to grab the extra heavy package. Breaking through three envelopes, Tavares found $40,000 in cash with a note that said: *Pay for school. I owe you that much. I love you, Tavares.* She knew the writing was Damien's but didn't know what to think. She'd already paid for school and he was right, he did owe her that much. So she wasn't sending the money back, that was for sure.

97

Tavares went upstairs to her king-size bedroom on the right side of the house. She buried the package of money in her closet and just fell on her bed and thought about Abdora. She missed him already, but she was going to take a shower and wait for Asia before she got caught up talking to him on the phone. When she did call him later that afternoon, Tavares didn't talk to Abdora for too long because she wanted to talk to Asia. Asia and Tavares kicked it well into the wee hours of the morning.

"Nigga, we got class at nine in the morning. Inda, Davenia, and Vachelle are meeting us at Loco's for lunch at twelve."

Tavares loved her school crew because they were all just alike, living the high life but doing their thing in college. No one balled out or did it better than they did. Tavares took a shower, laid her clothes out, and crawled in bed. Before she could debate to call Abdora back or not, her cell phone was ringing.

Tavares just laughed and answered, "Yes, stalker."

Tavares talked to Abdora until the wee hours of the morning, and finally hung up at 6:00 a.m. with the hopes of getting two hours of sleep before her 9:00 a.m. class. She went to her 9:00 and 10:30 a.m. classes before she headed downtown to meet her crew. Tavares was the last to arrive and heard her friends before she even made it good into the restaurant. They were in the corner sipping on sangrias and stuffing their faces like they didn't have classes to go back to in a little while.

"Hey bitch," Inda said, spotting Tavares.

Tavares slid in the seat and threw her hand in the air, trying to flag the waiter down for a drink.

"Look at your bougie ass all iced out and shit," Inda said, blown away by the diamond-encrusted necklace and charm bracelet.

"Christmas gift," Tavares said flatly, "And I know you ain't talking with those five platinum carats dangling from your wrist. I'm just catching up," Tavares joked.

Her girls balled like she did, so her jewelry was nothing to them. It was just the newest and hottest pieces for them all to admire.

"I need a friend," Vachelle only half-joked.

She was spoiled rotten by her parents and three older brothers and had no boyfriend. She only dated and they had to be straight hustling, balling niggaz who were getting money on top of money. Vachelle's attitude was you had to pay like you weigh to even be around her.

"Alright, so are we throwing a back-to-school party?" Davenia asked, loving to always party for no reason or occasion.

She just made up reasons like she was doing at the moment. Davenia's dad had passed away and left her and her moms millionaires, so blowing money was a sport to her.

"Oh hell yeah, shawty. That's what it do," Vachelle said.

"Oh no, we gotta get ready to go away for spring break and y'all want to throw a back to school party?" Asia asked, always being the frugal one in the crew.

There was one thing Asia didn't limit her own personal money to and that was maintaining her looks, shopping, and eating well. After those things, her money was always questionable.

Tavares shrugged her shoulders and said, "I'm in, but we ain't giving the party at our crib. I hate that even after we clean up, it still feels dirty. Then we gotta jerk another $200 for the maids to come."

"So, what we'll do," Inda said, cutting Tavares short like she had the answer to that problem, "is just throw the party at someone else's house. Like really," Inda said with a *get serious* look, "who ain't gonna let us host a party at their house?"

"I know, right, so uhhh, let's see," Vachelle said, thinking out loud.

"Location is important, because we need a lot of space," Asia reminded, forgetting that just thirty seconds ago, she wasn't even in.

"We can so give it at one of the baseball players' houses," Tavares suggested, rationalizing that they had the most spacious and nicest apartments in the complex where the school teams were housed off-campus.

"Hell mufuckin yeah," Vachelle said.

"I'll call Reef, Poppy, and Campbell tonight."

Nathaniel Reefs, III, London Poppy, and Kentrell Campbell were all fine without a doubt and had made men in tights sexy to a woman. The girls started out going to the games to see their fine, sexy asses in tights. The starters noticed the hot girls, and after a few conversations they all became cool as hell.

"After we buy $2,000 in food and a $4,000 in liquor, we'll be straight," said Davenia.

Everyone agreed and their party was in motion. As they exchanged stories about Christmas break, they drank and got fucked up. Before they knew it, it was 2:00 p.m. and they were all drunk. Deciding to blow off class for the rest of the day, they headed to the island to Asia and Tavares's house to get even more fucked up. By the time they arrived at the house, they all were impressed by Abdora.

"Yo," Vachelle said. "That nigga is that dude. I had been hollered at my peeps up top in New York, and they say that your mans and them is bigger than New Jack City."

"Vachelle, I don't care about that nigga's dough."

"Nah, only Vachelle does," Inda joked.

"I like him for him. That's it. Nothing more. Nothing less."

That comment brought on a debate about if money was important in deciding to deal with or be with a man. After debating about if money was important or not, Vachelle and Davenia lost with their two votes.

"Vachelle, the only reason your fucking ass don't think that love is more important is because you got your feelings hurt once. You can't let one time of pain deter you from loving, Bitch."

"What the fuck ever, hoe. I ain't getting my feelings hurt ever again. I get what I want, be cool, have fun, and go with the flow and don't even fuck them, so it works for me. There's no room for me to get my feelings hurt. Fuck love."

Tavares wanted the opposite.

"Nah, bitch, I want to be with a nigga to love him and to let him to know that he challenges me to do better and makes me aspire to know more and have more. I want a nigga to take care of me. And I don't mean with money, but to take care of ME... Feed me, run my bath, rub my back and my body from head to toe. One that will give me sex like he invented the concept. A nigga who lets me know and feel that every day is about me. Every motherfucking day and there ain't shit that can tear us apart. He holds me and my stress disappears. The problem ain't got to be fixed, but with him lying there, I know that the pain, problem, or burden is going to be taken away. It's like you're loving him and loving him and he's loving you back even more, so why would you want to leave that or break up with him."

"You wouldn't," Inda said with a look that said *unless you're a silly bobble-head chick.*

"Exactly... and none of that has got anything to do with money," Tavares said. "But y'all know me, so you know that even though I'm going for love, it's nice that he got dollars."

Everyone busted out laughing while Inda and Vachelle twisted two more blunts apiece. They took shot after shot, getting fucked up reminiscing about their winter vacations and how it would be weird for Tavares and Damien not to be together. But like her girls back home, they, too, were Team Abdora!

Damien was in the hood with his niggaz getting fucked up like he'd been doing since Tavares left.

"My niggaz, Tavares ain't even call me and say shit before she bounced back to school. I thought she was going to call and ask for me to pay for school but she didn't. I know that nigga ain't dishing out cash for school. I came home and found my car key in the kitchen with a note. Tavares is on some real bullshit."

Rollo looked at his brother who was looking for sympathy and he had none for him.

"Dame, nigga, I love you to death, but do you think you deserve for her to call you? You had Tavares right where you wanted her all this time. She took your bullshit and put up with your bullshit any way you dished it out, but some shit she just ain't going for. Did you think this was going to ride? My nigga, you really don't know your girl then. I love Tavares like a big sister and knew better than that dumb shit. The only way Tavares will talk to you is if there's a sudden death."

"Man, fuck you niggaz. I don't want to hear this fucking bullshit. I fucked up, but her ass was out of teezy stunting with niggaz, so she ain't no fucking better."

"Nigga, please," Rollo said. "She might have been, but nigga, you know that was your slip up. We be deep in the streets, and all the years you and Apple been together, you ain't never heard a nigga say that he was fucking with your bitch or had anything with your bitch other than she fucking loves you or is cool as fuck. You know Nana says what goes around comes around, and you reap what you sow. So, nigga, you just got what you deserved."

In the confinement of his office, Holton went in his desk drawer and obtained the contents that he'd put away a few days earlier. He never recognized that the contents weren't in the same position that he'd laid them in and he opened the envelopes and laid everything all out. He learned things that he wouldn't believe if he wasn't looking at them with his own eyes. Tavares was the daughter of Dolonda De Gada. She'd just turned twenty-one years old and came from a hard life. She was in foster care, till she ran away. She'd been on her own since. She lived with Dame and his family.

They were the closest thing she had to any family. She had spent the years working, going to school, and hustling. She was an honor roll student, who all her teachers loved.

People in the streets, men especially, were crazy about her. Women were envious. Her pretty face and keep-it-real attitude had her well-respected in both her worlds of school and the streets. She was a fighter who had no problem stomping a person out - something she clearly got from both her parents. Tavares was strong, independent, outgoing, and outspoken. She was in a six-year relationship with Damien up till a few weeks ago, but had been going hard with Abdora for months. Yet she still had maintained loyalty to Dame and was friends with Dora till they broke up, according to the report. Tavares was soon to graduate and was top in her class.

Holton was impressed and proud of what he read. However, he was knocked off his feet when he read Holton Montiago was her father, who had left her mother and never was a part of her life. From the math, he calculated that he indeed was her father. He and Dolonda had dated and were very much in love. So, it wasn't hard to believe she was his daughter, although he thought Tavares had been aborted. Holton was blown. He had no idea what to think or how to feel. No matter what he'd told Dolonda all those years ago when he kicked her to the curb, had he known that she had the baby she said she aborted, he would have been there.

"Damn, how the fuck am I going to tell Lilly this?" Holton asked himself over and over.

Lilly was sure to bug out when she found out that he and Dolonda had a baby together. Holton knew her eyes were all too familiar. They resembled his mother's in look

104

and Dolonda's mother in color. *Fuck*, Holton kicked himself in the ass. How the fuck was he going to work this out? Holton didn't know, but he locked the contents away for the moment till he came up with a solution. First and foremost, he had to find Dolonda.

Damien and his two boys headed to the Mattapan Tavern. Seeing them come through the door together had the women like *whoa, who the fuck,* and *goddamn.* They were all fine and had their own individual swagger. Trizzy was ruggedly sexy. Rainy was the pretty ball-playing thug. Damien was a chocolate delight from the looks to straight hood swagger.

"These bitches are rougher than me," Trizzy said, looking at the females who had a rough presence to themselves.

"Tell me about it," Dame said. "These bitches are bitches that you ain't even gots to wine and dine. You can tell them you got some weed and liquor, and they'll be straight ready to give you some."

Trizzy and Rainy fell out laughing. Dame stayed talking shit, but he was usually telling the truth. He just didn't like when someone told him the truth. Damien decided to drink up and bag him a broad to spend the night with. He was headed to the bar to hit on the cute bartender when his baby's mother came through the door. Damien just sucked his teeth and knew this night was about to go downhill. Damien kept on about his mission and wasn't even about to worry about his drama-filled baby's mother.

"How can I help you?" the small, chocolate bartender with pretty gleaming white teeth and a huge smile asked.

"I'll take two double shots of Patrón, one double shot of Remy, and your number."

The bartender laughed at the charismatic handsome dude, who she'd seen come into the bar from time to time.

"Uhhh, excuse me," Shaunda said, looking at the bartender talking to her baby's father.

"If you're done flirting with my baby's father, I'd like to order."

The friendly bartender looked at Shaunda like she was slap-dead crazy.

"Well, how about when I'm done flirting with your baby's father, who's also flirting with me, I come take your order?"

She knew the chick was just trying to bully her, so she shut her down right then and there to let her know she had the wrong one.

"Yo! Forreal, Shaunda. Like forreal forreal, please don't get embarrassed in this bar in front of everyone. Matter of fact, you need to order from the other bartender for the rest of the night," Damien snarled.

Shaunda wanted to test the waters, but something told her not to do it. For the rest of the night, Damien kicked it with the bartender buying rounds, while his boys played pool and clowned all the hoodrats that were on them like white on rice. Shaunda was mad that her friends had even convinced her to come out. Had she not even come out, she wouldn't have even seen Damien all in the next bitch's face. Shaunda was mad as hell that Damien was doing him right in front of her face.

He knew that Shaunda still wanted him, but he wasn't considerate of her feelings. Damien had left Shaunda and her bullshit alone for good when he got with Tavares. Nothing in hell would make him fall backwards and deal with his baby's mother past their being parents. Even if he had been stupid enough to do so down the line, she ruined that by messing with someone from a rival hood. Shaunda just watched and welled up inside with anger as her friends sat and talked shit to her about Damien doing him.

"Girl, if that was me," Shay Shay said, "I'd bust that nigga up."

"How you just going to let him do that shit?" Quoia asked, rolling her big eyes and snapping her already too small neck.

"And when Dame fucks me up, who the fuck is going to help me? I know it ain't going to be you two stupid bitches. So just leave me fuck alone and let's go. I want to go get my kids and go the hell home. Fuck Damien," Shaunda said, getting up so fast and so mad that she damn near knocked the bar stool over.

Shaunda's home girls could feel her pain as a baby's mother, so they just got up and followed suit. Damien just laughed because he knew the deal.

Over the next week, Holton searched high and low for Dolonda. Her mother had passed away, according to public records, and there was nothing listed in her name that made her traceable. *Damn, I taught Dolonda all too well,* Holton thought, frustrated. Lilly had oddly been picking at and talking shit to Holton for the last week. Holton was in the kitchen listening to Lilly flap her gums and had had enough. He didn't say two words. He grabbed his leather coat, hopped in his Cadillac, and headed to Boston to the one place he knew for sure that someone had seen Dolonda. Last he'd heard of her, she was still running rampant off that shit he put on the streets every day.

As he was approaching the projects, Holton parked on the corner in front of the liquor store. He hadn't been in the projects in years, but he had no problem hitting the streets when it was called for. Holton hit the corner of the broken down projects that had junkies and dealers everywhere. He spotted Damien. Damien saw a sight that he hadn't seen in years. Holton was walking through the hood. It had to be a serious problem. Damien was the one running the bricks, so if anyone knew Dolonda's comings and goings, it would be Damien.

"Yo, Dame, let me holler at you."

"Yeah, what's good?" Dame was really pondering what could be so major that Holton was out and about in the projects on foot.

They hit a backyard for some privacy, and Damien waited patiently for Holton to reveal what had dragged him out the 'burbs.

"Yo, I'm looking for this chick. It's real important that I find her. I been looking for her, but ain't got nowhere. Word is that she get high down here. Older Lady. A pretty Dominican. Her name's Dolonda."

"I got good fiends that are Dominican, but none named Dolonda. Yo, Holton, I don't know who that is, but I'll put my ear to the street to find her."

"That's what's up, because I know these are her stomping grounds."

Holton wanted to ask Damien what had happened with him and Tavares, but decided against it for the time being.

Damien was going to put his ear to the street for Dolonda, because he'd never heard that name and it was obviously important to his boy. Damien and Holton kicked the shit for a few minutes, then departed. They gave each other dap with the agreement that Damien would call Holton when he found out who Dolonda was.

~Chapter 6~
Uhhhh oh, I Think We Got a Problem, Houston

Davenia, Inda, Vachelle, and Asia along with Tavares had been running rampant for the last week and a half for their upcoming party. It was two days before the party and everything was all set. The DJ, the food, the liquor, and the chairs were all paid for, and now there was nothing left for them to do but drive to Atlanta to get their outfits.

"Oh my god, but is Davenia really in there putting on makeup?" Tavares asked, getting aggravated after sitting for fifteen minutes in Asia's Cadillac Escalade waiting for Davenia to come out.

"Y'all know Davenia has to be a top model no matter where we go," Vachelle said. "Just beep the goddamn horn until she gets aggravated and comes the hell out."

Just as they all laughed, Davenia came off her porch looking like she was going to the club or on a hot date rather than on a four-hour drive to the mall in Atlanta. They were driving up, going shopping, and driving right back to make class the following morning. Davenia was ready in her four-inch turquoise stilettos looking sexy in her skinny jeans and wife beater and pretty turquoise eye shadow that was very complimentary to her complexion.

"Ahh, you mufuckin trick hoe bitches, shut da fuck up!" Davenia snapped real fast like she was serious.

Everyone laughed because that was how they talked and joked.

110

"Ahh fuck you, you slow, turtle-paced pampered princess."

Inda pulled out two of the five blunts that she'd rolled before she and Vachelle headed to Asia and Tavares's house.

"I know that's right," Asia said all sexy and sassy before she burst out laughing.

"Y'all are so damn crazy," joked Tavares because she loved them to death and was just as crazy, if not crazier than them.

Their mini adventure was a success and by 4:30 a.m. everyone was home and in bed. From that point on, it would be countdown and no sleep till after the weekend was over, but they were used to it. Balancing partying and schoolwork was what they did for a living like it was a profession. By Friday night at 11:00 p.m., the ladies had started their pre-party over at the baseball trio's five-bedroom townhouse that had a front deck and back deck, five bathrooms, and enough space to hold all the people who would be in and out the following day.

After everyone smoked and drank, the ladies each went and got two to a bed with the exception of Asia, who was going to be cuddling with London Poppy's Trinidadian and black sexy ass for the night. The ladies had done everything, so the party just had to start and that it did. By midnight, it was out of control. There were people in every inch of space of the townhouse. The girls expected a big turnout, but the party had become plain insane with people everywhere. Tavares was locked in a bathroom smoking a blunt with Inda when there was a loud thump at the door.

"Oh hell no, you motherfucking bitches! Open this door right motherfucking now. This bathroom line ain't moved in fifteen minutes. I know y'all in there, so open this motherfucking door and pass that blunt y'all got in the air."

Inda and Tavares looked at each other and just started laughing. Tavares went to get up off the toilet to open the door, but Inda motioned one minute with her pointer finger. After Vachelle cussed them again, they laughed even harder than the first time and opened the door. After putting the last of the people out at six in the morning and being high and drunk, the ladies decided to go to one house. They headed to Davenia's house, and they were ready to shower and climb into one king-size bed like they always did when they crashed at one place.

"Once again, we threw the party of the semester," Asia said.

"It never fails, and I love it!" Inda joked.

"Girl, we too fly to fail," Davenia said with her stuck up self.

Tavares was in deep thought about her boo, who she hadn't seen in a few weeks and she was missing him. Later that week, Tavares was leaving class extra tired for some reason. The effects of the weekend seemed to have been kicking her ass and doing a really good job at it. Her cell phone began to ring, and she saw that it was Abdora calling, so she picked up with a smile.

"Hey babe, what's going on?"

"I just called to see how class was."

"It was good. I'm tired, though. I'm about to go home and lay it down for a little bit."

"Girl, you better go get some vitamins. You stay tired."

"I know, huh? I been ripping and running with school, going out with the girls, and our back to school party, so I just need to get some sleep. I'll call you when I get up, though."

"Alright, Sweetness. You do that."

Tavares wasted no time getting from campus to her apartment to get into her bed that was longing for her. She was curled up in her bed dead to the world asleep when she heard her girls downstairs. Dragging herself out of bed, she made her way down the stairs.

"Damn, y'all are loud as fuck," Tavares said in a grouchy tone and looking like hell.

"Whatever, Bitch. It's motherfucking 8:00 p.m. Wake your ass up," Inda said, not worrying about her home girl.

"I'm tired as fuck."

"Bitch, you look more than tired," Vachelle said snidely.

"What's that all about?" Tavares asked.

"Girl, you look like hell and all you been doing is sleeping."

Tavares laughed because she was hip to what her friend was implying.

"Oh hell no. I'm not pregnant. I got a period and..."

Then, Tavares realized that it was February and she hadn't had a period since December. Terror took over her face.

"Tavares, don't look like that," Inda said, always being the calm one.

The only absolute thing that stressed Inda was when the blunt wasn't being rolled when it was supposed to be. Asia looked at Tavares with a knowing look. Tavares had this look before, but she wasn't going to be the one to put it out there. Tavares said she wasn't having any kids till she graduated, so they'd taken a few trips to the clinic messing with Tavares's fertile ass and Damien's potent sperm.

"Listen, me and Abdora are going to Vegas for Valentine's Day, so after that I'll go to the doctor. But word, I don't think I'm pregnant. I can't be pregnant. I ain't seen Dora to have no dick. I'll be tired but in Vegas he'll give me all the energy I need to stay awake, so I'll be good."

The ladies kicked it, smoked, and planned for spring break. Tavares headed back to bed and couldn't help but know deep in her heart that she'd slipped up majorly somewhere. She knew that she was pregnant because she never missed a period, and the sleeping and eating only cosigned it. *Why me?* Tavares asked herself as she drifted back into her sleep that she wanted so badly.

For the next week Tavares went to school, ate, and got back in bed the same way she had been for the last few weeks. Before passing out, she made a call to her girls to inform them of the sticky situation she was looking at. Consoling words got Tavares through the next few days till she met Abdora in Vegas for five days. As they flew over the lit up strip of Vegas, Tavares had big plans to see the town and party hard. However, that all went out the window when she and Abdora arrived at Caesar's Palace Hotel. They didn't leave the hotel for anything. They ate, shopped, and gambled in their luxury hotel. They ate and slept together for hours on end in the platform king-size bed.

"Tavares, what the hell is wrong with you? You got me sleeping like a mummy," Abdora said as he lay in bed cuddled up with Tavares.

"I don't know, Abdora. I'm just so relaxed that this is all that I want to do."

"Babygirl, you better go see a doctor, because all this sleeping we're doing cannot be healthy. Get up and get dressed. We're going to play the strip."

Tavares didn't want to go, but she didn't object. Doing as she was instructed, Tavares and Dora headed out of Caesar's Palace for the first time in three days. After dinner at the Bellagio, a gondola ride through the Venetian Hotel, and a helicopter ride over the lit up city, Tavares was exhausted and ready for some loving and some more sleep. She and Abdora didn't leave the hotel for another two days, repeating their vicious cycle of the last three days.

Departing ways at the airport was sad but cute. Neither of them could let go or stop kissing.

"I really do have to leave. My plane is going to leave in twenty minutes. I can't miss it. I have class tomorrow morning," Tavares said, dead serious.

"Go ahead, Babygirl. Catch your flight, because you do need to be in class tomorrow. Call me and let me know you landed safely. I get back an hour before you."

The couple exchanged a long, intimate kiss, then turned and went toward opposite ends of the busy terminal. Tavares felt tired and ready to sleep all the way back to Georgia.

It was back to business as usual when Abdora got back to Jersey. He was so used to taking care of other people and having no alone time that being with Tavares was what he'd been needing. She was addictive to him like a powerful drug habit that he couldn't kick. Tavares was back at school and keeping busy so it was only daily multiple phone calls for him. He had nothing else to do but go hard with business. He was always occupied because of people always needing something, problems in the hood, things to be handled at the club, barbershops, and not to mention things that came his way daily.

Abdora was in his office at the club when his personal line rang.

He picked up the phone and said, "Dora speaking."

"What's up my nigga?" Kollar Dollar said.

"I was sitting here going over some business shit. What's up?"

"Yo, my nigga, we got a problem. Meet me on 11th Street."

"I'm on my way," Abdora said as he grabbed two guns, his short hooded mink, and car keys.

Just as Abdora reached 11th Street, his cell phone rang.

"Hello?"

"Hi, Abdora. It's Angelica. I hate to bother you, but my mom's been gone for a week and rent for this month wasn't paid. The landlord said he's going to call child services if my mother isn't back before the end of the weekend, because the first is Monday and she'll owe him two months of rent. So, we need somewhere to go," Angelica said through her teary eyes.

"You ain't gots to cry, Babygirl. Have I ever let you down?"

"No," Angelica said in a muffled tone.

"OK then. I'll be there in about an hour. Call the landlord and tell him to be there in exactly an hour."

Abdora hopped out his Porsche truck, approached the stash house, and went around back to the basement where he knew his niggaz were waiting for him. As he entered the basement that had been converted into an apartment, Abdora found some of his comrades at the bar and others in the kitchen. Bryce was on the computer in the office and the video game heads were in the den playing NBA 2k Live.

"Alright, I see we got a full house, and I got something important to handle in an hour so let's get this shit moving."

Buddah stood up, swept his long, pretty dreads over his back, and informed Abdora that word was Rocco from Tremont Street Projects was plotting on him. There were no details other than that he'd been paid a lot of money to take Abdora out. Unbeknownst to Abdora, it was Damien who had invested in having him killed. Rocco was only a gangsta nigga in the world he lived in, but in Abdora's world he was a small person who just wanted to be big. Abdora looked at everyone standing around them as if they'd lost their minds.

"You niggaz called me here for this shit? I'm not thinking about that bitch ass nigga. If he wants to go to war with me, then let him get himself killed. I'm true to this shit. I survived this long in the game by living with caution and never getting caught slipping. Get me Rocco's number. I'll call that nigga personally and let him know to get his army up."

"We got Rocco. We just wanted to put you on," Bryce said.

"Rocco is going hard recruiting niggaz and some more shit, but he'll be crushed before he even goes to make a move," Mid said with murder all in his thoughts.

"Do what y'all do, but if I see the nigga first, I'm taking the lead and going to walk that nigga into his own death."

"You sick," Mid said to his big brother.

"Alright, well let me get out of here," Abdora said, giving his niggaz their special dap.

Days later, Rocco's body would surface in the Hudson River with no fingers, eyeballs, or teeth and no evidence of who laid him there.

Abdora headed across town to meet Sherese's landlord and to drop off the $500 worth of groceries that he'd just picked up. Abdora parked in front of the purple and white house that was in desperate need of a paint job, got out, and just looked around. Judging from the people on the porch, this was obviously the hot spot for crackheads. Abdora gave two of them $10 apiece to carry the bags up to the third floor. When Abdora got upstairs, the landlord who was clearly a slumlord from the looks of the house and apartment was waiting with greed in his eyes.

"Hi, nice to meet you," the landlord said as he extended his hand to Abdora.

"I bet," Abdora said, not extending his hand. "Yo, Angelica and Gianna, y'all go take those groceries and put them away while I holler at your landlord."

Doing as they were told, they rolled their eyes at their ignorant, compassionless, pale-faced fat white landlord and went to the kitchen to put the food away.

"Listen here, son, I'm about to pay you a lot a money. Because never again do I want to get a phone call from one of them girls talking about you're going to put them out or call child services. Because if I do get another phone call, that's going to make me very upset. I don't like to be upset. Making me upset doesn't usually result in good things," Abdora said with a tone that was more than clear.

The man didn't know what to say because he more than got the drift. Abdora handed the man an envelope.

"Sherese's rent is $700 a month. I just paid you for the next year. So, should I ever get a phone call about you making threats not fixing shit in this apartment or giving Sherese or those girls a hard time, we're going to have a little chat."

"No problem, sir. We're all set," the obviously scared man said. "Thank you and have a good day," the money hungry pig said and hurried out the door.

Abdora entered the kitchen where the girls were jamming to the radio and putting the groceries away.

He clapped his hands and was like, "Damn, y'all make me wanna invest in a recording studio."

"Whatever, Abdora," Gianna said with her small raspy voice and cheesy smile.

"Listen, ladies. Take a seat. We need to have a serious talk. I'm going to speak with your mother, but I want to talk to y'all first. Y'all are big girls now. Y'all aren't grown, but y'all are definitely way past your times and capable of taking care of yourselves and each other. I'm going to put y'all in a position to do so by giving y'all an apartment and a healthy weekly allowance. All y'all have to do is go to school and keep your grades up."

They looked at each other in disbelief and their eyes popped out their high yellow bright-eyed faces.

"All we have to do is go to school?" Gianna asked, puzzled.

"Sounds too good to be true," Angelica blurted out, knowing her sister was thinking it, too.

Abdora laughed.

"Calm your little feisty ass down. You remind me so much of my girl. There's no catch. Y'all take your grown asses to school, get Cs or better, and from here on out, y'all ain't ever got to worry about nothing. When you turn eighteen, if you go to college I'll still help you, if not you're on your own. I watched y'all come up and love y'all like sisters or my own children, so I want the best for y'all. Y'all just have to do your part on reaching for the best and that means going to school.

"I'm going to get y'all a driver, an apartment with good amenities, furnish the apartment with all that y'all could need, and pay all the bills. I just paid your mother's rent for a year, so she's straight to do this bullshit and not let it hurt or affect y'all. Y'all can visit her whenever y'all want, but this environment ain't good for y'all because if something happens to one of y'all, it will be major problems."

Gianna looked at Angelica. Angelica looked at Gianna together they looked at Abdora with shock in their faces.

"Abdora, say no more," Angelica said. "We'll go to school and maintain our apartment appropriately."

"Oh my god," Gianna said. "This is so unreal, Abdora. Everyone talks about you, but now I really see why. I can't believe that you would do this for us just because you watched us grow up and have nothing because of my mother's getting high."

"Gianna, I got y'all. I love you little divas. I'm going to fly my girl out here to take y'all to get everything y'all will need for your new apartment. I know y'all will like her, too. She got a lot of attitude like y'all and those crazy eyes, so that's two things alone y'all have in common."

"Hmm, we'll see," Angelica said, overly protective of Abdora.

"What made her so special to be your girlfriend?" Gianna questioned.

"Because she's a special lady who has her head on straight and makes me more than happy."

"Well, we're going to have to check her out and thangs," Gianna said.

"And mean it, hunnie," Angelica said, laughing.

Tavares was in the library when Abdora started blowing her up. She missed him and wanted to see him so bad, but she'd been dodging him due to her situation growing inside of her. When she came back from Vegas, she went to the doctor a week later and, as suspected, found out that she was eight weeks pregnant. Tavares knew that she had slept with both Abdora and Damien, but she was almost positive that it was Damien's baby because Abdora never came in her - at least not that she knew of. On her, always, but never in her. She hadn't gained any weight yet but her body was totally out of whack. Hell, she felt like it was a major task to stay awake for eight hours of the day. Sleeping had become her new best friend.

Only her inner circle and diva squad knew of the baby on the way. Tavares had instructed her girls not to tell anyone. Everyone held their word, so Tavares hoped. Damien finding out that she was pregnant was the last thing that she needed on top of being pregnant and trying to go two more months until graduation. When the baby dropped, she would call him. Tavares knew that she couldn't hide from Abdora forever. He'd offered far too many times to come to her and she found every excuse in the book to refuse his offers. Tavares would be running out of excuses any day now, and she knew that she would soon have to tell Abdora that she was pregnant and didn't think it was his baby. Looking at his number coming across the screen, Tavares got up from the table in the center of the circular library and walked to one of the private quiet rooms so she could take Abdora's call.

"What's wrong?" Tavares asked as she answered the phone.

"Listen, I got a project for you."

"A project?" Tavares asked like he was crazy.

"Remember the two little mamis I was telling you about? I need you to come here and take them shopping for the new apartment that I just got them."

"You got them an apartment?" Tavares asked, shocked, admiring, and jealous all in one.

"Yeah, they needed to get out of the apartment with Sherese. She ain't shit."

Looking at her stomach, Tavares said, "Baby, I would love to, but I have to finish two papers and study for my four tests that I have next week. This weekend isn't good."

"Well, you can come next weekend after you ace your tests and shit."

Tavares didn't know why, but she said okay before she could catch herself.

"Where are you?" Dora asked.

"The library. I'm in a private room using my phone because phone calls aren't allowed in the library."

"Let's have phone sex," Abdora said.

"Oh hell no," Tavares said, way too loud to be in library. "You're so fresh," Tavares said, having to laugh at how spontaneous Abdora was.

"Alright. Well, get your study on and I'll call you later. You sound tired. Go home and get some rest. You're naturally smart."

"I will," Tavares said, more tired than he even knew.

Tavares was going to have to face the music next weekend, so she was stressing now. She grabbed her books and Gucci satchel and exited through the library turnstile and headed home to get into her bed. Tavares called Mona-Lisa.

"What the hell am I going to do? I really like him and want to be with him, but how can I ask him to be with me when I'm having Damien's baby?"

"Apple, that nigga loves you - like loves you to the core. Do you think that he would turn you away because of a harmless, innocent baby? He got too much heart and realness for that. He doesn't care about Damien. He might not want Damien in your life but that comes with the baby, so he'll understand that. Are you really showing yet?"

"Nope, not even. Just getting thicker than a snicker."

"Shit, you were already that," laughed Mona-Lisa. "So you're good money. I suggest you just keep it real with him. Sometimes honesty is the best policy."

"I guess you're right," Tavares said, not fully convinced.

After twenty minutes of baby talk, Tavares called it a night and went to bed.

A week of stressing went by and the day to face Abdora was finally here. Tavares took her tests and headed to the airport to go to Newark, NJ. Damien was in Boston being an official hoe. Going to the clubs and taking chicks home became a vicious cycle. He was fucking and going through women like water. Every night he had a different chick swallowing his babies. Since word that Tavares had left Damien had hit the streets, he was the hottest commodity up for grabs. When he entered Vertigo, The Rolls, The Tavern, or Back Stage, it was no time before chicks were throwing themselves at him. Little did they know, he wasn't settling with none of them. They were just good for the moment.

Damien hadn't slept at his brownstone since he got word that Tavares was pregnant. He'd called her about twenty times, and with no answer or any calls back, he was feeling some kind of way. The bitches, as he loved to call him, helped him fill a void that he was having a hard time filling without Tavares in his life. He got an apartment in the hood on Georgia Street and just started stunting off with his broad squad and kicked it with his niggaz. He was still getting money, but he felt like it wasn't the same without Tavares there to manage and take care of it all. He even missed her spending his money.

Damien looked at his ringing phone and said, "Damn, what does this bitch want? What's up, yo?"

"Shit... I just called to tell you that Tavares is alright. The baby is alright, and the pregnancy is going good."

"That's what's up," Damien said. "Does she need anything?"

"Nah, she just been going to class and sleeping a lot. She has a doctor's appointment in two weeks, so I'll call you then. Unless you want to see me before then," the female on the other end joked, but really meant it.

"Alright, well let me go," Damien said as he pulled up to his brownstone. He wanted to sleep where he once had peace and love.

Tavares exited the airport in her blue jeans, red patent leather moccasin shoes, white long-sleeve tee, red wrap sweater, and a chocolate brown DG purse. It was freezing so Tavares bundled up a bit more as she spotted the red Porsche. As she got into the car, Tavares gave Abdora a big long, wet kiss.

"Damn, I missed you, too," Abdora said, ready to rip Tavares out of her clothes.

"I see that look in your eyes. Don't even think about it. I want to meet the little princesses that we're going to get right."

"They're at my club anxiously waiting to go shopping with you. I'm going to give you one of my business credit cards. I made you an authorized user for the occasion, so you should have no problems using it. You can spend as much as you want."

Tavares was thinking when and how was she going to tell this man that she'd truly fallen in love with that she was pregnant and not with his baby. She decided she would tell him tonight after she came back from shopping. As she approached Abdora's nightclub that took up a whole block, Tavares looked at the huge sign that read *King's, Inc.* The cute couple entered the first floor and found Angelica and Gianna at the bar drinking Shirley Temples.

"Hey, Babygirls. This is my girlfriend Tavares."

Tavares and the girls exchanged hellos.

"She's going to set y'all straight," Abdora said as he tossed the car keys to Tavares.

He caught the young ladies with a look on their faces that all women had when they were going shopping.

With a huge smile on her face Tavares said, "Abdora wants you guys to get it all, so I think we're going to have a ball today."

Eagerly, they both said, "We're ready."

Tavares looked into their eyes. One had gray eyes and the other had green eyes. They were both beautiful and reminded her of herself in so many ways. Dora knew he was in for major damage when the bill came, but he was happy because he saw the girls as an investment. They were going to go to school and do something bigger than the hand they'd been dealt. That in itself was the payoff on his investment.

"Well y'all go on ahead and just call me when y'all are on the way back," he said. "I'll be out ripping and running, so I'll just meet y'all back here."

All three ladies gave Abdora a hug and headed to the girls' new apartment. Tavares and the girls hit it off immediately. Tavares talked to them about her life, the obstacles she'd faced, and how she'd been getting past those obstacles. She also discussed what it was like to go down south to a small town when you're from a major city. Fashion, men, hating ass women, and how wonderful Abdora was passed the rest of the time to the house. The girls were loving Tavares. Gianna loved Tavares's style, how she moved, and her natural beauty. She was also feeling the fact that Tavares wasn't stuck up about it like she was. Angelica liked the idea that even though Tavares was from the streets and had it in her to be hood, she wasn't a product of her environment. Instead, she was in school and classy. They concluded that she was nice and down to earth, so they could connect with her. She wasn't stuck up even though she was pretty and had a lot going for herself.

"So tell me, ladies, what do you have in mind?" Tavares asked as they gave the two-bedroom split-level condo a walk-through.

Gianna was upstairs with the kitchen, living room, her bedroom, and her bathroom. Angelica was downstairs with the den that had a huge flat screen TV, surround sound and DVD players and a stocked library of movies, her bedroom, bathroom, and laundry room.

"I want soft, pretty colors," Gianna said.

"And I want loud, bright colors," Angelica said, not liking Gianna's idea.

"Ok," Tavares said, seeing that she had a challenge ahead of her. "Well, this is what we'll do. We'll do the common rooms in neutral colors. Each of you can do your bathroom, and y'all can each obviously decorate your own rooms."

"Cool," they both said.

After spending the day in and out of furniture stores, going to Walmart, Target, Ikea, and Bed Bath and Beyond, the ladies were worn out. Tavares was proud of their choices and had a ball with the ladies. Gianna ended up with a red, white, and black pocketbook-themed bathroom, while Angelica went with a pink and purple princess theme.

Gianna's room was red and black. Angelica went for brown and turquoise. It was too cute to see them swap color themes with each other because they were so different but so much alike. When they got back to the club, they were all smiles and laughs. Abdora was so happy to see them all laughing. Tavares handed Abdora his car keys, credit card, and receipts.

"Thank you," he said, kissing her and feeling that there weren't sixty receipts like he'd anticipated.

"Damn, what did y'all get? Nothing? There aren't a lot of receipts," Abdora said playfully.

"Ohhhh shoot," said Angelica. "Let me find out he wants us to go spend more, because I'm so with it."

Gianna said, "Nah, Dora. We got more than we needed. Tavares took us to all the right places and made the shopping too easy. And, the best thing is that every store is going to deliver on Monday."

"Is that right?" Abdora said, smiling at Tavares, who was getting her props on the low for attacking the mission so well.

"Yes, it is so," Tavares said seductively with a snappy attitude.

"We went to the furniture store and got their bedroom sets, the kitchen set, and the living room set. We hit a few other places and got towels, sheets, comforters, dishes, kitchen appliances, bathroom sets, pots and pans, cooking stuff, and picture frames," Angelica informed him.

"Then, we went to Best Buy for electronics and got this cool red stacked washer and dryer. Next, we went to IKEA for all the decorative stuff like vases, frames, and small stuff.

Lastly, we went to Target and Walmart for whatever we forgot," Gianna included.

"Point taken," Abdora said, proud of Tavares.

"Well, Abdora, we're going to stay at our mom's tonight. You have fun tonight and don't worry about us," said Gianna.

Tavares was tired and ready to head to Abdora's condo in New York to lay it down.

"Meet us downstairs at the car," Abdora said to the girls. "Baby, we're going to have to hang out here for a while. Bryce had some shit to do, so I have to wait for him to come. It's ten o'clock, so he should be here soon."

"I'll take the girls home and come back," Tavares said, kissing Abdora and heading out the club that was already filling.

Tavares came back an hour later and couldn't believe the line that was out front of the club. She parked the car and came around the corner to a line that had wrapped around the block. Everyone eyed Tavares as she kept going and going, never trying to get in the line. Bitches thought she was bold and niggaz were wondering whose bitch she was because she was bad in jeans and a sweater. Seeing that Oh So was at the front, Tavares knew him and knew she was good.

As she approached the front a female said, "Excuse me, the line is back there," pointing to the long line behind her.

"Is it really?" Tavares asked the hoodrat and gave her a hell of an attitude. "Too bad I don't do lines, huh?" Tavares asked in a demeaning way, like the bitch and the line were beneath her.

"I don't give a fuck who you're fucking, the line is back there, Bitch. You need to stand in it just like everyone else."

Tavares jerked her neck back, having to stop herself from Hulk-smashing the chick who was asking for it. Knowing that she was pregnant and couldn't fight, Tavares embarrassed her and hit her where it hurt.

"Bitch, you got on a ten-dollar outfit, eight-dollar Payless shoes, and now you done stood in the motherfucking line for nothing because you ain't getting in."

Tavares felt fucked up using power that she automatically knew Abdora would back her up on. But fighting wasn't an option and she had to do what she had to do.

"You see, I'm engaged to the owner and your mouth just wrote you out of a ticket to enter. So you say goodbye to your friends and have a good night, you raggedy ass bitch. Furthermore, you got one more time to call me a bitch before I shove my shoe down your throat, you stinking bum ass bitch!" Tavares spat.

"Please miss. I'm sorry," the pathetic chick begged, truly regretting her mouth.

"It's my birthday and we been planning this for weeks. I'm so sorry."

"Bitch, do I look like I give a fuck about your sob story?" Tavares said, then looked at Oh So.

Oh So just laughed at how much this chick was like her man and stepped aside for Tavares to enter the club. Before Tavares made it upstairs to Abdora's office, she spotted Bryce on his cell phone cracking up laughing in one of the glass VIP rooms. He was waving for Tavares to come where he was.

Tavares opened the door and Bryce said, "What's going on, Miss Lady?" in his cool, always serious tone.

"Nothing much. Just dropped the girls off and had a situation out front. I was just laughing at you putting that bum bitch out of the line."

Tavares looked at Bryce, puzzled by the fact that he found out that fast when it happened all of three minutes ago.

Seeing her look, he said, "Nah, Ma, nothing happens that me and Abdora don't know about. I commend you, though, for being a woman and simply putting her out and not being a hoodrat, fighting, and bringing negativity right in front of the club. You hit her where it hurt in front of a lot of people. So she's bruised enough," Bryce said, respecting how Tavares had handled things. "Abdora is taking care of something, but he said to get comfortable. Page a waitress and order a bottle or some drinks, and he should be down in about ten minutes."

Don't I wish, Tavares thought.

"So, how's school?" Bryce asked.

"Almost over. Thank God. I'll be walking across the stage in May, God's will," Tavares said so gratefully.

"That's what's up, Ma. You're a good chick and I like you for Dora. You keep him grounded and make him smile. If you can do those two things, you're all to the good with me."

Tavares laughed because everyone thought her sweetheart was so hard at the core, but he was as sweet as pie.

"I like Dora. He's good people," Tavares said, unable to control her ear-to-ear smile.

"Y'all two are perfect for each other," Bryce said as he shook his head at how much they were alike. "Well, get comfy. Dora will be down shortly," Bryce said, making sure Dora's girl was comfortable before he went on to handle his business.

The private chambers were lined up in two rows with one row on the bottom and one on the top. They resembled jail cells, only there were no bars. There were sliding glass doors that opened and closed with a button. They were four times the size of jail cells and came with a private bar, plush couches, chairs, and tables. Tavares looked out the private room and loved King's, Inc. King's, as everyone called it, was an upscale establishment that everyone loved to frequent just because of who the owners were. There were five different rooms on the first floor. Each room had four bars that were positioned in each corner of the room. Each room also had tall private V.I.P. booths that were built up high overlooking the room. They were roped off and went all the way around the room.

The dance floors were square with two double staircases serving as the perimeter of the square. They had lounge areas downstairs in the basement for the patrons that just wanted to fall back and chit-chat and kick it without the loudness of the music in the rooms. The lounge areas only played Neosoul music at a low volume for those who wanted to get their groove on. There was also a soul food kitchen downstairs that was set up with tables and chairs for those that wanted to dine in the kitchen. The line was always crazy right before the club closed. Everyone always tried to get the finger-licking good food for their late night snacks, especially the fried chicken wings that tasted like someone's mother was back there frying.

All the space upstairs on the second floor was converted into two rooms. One room was the "U-Room" because it was supposed to be all about you when you went in there. It had a huge glass bar that was U-shaped. The interior of the U had tall chairs. Huge swinging birdcages were in each corner of the room. However, the cages didn't have birds, they had broads dancing in nothing but G-strings. There was a large stage split into three sections in front of the U. The stage contained three poles and three strippers all dancing at once. The center of the stage was raised for whichever girl was in the middle. There was money all over the floor from the men throwing dollars that the strippers couldn't pick up. They didn't work off tips. They only stripped and played in the money that accumulated on the stage every night. Patrons paid for dances by purchasing tickets from the bar or the waitresses.

Cameras picked up everything, so there was no getting slick. Everything was house money and they were paid $500 a night. Some liked it, some didn't. Those who didn't like it didn't have to work there, was Bryce and Abdora's motto. They figured there were plenty of chicks who would like to make $2000 a week after taxes and deductions. They received evaluations like any other job, and they all got bonuses. The money they worked for was even taxable.

Abdora finished conducting his business in the King's Playpin. King's Playpin was the V.I.P. of the V.I.P.s. It was broken down into multiple rooms that had beautiful beds and bathrooms. The playpin was where men received massages. Well, they got massages on the books and whatever else they could afford off the books because women didn't come cheap in the playpin. To even think of going in the playpin was $1000. It was nothing for the girls to be giving massages or doing some extra things for a little more in the playpin.

"Well my lil nigga, you know it's always good doing business with you. It ain't got to be business for you to hit me up, though," Abdora said to Trendell, who was one of his youngest comrades.

Abdora loved Trendell because he was young, but he was smart, wise, and a go-getter. He was a lot smarter and wiser than men Abdora's age.

"Abdora, I need a chick, my nigga."

"All these young bitches be chasing you, so what you mean you need a chick?"

"I need a chick I can wife. I don't want one of these busted-down hoodrats."

Abdora laughed because he could dig it.

"Lil nigga, get this money and your woman will come because mine sure did. I got her downstairs waiting on me, so let me run."

Abdora said goodbye to his lil mans and them and went to meet his shorty.

Damien was hot listening to all the inside information about Tavares. When he pulled up to the house, he was past angry. He felt like Tavares ripped his insides out by going hard and getting pregnant by homeboy. On top of that, her ass was so happy and in love with this nigga.

134

"Damien, why are you so mad?" the unsympathetic-speaking female asked who had just informed him that he wasn't the baby's father.

A hater was the last thing that Damien was, so his dislike and contempt for Dora was for one reason and one reason only. Dora had stolen his broad right from under him. Deep down, Damien knew it was his own fault for all the bullshit that he'd done. Damien had failed her in the lover department.

"Mad?" he asked her like she was stupid. "Don't I have the fucking right to be mad? Tavares is running around here pregnant with another nigga's baby after me and her were together for years."

"Damien, you think she meant to get pregnant?" the chick asked him with a tone that said *Nigga, get your mind right.*

"She didn't have to mean to, because, regardless, it still happened, and she now she's having that nigga's baby."

"Whatever," the chick said, tired of the conversation they'd been having for the last fifty-nine minutes.

She wasn't about to make it a whole hour.

"Dame, how about you put the movie in and twist a blunt up," the female said, getting up to go make drinks for them.

After a long night of taking shots of Remy and smoking blunts, Damien did what he did best. He took the chick to her room and laid his pipe game down.

He was getting up to get dressed when the chick rolled over and asked, "Why you leaving?"

Damien looked and almost said *because, bitch, I only be bothered with you for information.* Instead, he said, "I got some shit to do."

He bounced to go home to think about how fucked up shit was. Damien's phone rang as he headed to his house. He'd been calling Rocco for weeks and weeks and Rocco was finally calling him back.

Damien answered saying, "Damn, my nigga, I thought you was dead."

Damien was shocked to hear a female's voice on the other end. It was Rocco's girl returning his calls. She let Dame know that Rocco had been murdered. Damien thought that he was gonna get rid of the pain in the ass named Abdora once and for all, but his plan failed. Damien didn't know if he felt worse for the young man who had lost his life doing a job for him, or if he was angrier that Dora was still alive. He thanked Rocco's girl for letting him know the tragic news, and he continued on to his house.

Damien was in his big empty bed - in his big empty house, all alone. His phone interrupted his heavy thoughts. Looking at the clock that read 4:30 a.m., he knew he wasn't moving. *So, why even bother answering the phone?* Damien thought. As Damien ignored the phone, he tried to watch Sportscenter. The cell phone's constant blaring was interrupting his focus on the highlights, and Damien was getting aggravated. He finally got up and walked to the chaise to answer the ringing phone.

"What's good?" Damien asked aggressively.

The female on the other end said, "Dame, why haven't you been answering the phone?"

Dame looked at the phone and thought *this bitch has lost her mind.*

"Do you see what time it is? Maybe that's why I haven't answered the phone. What's up, though?"

"I need to talk to you face to face," she said with a deep urgency in her voice.

She didn't sound like she was fiending either, so Damien knew that it had to be serious.

"Are you in the city?"

"Yeah, but I'm headed home, so I can meet you by the highway. Meet me at the On the Run gas station by the highway on Mass Ave."

"I'll be there in about twenty minutes."

What the fuck could she really need to talk about this time of morning? Damien thought as he got dressed with all types of thoughts running through his head. *Did something happen to Holton?* Damien wasn't sure, but he was definitely about to find out. Ten minutes later, Damien headed out the house in a white tee, gray polo sweatsuit, some wheat Timberlands, and a fitted B hat as he hopped in his car in the brisk morning air.

Lilly was lost in her emotions about the information consuming her as she pulled up to meet Dame. While she was in Holton's office looking for the spare key to her car, she ran across an envelope that had Tavares Del Gada written on the front of it. Seeing Tavares's name sparked her curiosity to open it. *Why would Holton have an envelope with Tavares's name on it?* Lilly thought to herself. When she read the contents, she got the surprise of her life and tears instantly flowed. Lilly was crushed and brokenhearted to learn that Tavares was the daughter of her husband and her

137

archenemy. Her heart shattered more and more as she read the sentence over and over, *"Tavares is the daughter of Holton Montiago and Dolonda Del Gada."* Lilly thought her world stopped, and then it hit her that Tavares was the child that was never aborted. Dolonda had one up on her, again.

Damien crawled into Lilly's car mad as a motherfucker that he was outside.

"Lilly, what's so important that you got me out of my bed this time of morning?"

"Damien, I need to share something important with you. Holton doesn't know that I know, and I didn't know where else to turn."

"Ok, what's up?"

"Holton did a background check on Tavares."

Damien's face was really confused.

"Why would he do that?" he asked, not understanding.

"I don't know, but the information that came back is why I'm here."

"Lilly, stop beating around the bush and spit it out."

"Tavares is Holton and Dolonda's daughter."

Damien's eyes popped so far out of his head that they could have hit the floor. He thought his ears were playing tricks on him.

"Lilly, did you just say that Tavares is Holton's daughter?"

"You heard me correctly."

Damien couldn't find any words. He was speechless for a whole two minutes. Then he asked, "Who the fuck is Dolonda?"

Lilly was saying the name like he knew Dolonda or some shit. Lilly gave Damien a blank look with her face screwed up.

"What do you mean who's Dolonda? Damien, are you kidding me? You deal with Dolonda on a regular basis."

"Lilly, I don't know a Dolonda. So, I don't know what would make you assume I deal with her and on a regular for that matter."

Lilly thought Damien was losing his mind.

"Dolonda's who I was fighting with in the projects."

"Dollar?" Damien asked hesitantly.

"Uhhhhh, yeah. What did you think Dollar's real name was?"

"I met Dollar years ago, and she said her name was Londie. Because of how she always spent big and never was a dollar short, I started calling her Dollar shortly after we met."

So many thoughts ran through his mind at once and his body was covered in goosebumps.

He didn't know what to think or what to say except, "Dollar's Tavares's mother? How the fuck have I been serving Tavares's mother all these years and had no clue?"

Damien felt his heart break into two pieces. *Dollar and Holton are Tavares's parents. How the hell am I going to break this news to Tavares? I can't tell her this,* Damien thought. *At least not right now.* Damien decided that he was going to wait till after the baby was born.

"Yo, listen here, Lilly. Tavares got a lot of shit on her plate right now. This ain't the time to spring this shit on her with her graduating soon. Not to mention, she's pregnant."

Lilly and Damien talked about the crazy coincidence for an hour before they parted ways, making a deal to keep the info under wraps. Only Lilly had no idea that Dame would be calling Holton and taking him right to Dollar's door.

~Chapter 7~
Mama's Baby, Daddy's Maybe

Tavares was exhausted, but after Abdora dragged her on the dance floor, she found a burst of energy. They danced the night and the morning away as if they were the only two people on the floor. Abdora stayed until the club was closed down, and they ended up back over the bridge to New York. They didn't make it to the house until 5:30 a.m. Tavares felt like she wasn't going to make it from the garage to the house.

"Damn, baby, you look beat. You want me to carry you?"

"No," Tavares said with her eyes half open as she dragged her body toward the elevator.

When they finally got into the house, they dropped Tavares's bags at the door and went to the kitchen to get something to drink before they headed upstairs.

Tavares was so out of it and discombobulated that she mistakenly said, "This baby got me starving," and grabbed a bag of chips.

Dora dropped the cup in his hand and his eyes gouged out of his head, looking at the belly that was in front of Tavares. Tavares realized her slip up and began to try to explain herself to Dora.

"Abdora, please wait. Just let me explain."

"Tavares, what the fuck? You're pregnant and not just a couple weeks. So what the fuck do you mean let you explain?"

Tavares knew she was wrong for not telling him all this time, but she didn't know how to break the news to him.

"Abdora, listen."

"Listen to what?" Abdora asked, feeling like he'd just gone from zero to a hundred. "I would love to hear what the fuck you can say to redeem yourself from this."

"I found out around the time we came back from Vegas, so it's only been a month and some change that I haven't said anything."

"ONLY? Tavares, miss me with the fucking bullshit. You speak to me every motherfucking day. How hard would it have been to say Abdora, I'm pregnant?"

"Don't you think that I wanted to tell you? Shit, I was tired of making fucking excuses as to why I couldn't come see you. But, I was afraid that once I told you that I was pregnant with Damien's baby that you wouldn't want shit to do with me. So please don't make me feel awful. I really did want to tell you."

Abdora just cupped his face with his hands and shook his head at the fact that the female who he would have given the world to really just didn't get how much he was into her.

"Tavares, you just don't get it, Ma. You ain't got to hide shit from me. I'm a real nigga. I'm not some bum ass bitch ass nigga. If I love you and want to be with you, then I'm going to accept and love your baby. What don't you get about the fact that I've fallen in love with you? I've had some bad bitches in my day and seen the best of the best. But, Ma, it's you I want to give my heart to. I never thought I could fall in love. And, the fact that you got me totally in love should let you know that there ain't a motherfucking thing you can't tell me about. How do you know that it's not my baby?"

"Excuse me?" Tavares said like Dora was crazy.

"You heard me."

"Well, smart ass, to my knowledge you've never ejaculated in me, so it can't be your baby."

Abdora stopped and thought about when he thought he'd pulled out. Ultrasounds were off sometimes, so even though Tavares was convinced, he wasn't going to dismiss the thought just yet.

"Trust me. I wish it were your baby. It would make this whole situation perfect and end in a fairytale way, but unfortunately this is real life. Please, just don't be mad at me."

"Tavares, I ain't going nowhere. I'm going to love your baby like it's mine. To be honest, I'm not convinced the baby isn't mine. Your baby's father isn't going to be feeling us, but as long as you're riding, I'm riding with you."

Tavares started to cry because she wanted to believe that he loved her, but after Damien, she didn't believe that true love existed. Dora grabbed Tavares and kissed her so passionately that she got goosebumps. Tavares let go of his lips after five minutes and headed upstairs to take a shower. She needed to take a long, hot shower after the load she'd dropped on Dora. Dora cleaned up the mess he made on his tiled kitchen floors, had a drink, and headed upstairs to meet Tavares. Tavares was passed out. Abdora lay down next to Tavares, watched her sleep, and wondered how all this was going to play out in the end. He loved this girl and just hoped that she didn't break his heart because he wasn't going to do anything to break hers.

After what seemed like a short nap, Tavares woke up out of instinct. When she and Dora slept together, if he got out of the bed, she woke up within minutes of him deserting her. Not wanting to get up just yet, Tavares was mad as hell at Abdora for getting out of the bed on her. She rolled out of bed and got up to give him the business like it was his fault she woke up. Tavares washed her face and brushed her teeth before she headed downstairs. She could hear Dora on the phone and so she stopped to ear hustle.

"Yo, is this what the fuck you called me for? You're talking some dumb shit on my jack right now. You ain't my girl."

Dora was using a hard and harsh tone Tavares had never experienced.

"So what if that's the person from the party I took you to? What the fuck is that supposed to mean? It's none of your business where I met her. I ain't tapped you since after the New Year."

The New Year? Tavares thought. *We became a couple shortly after the New Year.* There was silence for a moment.

Then, Tavares heard him say, "You know what, Jade? Lose my number. I got a girl," and he hung up the phone. "I hate bitches," Dora said out loud just as Tavares entered the kitchen.

"Well, you don't hate this bitch, so watch your mouth before I pop you in it," Tavares said, kissing him.

"Morning to you, too, and you ain't no bitch. So, don't ever fucking refer to yourself as a bitch again. You're my Queen, so don't let me hear you ever say that shit again."

"Alright, killa. Relax. Don't get all serious on me."

"No, I'm very serious. Don't let me hear you say that again."

Tavares rolled her eyes and said, "I fucking heard you. And don't be giving me no 'tude because you just got into it with one of your little girlfriends."

"Well, since your nosey ass heard my conversation and conveniently came in after it was over, then you obviously know you can cut the slick shit, Ma."

"I wasn't being slick," Tavares said, rolling her eyes as she took a seat at the circular-shaped island. "I heard you. So yes, I stopped on the stairs to listen," Tavares said, smiling and dangling her feet since her legs weren't long enough to touch the floor.

"I'm hungry. What are you cooking?"

"I bet you're hungry. Don't come in here trying to eat me out of house and home because you're eating for two now."

"Whatever. Just get to feeding me because now that the cat is out the bag, I'm looking for the pampering to start," Tavares joked.

"I gotta pamper the baby first, but I'll see what I can do for you," Dora said, going into his double-door fridge and pulling out some eggs, turkey sausage, green peppers, and onions. "How about you be helpful and get the batter down and make the waffles. The Belgian waffle maker is in the closet right behind you," Dora said as he got busy making the omelets.

"I thought we just talked about this," Tavares jokingly scolded.

"We did, but I don't recall saying ok. So, if your hungry ass wants to eat, get that waffle maker out."

Tavares just rolled her eyes and did as she was told. As they cooked breakfast together, they laughed, joked, and listened to music. When breakfast was done, they had Western omelets, waffles, and turkey sausage. After stuffing themselves, they developed nigga-itis.

"How about you go take a shower, and I'll load the dishwasher," Tavares volunteered, really not wanting to move.

"Ahh, you're a doll. I'll take you up on that."

Dora got up, rinsed the dishes out, and stacked them by the dishwasher before he headed upstairs to take a long, hot shower. He was definitely ready to crawl back in bed for a little while. Tavares loaded the dishwasher, watched the rain out the window over the sink, and listened to the downpour. Tavares loved the rain. It made her want to relax to the hundredth degree. She thought about the fact that she was having a baby and her mother would never know it. One of the most important events of her life was happening and she had no family to share her joy with. It made Tavares sad. After washing the counters down with water and bleach, she hit the light and walked upstairs.

"Damn, was I gone that long?" Tavares asked, looking around the room that had been straightened up and the bed was now fully made.

She joined Dora in the bathroom to see what he was up to since she didn't hear the shower running.

"Dora, what are you doing?"

"I was laying a towel out and some new pajamas for you to take a bath."

Tavares turned her head to the corner where the Jacuzzi-style bathtub was and saw it filled to the rim with bubbles.

"Ooooh yes," Tavares said, starting to strip. "You better hope I make it out alive, because the rain might put me to sleep in here."

"Trust, I ain't going to let you drown our baby."

Tavares thought to herself *our* and just smiled.

"Call me when you're ready, and I'll wash you up," Dora said, kissing Tavares and closing the door as he exited the bathroom.

His body smelled so fresh like Dove soap that Tavares had to resist grabbing him back. Tavares threw on her Jazmin Sullivan CD, dimmed the lights, and crawled in the huge tub to let her mind, body, and soul rest. Thirty-five minutes later, Dora went into the bathroom and couldn't believe that Tavares was true to her word and had fallen asleep. He kissed Tavares awake.

"Damn, I really did fall asleep, huh?"

Tavares sat up enough for Dora to change the water and give her a sponge bath. The bath felt so good that Tavares didn't want to get up, but she knew that her new PJs and the bed were going to feel twice as good. She motivated herself out of the tub, got dressed, and slid back into the bed.

Tavares asked Dora, "What are we going to do today?"

"What do you want to do?"

"This."

"This?"

"Yeah, I want to lie in bed and watch the football game."

"Girl, you be killing me acting like you're this big ass football fan."

"Don't hate because I ain't like every other chick you had just pretending when they didn't know the difference from a field goal, sack, and a punt return."

"Ok, Miss-I-Know-Football-Terminology, let's get in the bed and get this party cracking," Dora laughed.

Tavares was snuggled under Dora real closely when she heard her phone start vibrating on the dresser.

"Can you get it?"

"You sure you want a nigga answering your phone? I ain't trying to make no one mad," Dora joked as he got up and picked the phone up.

"I told you to answer it, and you didn't. So, give it here."

"Hello," Tavares said, sounding as relaxed as she felt.

"Hey, Stranger. Where you at?" asked Doll.

"Hi, Ma. What's going on?"

"Shit. I was sitting here looking at all this rain and thought about you because I know how much you love it. I ain't heard from you, so I just wanted to call and check on you."

"I'm good, Ma. I'm just lying here watching the game."

"Well then, why you ain't called me the last week or so? Don't get cute and get beside your little pus-colored ass because you and Damien aren't together."

Tavares snickered because Doll was too serious.

"Ma, would you calm your crazy ass down. I had mad tests the last week and then I came out of town this weekend."

"Where are you at?"

148

"I'm in New York."

"With who?"

"Here you go, Lady. I'm with my booface!"

"Ok, say no more. Momma gets the drift," laughed Doll. "Shit, I ain't no motherfucking fool. I'm just glad you woke up and realized that one monkey don't stop no show. You have fun and give me a call when you get back to school. Be safe."

"I will and I love you."

"Love you, too," Tavares said and the line went dead.

Tavares gave her attention back to Dora, who looked like he wanted to ask a question.

Tavares was learning him just like he was learning her, so she asked, "What's on your mind?"

"I'm good, Ma."

"Stop lying before I slap you," Tavares said, laying a playful slap on his forehead.

Abdora couldn't help but laugh at the pint-sized bully.

"I'm just curious. What does homeboy and his peoples think about you having his baby and being with me?"

Tavares just laughed, because he was looking too serious for something that wasn't even that serious.

"Oh, they don't even know I'm pregnant."

Dora was confused.

"What do you mean they don't know? Don't you plan to tell them?"

"Yeah, but not right now. I'm just not ready. I'm trying to get Damien out my system as a whole. And, baby's father or not, I'm not ready to open the fresh wound. Nor do I want him using this baby as a reason to harass me to take him back. He can be a father, but he has no bearing on our relationship."

Hearing that made Abdora feel good, because he knew that this shit wasn't going to be easy, but her words were soothing. They watched the Patriots and the Giants play and Tavares was getting worked up.

She started screaming, "Come on, Brady! You know that's not how we do things! Get your fucking mind right!"

"Girl, calm down. You're working yourself up like he can hear you and shit."

"Leave me alone, Abdora."

Tav slapped Dora as she lay with her head on his chest. The day seemed to pass them by in a blink of an eye as they watched football, had sex intermissions, and ate. It was nine o'clock when they'd bathed for the third time and had sex five times.

"I need you to do something more than try to rape me," Dora said, coming out the shower wrapped in a towel.

He was looking so sexy that Tavares was truly ready to attack him again. Tattooed from head to toe in every place and space on his body was the sexiest to Tavares. The muscles were just the icing on top of the cake. Most people lost their sex drive when they got pregnant, but Tavares's had heightened way too high.

"Whatever, you know you want to give it to me. I'm good, though. My poor baby is tired of you poking him in his head with your big ass dick."

"Whatever, Tavares! Tell your baby his momma can't help it that she's a freak."

Damien hit Holton up and told him that he'd located the woman that he'd been looking for. He failed to tell Holton that he'd been selling crack to Dolonda for years and had no clue that she was his girlfriend's mother or that he was his girlfriend's father. They agreed to meet at the Brockton Mall and Damien would show Holton the way to Dolonda's house. As they pulled up to Dolonda's house unannounced, they were ready to tear her a new asshole for separate reasons that were one in the same.

Hearing the bell and not expecting company, Dolonda dragged herself out of bed and said, "Hello," groggily into the bell.

"It's Dame."

What the fuck is Dame doing here? Dollar thought as she buzzed the bell and cracked the door. She went to her room to throw on some jeans, a bra, and a shirt. Damien and Holton entered the house and took a seat on the couch with each of their blood boiling. Dolonda came out her room and got the surprise of her life. Holton Montiago, the man she'd loved and who had walked out on her when she needed him was standing before her. It had been twenty-two years since she'd seen Holton, and he still looked the same. He was as fine as fine got.

Holton looked at Dollar and could see that, past the addiction, she still had it if she wanted it. She just had to get it back. She just needed to put down the crack pipe. Had it not been for Lilly, he would have married Dolonda. She was bad as bad got in their day. He loved Lilly from a small child and couldn't walk out on her, but he'd been in love with Dolonda. Dollar looked from Damien to Holton, then from

151

Holton to Damien, and was afraid that she didn't want to know why they were both in her living room and together.

"Yo, Dollar, you ain't shit!" Dame spat real calmly. "All the times you looked me right in the face and said you had no kids was a lie. You straight denied Tavares and her existence. What type of fucked up shit is that? I watched your daughter grow up hurting and aching silently because you weren't around. Yet, you spend your days denying her and getting high to make yourself feel better. You should feel as fucking low as the fucking crack you put in a pipe and blow into the fucking air. Right now Tavares got a lot on her plate, but oh you betta believe she's going to know that I know where her mother is. It's going to break my heart to tell her that I been selling to you all these years, but I'm going to do what I got to do."

Dollar's eyes showed hurt on a whole other level. After Damien asked her the first time about why she never had kids, she prayed time and time that he never found out about her being Tavares's mother. Dollar was ashamed that she bought drugs from her daughter's boyfriend, all while denying having a child. Dollar was crying like a baby, but no one felt bad for her. Damien continued to dog her out about how she missed knowing a wonderful, great, and gifted person.

Holton gave it to her next. He wasn't trying to attack her, but she earned the harsh words they were giving her.

"You ain't shit, Dolonda. What type of fucking woman keeps her daughter from her father? You outright lied and said you aborted the baby. If you were fucked up, I would've stepped up and took care of my daughter had I known she ever existed."

"Get the fuck out of here!" Dolonda said, flipping out.

It hit her that had he been around, maybe she would have had a chance at having her daughter in her life at the present moment.

"You got brand motherfucking new," Dolonda said, shaking her head and her Dominican accent coming out thick as her long hair swung with her anger. "I told you that I was having a baby, and you let Lilly convince you to turn your fucking back on me. You decided to be less of a man. It wasn't my fault that you were a punk bitch. So, no, you didn't deserve to know that I had my baby. I did what I could till I got hooked on that shit. I did it all on my own. Without you or my fucking mother. So, I don't need your no good motherfucking ass standing here trying to tear me down no more than I already tear my fucking self down every day that I get high. I feel fucked up every time I see Damien. Every time I hear Damien brag about how great his girlfriend is. So you want to do something? Get the fuck out my house and act like you never knew me!"

Holton knew for sure that Dolonda had lost her mind smoking that shit. He stopped to make sure he wasn't hallucinating over the way he was just spoken to. In the snap of a second, he raised his right hand and backhanded Dollar so hard that she went flying.

"You no good, stinking crackhead bitch. You had a baby and told me you aborted it. You're the reason that my daughter grew up in the streets with no mother or father. You better hope and pray, Dolonda Del Gada, that you can make it right with me and my kid. Because, if not, you're going to have way bigger problems than trying to figure out where your next hit is coming from."

153

Dollar lay on the floor not knowing if she would ever be able to come face to face with her daughter that she hadn't seen in over eleven years. Holton continued beating Dolonda down with hurtful words before leaving her there curled up in a ball, crying like a newborn baby. Damien and Holton ended up spending the whole day together talking about Tavares. Damien told Holton all about Tavares. He informed him of all the monumental things that he'd missed in Tavares's life.

"Holton, it doesn't surprise me that Tavares is Dolonda's daughter, but I'd have never guessed that you would be her pops."

Damien was amazed that the biggest connect he knew from a kid was Tavares's father.

"She got you in her, though. Word, she does," Damien said, realizing that Tavares's drive, hustle, and street intelligence came from Holton.

"Thanks," Holton said. "I won't even lie to you youngin. I was checking your little lady out. I kept looking at her and looking at her but never thought that she could be my flesh and blood. Her eyes, though. Her eyes are what kept me pushing to want to know who she was. Her eyes look like my mother's but are the same color as Dolonda's mother's eyes."

"You and Dolonda made a beautiful daughter, Holton."

"Thanks," Holton replied, not surprised because Dolonda was badder than his wife on any given day. "I'm tight with Dolonda," Holton blurted out. "She birthed my first daughter and when shit got rough, rather than come to me and tell me I had a kid, she left my Babygirl out there fucked up. I can't believe Dolonda got fucked up on that shit. Dolonda was never the type to be a follower and do some dumb shit. I can't believe she lost Tavares either. Everything about her was together back then. She's always been headstrong and had her shit together. She worked hard and went to school with the hopes of being a lawyer one day."

That made Damien think the apple doesn't fall too far from the tree because that was Tavares's dream. Damien could hear in Holton's voice that he loved Dolonda somewhere deep inside him.

"So, when do we tell her?" Holton asked.

He was ready to track Tavares down to tell her right then and there.

"Holton, Tavares got a lot on her plate right now."

Dame explained the circumstances of their break-up, school, and her being pregnant. Holton felt some type of way about Damien dogging Tavares out, now that she was his daughter. He didn't say anything, though, because they were grown. After hanging out for four hours, they both decided that Tavares would know about her parents, just not anytime soon.

"She's graduating from school and having a baby shower in three weeks," Damien informed Holton. "She has no idea, but a bunch of us are flying down to surprise her for both events."

"I'll be there," Holton said with a tear truly sliding down his face.

He missed so many years of his daughter's life and just wanted to be a part of it going forward, even if she didn't know he existed.

Graduation was two weeks away, and Tavares didn't know whether she was coming or going. It was one thing after another. She was miserable, writing papers left and right, while preparing to walk across the stage when she wasn't sure if it was going to happen. Stress and misery were driving Tavares crazy. One of Tavares's grades was looking shady. She was a pro at writing, but numbers were a monster to her eyes. Having waited until her last semester to take the required calculus class left her unsure if she was going to pass. Tavares had failed all her tests but went to every single class and tutoring session, despite her miserable pregnancy that was kicking her ass. She turned in all her homework and even got tutoring to prove that she was trying. Numbers just weren't for her, unless it was measurements with coke and counting money - the only two things she'd ever needed numbers for. Tavares hadn't even informed her friends and Abdora that she might not be graduating.

She exited the math building and waddled across the street to Payne Hall, where all her other classes were located. She stopped at the vending machine and got some cupcakes and milk to enjoy before her class.

"Tavares, girl, what you do doing eating that stuff? You know that stuff isn't good for that baby," Dr. Pooler said.

Dr. Pooler was old but sexy. She was fiery and stunning. Dr. Pooler was Tavares's advisor and department head and she was smart as a whip. She was pretty, petite, sexy, and fitter at sixty-five years old than a twenty-five-year-old was. She ran marathons as a hobby, and she only wore the hottest shoes, purses, and suits. Her only flaw was her bad weave that just was never looking good. It was always raggedy and shifty - even when it was new. She kept weaves in for what seemed like forever, but other than that, she was definitely a role model and a strong black woman.

She was a girl born and raised in the woods who dreamed big and got hers off top. She went to school, earned her doctorate degree, and pursued her dream, and she was definitely Tavares's role model. Dr. Pooler came to love Tavares for her smarts, but Tavares had stolen her heart in a time of sadness. She officially became her favorite student when her husband had passed away and Tavares came to check on her every day. It was sincere, and woman-to-woman, not student to professor. She respected and loved Tavares.

"Girl, I told you to eat vegetables and fruits. That's why you and the baby are getting so big. Come with me and throw that mess away."

Waddling down the long narrow hallway, Tavares entered the end office and slid down on the couch.

"Tavares, why are you sitting out there eating all that junk and looking like that?" Dr. Pooler said, leaning back in her leather chair really waiting for an explanation.

"Oh my goodness, Dr. Pooler. You don't even understand. I'm stressed out and there's no going out to have a drink, so eating is all that I got."

Tavares gave her a sneaky smile.

"Make me understand. What's the problem? You're graduating in two weeks, have a scholarship to law school, a job lined up if you want it. Not to mention, you're doing pregnancy justice."

"Dr. Pooler, not only is this baby killing me, I don't know if I'm graduating. I'm not passing Dr. Allendale's class.

157

I'm going and trying, but it's not working out," Tavares said with a sigh.

"Tavares, close my door," Dr. Pooler said with a small chuckle. "Tavares, have you gone to every class and done every assignment?"

"I sure have, but the tests are killing me."

"If what you say is true, Tavares, then you'll graduate, sweetie. All you gotta do is trust in it and believe in it."

"What?" Tavares said. "Please don't play with my emotions right now, Dr. Pooler. What do you mean?"

"Like I said, if you've done all that you've said you've done, then you don't have to worry about you and that baby getting your dual degrees in Criminal Justice and Social Work."

Days before graduation, Tavares would learn that Dr. Allendale passed Tavares because Dr. Pooler informed him that if he didn't, he would be on the couch and getting no nookie. Consoling her, Dr. Pooler reassured Tavares that she was going to be ok. She was stepping toward her destiny, and this was a milestone that she was going to reach. It was on and popping now. Tavares went to class full of a burst of energy. She didn't have to worry about disappointing the few people she had mailed invitations.

With black being the required graduation color, Tavares bought every black dress and shoes in her size that she could find. She was finally anxious for graduation to come. She called her friends and Abdora every day for the next two weeks because she was so excited and ready to see all eight of the people that she'd invited. Tavares didn't know that she was really getting on everyone's nerves with calling them all day every day when she wasn't in class, stuffing her face, or sleeping. They were trying to coordinate her surprise baby shower, and she was busy beeping in on everyone's phone line.

Tavares was officially done with school four days before graduation, so she spent that time preparing her acceptance speech for her law school scholarship and pampering herself. Graduation was at four o'clock in the afternoon, and everyone was flying in at ten that morning. They would go to the hotel to get dressed before meeting Tavares at the gymnasium where graduation was being held. Tavares was in the procession line looking beautiful as she kicked it with the Diva Squad, who were also graduating. They were all being sentimental while Tavares was trying to hold back.

"Listen, I'm not about to smudge my perfectly made up face from MAC."

Tavares's hair and makeup were flawless from her morning appointment. She was flawless in a fitted black dress with a v-neck in the front and the back. The dress hugged her small body and big belly. She also wore black stockings and cute black Chanel slipper-like flats. She was a diva - pregnant and all.

With everyone around her, hugging and congratulating her, it was so surreal that she was pregnant, graduating Salutatorian in her class, and getting a scholarship for law school. Asia was graduating number one and heading to med school, so Tavares was okay being number two. Tavares was really proud of herself and wished her mother could see her, because she would be proud of her. Tavares also wished that Damien and Doll had been there to share her accomplishment since they had been her only family.

Tavares had talked to Doll every day for the last three weeks but had lied and told her that she wasn't graduating because she wasn't ready to tell them that she was having a baby. Tavares felt awful lying to Doll.

As Tavares entered the gymnasium that was to capacity with people in the seats and standing around the circular standing level, she started to look for her friends. It was too many people, though, so she didn't even bother. Tavares listened to all the boring speeches and wished they would hurry up because she was ready to get her degrees and scholarship. Plus, she was ready to get out of the black robe that she was burning up in. Finally, Dr. Pooler approached the podium.

"We have a young lady who is being awarded the Founders Club scholarship along with three other urban scholarships, as an opportunity to continue on the road of higher education to law school. She is a beautiful, bright, and gifted young lady who is going to go far in life. She is going to have company with her when she comes up here, so don't be shocked. Please give Tavares Del Gada a round of applause!"

Everyone was clapping, but as she walked she could still hear *Go Apple, Diva Mom, and Tavares* from one whole section. When she turned around, she got the surprise of her life. One whole section was filled with everyone that she could have imagined. Tavares was frozen and couldn't believe her eyes. There was Damien, Doll, and their whole family, Dora and his friends along with his family, Gianna and Angelica, Lilly and Holton, and of course her friends. Both Damien and Abdora's brothers were there with their wifeys. It was crazy that she had a whole section full of people and had no idea any of them would be attending. Tavares started to ball because she never imagined so many people would show up. Tavares was still in shock when she made it to the podium.

"Please give me a moment. Before I say thank you for my scholarship, I just want to thank that whole section of people over there who are here by surprise," Tavares said, pointing to the right. "As you can see, they're very full of spirit with their signs and cheers. I have no family. I grew up without a mother or a father. They're my family, so I want to say thank y'all very much for flying here to celebrate with me."

Holton's heart hurt. Damien felt bad for both Tavares and Holton when he heard that.

"When I applied for this scholarship, I thought it was a long shot that I would get it, but I still applied. I put my faith in my essay, and my recommendations in the hands of God. I see that GOD is good, because this gives me a chance to further my education not only for myself, but also for the two babies that I'm carrying."

Everyone in Tavares's sections was shocked. Their eyes popped out their heads, they said *huh, what,* and *oh shit.* No one, not even her friends, knew she was having two babies. Tavares didn't even know till her last visit, when they found her second baby hiding behind the first baby. She'd saved the good news for graduation day.

"When I saw the essay topic, I never in my wildest dreams meant to touch people or affect them in the way I did with my life story. I just wrote from the heart, so I feel honored and blessed that I was chosen as the most deserving person to earn a way to law school. The question said: Tell us about who you are, how you got to where you are, and why you should be awarded this scholarship to continue your higher education. My life ended before it really started. From the age of ten, I was on my own growing up in foster care. It was a long, rough road for me but GOD looked out for me. He gave me a chance at life past what I was destined for. With that opportunity, I never stopped working for and wanting more. I never saw this in my future, so it feels amazing. I'm having two beautiful babies," Tavares said proudly, "and I hope that I can instill in them everything that makes me who I am and got me to this point. Thank you," Tavares said with tears streaming down her face and everyone on their feet clapping.

After graduation, Tavares met everyone outside and accepted tons of cards, gifts bags, balloons, hugs, and kisses. She couldn't believe that Damien and Abdora were in the same place being cordial on the strength of her. Tavares thought she was going crazy but was more than grateful. She and her entourage took about two hundred various pictures. As everyone started to make their way to their cars, Tavares remembered that Asia had driven to graduation.

"Uhhh, excuse me," Tavares said to the few still making their way to their cars. "I need to ride with someone to the restaurant."

"Tavares, calm your nerves," Damien said. "There are plenty of cars out here," he said, laughing at how cute she was being pregnant and so dramatic.

Tavares just stuck her tongue out at him and gave him the middle finger.

"Well, how about you drive yourself," Abdora said, trying to hand her some keys.

Tavares just sucked her teeth and asked, "How about I don't? Today is all about me, so I'm doing no such thing. I'm not doing nothing that isn't about me today and driving seems like it's not about me. Someone needs to drive ME."

Everyone just laughed, because she was serious and looking at the keys dangling before her like they were a foreign object.

"Well, what you going to do with your car?" Abdora asked.

"Those ain't my keys, and I didn't drive," Tavares said sarcastically.

"Tavares, you're book smart as hell, but sometimes you ride the slow bus," Abdora said, shaking his head.

"What?" Tavares asked, holding all her bags and balloons with her blue eyes glistening as they popped out her head.

"Whose keys are these?" Tavares said, mad as hell as she snatched them.

"Yours," Abdora said, walking away because she was getting on his nerves, and they had a plane to catch.

Tavares had no idea Abdora was using his flying time to charter two planes to get everyone to Miami. She made it hard for him to really get mad because he loved that she was so feisty and cute. Tavares's girls and the Diva Squad were standing there looking just as clueless as she was.

"Click the fucking alarm and see where it beeps at," Mona-Lisa urged.

When Tavares clicked the alarm, everyone jumped back when they saw the cherry red Lamborghini truck in the center of the back parking lot.

"WHOOOA!" Randee gasped, thinking that she was about to pass out.

The ladies walked to the truck and quickly examined the wheels that were hot as fire. They were personalized with plates that read *Apple*. There was OnStar inside, a high-tech talking navigation system, and TVs with DVD players built in them. The system sounded like it was for a block party, and the interior smelled so new that it made the ladies want to scream.

"Girl, this nigga needs to do me a favor and NOT be balling so out of control," Asia said, blown away that her girl was about to be pushing a Lambo in the hood.

That wasn't what people in the hood did, except Abdora.

"I second that," Vachelle said.

Everyone just laughed because this dude that Tavares had snagged was really going hard. Tavares exchanged goodbyes with the Diva Squad ladies, who were going out with their families.

"The line that we're supposed to follow is almost off campus, and we're still over here running our mouths," Randee said as they got into the car.

The ladies opened the sunroof along with the windows and caught up to the long line that looked like a damn procession. Jazz was in the front listening to LL Cool J's "I'm Bad" on the satellite radio and digging Tavares's new ride. Mona-Lisa and Randee were in the second row, and Leslie was in the back row reclined, twisting up a blunt.

"Bitch, don't you dare light a blunt in my brand spanking new truck," Tavares said, looking through the rear view.

Sucking her teeth, Leslie said, "Damn, I can't wait for you to have them babies," and lit the blunt knowing Tavares was just trash talking.

"I can't believe this nigga copped you a Lambo," Randee said, inhaling the smoke.

"Who does that?" Mona said. "Of course, only our community boo," she said, answering her own question and laughing.

"What do you think Damien is going to say?" Jazz asked as she shook her head.

"Who cares? We're not together," Tavares said, rolling her eyes.

"He might want the truck and car back that he bought you."

"Bitch, Damien ain't getting shit back," Tavares said, feeling her temperature rising. "My cars are in my name, and he ain't no bum nigga to ask for them back. Not when he got three cars at home his damn self."

"Nah, Dame ain't like that," Mona-Lisa cosigned.

"Bitch, what are you going to do with three fucking cars?" Leslie asked.

"Shit, hell if I know," Tavares laughed.

She couldn't believe she'd gone from being homeless to graduating from college and on her way to law school with mad cash in the bank. Plus, she was about to be a mother and had really made it, but was far from being done.

"Shit, I need a new damn car, if you're giving any away," Leslie said.

The ladies laughed and joked their way all the way to the other side of Savannah, when Tavares realized that the line of cars was getting on the highway.

"Where the fuck is whoever is in front going?" Tavares asked no one in particular.

"Just follow the line."

"Where are we going?" Tavares asked. "Because it sounds like you whores know," she continued.

"Ahh, bitch, I got your whore," Jazz said, pulling Tavares's hair that was now to her butt from growing like crazy since she'd become pregnant.

"We're going to the airport," Jazz said, ruining the surprise.

"I thought we were going to eat. What the hell is going on?" Tavares asked, knowing that it was about to be something crazy.

As Tavares listened, she didn't even understand why she was ever shocked at anything that Abdora did. Everyone arrived at their airport and returned their rental cars while Tavares and her girls made their way to long-term parking. Tavares waddled to meet everyone and couldn't believe that Abdora had done all this for her. It was unreal. Not because of the money he spent, because money was nothing to him, but the extent he went to celebrate and put a smile on her face. Tavares looked around at her friends who had all somehow managed to forget they had no clothes.

"Uhhh, does anyone besides me realize that we have no bags with clean clothes?" Tavares asked sarcastically.

"No, Boo Boo, *you* don't have clean clothes," Mona laughed. "We have clothes on the plane. You're the only one who doesn't have clothes, because only you didn't know where we we're going," Mona laughed like it was really funny.

"Fuck you, bitch."

"Don't listen to her," Leslie said, slapping Mona's arm playfully. "Abdora said he got it covered."

By the time the ladies got to the runway, the two chartered planes were ready and waiting to take everyone to Miami for the weekend. The young people were on one plane blowing it down and taking shots while the older people were on the other plane.

"Abdora, thank you very much for my car. It's gorgeous."

"You're gorgeous," he replied. "So, your whip should be, too. That's your G-Ride. Usually niggaz call their rides their rides G-Rides which is short for a gangster's ride, but that's your gorgeous ride."

Tavares laughed because it was gorgeous, so it was for sure her G-Ride.

"I'm just glad you like it."

"But, hold up," Tavares said, remembering that she had no clothes. "Dora, where the hell are my clothes, because I sure don't have any," Tavares said, throwing her hands up in the air.

"Calm down. I don't want you mad at me. I swear to you, with doing all the last-minute stuff, I totally forgot that I was supposed to be the one to get your clothes. You can wear what you got on to the graduation dinner, then you can take some dough and go crazy tomorrow."

"What?" Tavares said like he was crazy. "So everyone has fucking clothes but me? Is that what you're trying to tell me, Abdora? You're not serious," Tavares said, getting mad.

"Babygirl, calm down. That dress is hot. You ain't gotta change," Dora said, trying to be convincing.

Tavares wasn't buying what he was selling.

167

"Abdora, do me a favor and don't talk to me," Tavares said, going to sit somewhere else.

By the time everyone got to the hotel and checked in, it was 8:00 p.m.

"Listen, Slow Poke Crew," Dora said to Tavares and her girls, "the party starts at ten o'clock, not at eleven or twelve o'clock, but ten o'clock. So, y'all need to have slow poke there on time," Dora said, giving an order but making it sound like he was asking.

"We ain't that damn slow," Leslie said, pretending to be rolling her eyes at Abdora.

Tavares made her way to the room but didn't know why when she had no clothes. She walked into the suite that smelt like candy and had a perfect view of the ocean. Tavares was blown away. To the left was a beautiful marble bathroom with eye-catching monogrammed towels. There were way too many free Dove products on the double sink that had personal shelves and mirrors over each sink. There was a large supply of soap, lotion, deodorant, shampoo, conditioner, face creams, and cleansers. There was a private enclosed area that contained the toilet, a phone, and a TV. The shower was twelve feet tall with a marble bench in it and a radio system built into the wall. A marble heart-shaped Jacuzzi was in the corner behind the door. There was a mirror behind it so big that you couldn't help but see what you were doing when you do in the Jacuzzi. *Whoever designed this bathroom had sex in mind,* Tavares thought, and she was already pleased.

Across from the bathroom was a living room that had congratulations balloons and red roses everywhere. The living room had a really nice-sized cushioned red leather loveseat and couch. There was a 64-inch plasma TV with all Dora's favorite video games, movies, and junk food. It was like the movie theater.

"This fool is crazy," Tavares said, thinking that he just didn't know how to quit. "Who does all this and still, I have no goddamn clothes?"

Tavares was upset for the first time not only that she didn't have any clothes, but that they were in a hotel room with no kitchen. Since she was pregnant, she was always starving to death. Ordering room service came to mind, but Tavares decided to go to the bedroom and lie down for a minute since she had nothing to change into like everyone else.

When she entered the all black bedroom, Tavares dropped her Chanel bag on the couch and was shocked as hell when she went to the cove to where the bed was. On the bed, there were pretty, bright, vibrant-colored dresses that were Tavares's style all day. Cute flat sandals lay in front of each dress since heels were out of the question. He even purchased panties and bras to match each dress. After trying everything on, Tavares couldn't believe that she really thought Abdora dropped the ball.

Abdora was gone to check on the beach party that had been secluded off exclusively for their crew. Dinner was in a private glassed-in patio area on the beach. He went with a simple decorative scheme, but it was still pretty. He knew that Tavares loved red roses, so he used them as an accent. Everything in the room was all white, including the table linens, china, draperies, and chair covers. Fresh handpicked rose petals were scattered on the tables. Tall red vases with long-stem red roses popping out of them were placed in the centers of the round tables.

Dora had roses weaved and sewn together to make decorative draperies from the ceiling. The massive red flowers against the all-white room set the beautiful scene. Abdora even had party favors vertically opened like a college degree. On one side of the favor was an image of a degree and a recent picture of Tavares while she was pregnant was on the other side. Abdora had dished out a whole lot of cash on this one weekend. Chartering the planes, paying for the hotel for everyone, and all the catered weekend events had topped any event he'd ever paid for, but Dora was happy because he felt that Tavares deserved and earned this weekend.

With everything all set, Dora headed upstairs to change and to see how Tavares reacted when she found that he was on top of things as always. Tavares walked out of the bedroom just as Abdora was stepping out of the common bathroom.

"Damn, where did your ass come from?" Tavares asked with her eyes popping out her head. "I didn't even know you were in there. I had the doors shut with the music going while I was getting ready."

"You did a good job," Dora said, admiring the fact that Tavares had chosen his favorite dress.

"Well, you put on your clothes, and I'm going to put on some makeup," Tavares said. "Lucky for you, I always keep a makeup bag in my purse. Because, if not, I would've been hit this weekend."

Tavares and Abdora finished getting dressed and headed down to the party thirty minutes late. Tavares chitchatted and made her rounds, thanking everyone for coming to celebrate her graduation with her. The lady of the evening was happy that everyone was having a good time. She couldn't help thinking this was too surreal. Tavares thanked everyone for coming and for drinking since she couldn't. People were laughing, but Tavares was serious.

Tavares's attention was grabbed by the dancing going on. Abdora's brother and friends were on the dance floor with their dates getting it popping. You couldn't even be mad at them. They were fine ass gangster niggaz, letting down their street life for the night and having a fun time. Tavares tried to slide by, but Dora grabbed her and dragged her on the floor.

"Damn you," Tavares laughed as he was playfully rubbing her stomach while they danced. "You know you don't have the sense that God gave you, right?"

"I know, but it's cool because you love you some me."

"Whatever," Tavares laughed as she and her two babies two-stepped and celebrated her milestone.

After working up a mild sweat on the dance floor, Dora and Tav made their way over to Holton and Lilly. Holton was torn down inside, because he was so proud of his daughter who didn't even know he was her father. Lilly was happy that Tavares had accomplished something so important. After giving congratulations, Holton and Lilly gave Tavares a check for $10,000. Tavares thought she was seeing wrong and had to move the check in and out from her eyes a few times.

"I can't take this," Tavares said, buggin' that they'd given her such a big gift.

"Man, listen, Holton. If she don't want that, I'll take it," Dora joked.

"Nah, momma. That's for you," Lilly said, knowing the true reason the gift was so big even though her husband thought she was clueless. "Between the graduation and a little trust fund for each baby, it's just enough."

Tavares was still looking from the check to Holton and Lilly. She was at a real loss for words. Tavares gave each of them a hug and said thank you as she left Dora standing there and made her way over to her friends who were in the corner doing what they did best - running their mouths.

"Who y'all over here talking about?"

Everyone fell out laughing.

"How you know we're talking about people?"

"I know you stuck up bitches, so I know what y'all are doing."

"Well shit, since we talking about people, let's talk about your ass," Mona-Lisa said with a slick chuckle.

"Alright, well let's do it outside," Tavares said with her friends already knowing what was good.

They slipped out without anyone noticing and headed out to the beach for some secret squirrel time to blow it down and do them.

"Apple, I'm so proud of you," cooed Mona-Lisa.

"Me, too," Randee said, holding back her tears because she didn't do sentimental. "I can't believe you're graduating, having babies, and probably about to get married at the rate you're going."

"Oh God, that's a force, Mona," Tavares said, thinking it seemed farfetched. "I don't know about marriage because we ain't talked about it, but I do know that I love him, y'all," Tavares said real soft, content, and clearly happy.

"Ahh, that's sooo cute," said Leslie.

"Awww, my bitch is in love forreal," Mona said sarcastically but seriously.

"Shut up, Mona," Tavares said as Randee passed Mona the blunt.

"I'm just saying, like I really, really love him," Tavares said, not really knowing how else to explain it. "Look at us, y'all. For real, look at us. We're really in Miami for the weekend and Abdora paid for everyone and everything. This shit is past surreal to me. I've never met or encountered a nigga like him in all my life. He's just so him that I gotta call him special," Tavares said, knowing that she was probably making no sense to her friends. "I never thought that I would fall in love like this, y'all. It's crazy.

"He's swept me off me feet for real. Even though everything about it seems too good to be true, it's not. He ain't never lied to me, ain't never did nothing but be good to me and take me for me. I love that he appreciates me more than anything. I thought love would never exist if it wasn't with Damien, but he showed me that love was hardly for real with Damien. Dora made me see that when someone says they love you, they don't show you with their words," Tavares chuckled with a big smile. "They show you with their actions, and it's a wonderful feeling. I ain't giving him up, ladies."

"Shit, you better not. I'll beat you up," Randee joked.

"I never thought that I could want to be in the house and not in the streets with you bitches," Tavares said, shaking her head. "I don't know how it happened or how it went down, but I'm glad it did. Even the shit with Damien, it happened for a reason. You gotta take the bad with the good. Now I'm taking the good with good, and I'm happy," she said, getting misty eyes as she started rubbing her belly.

173

"I can't believe you of all damn people are about to have not one but two babies," Leslie said. "I never thought I would see the day that you had a baby."

"Girl, please don't even tell me about it. I'm having fucking twins. Only with my luck I would get stuck with twins the first time I get pregnant."

"Why you didn't tell niggaz?" Jazz questioned.

"Because I didn't know - well, not till a few weeks ago when I went for my last appointment. The second baby was behind the other baby all this time. The baby is healthy though."

"I would love to know who the fuck has twins in their family," Randee said.

"Please don't get me to lying," Tavares said, curious also. "Maybe it's good, though. Because after this, I got one more in me, then I'm done. No if, ands, or buts about it. If I gots to handle being a mother twice over at the same time, that's too much and enough to make me say I'm only doing it once more."

Everyone just laughed because even though Tavares loved kids, she never saw herself having any. After kicking it with her friends for a hot minute, Tavares made her way back inside to see Miss Dhara and her table.

"Hi, Miss D," Tavares said, then gave her older-looking twin a kiss on the cheek.

"Hey, Meemaw," Tavares said to Dora's half-Cherokee Indian and half-Portuguese grandmother.

Meemaw was bad with that deep, rich, coffee-colored skin looking like Pocahontas's grandmother, but she was another gangster granny. It was crazy to Tavares how Dame

174

and Dora's families were so similar. Meemaw told Tavares that she better be ready for war with two babies at once.

"I am, Meemaw. I got this. If I don't have this, I know I'm prepared for the learning experience of being a mother that I've read about."

"Girl, cut that textbook mother shit out and get wit it."

Everyone fell out laughing because Meemaw didn't care what she said.

"Shit's real, you beautiful, mixed Barbie, but you need to know that your world is about to change forever. You're about to take on the world to make sure that those kids are always alright. It's no longer about you, baby. It's about them babies. So, you get ready, but know that me and Dhara got your back. Especially if you keep making Dora smile," Meemaw said and high-fived Dhara.

"You got my baby running around here all open and shit," Dhara said, shrugging her shoulders while asking, "What's up with that? My boy is real happy and living in his la-la land of love."

Tavares just laughed because they were on it rooting for their baby boy.

"Miss Dhara, you better stop! We're chillin'."

Mid's date was feeling the heat on Tavares and helped her out.

"So what sexes you having?"

"I said I didn't want to know," Tavares said with a slight smile. "That's why I told my friends I didn't want a baby shower. It would have been too much unless people gave me only gift cards and money."

"Speaking of which, Meemaw, I heard you got in on the pool," Tavares said with her hands on her belly and shaking her head.

"Oh hell yes, I did. I think I got it, so whoever is in is going to hit if they know like I know."

"What pool?" Mid's date asked as the only clueless one at the table.

"Well..." Tavares said, looking at everyone at the table. "Once I decided that I wasn't going to find out the sex, Abdora decided that he was going to take bets on if it was a boy or a girl. But, now it's going to get juicier because they can bet if they're two boys, two girls, or one of each. I mean, he's dead ass forreal with this prediction bet. You would think he be taking March Madness bets or something," Tavares laughed. "Girl, when you make your bet, you pay and fill out this personal information form in case you're in the winner pot.

"Then, Dora's secretary gets the prediction and the money. She's tracking every bet and sends you an electronic receipt. Bets start at $100 and go up to $500. Then, she updates your prediction on the website little blog thing that they're tracking the predictions on. It even shows you there are this many people in this pot and the total in the pot is this much and I just be laughing. And, girl, I really want to say, the last time I looked the total pot was up to like $80,000. It's purely crazy," Tavares said, not believing that they'd gone so far with this.

Everyone was laughing, because they had for sure submitted their $500 and had their baby lottery ticket. "Girl, it's amongst his friends, my friends, his family, and people at the club. I don't mean just the workers. If you're at the club partying, you can submit your prediction. They're taking payments in the barbershops and in at least one place in every hood. You can even mail the money in. It's like a hood lottery, and I'm bugged the hell out about it. I just feel bad for Dora's secretary, because it's going to get hectic when people go to change their bets now that there are two babies. God bless her," Tavares laughed, but seriously felt bad for how hectic it was gonna get for Talia. "I just want two babies that each has ten fingers and ten toes."

"Girl, you going to get it," Meemaw said really convincingly. "And, I'm going to get me some damn money," she laughed and nodded her head.

"We'll see," Tavares laughed.

Tavares talked for a while and stalled before she made her way to the one table she had avoided.

Tavares was blushing as she approached the table with Doll, NaNa Dancy, Damien, and Rollo.

NaNa said, "Girl, get your butt over here and let NaNa rub them grandbabies," Dancy said as proud as she wanted to be.

"NaNa, these kids do not need to be rubbed. They need to be beat. They be moving all the time and just working on my poor body."

"Girl, shut up. They ain't worked your body yet. Wait until you get to push their big-headed butts out. Then, they will have officially worked your body," Dancy said.

Tavares kicked it with the only family she had ever known or ever had since her mother abandoned her. Doll was her mother, Dancy was her grandmother, and Damien's brother was her brother. It was just hard because now that they were on bad terms, it felt like Damien was really theirs so she had to step back for a moment. Tavares knew that Dora was somewhere watching her. She didn't have to look around, because she could feel him. Whether he was cool or mad, Tavares didn't know, but she knew she could feel his eyes on her.

Damien's whole family was at the table and couldn't believe that Tavares was really having two babies. Damien and Doll rose from the table.

Doll said, "Come with us. We need to talk."

Tavares knew she was about to have the talk she'd been trying to avoid as she followed Damien and Doll down to the beach for a quieter environment.

Doll started the conversation.

"Tavares, just tell me how could you really be pregnant and not say anything? You called me every other day and never once mentioned a baby," Doll said with hurt in her face and voice.

"Ma, I wanted to. I really did. Do you really think I wanted to go through this alone?" Tavares said with her head hung down.

"Tavares, you know that I love you like a daughter - past what you and Dame have or had. I will never stop loving you or being a part of your life unless you make it like that. You're my daughter just as much as he's my son. You're the daughter I never had. I just want you to know that I love you, and I'll be calling you every single day to check on my grandbabies," Doll said with happiness at the fact that she would have two grandbabies to spoil rotten. "I'm going to leave y'all, but don't be too long," Doll said as she headed back toward the party.

Damien just looked at Apple with mixed emotions. He was proud, hurt, and still filled with love for her. More than anything, he hurt for the information that he was holding on to but couldn't reveal yet.

"Tavares, you're beautiful pregnant and all. I'm proud of you. Let me say that first and foremost."

"Thanks," Tavares said, leaning on her right leg not knowing what to say.

Damien had crushed her yet she still loved him. Regardless of what came of them, she never thought he would do what he'd done.

"Tavares, why didn't you call and tell me that you were pregnant? I love you and still will do anything for you. Even if I did fuck up and you're with that nigga and having his babies, you still could have called me."

What? Tavares thought, totally shocked by his last sentence. She didn't know that Damien thought that she was pregnant by Abdora.

"Damien, I don't recall telling you that these are *his* babies."

"What?" Damien said, now totally shocked because someone had told him different.

"So, whose fucking babies are they?"

"I'm not even entertaining that if I just told you they ain't his. What you think I just been running around here throwing my pussy on whomever? Get real, please."

"Tavares, you're telling me that you want to be with this nigga and have my kids?"

"What type of shit are you on?" Damien asked, looking at her like she was crazy.

"Damien, what do you want from me? I didn't expect to be carrying your babies when I moved on. And I'm just supposed to be with no one and not be happy? Come on, you know that ain't right. Especially since I don't want that for you. Plus, you fucked up, not me. I want you to find someone, treat her good, and love her hard."

Damien was floored, because he knew Tavares meant it. Damien couldn't believe that even though Tavares was carrying his twins, she still had no desire to come back to him.

"Well, can I at least be there for you till you have the babies? Don't just cut me out, Tavares. We had something too long and too real for you to be like that."

"Damien, I'll call you and let you know that I'm alright, but past that, I'm not trying to go backwards - your babies or not. Plus, you know that NaNa and Ma are going to be calling me every day," Tavares laughed, knowing that they were going to drive her crazy checking on her.

Damien and Tavares chatted for another few minutes and then returned to the party. When they came back, all eyes were on them because everyone was seated waiting for Tavares so that she could make a small speech. Tavares knew what everyone was thinking, but she didn't give a fuck. She knew that her walking in with Damien was innocent. Abdora had a look in his eyes that said he felt some type of way even though he knew it was nothing. Tavares just ignored his look, grabbed his hand with a swift movement, and pulled him up on the stage with her. Abdora thought, *she thinks she's so slick, now I gotta smile.*

Getting up on stage, Tavares said, "I just want to thank my ohhh sooo sweet boyfriend, Abdora, for making this more than a memorable graduation. I got a new car and a weekend in Miami for a wonderful graduation party with all the people I love. What more can I ask for? Absolutely nothing. I just want to thank each and every one of you who is dear to me in one way or another for coming to be a part of this special occasion with me, my babies, and my honey."

Abdora gave Tavares a long kiss, and everyone cooed and clapped before they went back to partying. After a long, hard night of partying, everyone headed to their hotel rooms ready to do it all over again, unbeknownst to Tavares. Tavares and Abdora made their way to their room. Damien felt some type of way watching his girl of six years going hard with a nigga that she'd only been with for months. He didn't know if he was more upset with Tavares or himself. Now that he found out they were his kids, he was tight about her going to lay up with her new boyfriend and his babies. However, Damien knew that it was his fault that he'd lost her, but to see her with someone else, really happy, and not even worried about him, stung a little.

Tavares woke up to Dora kissing all over her face. She wasn't trying to get up.

"Wake up, Baby. You have to get up and get dressed."

"I don't want to," Tavares whined as she snuggled under Abdora with her naked body keeping warm from his body heat.

"Baby, you have to get up."

"Nope," Tavares said flatly with her eyes closed. "I did all that I was supposed to do yesterday. I graduated, remember? It was a great day. I graduated, ate, partied, and fucked you," Tavares said, slightly snapping.

181

"Ok," Dora laughed. "Like all that was cool and well, but today is a new day. We're doing new thangs, so I need you to get your pretty, big bellied ass up outta da bed and get dressed."

"I want to rest," Tavares said, really not trying to get out the bed if she had her way.

"Babygirl, please get up," Dora said with a tone that said he wasn't going to ask again. "We have an appointment at noon."

"Alright," Tavares said, snatching the cover back and getting up mad as all hell.

Tavares huffed and puffed the whole time she was getting dressed. Dora just laughed because she couldn't help putting up a fight about everything. After complaining about getting dressed, Tavares still turned out beautiful through all her bitching. Her thong sandals decorated her perfectly manicured toes. Her sandals had pretty rhinestones on them and made her pretty red toes stand out even more. Tavares looked naturally pretty in a floor-length strapless flowing white sundress that was nice and snug. With her hair blown straight, Tavares unwrapped it and was ready to roll.

Abdora had on his white linen outfit and crisp white Pradas and was ready to lead the lady of the hour down to the beach. They entered the double doors and walked down the stairs that led to the private reception area.

Tavares asked, "Where the hell are we going?"

"Stop talking and keep walking, and you'll find out," Abdora joked.

When they entered the beautifully decorated hall, Tavares looked around at all the beautiful green, pink, and purple decorations everywhere. There was a huge table full of

182

nothing but cards. There was an oversized chair that resembled a throne with green, purple, and pink decorations especially for Tavares.

"Oh my God," Tavares said, totally surprised. "How did you all pull this off?" Tavares asked with evil eyes.

"Don't worry about it. Just enjoy it," Abdora said.

Tavares did just that. She never expected a baby shower, so one of this magnitude was greatly appreciated. Tavares couldn't have been happier. The dessert bar was full of cookies, brownies, cakes, and pastries. The centerpieces and décor were flawless. Guests were playing games and winning gift cards for massages, to the mall, and high-end restaurants such as Morton's and Ruth's Chris Steak House. Some of the guests won gift baskets and there was even a raffle for a 50-inch flat screen TV. Those that wanted to win the TV had to buy a $20 raffle ticket. They basically got a TV for a minimum of $20 if they won, and if they lost, it was a good shot at it. There was food galore with shrimp, steak, chicken, ribs, rice and peas, mac and cheese, salads, pasta dishes, and mounds of dessert to feast on. Everyone ate, laughed, and took pictures all while having a ball.

When it came to opening presents, Tavares couldn't believe the money that was dished out for her unborn babies. She received everything that she could have possibly wanted. The only problem was that she was having two babies and no one knew, so she would have to go out and use the thousands of dollars in gift cards to get the other twin's stuff. The best gift was two checks for four thousand each from Holton and Lilly. They had weirdly been big spending all weekend, and Tavares was real curious as to why. By the time the baby shower was over, Tavares was

183

totally beat. Her loved ones had drained her and her two babies with all the fun, food, and festivities.

Tavares said goodnight to everyone and was heading out of the function hall up to her room to meet Abdora when Damien stopped her.

"Yo, Tavares. We need to talk," Damien said in a real serious disposition. He was ready to spill a whole lot of secrets. Now that he knew he was the father of her twins, he wanted to start on a clean slate and at least be Tavares's friend.

"Damien, I'm fucking beat, yo."

Tavares had tired all in her voice, demeanor, and eyes.

"Y'all done wore me and the babies out. Can't it wait till tomorrow or when we get back?"

Damien really wanted to take advantage of the liquor that he was feeling but decided that he would stay true and wait till the babies were born.

"Tavares, I just want to tell you that I'm definitely proud of you and the fact that you're going to be my baby meezy."

"Uhh, thanks for the compliment with the exception of you being proud that I'm going to be your baby's mother. I'm definitely not thrilled about being a baby's mother, yours or anyone else's," Tavares said with a tone that let Dame know that she was serious.

They exchanged brief hugs and went in opposite directions. Dame had his Miami mami come through to keep him company, and Tavares was going to meet Abdora.

Dolonda lay in her house smoking the last piece of crack that she would ever put to her lips again. She had a good run with crack, but now it was time to let it go. Seeing Holton in her living room a few weeks ago did something to her. He made her think back to the past. More specifically, she thought about the successful path that she was on when she'd loved and lost Holton. Looking at Holton made her ashamed of what she'd become, even though she turned to crack to shield her pain of losing him. She lost control of her life, and lost her daughter, the only person she ever loved more than herself, due to crack and not being able to beat it.

Crack had taken her off her path. It caused her to smoke away her dreams of being all that she ever wanted to be, a good parent. Damien made her know that it was her loss walking out on Tavares. Her daughter proved to be strong and had survived a world where she was left to fend for herself. Damien voiced that her being absent took something from Tavares that she could never get back. Dolonda knew that if her daughter was anything like her, forgiving her was nothing but a hoop dream. But, if she lived to see the day, she would be clean when it came. Dolonda smoked an eight ball, cried for four hours, and then got up to pack her bags. The next day she would be checking herself into rehab for as long as it took to get her life back.

Tavares made it upstairs to her suite. She was ready to take a shower and go to bed. Her body and feet were aching. When she entered the suite, the pregnant beauty found Abdora sitting at the desk in the plush living room. He was studying the contents in front of him in depth.

"Mr. Hella Handsome, whatcha doing?"

"I was waiting on you and trying to figure out where are you going to live when you get home."

185

"Hmmm, that's a good question," Tavares replied, clueless to the answer.

Tavares hadn't even thought about where she was going to live, even though she would be back in Boston permanently in less than five days.

"I won't lie to you. I didn't give it the least thought with trying to graduate and get through this pregnancy. I got some time to buy, though," Tavares said, plopping onto the couch. "I still gotta go back to Savannah to ship my two cars. The house is empty. Asia and I gave everything to the Goodwill with the exception of our wardrobes. All that other stuff, we had no time to be trying to divide and share. It will be a nice little tax write-off," Tavares said, winking her eye at Abdora, who was sitting across the room from her.

"Well, this is what you do," Abdora said, giving her an order. "Get all your stuff packed. I'm going to have two of my soldiers go put that shit in your two cars and drive your cars to you. So, do it when you get some time, Miss. Look at the houses that I printed out for you and pick two."

"Awww, that was nice of you," Tavares said, showing her gratitude with sarcasm. "And, I don't need two houses. That's just too much and too ridiculous!"

Dora got up and joined Tavares on the couch. She sat on the end of the couch, and he stretched her legs out into his lap as her head fell back in a relaxed position. She thought she was going to pass out from the pleasurable foot rub.

"You do need two houses because you're gonna be living in between two places."

Tavares was listening but she wasn't paying Dora any mind about the houses.

186

"Oooooh, yes," Tavares said to her massage and not his comment.

Dora stopped rubbing. Tavares's eyes opened and her head snapped up with a puppy dog look all on her tired, pretty face.

"Damn, why did you stop?"

"Because you wasn't listening."

"I was, too. I heard what you said. I'm going to get a crib in Boston. Then, I'm going to get a house in Jersey or New York that'll be for me, you, and the babies. I heard every last thing you said. Now, can you finish rubbing?"

Dora just laughed because the more Tavares's pregnancy went on, the snappier and more demanding she became. He wasn't bothered, though, because he loved it. As Dora rubbed her whole body, they did as they usually did, and kicked it about any and everything under the sun.

"Do you know that you got a total of $26,000 in checks and $10,000 in gifts between your graduation and baby shower?"

"Damn..." Tavares said, not believing that she could have made out so well. "Oh, I'm going to be good when the babies come. Yo, let me ask you a question," Tavares said, sitting up because she needed to look Dora in the face.

"What's up with Holton?"

"What you mean?" Dora asked, confused because Holton was the most up and up man that he knew and respected.

He reminded him a lot of his pops, who had died in a bank robbery gone bad when he was young.

"He's a good dude, why?"

"I know his wife, and I just can't figure out why they gave me damn near $20,000. For the graduation, they gave me $10,000. Then they gave each twin $4,000."

Dora thought it sounded like an awful lot of money to him, too.

"I don't know, Ma. Holton got money on top of money on top of money. So, maybe he did it on the strength of knowing me and Damien. Wait, but you said you know Lilly, so maybe it was her doing."

Tavares gave Dora a looked that read, *I highly doubt it.*

"Me and Lilly go back and are close as hell, but $18,000 is a lot of money considering the nature of our relationship."

"What the fuck does that mean?" Dora replied, knowing that he really didn't even want to know.

"Don't ask and I won't tell," Tavares winked. "I don't know, babe. Maybe I'm overreacting, but I feel like they gave me too much of a gift."

"Listen, Babygirl, I don't know why Holton gave you so much money, but Holton's good peoples. He's a nigga I respect and admire, so I know that no matter what, the money came with good intentions."

Tavares still thought it was excessive, but she let it go. They showered together and climbed in the bed. Tavares drifted off in deep thought for a second without even realizing it.

"Hello, Earth to space cadet... Pass me the remote."

Tavares passed Abdora the remote and thought about how her life was moving fast with twins on the way that weren't her boyfriend's, who she was truly falling in love with more each day.

"Yo Abdora, I be scared about what if this doesn't work. I'm not trying to love you any more than I already do, just to get hurt again. I never thought that I would be having kids and not married. That was my one promise to myself, and why I never had kids all these years. Thanks to you, I'm not doing this alone, but sometimes I be like what if shit doesn't work? That's my fear, but on the other note, I know that you're the greatest man ever. Your personality, character, morals, values, looks, swagger, sex, and everything you believe in and stand for. There's not one thing don't I love or adore about you.

"It's not hard to tell that you're head over heels for me. I love everything that you do or give me, but I don't be caring about the money, the gifts, the trips, or none of that shit. I just enjoy being with you. And I don't care what anyone says about me being with you and not Damien. He had his chance and he blew it. I know that you're going to hold me down until the end. You proved that to me early on. You love my babies already, and they aren't even here. That shit amazes me. I just need you to do me one favor. Just never take my love for granted like Damien did. When I love, I love hard. So, I'm just not trying to get burnt twice."

Abdora felt where she was coming from, but because of the love he had in his heart for her, he was a tad bit insulted.

"Tavares, I fought for this spot. Coming to your wack ass office visits, letting you give me the blues. I stayed around for months with no pussy, no nothing, just conversation, and that shit wasn't about nothing. I just enjoyed being with you and the fun that we had together. Our chemistry and the way that we rock is mean, so I was good with our platonic friendship. While you..." he chuckled, "you was stuck on homeboy and all his bullshit. I ain't no on-the-side-type nigga! But, I knew that you was made and meant for me. So, I just went with the flow.

"Damien fucked up a good thing. That's his loss. I don't feel bad for son. My man should have done better if he knew better. I ain't never been that nigga into one woman, but when you got a good one, you hold on to her. Especially one that feels like your best friend, your twin, and who gives you sex that's absolutely ecstasy. He ain't gotta worry, though, because I'm not going to make his mistakes. You're too easy to love and make happy, so I got this. I wanna hit that sweet little tail three times a day. You got the sweetest pussy in the world," Dora said with a sneaky smile.

Tavares gave Dora a fake mad look as she listened.

"I want to provide for you and give you and the kids everything. I ain't trying to hurt you. I just want to love you, protect you, and take care of you. We gonna be married and have us like ten babies. Shit, we can get married tomorrow if you want to," Dora said with a serious look.

"Oh, you've for sure bumped your head," Tavares said as she fell out laughing. "I'm not pushing out or taking care of that many mini yous. And, I want to get married but not tomorrow," Tavares laughed.

"Girl, we can do anything you want short of going to the moon. You can have ten babies, and you'll still be good because I got it, and I got you," Dora said. "We can have nannies. It's nothing."

Tavares thought she'd heard him wrong.

"Don't play yourself, Babe. I ain't having no more than three total."

Dora laughed because Tavares didn't know he was going to keep her barefoot and pregnant.

"I can't see myself without your crazy ass," Dora laughed, "you're too much of my twin. Believe in me, Tavares, but more importantly, believe in us. Babygirl, we're in this to win it. There ain't no stopping us. I've loved you since Red introduced us. Do me a favor, Ma? Just stay true, and let me worry about the rest. You're set for life."

Tavares said nothing because Dora had said it all. Snuggling under Dora's frame, she kissed him, lay in his arms, and watched Sportscenter.

~Chapter 8~
New Chapters, New Beginnings

Dolonda Del Gada had just finished her ninety days of treatment and was told that there were no available sober houses open in Boston or the surrounding area. However, if she wanted to apply to other states, funding was available. The mission was to stay clean after leaving their detox center. So, Dulcies, the non-profit agency helping Dolonda, paid for a rent stipend to a sober house for up to a year. Dolonda wasn't too happy about having to move out of state to go into a sober house. Then, she thought about how she would eventually have to deal with Holton, Damien, and her daughter. She didn't know if she was ready for that, so maybe leaving wasn't such a bad idea. She was going to apply in New York, Philly, and Jersey. Whoever called with a bed first was going to be her new stomping grounds.

Dolonda decided to go shopping for whatever was ahead of her. She had a lot of thinking about life and getting it together to do. When she fell onto the crack wagon, she had just graduated with her bachelor's, so now it was time to do something bigger and better. Dolonda knew that crack had its way with her for too long, and that was definitely over for her. *I'm going to go away and start a fresh new life. When and if I get completely right, I will come back and face my demons*, Dolonda thought as she hopped on the Silver Line to go to downtown Boston.

When she made it downtown, Dolonda went in Macy's, H&M, and DSW and bought herself a whole new wardrobe with the money she'd saved over the last three months since she had stopped smoking. As Dolonda hustled and bustled from store to store shopping, she realized that it felt good to have money to spend. When she was smoking, money came and went no sooner than she had it. As Dolonda handed $300 to the cashier for the six pairs of shoes she bought in DSW, she thought, *Damn, once upon a time the only person I was giving my money to was the crack man.* She felt good inside as she took her change of $18.00. By the end of the day, Dolonda had shopped $3000 away and was proud that she even had the money to do it.

She didn't take any of the tags off the stuff she'd bought. She purchased two suitcases, and dropped all her new belongings into them, then headed toward the Boston Commons for a nice walk just to think. As Dolonda walked and saw the natives, tourists, and children running and enjoying themselves, she realized that she'd really missed out on the last eleven years of life. Always being high or needing to be high had been her only focus. Dolonda thought about who she should call to tell them that she was leaving, but she realized she had no one to call. Her mother had passed away and she was an only child. The only people in her life for the last ten years had been crackheads. Dolonda almost hit a down spot but refused. She kept walking through the Boston Commons, the public garden, and ended up back at Dulcies optimistic and ready for the world.

"Baby, you sure you don't want to go with me?" Dora asked Tavares as he was getting dressed.

She was laid out in the middle of the bed wearing nothing but a pink wife-beater and some purple and pink striped boy shorts. Tavares was looking like she was just fine where she was.

"Nah, Babe. I'm good. I'm going to lie here and relax. It'll be peace and quiet with you gone."

"What you trying to say?" Dora asked, pretending like he was offended.

"You heard exactly what I said. If you didn't, go get your ears checked," Tavares said, laughing as she got up to go make something to eat.

"Ok, hungry hungry hippo," Dora said as he watched Tavares waddle out the room and down the stairs toward the kitchen.

Tavares was in the kitchen frying wing-dings, catfish, and French fries when Abdora came in with his jokes.

"Damn, Ma. Is that lunch or a Thanksgiving dinner?" he said, attempting to put a wing-ding in his mouth.

Tavares didn't even entertain Abdora and his big or pregnant jokes anymore. She knew that when she reacted, it got a rise out of him, so she stopped paying him any mind.

Snatching the wing-ding right out of Dora's mouth, Tavares said, "It's not yours, so I guess it really doesn't matter what it is, now does it?"

"Aight, you got that, big girl. Get your grub on. I'll be back in a little while. Don't overexert yourself either. Your little ass needs to take it easy with the babies on the way next month."

"Yeah, yeah, yeah, Daddy Dearest," Tavares playfully said as she stood at the stove cooking her huge lunch that looked small to her.

Dora had to handle some business real quick, but knew Tavares would be long gone when he got back. She had her truck in the garage and never hesitated to get in it. Tavares didn't ask questions when Dora had to leave. She

194

just kept busy doing her own thing. She would go eat alone, and she would go get her nails and feet done. One of her new favorite pastimes had become getting a pregnancy massage. Tavares loved that she was so independent and didn't need Abdora to always be near her.

Dora went to the Tremont Street projects that were truly a sight to see. There was a youngster on every corner who stood and yelled five-o when he saw the police coming. This job paid $500 a week to kids older than age thirteen. Then there were the youngins who held packages, and they made $1500 a week. They ranged from fifteen to sixteen years of age. The hallways of the projects had niggaz standing in a line next to each other with fiend after fiend trying to get the crack that was flushed in the projects. Everyone passed their money, then the runner went upstairs to get their product. Runners made $5000 a week, but they had to be over eighteen to get runner money.

The project buildings were connected, so runners would go upstairs out on the rooftop, over two buildings or so, and down into the next building of the closest stash house. When they came back down with the product, the people never knew where it came from. There were niggaz who sat on top of the rooftops to ensure that everything went right below them and through the passing of buildings. All the projects in Jersey were controlled and moved like a mean business operation, and all operational fees were paid to Dora and the Murder Mafia. Dora would let anyone eat if chose, but they had to get in where he and Murder Mafia let them in.

Dora was passing through the bricks just to holler at his niggaz, and he respected how smoothly things ran. It was money on top of money, and because of the order, everyone was getting money. *Prince had done a good job with the organization and the managing of his projects*, Dora thought to himself. By the time Dora made it to the top of the projects where the basketball court was, he noticed that niggaz were sleeping. He whipped out his gun and busted off in the air and made niggaz duck and dodge. Dora busted out laughing.

"That's what you sleeping ass niggaz get. Don't ever sleep on a nigga coming in the bricks. Get on your shit, because that could have been one of you niggaz lives," Dora said with a serious tone. "I get that niggaz is gambling and bullshitting, but don't get caught slipping. Slipping can mean death in this game."

"Whatever, nigga," Prince said. "That fucking shit ain't funny. How the fuck you gonna come in the hood and bust just because niggaz was sleeping?" Prince said with his small frame trying to get mad.

"Nigga, I bet that will be the last time you sleep," Dora said, ending that conversation.

Dora's phone rang with Tavares's "Miss Independent" ringtone and he already knew what she was calling for.

Tavares didn't go too long without calling to say she was doing something she had no business doing.

"Hold up, you cry baby ass niggaz. What up, Babygirl?"

"Nothing much, Sweet Cheeks. I just called to tell you that I'm going to Jersey Gardens Mall to get some stuff for the new house."

Dora laughed because Tavares just had to be shopping.

"Do you, Ma. I'm in the hood. Just be careful and don't burn a hole in your pocket."

"What?" Tavares sassed. "Trust me, I ain't gonna do that, because I'll have all the receipts ready so you can reimburse me."

Dora was just laughing as he listened to Tavares in one ear and listen to his niggaz in his other ear talking about some birds trying to flaunt through the court to be seen but looked like a broke down mess.

"Babygirl, I told you, do what you do. When you're on your way in the house, just call me. I got a few more things to handle, then I'll be ready to come in the crib, too. We gotta find you some friends, though, because you just entertain your poor self at the mall every day," Dora laughed.

"I know, right," Tavares said sarcastically because he was so right.

"I got a friend. Bella, and she's enough. I can rock with her because she's my speed all day. I ain't too receptive to new friends, but every time she and I are together, we get along really well."

"Shit, Bella got just as much of a shopping problem as you do, so that friendship might break the bank fucking with you two," Dora laughed.

"Shit, if a chick can shop how I shop, she's a friend from the friend gods," laughed Tavares.

Dora told his girlfriend, "I'm gonna get back to my business, but make sure you hit me when you're on your way back to the house. I love you."

"Love you, too, Sucker," Tavares said and hung up.

Abdora was in the projects when he saw the same car that he had seen earlier coming through the back parking lot of the projects. The same unfamiliar face was staring at Dora. Dora wasn't too much into staring, so he wasn't going to play that game.

"Nigga, what up?" Prince asked. "It's a problem, my nigga?"

"Nah, it's all love, Prince. That nigga don't know the next time he see me, he'll be going into a body bag. You know that nigga?" Dora asked, trying to figure out if he'd ever seen the nigga before today.

"Nah, I ain't never seen that nigga, but we can lay that nigga to rest before he even get to the front of the bricks. Just say the word, nigga."

"Nah, I don't wanna lay the nigga to rest for a coincidence, but if that nigga makes it three times in one day, he's going into a body bag," Dora said calmly like it was nothing.

Dora had a mean sixth sense that never steered him wrong, and his sixth sense was telling him the unfamiliar face was trying to get the drop on him. For who and what, he didn't know, but it wasn't going to matter if he saw that car a third time today. Dora kicked it in the bricks talking with his niggaz, throwing back shots, reminiscing about being kids and taking over the streets. Before Dora knew it, he'd blown down multiple blunts, taken mad shots, and still hadn't heard from Tavares. Whipping out his phone mid-conversation, Dora called Tavares. With no answer, he called back three more times.

"What the fuck?" Dora cussed the phone like Tavares could really hear him.

Dora called back with his anger starting to boil, and Tavares answered cheerfully.

"Hello."

"Why you ain't picking up your jack?"

"Who you talking to like they six years old?" Tavares asked no sooner than he got his question out.

"What did I tell you about answering a question with a question?" Dora said.

"Ok, I see where this is going. I was in the shower. Is it ok if I wash my tail?"

"Well, why you ain't hit me and say that you was home?"

"I was going to but my phone died. So, when I came in, I threw it on the charger and got caught up putting the stuff away. Then, I got in the shower. I figured you would come in when you were done doing what you were doing."

Dora smiled because his chick wasn't a headache. It was weird to not have a woman who nagged or asked forty million questions.

"You on your way home now?" Tavares asked.

"Yeah."

"Alright, I'll put your food in the microwave. I got us some fried lobster, spicy shrimp, and shrimp fried rice from this authentic Chinese place downtown on the water."

"You're the shit, Babygirl," Dora said.

"I know."

Dora smiled while saying, "I'll see you in a little bit."

Tavares sighed and said, "Ok," and hung up.

Tavares loved their new house even though it felt more like a city than a home. She couldn't wait till it was all finished next week. For now, she was thugging it out in Dora's condo. Getting in the bed, Tavares flipped on the drop down plasma TV and began to watch her favorite channel,

Lifetime. Tavares was deep into her movie that was halfway done when Abdora's loud phone rang and vibrated in the bed, scaring the hell out of her.

"Oh damn, Dora left his other phone," Tavares said, finding it under the blanket and throwing it on the nightstand.

Tavares wasn't into checking phones. She kept watching her Lifetime movie while Abdora's phone kept blowing up.

"Now this is just plain fucking aggravating," Tavares cussed out loud.

She answered the phone in a very agitated voice.

"Can I please speak to Abdora?" the woman asked hesitantly as she heard another woman's voice on the other end of Abdora's phone.

Abdora hadn't picked up her calls in forever and now when she thought she was in luck, her feelings were crushed.

"He's not here," Tavares said real nonchalantly as she lay out on Abdora's California king-size bed.

"Can I take a message?"

"Who the fuck is this?" the now angry woman on the other end asked.

"Oh no, sweetheart, you've bumped your fucking head questioning me?" Tavares said real calmly, looking at the phone like the woman could see her. "So, either you change your tune, or this conversation will be terminated," Tavares said in a taunting voice. "Now, can I take a message?"

"Nah, I ain't got a message," the chick said. "But..." she paused long and hard, "I would like to know who this is answering my man's phone."

"Your who?" Tavares asked, trying to hold back her laughter but slipping a little.

"You heard me. MY MAN. So, whoever you are, please know that it's going to be problems when he finds out a jump off was answering his phone."

"Is that right?" Tavares asked in an unconvinced tone that was upsetting the irate female even more.

"Sweetheart, I ain't got time for this shit. You're interrupting my movie, which you should be starring in because it's about stalker exes who can't let go. But, let me just tell you something, whatever you're talking about is of no relevance to me. If you got something with Abdora in your mind, guess what. That's cute and nice," Tavares taunted. "But if Abdora is your man, as you say, then you need to be lying in bed with his phone aggravated like I am, because a crazy, deranged bitch ruined her movie. How about I do you a favor, though, since you were interrupting my movie with your back-to-back calling? Im'ma have Dora call you as soon as he comes back, because he's out at the present moment. Is that alright with you, Jade?"

The woman gasped as Tavares said her name.

"Because, if I'm not mistaken, he shut you down already, right? But you know, maybe I heard wrong. So like I said, I'll have Dora call you when he gets in."

"Yeah, you do that," the angry, steaming-mad woman said before slamming the phone down in Tavares's ear.

Doll was thinking about Tavares and her grandchildren that would be here very soon and decided to call and check on them. While she waited for Tavares to answer, she jammed to her ringback tone that was playing "Get Me Bodied" by Beyonce.

"Hello, crazy lady," Tavares answered.

"Hey, my pregnant butterball. What're you up to?"

"Nothing. Just chillaxing."

"Your mother was just sitting here thinking about you and wanted to call and check on you and my babies."

"I'm just sitting here debating what I'm going to do tonight. Everyone is going out to dinner and to Abdora's club to kick off Labor Day weekend. I feel way too big to be at the club."

"That's because your motherfucking ass is," Doll chastised.

"I am not, Ma. I just meant clothes-wise. I can't wear my cute stuff anymore."

"So what if you ain't big? You need to be sitting your ass down and chillin."

"Ma, I feel fine. So, why do I need to be all cooped up in the house? Most people feel miserable this late in the game when they're pregnant. I'm feeling great and want to hang out. I just need to get into something that I feel like I look cute in and not a beached whale. Oh damn, I'm not feeling this bow," Tavares said as she looked in the mirror at her dress that was doing too much.

"Tavares, you're due in a month. This better be the last motherfucking time you take your ass out. Do you hear me?" Doll barked.

"Yes, Ma. I hear you," Tavares said like she was a small child answering to her parent and not a grown woman.

"So, what else is up?" Doll asked.

"Nothing much. I been shopping, eating, and sleeping. The house will be done at the end of this week."

"Oh that's nice," Doll said, truly happy for Tavares. "Abdora be handling his business. I like that about him."

"Yeah, he do, but Im'ma give him the business when he comes in here, Ma. I was just sitting here and one of Dora's chicks called. I answered his phone. I mean, I know that she's no one, but it's just the principle. I'm not about to be going through all the same bullshit that I just went through. If so, then I can be alone."

"Girl, that's just your pregnant hormones and emotions, so stop it. Has that man ever gave you a reason to feel like you can't trust him? Has he ever lied to you?"

"No, he's never lied to me or made me doubt him. He told me that if I just trust him and love him, he would be here through anything. He said that he would never be disloyal to me. He wants me and the kids to live with him in Jersey in the new house fulltime and still have a house in Boston."

"Oh hell no!" Doll yelled. "I need to see my goddamn grandkids. So, you better be planning to live in Boston and have the vacation home in Jersey. Girl, you done lost your damn mind," Doll said angrily. "If Abdora don't like it, you tell him to call me," Doll said with sternness.

"Ma, I want to be wherever he is. I don't care if it's on the goddamn moon, as long as me and my babies are good money. He makes me feel like this can't be real. But, then he shows me every day that it is real, and I know that I'm not dreaming. I mean literally, every day I wake up and pinch myself to remind myself that it's as real as real gets. I thought me and Dame was real, and I got burnt. I'm not trying to get burnt again, but I don't think Dora will burn me. Ma, he makes me feel like I should give it all to him," Tavares said, smiling. "He makes me feel like love is real. Like, I mean that from the bottom of my heart. I be like *oh my god this is too damn good to be true, please help me!* I don't know where it ends, but if he never stops loving me the way that he does, I will be grateful and happy. Ma, like Keisha Cole says, *I love him, I trust him, I want him, I need him, I breath him, I would never leave him!!*"

"Well the shiiiiit," Doll said in her small, squeaky voice. "What is the motherfucking problem?"

"Ma, I just think about all that I went through with Dame and the flashbacks make me wonder if this is going to happen here. Damien scarred me, and rather than let my wounds heal, I moved on with open cuts and wounds. So, I'm buggin' out a little."

"Baby, let me tell you one goddamn thing. You better get your goddamn mind right, Girl. Don't be no fool," Doll said as a mother telling her daughter the right thing. "I know you love Damien and that Damien loves you, but guess what, Boo? That's a closed chapter of your life, and you deserve to go on and have happiness. I love my son to death, but he had his chance for six long years. You deserve to be happier than you know. All that you been through, shit, you better get your mind right and let the man love you till he can't love no more. Because you're right, love is real, and when it picks you up off your feet and keeps you floating in your heart, then you know that it's real.

"That man loves you with everything in him. I saw it your graduation weekend. At the baby shower, you would have really thought that they were his babies. He didn't skip a beat tending to your every need and making sure that it turned out nice and went smoothly. He got you that nice ass truck you been sporting around all summer, so you better open your goddamn eyes. So what some huzzy called? How you know she just won't stop calling? Some niggaz can't be trusted, but Abdora comes across like he really cares for you. I'm your mother, so if shit didn't seem straight, you already know that I would be letting you know it. His only downfall is wanting to take you away." Doll joked.

"Ma, I feel you. I just don't know, though."

Dora came through the door, excited to tell Tavares about the twin carriers that he'd ordered from Gucci. She wasted no time letting him know about the phone call from Jade.

"Ma, let me call you back, Abdora just came in."

"Girl, don't start no bullshit. Leave that boy alone."

"Nope."

"Why don't you leave the boy alone?" Doll said, laughing while she tried to talk some sense into the girl she loved just like a daughter. "Tavares, did you hear what I said?"

"Yes, I did," Tavares replied real bubbly. "I'll call you back. Love you, Ma," Tavares said and hung up. "Uhh, you need to talk to your bitch, Jade. She called here all aggressive and shit. Then, she told me that you were her man and that I was going to be in trouble for answering your phone. You better let her know something," Tavares said with an uncompromising look.

"Wait a minute," Abdora said, confused and laughing on the inside. "You answered my phone?"

"Yeah, I did. Is that a problem? Because, if so let me know," Tavares said with a huge belly, small body, and her hands on her hips challenging Abdora. "I didn't see the problem considering that you sleep in the bed and be a pain in my ass every day and every night. If you got something to hide, how about you don't leave your phone lying around. And, definitely not blowing up disturbing my movies. A few other people called, but Jade was the only chickenhead," Tavares said.

Abdora wasn't even mad. He loved his crazy ass shorty.

"Yo, Tavares, let me tell you something. I can't keep people from dialing my number. You know goddamn well I ain't that bitch's man. You been heard me shut her down. I can't help it if she wants to call and hang on to what was. I don't even know why you answered her calls, because I sure as fucks don't," Dora said in a tone that confirmed he was speaking the truth.

"Girl, you're the only one for me. Do you know what you do to me? I can name five reasons why I love you off the top of my head. You got hands of magic. You drive me crazy with those soft ass hands all over my body. As soon as you put that massage oil on my back and slide your hands up and down, my dick gets rocks hard. I be trying to not get so lost in the moment, but you be having a nigga on lean. Every man can appreciate not only a massage, but a good massage from his woman. Not to mention the fact that you give massages without a nigga having to ask. That's the ultimate win right there.

"You don't mind paying when we go out. I find that shit sexy as hell. Bitches out here be looking for a free date and a come up. You ain't like that. Even though you know that I hate for you to pay, you do it to show me that you're independent and got money, too. Your offering to pay shows me that you don't care about my money. And, the way you spend on me is too cute. You be knowing that whatever you want, I'll get. Yet, you go out and get your own shit and don't even ask me for nothing. Who doesn't love an independent woman who doesn't just talk the talk but she walks the walk? I respect that you're strong in your place and position.

"You don't trip on me even when we're in the same place with our friends. You and your pregnant ass go out and don't even be worried or bothered about me and what I'm doing. You know that I'm yours sexually, mentally, and physically, so you're strong in your spot and do you. You're secure in yours, and that shit is so fucking raw to me. You don't do like most chicks and be across the room trying to spy on what's going on. Every man needs a secure woman who's strong in her spot.

"Girl, you read me like you're my fucking twin. We ain't even going to mention the fact that we have the same birthday. So, it's really like you are my twin, but you be knowing just what I need even when I don't know what I need. Sometimes I be aggravated, then you'll just bring me back down to a calmer place after we talk and kick it about it. When I'm wrong, you're the only one who'll tell me that I'm wrong without any hesitation. I be wanting to snap niggaz necks for the dumb shit they do out in the streets, and then you will let me know I'm trippin' and just don't pay me any mind.

"You are a Dominican, Trinidadian, and Italian combination of nothing but raw beauty. Your beauty, your sexiness, your body are ALL me. You're the most beautiful mix-breed that I've ever seen. You got eyes that bitches hate every time they look at you. They're to die for. Who doesn't want to wake up to you every morning? You're bad even while pregnant, so come on. People know that you're bad without that belly, and guess what. You're all me. Only I hit that. Only I hear you moan and beg and plead for more. Only I make you cum till you beg for mercy while you're in tears because you've orgasmed so good. I love your pussy and the fact that it's all mine. I don't ever want no one else hitting that, so trust I ain't about to be hitting nothing else.

"I'm fucking truly, absolutely, positively in love with you, so you better know this is real. Please don't ever think that I'm leaving you. I can go on with why I'm never leaving you, but you get the fucking picture, so cut the shit. You just better know that there isn't another woman who can take your spot."

Tavares could hear the sincerity in Dora's voice and she felt bad for confronting him about Jade. She already knew he was down for her.

"I love the way you love me, so if you never hurt me, I'll give you all of me. I mean, my mind, body, heart, and soul. And, I'll never leave or hurt you. You held me down when I was having these babies and never did you think to bail on me. Never have I met a man that's more amazing than you. You got my heart, and it's fragile. I just hope you do the right thing with it, because I'm full of love and just want the same love in return. I know that you're irreplaceable. So, I'm not going anywhere.

"We can weather any storm that comes our way. Nothing or no one can come in between us. We've proven that with our feelings and genuine attachment to each other. I know that getting pregnant threw a monkey wrench in things real quick, but you stuck with me and rode with me. How can I not love you? You stuck around knowing that I was carrying another man's baby, and then you didn't run for the hills when you found out it was not one but two babies. I have no choice but to love you and always be here," Tavares replied.

"Don't be giving me no fucking hard time then. Just relax and be pregnant, and wait on the babies. You be buggin' the fuck out, Babe."

"That's alright, because I'm about to drop the babies and be good. So, later for you," Tavares said as she ate her mocha chip ice cream with chocolate sprinkles and peanut butter chips.

"I'll be glad when the babies come out and you heal up. It's going to go down like you ain't even ready for," Dora said, getting kind of excited. "That's why I'm going to let you heal, real good and shit."

"You're justa plotting and planning. Damn," Tavares laughed. "I ain't mad at you, but you're forreal on the prowl like a thief in the night," Tavares teased.

She couldn't get it all the way out before she was cracking up at her boyfriend who was waiting patiently for her to drop her joy of double trouble.

"I remember the first day I met you. I was like *oh God who is that,*" Tavares chuckled. "I was like damn, he done swept me off my feet. I was never expecting to see you again. Then, I saw you at the club in the cell, and I'm like what the fuck. I didn't know what to do. I just knew that I was feeling you and was trying to fight it. I'm loyal. So, I was trying to really fix and hold on to what I had with Damien even though he wasn't taking care of home. But, you. You take care of the home, the attic, and the garage. I decided I couldn't do that anymore, after I caught him in my house.

"I wanted what I had with Damien, but you showed me that shit wasn't right and that I so deserved to be loved. I feel so bad because I was letting history hold me back. I was missing you, wanting to be with you, wondering what you were doing, who you were with, and just like wow, *I'm feeling him*. I was so mad at you when I saw you with Jade at the Christmas party. I wanted to so flip out, but I knew it was a no way, no how. I just was like *okay, he got that*. You had me tight, so I had to give you your credit. That's how I knew I had officially fallen for you. I was so mad," Tavares said, shaking her head.

"I'm glad we're on the same page, because you're everything that I want and need. I can't leave your crazy little ass alone if I wanted to. I'll move mountains for you. Chicks might wish that they could have a nigga like me. Be glad you got me, because there ain't too many niggaz in the world like me," Dora laughed. "So, are we going out tonight?" Dora said, kicking off his red and white Air Jordans, "Or, are we laying up with me rubbing and playing with your belly?" he asked as Tavares was lying on the bed rubbing her protruding stomach.

"I want to go out, but I ain't feeling nothing I tried on," Tavares said sadly.

"Babe, you be killin' me acting like you're mad big. All you got is belly to match all that ass and those hips. You filled out. Get over it! Throw something on, and let's go to dinner. We ain't gotta hit the club," Dora said slowly, kissing Tavares's stomach in between his words.

"Get out of here then," Tavares said, lifting Dora's head up. "Before you know it, you'll be out those clothes and in then bed. So, go get in the shower, and I'll lay your clothes out. And, I'm gonna make something happen with my big ass," Tavares said, not sounding real convinced of her own words.

Kissing Tavares made Dora want to do some nasty things, but he declined with her so far in game about to drop the babies. Instead, Dora took his rock hard dick to the shower to think about his pregnant girl and her waterfall wet pussy while he beat his dick.

Two hours later, Tavares was getting ready to walk out the door when Dora stopped her.

"You're fucking beautiful. And you look good in anything you wear, so save that bullshit from here on out."

Tavares had to admit that she *was* one sexy pregnant lady. You couldn't tell her nothing in her charcoal gray skinny jeans, black off-the-shoulder shirt that complimented her belly, and some black lace peep-toe ankle bootie sandals.

"So, where are we off to?" Tavares asked as they approached the elevator.

"Don't worry about it, nosey lady. Just get in the truck, lay back, max and relax, and I got this. You look good as fuck, pregnant. Niggaz are gonna be checking for you pregnant and all, so don't get a nigga killed tonight," Dora laughed, only half joking.

"Abdora, please! Ain't no one checking for the pretty pregnant girl but you. Believe that, so save your little threats," Tavares laughed.

Damien was in Boston enjoying the fall air. He and his boys were at the park shooting the shit and drinking Privilege. Dame was physically there, but his mind was miles away. He was thinking about Tavares and his kids that were coming soon. He still needed a way to tell her about her parents. Tavares was going to bug the hell out, but he knew that he had to tell her. *Damn,* Damien thought, *when is Tavares going to get a break?*

"Hello? Nigga, what you over there thinking about?" Rollo asked. "Take the fucking blunt and get your mind out of space."

"Nigga, I got a lot on my mind," Damien said, knowing that he wasn't paying anyone any attention.

Damien decided that he had to go, so he gave his niggaz dap and headed to his 745. He hopped in prepared to take a long drive and get his mind right. Damien was in his car for over an hour cruising the city when he still hadn't come up with a way to get his chick back. He thought he knew how critical Tavares was to his life, but he realized he really didn't have a clue till she was gone. It had officially hit him that Tavares was never coming back. She was happy where she was. He knew that even if she and her dude didn't work out, she still wasn't coming back. She was hurt way too bad and too strong of a woman to come back. *I can respect it,* Damien thought to himself. He'd really lost his girl and it was all his fault.

Damien couldn't help but ask himself over and over, *how did I fuck something up so good, and how can I get her back? Maybe seeing me with my kids,* Damien thought. *If she sees me being a good father and coming around all the time, maybe she'll see my good intentions.* He was really trying to brainstorm. Blowing blunt after blunt, it was hours later and Damien had seen the city enough times and still hadn't come up with a way to score Tavares back. He was frustrated and decided that he was going home to get in his bed. Before he made it home, his phone was ringing.

"What's up?" Damien asked the chick on the other end of the phone.

"Shit. I was just lying here thinking about you and was hoping that you were on your way to come see me."

"That sounds like a plan. I ain't got shit else to do. I'll be there in ten minutes."

Damien detoured in the opposite direction and made his way to where he knew he had no business going.

After dinner, a movie, and a horse and carriage ride, Tavares had a great night with her gangster knight in shining armor. Just as Tavares went to ask where they were going next, Dora's phone went off.

"What's good, my nigga?" he answered for his best friend.

"Ain't shit. We all at the club wondering where the fuck you are," Bryce replied. "It's been like a month since we saw you at the club on a Saturday."

"I know, my dude. Wifey keep me on lock," Abdora laughed, although he loved it. "I was debating coming through. Me and wifey just left Times Square. I'm about to shoot her to the crib, tuck her in, and then Im'ma take that ride over the bridge."

Tavares was staring at Abdora with a look that would have killed him if looks could kill.

213

"Aight, son. Im'ma see you when you get here, and don't bullshit," Bryce said before hanging up.

"What's the crazy look for now?" Abdora asked, trying to hold back his laugh from Tavares's ill grill.

"WHY are you taking me home? I'm a big girl, and I want to go to the club, too."

"Oh hell fucking no, you're not," Abdora said, letting it be known that the issue wasn't up for debate.

"Abdora, I'm not a child, and just because I'm pregnant doesn't mean that I can't go out and enjoy myself. I haven't been to the club since I got pregnant. I want to go hang out, eat, listen to the music, and chill out."

"It's not happening, Tavares. So, stop pleading your case."

"Fuck you," Tavares said, mad as hell.

Abdora thought he'd heard his girl wrong and just gave her an ice-cold look for a response.

"Why the fuck can't I go to the club? Because I'm big and pregnant and you want to go there and push up on some bitches?"

Truthfully, Tavares didn't believe what she was saying, but she knew it would guilt Abdora into feeling bad and letting her go.

"Not even, so cut the shit. You don't need to be at the club around no drunk ass people. God forbid something happens, and then what?"

"What's going to happen, Dora?"

Dora didn't know if something would happen, but he wasn't trying to chance it. Tavares's ocean blue eyes got big and dropped like she was going to cry before she said, "Are you embarrassed of me?"

She knew she was laying it on thick, but she didn't want to go home. Abdora knew he was about to go against his better judgment for this spoiled brat.

"Fine, Babe. You can go, but you're sitting your ass in one of the private chambers where you can see everything, eat, listen to your own private DJ, and watch the scene. Don't you dare leave for nothing but to go to the bathroom," Abdora said, dry as hell.

"Awwww, I love you," Tavares said, full of life like she wasn't just playing sad twenty seconds ago.

When they arrived at King's, the line was around the corner as always.

"Baby, you really need to open another club," Tavares said. "This line is always around the corner and down the block like this is the only club in Newark."

"Baby, it's the best club in Newark. So, what do you expect?"

Dora parked in his designated spot and they made their way in the back door. They spoke to Buddah as they made their way inside. Tavares loved to dance and was two-stepping no sooner than she hit the hardwood floor of the entrance door.

"I gotta go to the bathroom. Which room are we going in?" Tavares asked.

"Oh, no, Miss Pregnant-at-the-Club. We ain't going in no room," Abdora said with a look that asked *are you stupid?* "We already discussed and established this, so cut the shit. We're going into a private room where you'll be hanging and dancing all night."

"Oh hell no!" Tavares screamed over the music of all the different rooms and crowd around them as they stood in the center of the club. "You was serious about all night?" Tavares asked, pouting as she walked to the bathroom a few feet behind her.

Abdora loved his spoiled rotten chick. As Abdora walked toward his own personal private chamber, he saw his niggaz in what most coined the gangster room or G-Room. It was where all the gangsters, hustlers, and ballers congregated, because it played Jay-Z, Lil Wayne, Tupac, Biggie, Dipset, Meek Mill, and lots of other music that they listened to and identified with.

"Awww, now you niggaz put the private rooms in the common areas," Dora teased.

"What's good?" everyone said to Abdora as he dapped Bryce, Nas, Hawk, Pure, and Bam-Bam.

"Nigga, I know you ain't talking when Tavares just let your punk ass outside thirty minutes ago," Bryce joked and finished it off with, "So, nigga, please!"

"Whatever, nigga. Shut the fuck up," Dora said, giving his best friend evil eyes.

Everyone just laughed because their shit-talking was how niggaz played and showed love.

"What can I say?" Abdora defended, "I found someone who makes me want to do more than handle business. My shorty's a bad bitch, and I don't just mean the eyes or ass. She got it popping in every area: beauty, books, business, and brains. And, I don't mean the brain in her head," Abdora said letting niggaz know real loud and clear that his household was past good in every walk of life. "She's badder than a motherfucker, pregnant and all. She handles business in the corporate world, but can go to the streets and not be lost and get it in like a hood bitch. And, her head

216

game could make a grown ass man cry. It's so serious," Abdora said, proud of what he stayed lurking for till he got what he wanted. "I gots no reason to be out, but I still love you niggaz," Abdora said, shrugging his shoulders and laughing like he couldn't help them out.

"That's what's up, nigga," Hawk said, knowing his close friend very well.

Hawk knew that he was happy. Dora wasn't beat for no chick. He had chicks at him all day every day, literally. So, if he was talking like this, Tavares was the one.

"Everything she do make a nigga smile. I can't beat that," Dora said. "Only a fool would fuck up with her. Ma got a heart of gold, past all her beauty. And she's still a baby, so just wait until she's late 20s early 30s in her prime," Dora said like he was yearning for that time because he knew what was in her.

"Yo, I even smile when she cusses me out."

"She be doing what?" Bryce said with his eyes bulging out his head in total shock. "Nigga, I ain't heard a motherfucker cuss you out or think to cuss you out since we was in middle school. Tell Tavares to let me know just how the fuck that shit works," Bryce laughed. "Yo, my nigga. Did you just say that she cusses you out? Fuck the *you be smiling about it* part," Bryce said, looking at his friend playfully like *nigga, let me find out.*

"Yeah, she be cussing me out. Her little sweet ass will straight flip and go off if she say I'm wrong or out of pocket. I love that she's pretty and raw. She gives it to me like I be out here giving it to niggaz. I be cracking up, like damn is God paying me back. She's the only one who can talk to me how she talks when she goes off. She doesn't hold any punches

217

with your boy. She'll cuss me out like she don't even know what I would do to her if she were someone else! So, I gotta respect it, because she got heart."

"I can't lie. Tavares is that chick," Bam-Bam said, wishing that it had been him who had bagged Tavares, because she was for sure a diamond in the rough.

Tavares went up to the Mezzanine, which separated the first and second floors. This was where the glass sound-proof private rooms were located. Tavares walked past all the private rooms, and approached Dora and Bryce's private room that was in the center and overlooked the entire first floor of the club. The room was empty. Tavares buzzed a waitress and wondered where the hell Abdora had slipped off to. The young, beautiful, sexy Latin waitress came in the room in what looked like boy shorts and a wife beater, and Tavares couldn't help but think those uniforms really needed to be changed.

"Uhhh, may I please have a water and a bottle of chilled Patrón with water on the side for Abdora? You can just swipe the door open with your card and leave the drinks on the bar. Thank you, and here you go," Tavares said, passing the waitress a $20 tip.

"Ok, no problem," the waitress said, liking Abdora's new girlfriend a whole lot better than the last one.

First and foremost, she tipped. And she was also polite, unlike the last lady in his life. She was asking for things and not just barking orders because she was with Abdora. The waitress and Tavares exited the private room and down the stairs together. The waitress headed to the bar, and Tavares went on a hunt to find Abdora, who had somehow forgotten that he came with her.

Tavares entered the G-Room to find Abdora and a good amount of his friends at the bar, laughing, joking, and talking like it was a mini reunion. She could see that Abdora missed hanging out with his friends. Not knowing that she was the topic of conversation, Tavares walked up with all eyes on her.

"Hello, fellas," Tavares said with her bright smile and pregnant glow.

Everyone said hi, hello or what's up.

"What are y'all doing in here?" Tavares asked like she was chastising them. "Isn't this where the players, gangsters, hustlers, and ballers hang out?" Tavares asked.

Then, she chuckled as she looked around the room at too many niggaz who were trying to be hard, fresh, and cool all at the same damn time.

"Yeah, you know we party in the common areas from time to time to get our clown time on," Hawk said, laughing because Tavares was right on point.

"What kills me is half the gangsters ain't never shot no guns or did no time," Nas added. "And, they're stupid hustlers that hustle for nothing. They do that shit just to get a new pair of Airforce Ones or Pradas and a new outfit to come to the club and spend all that they hustled for on a two-dollar bum bitch just to fuck her at the end of the night," Nas said. "That shit is stupid to me. It doesn't make sense to me and sure shouldn't make no fucking sense to a nigga who put his life on the line everyday hustling out here in these streets."

Nas was mad because niggaz wasn't the same from when they'd come up. They were recycling money, not stacking paper trying to get to where he and his friends were.

"Anyways, Tavares. What the hell are you doing in the club, period?" Bryce said, letting it be known with his body language that he didn't approve.

"Well," Tavares said, dragging her syllables, "I was – no, *we were* - bored and decided to come out."

"We?" Abdora said to Tavares. "I don't know if we were bored, or if you were begging to come out."

"Whatever," Tavares said since Dora had thrown her to the wolves. "I wanted to fucking come out, so that's what we're doing out. I'm pregnant, not fucking dead. Shit, just because I'm pregnant doesn't mean I gotta be cooped up in the house feeling all miserable. I feel good. I wanted to come out and listen to music and dance, even if I can't drink."

Everyone was just amazed at how fast she politely checked everyone who was looking at her crazy.

"Damn, Tavares, I didn't know you had all that in you. Give me some dap," Bryce said, extending his hand.

"Whatever, Bryce," Tavares stated while playfully hitting him.

"Dora told me you don't be taking no shit, and I ain't mad at you."

"Oh no, not me. I don't know about other women, but I definitely will let a nigga a have it with no ifs, ands, or buts. That's why I feel Katt Williams when chicks say that a nigga be messing with their self-esteem. How the fuck and why the fuck should a man dictate your fucking self-esteem? It's all about you. And, I fucking love me to death," Tavares said, stressing every word. "So, no, I'm not taking no bullshit."

As everyone just listened to Tavares, they knew for sure that she was Abdora's twin. *She's meant to be the boss's wife*, Nas thought. She sounded just like Dora when she spoke with her soft tone but harsh seriousness.

"You're a piece of fucking work," Bryce said, "but I love your little nutty ass."

"I love you, too," Tavares said to Bryce, who she saw every time she and Dora came to Jersey.

Whether it was by accident or on purpose, at the office, in the streets, or at one another's houses, Dora and Bryce were together every day.

The group had been shooting the shit when they were interrupted.

"Excuse me," a chick said. She was tall, thin, and pretty with dreadlocks that were dipped gold on the ends. With the conversation interrupted, everyone gave their attention to the pretty, unfamiliar chick.

"Nas, that dude at the table over there told me to bring you this drink."

People sent drinks all the time. Wanting to return the favor, he asked where the guy was sitting.

"Over there," the chick pointed.

When everyone looked in the direction she pointed, she raised her hand and went straight across Nas's cheek with a straight razor. Tavares screamed out of shock at all the blood gushing from Nas's cheek with white flesh hanging. She'd cut him deep. Everyone whipped out their guns.

Bryce looked and quickly said, "Is you niggaz crazy? Put that shit away! Y'all will kill too many innocent people."

Dora went to another place. His natural being caused him to lunge at the woman before the guns came or Tavares had screamed. His big, strong masculine hands grabbed the suicidal woman by the neck and he was choking the life out of her. The sliding doors at the entrance of the room closed and locked before Tavares could blink her eyes. Shit was happening faster than the speed of lightning.

"Get that nigga to the hospital right fucking now," Bryce screamed as he pointed to three of his niggaz.

Security cleared the way and they carried Nas out. Once Nas was out, the crowd went out the emergency exit that every room had for situations like this. Security and the Murder Mafia were ushering the people out who were glad to leave after seeing the chick who'd signed her own death papers. Abdora was the last one that you wanted to fuck with in the hood. So, if she didn't know what she'd just done, she was going to wish she had. Everyone knew that if they even thought they'd seen anything, they would regret it later. So, they left without any commotion even though there was a girl being beat to death just feet away from them.

Tavares was in total shock and didn't know whether to move, stay, or scream.

"Stop, Abdora, stop!" Tavares yelled.

He didn't even hear her words as he was busy screaming, "Bitch, who sent you?!"

The chick was spitting blood as she was saying, "I ain't no snitch."

Abdora was constantly beating the woman in the face, and she was bloody and barely conscious.

"Who the fuck sent you?" Abdora was yelling.

Letting her neck go, he let her fall to the ground and starting breaking her bones with his feet.

"Ok, ok, ok," the woman was barely mustering up. Abdora stopped. "Please don't kill me. I'll tell you who sent me."

Abdora took his foot off her throat where he'd been kicking her.

"Please just let me live," she said in between gags of blood coming out her mouth.

"Ok, you got that," Dora said like he was playing fair.

"And you'll let me live?"

"Yeah, it's a favor for a favor."

"Ramol sent me."

"Ramol?" Dora said and gave his infamous chuckle when there was something ugly to follow.

Ramol had been one of Nas, Maniac, Bryce, and Dora's childhood friends. He was never a member of the Murder Mafia because the older they got, Dora just felt like he was weak no matter how tough he tried to pretend he was. Ramol was always the dude picking on the weakest person in the room. He would never get tough with a dude who was about that life, but he would pick on a dude he knew he could bully. Ramol was also a woman beater, and that was bottom of the barrel in Dora's book. Dora thought bullies were wack and weak, and he just didn't rock with Ramol past *what's up*. Having come up from the sandbox, Nas always had love for him.

Ramol had some smoke with some dudes one night at an after-hour joint and called Nas. Nas came through even though his right hand mans said for him to leave Ramol stankin. Words were exchanged and guns were shot. Nas got away, but a witness gave Ramol's name because he always frequented Nikki's. Next thing Nas knew, the police were at his door asking his whereabouts a few nights prior. No one knew him, because that wasn't a spot he rocked in. They sure as hell didn't know his address for the police to come knocking.

After that, Ramol became known as a snitch. Once the paperwork came back, it was official and niggaz wouldn't fuck with him. He couldn't even cop no work in Jersey or the surrounding states. He had to travel south. So, he always had a personal with Nas. He thought because he didn't tell them his full name Naseem Harding and just "Nas," he didn't snitch. But, he indeed said he was a witness and thought it was Nas who was the problem.

"You let a rat ass nigga walk you into your death. That nigga is a bitch ass nigga and put you up to do his dirty work, KNOWING you wouldn't leave here alive," Dora laughed.

Then, he pulled out his gun and she screamed, "Wait, wait! I thought you weren't going to kill me!"

"I lied, Bitch. You buck-fiftied my man's face, and he'll forever have a scar. You actually thought you would walk out of here alive?" Abdora asked very seriously.

He didn't give her time to respond. He shot her twice in the head.

"Get that bitch out of here. A stupid bitch who died young," Dora said.

Tavares didn't know who the person was that she'd just seen. That person wasn't the person that she slept with at night. Tavares was very clear on who Abdora was and how she'd heard he got down, but the person who'd just murdered that girl in cold blood without any conscious thought wasn't her boo. Abdora had blacked out fast seeing

the razor go across Nas's face. When he came to himself, he turned around and froze. Tavares's face was white as a ghost. He never realized that she was watching all this.

"Say word, my niggaz! You fucking niggaz didn't take my motherfucking wifey up out of here? What the fuck, Yo?!"

Everything happened so fast that no one thought to usher Tavares out with the crowd. Bryce had cleared the rest of the club out with the push of a button but dropped the ball on getting Tavares out.

"My nigga, I fucked up," Bryce said, knowing that was his job and place but he got caught up trying to clear the club out because he knew it was about to be a crime scene.

"Dora, I'm ok," Tavares said, trying to ease the blow that she knew they were going to catch in the near future. Tavares was shaking and clearly not okay.

"I gotta get wifey home, this is fucked up. Ramol will be taken care of in the morning," Dora said, feeling fucked up that he just blacked out and his shorty saw the monster in him.

Tavares had never seen him put his hands on people, use guns, or even do anything violent. Abdora was always loving, kind, romantic, and sweet. The ugly sight that Tavares just saw was shocking.

~Chapter 9~
All Women Don't Break Under Pressure

All of Abdora's boys cleaned the crime scene without leaving a trace of the woman that had just been murdered. She was going to disappear without a trace thanks to Buddah's specialty of chopping people's bodies down. Buddah took the body to the basement and chopped her body to beef stew-size pieces. Abdora, Bryce, and Tavares came out the G-Room, went down to the basement, out the kitchen door, up the three flights of stairs, and slipped through the crowed. No sooner than they hit the street, they knew they'd come out the wrong door. Two dudes were arguing like they were about to whip their pistols out at any moment.

Abdora never forgot a face, and that was the third time that he'd seen this nigga. *Now this nigga's at my club making my spot hot,* Abdora thought. He'd just had his third strike, and he was for sure going in a body bag. Abdora never removed his eyes from the future murder victim while telling Bryce to take his wifey home.

"Where are you going?" Tavares skeptically asked.

"Im'ma deal with the bullshit and get niggaz off the block making shit hot."

"Bryce and I will wait in the parking lot."

"Nah, Bryce, take her fucking ass home."

"Bryce, I'll stand right here and not fucking move. I know you can't pick my big fucking ass up. So, either we wait in the parking lot, or we wait here in the crowd," Tavares said, not backing down.

After a stare-down that Tavares didn't back down from, Dora said, "Aiight, go to the car. Give me five minutes."

Abdora wasn't going to kill this nigga. He was just gonna get his license plate for a date in the near future. He really wanted to shoot him in the middle of the street, but dude had a pass tonight on the strength of Tavares. She'd already witnessed one murder for the night.

Amari saw Abdora watching him and giving him a look that he really couldn't read. He was a stone-cold buster from South Carolina. He and Ramol met through his cousin who was in Jersey. Ramol gassed Amari up to believe that if they could kill Dora, they could take over the city. Ramol never informed Amari that he was a rat, nor did he mention the type of stone-cold gangster Dora was or that he had an army behind him. He only said follow him and get the drop so they could take him out and take over the city. Being a small-time country boy, Amari never knew he had no chance against Dora. All he'd done was let Ramol walk him into his death.

Amari had been outside waiting for Ramol's girlfriend Shelby to come out. She was supposed to go in, buy Nas a drink, flirt with him, and get him to leave with her. Something must have gone very wrong because the club had been emptied, and she was nowhere in sight.

Amari called Ramol, "Hey boy. Yo' galfriend went in dis club and ain't come out."

"What the fuck you mean she didn't come out? The club isn't even closed yet."

"Well everyone's outside, and I just seen that Abdora, some pregnant girl, and a big light-skinned guy come out a side door. Something don't feel right," Amari said in his heavy country accent.

227

"What the fuck?!" Ramol yelled.

"I hope Shelby didn't do no dumb shit and tell them niggaz my name."

Amari took that sentence as a red flag that Ramol was all about self.

"Yo galfriend missing and that's what you say? What the fuck you want me to say if she did some dumb shit?" Amari was a country boy, but he wasn't stupid. Ramol was grimy and now he was on his own. Amari was gassing up his car and heading back south in the morning.

Tavares and Abdora were dropping Bryce off at home to get his car. Tavares was very quiet and distant.

"Yo, Tavares, you aiiight up there?" Bryce asked as he looked at the quiet Tavares in the front seat. "Tonight was a real crazy night," Bryce said, stressing each word to the fullest extent. "I just want to make sure you're good and can handle what you saw."

Dora had said that Tavares was his ride or die, but he was testing the waters for himself.

"I'm good, Bryce. Yo there ain't much that I ain't been through in life. So, tonight was just another notch on the belt. Ain't nothing that I can't handle, though. Plus, I didn't see nothing, because NOTHING happened," Tavares said, dead serious.

Bryce just chuckled.

"That's what it do then, sis."

They pulled up in Bryce's driveway, and Dora and Bryce gave dap through the window of Abdora's black Lexus.

"Aiiight, my nigga," Bryce said. "I'll see y'all at the hospital."

Bryce saw Tavares in a whole other light tonight. She knew shit - shit that they didn't involve their wives in, and if she went to the grave with it, she was a rider like Dora bragged.

Tavares was asleep before they even made it back on the highway toward New York. While Tavares slept, Abdora drove and thought. Dora kept asking himself over and over, how did his girl just see the belly of his beast. He was beating himself up that his wifey had just seen him commit murder in cold blood. His street life was a world that he would never bring Tavares into intentionally. So, it was bothering the hell out of him that he'd reacted so fast that he didn't even think about Tavares. He just wanted to love her the way she loved hard in her heart, even though she really didn't give it to the world.

They'd been together for only a few months, but they were the ideal couple. They'd shed tears and shared hugs, laughs, pain, and struggles. There wasn't anything that he wouldn't do for her. Whether they were making love or fucking, there was so much passion that their love could be felt. Abdora wasn't trying to stress Tavares. He just wanted to give her the world. This street life he lived by came with too much, and he wasn't trying to bring harm's way to Tavares and the babies.

Abdora had the streets in his blood. It was embedded in him like his drug of choice. He didn't know how he was going to do it, but he had to lean back, far back from the streets. Dora knew that even though he was respected, a nigga or two would try to test his gangster if they thought he went soft and turned into a sucker-for-love ass nigga, which he wasn't. Then, they would make him show and catch a whole bunch of bodies. Dora was going to do what he had to in order to be with his shorty, but he was going to keep that fine line of him being in the streets.

"Wake up, Sweet Sugar," Dora said, kissing Tavares on her cheek.

Tavares woke up not even realizing she'd passed out and slept the entire trip home.

"Damn, why did you let me sleep all the way home?"

"You were out, so I just drove and got my mind right. Let's go in here, shower, and head to the hospital."

When they got in the house, before taking a quick shower together, Tavares and Abdora both stripped their clothes and dropped them in the fireplace to burn. By the time they got out the shower and made it to the car, they were wide awake like it wasn't four o'clock in the morning.

Seeing the stress lines in Abdora's face, Tavares said, "I love you. You're my angel. I'm never going to turn my back or shut the door on you. You're my everything, along with these two babies that I'm carrying. You're everything that any woman could ask for. You inspire me to want more, to have more, to do more, and to just be more. I know that you love me, and although you did wild out for the night, it doesn't change shit between us. No one knows what happened. So, unless you decide to do me like that, we're all good," Tavares laughed, trying to lighten the mood. "I'm sorry that you have to deal with all this stuff," Tavares said, feeling bad for Abdora and seeing the weight on him through his green eyes. "I just wish that I could love your stress away. You be doing a lot, taking care of a lot, and have a lot of people who truly depend on you."

"I know," Abdora said.

He did a lot for people, but it came with his life. He wanted the people in the hoods and streets to feel like he was giving back and not just getting rich.

"I gotta take a big step back from these streets. I don't know how or when, but it's coming."

Tavares didn't know what to say other than, "I love you, Abdora. And you do what you feel you need to do not just for us but for you, too."

"I hate hospitals," Tavares said as they pulled up to the emergency room parking area.

"Damn, Baby, you said that with such conviction."

"I don't know what it is about hospitals that bugs me out or what it is, but I really ain't a fan of hospitals. Every time we go to one of my appointments, I mentally prepare myself. Hospitals always make me feel and smell the sick and death lingering through the air," Tavares said as they were getting out the car. "Come on, because I know sometimes we gotta do shit that we don't want to do."

When they entered the emergency room and approached the registration desk, Abdora asked the middle-aged, blonde-haired, blue-eyed, way too dippy nurse where Naseem Harding was.

"You have to see the detective first."

"Detective?" Abdora said, already knowing that some bullshit was about to go down.

"You want me to get him?" the nurse said way too happily with her eyes wide open at 4:30 a.m. like she'd drunk too much coffee or took a toot or two of coke.

"Yeah, do what you gotta do," Abdora said.

Five minutes later, a petite, black male detective came out with a toothpick in his mouth and a smirk on his face.

"What's up, Abdora?" the detective said like they were old buddies, but they hadn't met a day in their lives.

"Ok, since you know my name, won't you tell me what's up? You coming out here strolling and shit like you got something to say, so put me on," Dora said, feeling himself getting mad.

The cop gave a smug smile and said, "Oh nothing's up. Just waiting for a body to turn up."

Apparently, the cop knew retaliation was coming.

"The police officer on duty saw your partners, homies, gangsters you know, whatever y'all call yourselves, come in and shit, and he gave us rang."

"Ok, so what's the problem?" Dora asked like he needed the cop to give him the missing clue.

"It's our job to serve and protect, so we just came to see if Naseem needed some assistance or wanted to make a statement against the culprit who cut his face."

Abdora chuckled because the cop thought he was slick, but Abdora was two steps ahead of him.

"Oh really? That was kind of y'all. Taxpayers like myself like to get their money's worth out of city workers, so thanks."

Abdora was so cool and slick that the cop was burning up with steam inside. His eyes said it all as he just looked at Abdora with *fuck you* eyes.

"So are you the one that's going to lead us back?" Tavares asked, tired of the tit for a tat game.

"Yeah, and who are you?" the cop asked Tavares as if she couldn't ask him any questions.

232

"I'm a worried friend," Tavares said, daring him to try her after the night that she had.

Lucky for him, he didn't. Although he made a mental note to find out who she was. Long before Tavares and Abdora found the hospital room, the voices of Abdora's friends guided them. They entered the room where Naseem was lying on the bed with a patch over his cheek. Bryce was leaning against the bathroom door. Hawk and Buddah were each sitting in a windowsill. Maniac and Pure were in the chairs, and Bam-Bam was at the foot of Naseem's bed.

"Goddamn, you niggaz are way too deep in here," Tavares said, walking by Bryce into the center of the room.

"Niggaz love me. What can I say, Tavares?" Nas said, shrugging his shoulders.

Tavares looked around the room at the black men, who were hood as hell, gangster in the blood but always loyal in their hearts to each other.

"These bum ass niggaz yo, they're my niggaz, Tavares," Maniac said in his deep, raspy voice.

"Bum ass nigga my ass," Hawk laughed.

"So what's good with the face?" Dora questioned.

"A nigga got two hundred fifty stitches and a hell of a lot of pain meds," Nas said like he was feeling real good.

"So, what's up with bitch ass detective meeting us outside?" Dora inquired.

"Nigga, don't get me to mufuckn lying," Bryce said. "His ass came in here talking some dumb shit about who did this and making a statement, and niggaz looked at that nigga like he was stupid. He talked some more and niggaz still said nothing. Then, he said he would be right back, but you and Tavares came in instead."

"He's still out there, probably listening," Buddah said. "But, who gives a fuck? We're the victims this time," he continued with a laugh at the fact that the real victim was gone with no trace.

There was a light rap on the door and in came the older white doctor that had Nas's discharge papers.

"Hi, Mr. Harding, if you'll just sign right here and be sure to go see your primary physician in two weeks for a follow-up."

Nas signed the papers and the doctor took them and scurried out of the room full of thugs. There were too many ears around in the hospital to discuss tonight or dealing with Ramol, so Abdora scheduled a meeting for later.

"Aiight my niggaz, I'll see y'all to shoot pool at noon," Abdora said, which was code for the U-Room at 4:00 p.m.

The time was always four hours later when they said see you to shoot pool over the phone. Just in case the officers were outside still lingering and ear hustling, Dora wanted to be careful. Tavares hated when they talked in codes.

"Alright, well you gentlemen have a good morning, get home safe, and stay the hell out of trouble," Tavares said like she was a mother talking to her kids and not her boyfriend's grown ass friends.

"Tavares, you don't worry about us, worry about your man who rode the slow bus to school," Bryce said, talking shit.

"Whatever," Tavares said, swinging her Gucci satchel over her shoulder and waddling toward the door.

Dora gave all his niggaz dap, and everyone headed out the door to lay their heads next to the chick of their choice for the morning. As they left the hospital, the fellas and Tavares had all eyes on them. People were staring at them like they'd never seen a group of black men with expensive jewelry looking flashy. Abdora and his friends were used to it. Only Tavares was uncomfortable with the stares and the funny looks.

Saturday afternoon came, and when Tavares woke up, Abdora was dressed in a brown Lacoste t-shirt and cargo khaki shorts with his brown Gucci bowling sneakers and iced out looking like a superstar with his bracelet, watch, ring, and chain. Tavares rolled out of bed and walked down the two steps that led to the floor without saying anything to Abdora. She went straight to the bathroom to wash her face and brush her teeth, so she could fully wake up.

She came back replenished, gave Abdora a kiss, and said, "Can you please bring me some Cold Stone when you come back? I want a strawberry shortcake serenade," Tavares said, getting back in the bed and lowering the 72-inch flat screen TV from the ceiling and turning on the power.

Abdora just laughed because Tavares wasn't out the bed thirty minutes and all she was thinking about was ice cream for later. Her eating was crazy since she'd gotten pregnant.

"And be sure to get me an extra-large. The babies really seem to like it," Tavares said, smirking while thinking *not more than me, though.*

"You got it, momma. I'll be gone a few hours, but I'll be sure not to walk in here without your ice cream," Abdora said, giving Tavares a kiss before heading to his club.

Tavares lay in bed and debated what she was going to do for the day. Shopping and eating seemed to be all she did these days, so she decided to get up and do something different. Her pregnant nerves were still uneasy as she thought about the night before, so she was ready to do something to take her mind off her thoughts.

By the time Abdora arrived at the club, he could see that he was the last one to get there. The club parking lot was empty, but coming on the main street of Avon, he saw all his niggaz cars blended with the street parking. Abdora parked in front of the club, clicked his alarm, and headed inside with his natural gangster limp. He entered the club and found over a hundred niggaz in attendance. Niggaz were in every room drinking. Abdora just looked around.

"Ohh, so this is how niggaz are doing it?" Abdora asked himself, mad as hell as he stood in the foyer that led in every direction to a different room.

Usually, Dora was laid back about mixing business and pleasure, but today wasn't one of those days, and they could already see it. Niggaz downed their last shots and hurried to the foyer where Dora was standing.

"I need everyone upstairs in the U-Room like yesterday."

Dora's green eyes were icy, and his tone was edgy, so everyone already knew what it was. As they headed upstairs, all Dora's niggaz knew that the quiet storm was about to attack.

Dora was the last one to enter the U-Room. Bryce was behind the bar. Everyone else filled in on the stage, the bar, the tables, and just stood around.

"What I'm about to say is for certain to the niggaz who wasn't on their job last night," Dora said. "I'm a real nigga, and I do real things. I want niggaz to know that I feel some type of way about my shorty seeing and being implicated in what happened last night. We aren't just niggaz. We put our lives on the line for each other every day. If the tables was turned and one of y'all flipped out, I would've made it my business to take y'all's shorty out the area."

Dora could feel the steam rising from his feet to his brain. From there, Dora just went off about a variety of things that he was fed up with. Someone on the stage took their hat off their head and dropped a $100 bill in it. By the time Dora was done going off, three hats that had nothing but $100 bills in them were given to him. Niggaz knew that homage was going to be paid one way or another, so they were happy to pay for it.

"Now that I got that off my mind, what's good with the nigga Ramol?" Dora said like he'd flipped his crazy switch off. "Ramol is to die a slow, painful death. Slow and painful," Abdora reiterated. "He caused havoc at my club in front of my shorty, so he's going to pay."

"Word is that he was trying to get back for Rocco's death, and Nas letting it be known he was a rat," Bryce laughed.

"But what I want to know is who hired Rocco in the first place?" Hawk asked. "That bitch ass nigga was no match for us, so who walked him into his own death?"

"And shorty was asking to die for the stunt she pulled. So did Ramol set her up to die, too?" Buddah asked.

"I don't know, but while Ramol is dying a slow, painful death, he can inform us. He should be dead by the end of the week," Dora said flatly.

Tavares went to the spa and had a manicure and pedicure that wasn't needed but was so relaxing. As she was finishing up, her hunger kicked in along with a gut feeling that something wasn't right. God had blessed her with a sixth sense and Tavares didn't know what, but something was wrong. She pushed the feeling to the side and headed to the Cheesecake Factory. While locking her car, she saw two pretty professional women getting out their car three cars down. After looking them up and down and thinking they looked nice, Tavares went on about her business.

Tavares was about to dive into her meal like a fat girl when the two women from the parking lot approached her and the prettier of the two said, "Tavares Del Gada?"

"And, who are you?" Tavares asked, pissed that her meal was being interrupted.

"I'm Agent DeJesus, and this is my partner Agent Moran. Can we please have a seat and talk with you?"

"You're asking like if I say no, you're going to keep it moving. So let's cut the bullshit, please and thanks."

Agent DeJesus took the lead while her blonde-haired, blue-eyed partner whipped out a pad to take notes.

"So, who is Abdora Santacosa to you?"

"Lady, no disrespect but you know who Abdora is to me. So, what's this all about?"

"You were at the hospital last night when his friend got cut. Were you there when the incident took place?"

"Nope."

"Do you know what happened?"

"How can I know what happened if I wasn't there?"

"Did Abdora mention to you what happened?"

"No, we don't discuss the things that take place with his friends. That's not my business."

"A witness informed us that Naseem Harding was assaulted by a woman at Abdora's club."

"Oh really? I doubt that. But, if so, it wasn't me."

"Do you know who she was?"

"Miss, again, if I wasn't there, how would I know what happened or who did it? My boyfriend had a friend in the hospital, and I went to support my boyfriend, bottom line."

Agent Moran wasn't buying it, but Tavares was good, very good. She wasn't sweating under pressure like most women did. Agent Moran tried another tactic.

"Miss Del Gada, we want to help you before it's too late and you're in too deep for us to help you."

"I don't need any help. Usually people who need help are in some sort of trouble, and I'm not in any danger, fear, or trouble, so I don't need your help. Now, unless you're arresting me for something, I'd like to get back to my meal."

"Miss Del Gada, you don't know who you're in a relationship with."

"And you do, Agent DeJesus, because of reports and what you hear?"

"I want to help you before it's too late."

"Thanks, but no thanks," Tavares said, straight-faced.

The women excused themselves and Tavares was pissed not because of the conversation, but because her appetite was ruined. She left the Chinese pot stickers, asparagus, and mashed potatoes on the table along with the money to cover it. Tavares called Abdora when she got in her truck.

"Hey, Babygirl, what's up?"

"Where are you?" Tavares asked with a bit of an attitude.

"I'm in the hood. Why, what's up?"

"I just had a spic and a white bitch ruin my lunch asking questions about you. Meet me at home, please."

Abdora didn't like the tone in Tavares's voice.

"I'll be there by the time you get there." They both hung up and headed home.

Abdora was in the green room where he smoked his weed when Tavares got to his condo.

"So, what you mean your lunch was ruined by a spic and white bitch asking questions about me?" Dora asked between pulls of his blunt.

"Babe, I was sitting down minding my business about to smash my plate, and here they fucking come asking about last night. Was I there? What happened? A witness told them that a chick did it at your club."

Abdora's eyes got big and his chest got tight.

"Yeah," Tavares said, rolling her eyes. "Then, they wanted to make you out to be the big bad monster and they wanted to help me. I told them I wasn't there, don't know who, what, when, or where, and I don't need help being saved."

"Don't worry about it, Babe. They were fishing because you was with us last night. And I seriously doubt a witness told them that. But, if so, that's no worries either. Now, get naked, and let me love you," Abdora said.

240

Tavares just laughed and followed the orders. She could use some cuddling and kissing.

Agent DeJesus wasn't done with Tavares and Abdora just yet. She was going to have a tail on Tavares, and she'd be waiting to make her cooperate with helping her send Abdora to jail. It was business, but it was also personal for her. Abdora had hurt someone she loved, and he was going to pay no matter what.

In the weeks following the events with Nas at the club, Dora and Tavares spent most of their time moving and shopping for a second house. Dora and Tavares had different ideas on houses. Tavares wanted something large and homely, and Abdora outright wanted a mansion. After a month of searching, Tavares found her house in Massachusetts and loved it. Even though she didn't see it in person, she knew it was her house, and Abdora did the rest. For now, she was relaxing in the mansion that Dora had purchased. Tavares was resting in bed when her phone rang.

"Hello," Tavares answered.

She heard four different voices and knew that it was all her friends on the four-way. Listening to Tavares run her mouth, Dora knew that he was good to go downstairs to eat. He stopped in the babies' rooms to notice that they were completely done being decorated. Tavares went with pretty colors that could go for both boys and girls since she didn't find out the sexes of the twins. They were both turquoise and brown with soft turquoise paint and brown furniture. Each room had a crib, a changing station, and a tall dresser with a mirror. There were turquoise designs and chocolate brown teddy bears laminated on the walls, and tons of stuffed animals on the windowsills. There were even chocolate brown his and hers rocking chairs for Tavares and Abdora for when they had to hold the babies at the same time. Abdora was more than proud that Tavares had gotten the rooms finished. Their rooms did look hot to death using the space in the over-sized rooms and the colors she chose.

Dora headed downstairs to eat his food. After going to work on the lobster and shrimp, he headed back upstairs to take a shower in his bathroom. He and Tavares each had separate bathrooms in their bedroom. Walking in the bedroom that was bigger than the average two-bedroom apartment, Dora found Tavares in the same place he'd left her doing the same thing she was doing when he left. Without interrupting her, Dora gathered his belongings to take a shower and sober up a little.

Tavares was running her mouth real good, talking about how much she was missing them when her line beeped.

"Hold on, y'all."

Tavares saw that it was Dame and debated if she should even answer. She decided to answer because when she didn't, all Dame did was bitch about her not being in Boston with his babies.

"Hello," Tavares answered dryly.

"What's up, Tavares? I just called to check on you to see how you was feeling and shit."

"I'm fine," Tavares said with no emotion.

"Damn, must you talk to a nigga like you hate him?"

"I don't hate you, Dame. I just feel there's no need to be bubbly with you. We're co-parents, not friends. Even though I let go of what you did to me, you be acting like you expect me to forget or some shit."

"Tavares, I didn't call to fight with you. I just wanted to know that you and my kids were alright."

"Well, we're fine, so you have no worries," Tavares said, sounding irritated. "Listen, Damien, I was on the other line with my home girls. I'll call you sometime over the week."

Damien hated feeling like he was being cut short, but he'd become used to Tavares giving him little to no play these days.

"Aight yo," Damien said and hung up, not even knowing why he wasted his time.

When Abdora got out the shower, he heard Tavares venting to her friends about how Damien aggravated her nerves when he called. Abdora kept going about his business. He rolled three blunts and laid them on the nightstand next to his side of the bed.

"Alright ladies, my booface is looking at me like I been talking to y'all long enough. I'll call y'all on Monday before I head to Boston. The interior decorator will be there on Wednesday, so I'll be there Monday night."

Everyone exchanged I love yous and hung up.

Abdora sat on the bed next to Tavares and passed her the lotion.

"Thank you," Tavares said half genuinely and half sarcastically.

She knew this routine all too well. It was a pain at first, but now it was cute since she got his twisted reasoning for it. Abdora would lotion his entire body, then would only ask Tavares to lotion his back. One day Tavares got aggravated because she was reading a book when he asked her to lotion his back.

She said, "Damn, like this is crazy. No one knows that your goddamn back isn't lotioned. How about you just put the shirt on and leave me alone?"

Dora looked from the lotion bottle to Tavares, back to the lotion, and asked, "So you don't have my back? You really ain't going to hold my back down? I did everything else, so what's asking you to have my back?"

After it escalated to a real debate, Tavares deciphered from their conversation that all he ever needed her to do was have his back. Even if it meant literally at the moment, Abdora was so twisted and weird in a way that only he could be. From that day forward, Tavares lotioned his way too soft back without any hard times or cussing.

"So, what's the word?" Abdora said, turning around and thanking Tavares with a kiss as she finished rubbing the lotion in and giving him a slight massage.

"Shit, Damien called and aggravated me when you were in the shower."

"What happened?" Dora said, just waiting for the day he could kill Damien.

"Shit. I just get aggravated talking to him. Pregnancy got me bitchy real late in the game, and only with him. It's all good, though," Tavares said with a sigh.

Holton was finally ready to break the news to Lilly about Tavares. He called Lilly to his office and told her they needed to talk. Lilly had been waiting months and months for this conversation.

With attitude she asked, "Talk about what?" •

"Lilly, what's with all your fucking attitude lately?"

"What do you want to talk about, Holton?"

"There's no easy way to say this. Dolonda and I have a daughter together. It's Tavares."

Lilly had mentally played this scene out several times for when Holton finally decided to tell her, but now she didn't know how to feel. Silence filled the room, and her tears began to fall.

"Lilly, say something."

"Holton, what the fuck do you suggest that I say? You and Dolonda have a beautiful, amazing daughter together. And me... My son is six feet under, and I'll never know the experience of being a mother."

"Lilly, I only found out a few months ago. Like you, I thought Dolonda had an abortion."

"Well, Holton, she didn't. And, once again, she has one up on me."

"Lilly, I wish I could do something to ease your pain. I do, but it is what it is, and I want to be in my daughter and grandchildren's lives."

"Do what you need to do, Holton. It's never been about me. Never. You've been here all these years out of guilt and feeling sorry for me because I lost my son. I love you and you love me, but we aren't in love nor are we happy."

Holton didn't know what to say. Lilly just got up without saying anything further and closed his office door behind her.

While Abdora loaded Tavares's car up for her, she was in the kitchen munching on English muffins with scrambled eggs and bacon.

"Damn, big girl, slow down with the fork. You look like you eating in a marathon."

"Oh, shut the hell up," Tavares said, putting her fork down. "Must I remind you that I'm not eating for one or two but three? So yes, I eat a lot and I like food. Please fucking forgive me, buff thug," Tavares said, rolling her eyes and finishing her food.

"Ok, Boo, you got that. Calm down. I was just telling you that the plate wasn't going to run away," Abdora said, chuckling and still talking shit. "All your stuff is in the truck. I'll see you Thursday. Sit your ass down till I get there. I don't want to hear no fucking bullshit about how you just ended up out on an accident. You better be at your new crib or in someone's house."

"Yes, sir," Tavares said in a voice like she was answering her drill sergeant.

Tavares arrived in Boston at the Copley Square exit off the Mass Pike and went straight to the hood to Leslie's house. She rang the doorbell and waited under the strong early evening sun to be buzzed in.

"Hello?" a small, squeaky voice answered.

"It's Aunty Apple."

"Hi Aunt Apple!" Tay screamed.

"Buzz me in, crazy," Tavares said to her friend's daughter who was just jumping up and down smiling.

Tavares was pooped when she made it up the stairs.

"Oh my God. That will be the last time that I climb those stairs until I drop my babies," Tavares said, plopping down on Leslie's bed.

"Apple, those stairs are a killer even if you're not pregnant. I don't even know how you did it."

"Girl, I don't either, but best believe it was the last time. Those stairs will cause a bitch to go into labor."

"How long you here for?" Leslie asked as she lit the blunt that she was rolling when Apple rang the bell.

"The babies' furniture for their rooms is being delivered tomorrow, and then the interior decorator is coming on Wednesday to put it all together. The painters did a good job on the colors. I'm doing the same colors for here and in Jersey but different furniture and different themes. I just picked neutral colors since I don't know which sex they are."

"What colors are you doing?" Leslie asked after she exhaled the blunt and passed it to Tavares, forgetting that Tavares was smoke-free.

Tavares said, "Chocolate brown and Tiffany blue," between pretend coughing from the smoke. "The rooms here are going to be painted more like an aquarium with brown animals as the theme, though."

"Awww, that's cute. Have you talked to Damien?"

"No, but something tells me that he'll be calling when his nose sniffs that I'm here. He be knowing I'm here before I can even fucking call him. That shit irks the hell out of me, too. I'll be here until Sunday, so I'll hit him up on Friday,"

Tavares laughed. "But I'm gonna go see Doll later. I miss her."

"Doll is fucking crazy," Leslie laughed.

"I don't know who's more hood with it... her or Miss Dhara. Girl, could you imagine if the two ever even bumped heads? They would never have a reason to, but Lord have mercy if they did. I would just back up as far as I can get," Tavares fell out laughing at the two "Original Gangsta" mothers who took no shit.

Tavares headed to Doll's house after hanging with Leslie. She knew before she left Damien's mom's house and made it to her car, Damien would know that she was in town, but Tavares didn't care. She rang the bell and waited patiently.

Doll opened her door and screamed, "Get your butt in here!" smiling from ear to ear with her dimples as deep as they wanted to be.

Tavares and Doll talked about the babies, life, and Tavares seeming happy.

"Boop, I'm so happy to see you smiling and doing you. I told you that you deserved to be happy, so I'm glad you took my advice. I just wanted to see you happy and smiling like you always seem to be doing these days. I even hear happiness in your everyday voice when I talk to you. I love my son, no doubt, but I love you, too. And I know that just because two people love each other doesn't mean that they have to be together. Damien will get it together one day. I did my job. He's a grown ass man now. You got my grandbabies, so I'm always going to be here for you and them as long as I got breath in me."

"Doll, I want you to know that, in a way, I'm relieved that me and Damien are over because I love you like a mother. Now it's not like we can have that relationship because you're not my boyfriend's mother. I know that you're Damien's mother, so you were between a rock and a hard place with the drama in our relationship. But, I do respect that you just stayed out of it all across the board. You chose no one's side, and for that I got mad love for you."

"Tavares, I love you like you're mine, so what went on between you and my son made me just stay neutral. I love you like the daughter I never had. Now, let me go in this kitchen and cook something real quick. How about you roll up? Go upstairs to my bedroom and look in the nightstand, on the left-hand side of my bed. There are three mango rollies are in there. I usually got some down here, but I took what was down here upstairs when I ran out last night."

Tavares just laughed because Doll was too serious. She played no games when it came to her weed. She didn't drink or touch crack, but she would forreal be acting crazy if she didn't have a blunt. Doll was the hood mother who everyone came to kick it with, talk to, and get advice from. At any given moment, her sons' friends or kids from the neighborhood would be at her door. She showed them so much love that there wasn't nothing they wouldn't do for her.

Doll went to the kitchen to whip up some smothered chicken breast, white rice and gravy, and string beans while Tavares slowly but surely made her way upstairs to get the rolling utensils. Tavares ate the night away. She was so stuffed that she couldn't move three hours later, so she stayed the night at Doll's. When the alarm went off at 6:30

the next morning, Tavares was up and out. Damien would be coming through between 7:00 and 7:30 a.m. after he left the projects from his morning work hours, and she wasn't trying to see him. She slipped out the door while the sky was still dark. When she got in the truck, she turned on the radio to try to wake up. After a yawn and a stretch, Tavares pulled off and headed home to her new house in Natick, MA.

Tavares pulled up to her new house and used the remote to raise the double garage doors. She entered the house through the door that led to the kitchen. Her house was cute, spacious, and not too much, so she loved everything about it. She slowly brought her stuff up the three stairs into the kitchen. One of the babies must have been sleeping on her bladder, because she got a sudden urge to tinkle. She dropped her bag and hurried to the left into the bathroom to empty her bladder.

She opened the doors to the right in the bathroom and looked at her new red GE stainless steel washer and connected dryer and loved it already.

"Ohh yes," Tavares said, excited about doing laundry in her state-of-the-art washer and dryer.

She relieved herself and washed her hands then exited her soon-to-be decorated red, orange, and brown bathroom. She went into the kitchen that had a huge, spacious living room connected to it and walked to the huge windows that were set back. The windows separated the kitchen and the living room. The door that led out to the patio and the huge enclosed backyard was between the huge windows. Tavares looked out the window for a quick moment, then at the kitchen.

As she headed to the foyer of the house, Tavares passed the living room that was for viewing pleasure only. She stopped to admire the spiral staircase but didn't go in the formal dining room. She peeped in from the stairs and loved how it had turned out. She proceeded upstairs where there were four bedrooms and one bathroom with another bathroom in the master bedroom. There were huge his and hers walk-in closets. Tavares was going to go crazy filling hers with new stuff after the babies came. She went into the babies' rooms and loved the Tiffany blue paint on the walls that would serve as the water for the aquarium theme. After Tavares went through every room admiring what had been done thus far, she headed to her bedroom to take a nap.

Tavares was sleeping too good when she heard her doorbell ringing. Thinking it was the baby furniture, Tavares hopped up and made her way downstairs. When she opened the tall brown door, Tavares didn't find a deliveryman or any furniture.

"What the hell are you doing here? Actually, no, how the fuck do you even know where I live?" Tavares asked the last person she wanted at her house.

"Damn, that's how you acting? You ain't going to let a nigga in?"

"Damien, you're not about to get on my last fucking nerve, so do us both a favor and make this visit a short one and your last one till your kids get here," Tavares said, stepping away from the door.

"Damn, that's a nice chandelier," Damien said, coming in the door and looking high above his head at the chandelier that was perfect for the décor of the house and the entrance. Damien went into the dining room and took a seat.

"It's ok to sit at your marble table, right?" Damien asked sarcastically.

"Damien, what the hell do you want? I can't believe that you're at my house already. I haven't even owned it a whole month yet."

"Did you forget that property deeds are public records? I didn't tell you to get no big, fancy house out here in the 'burbs and put it in your name."

"Whatever, Dame."

Just as Tavares went to ask a question that she knew was going to come back to haunt her, her words were cut short by the doorbell.

"Now, this better be the deliverymen or we're going to have a real problem," Tavares said, getting up and making her way to the door.

When she opened the door, Tavares saw a large truck that was ready to deliver and set up her babies' furniture. As the deliverymen brought the furniture in, Tavares went upstairs to give them directions on where to put the furniture. Damien just spectated and really missed her. After an hour, Tavares and Damien walked the movers out and made their way back to the dining room.

"I like what you did with the rooms. They'll work perfect for either a boy or a girl."

"Thanks," Tavares said. "But, to what do I owe this visit?"

"I just came to check on you since you tried to slide from my mother's house this morning."

"Yeah, I was trying to miss you," Tavares said with a look that read she was mad it didn't work. "What, did you see me or something?" Tavares asked, still trying to figure out how Damien had ended up getting her address so fast.

"I didn't see you. I got there, and when I went in the guest bedroom, the sheets were rattled like someone had slept in them. When I asked Ma, she got all tight-lipped, telling me to mind my business. It wasn't hard to figure out. Can a nigga get a beverage or something?"

"I have nothing. The fridge makes ice and water if you want that. I'm going shopping later."

She got up and walked out the dining room through the doorway that led right into the kitchen. Damien followed her to the kitchen and took a seat at the cream-colored marble island that was the shape of a half-moon.

"Yo, Tavares. I need you to be done with this little game and charade you got going on and came back to me. It's gone on long enough," Damien said with a straight face. "I know that I fucked up and trust me, I'm sorry. I'm really fucking sorry, and I know the error of my actions now. Yeah, it took for a nigga to lose you before I got it. But, I got it. We have history - six years, and there's no way that you can tell me that you're so far in love with him that you ain't willing to work out what we had. I'm willing to do whateverrrr," Damien said. "I know I gotta do a whole lot to earn your trust back, and I'm ready and willing to."

Tavares was holding the glass of water and just looking at Damien as she listened to the words that were coming out of his mouth.

"Tavares, you're my bitch. I love you," Damien said like he'd just given a compliment by calling her his bitch.

"I know that I deserve for you to be done with me, but Tavares, I love you, and I know that you love me. How can you really want to be with someone else and raise our babies?"

"Oh my God, Damien! You sound stupid and look dumb, and you must be crazy. You're sitting in my house trying to apologize? For what? You weren't sorry then, so don't be sorry now. I'm not being a bitch, but that's real talk. It's water under the bridge as far as I'm concerned. All I wanted was for you to be faithful to me, and that was too much for you. So, don't be sorry now for all the games you played, the lies you told, or the cheating that you did. You know why? Because, you aren't sorry for the things that you did to hurt me or us. You're sorry that I caught you and that I got up and left. It is what it is, though. I'm crushed, but it's no hard feelings.

"I'm going to do what I have to do as a mother. I'm young, but I'm not about to be out here on no baby daddy drama, acting crazy with you or over you. We gotta be cool on the strength of the babies, and that works for me. I thought I would forever need you and have you in my life on a relationship note. However, now I feel free, and I wake up smiling and stress-free every day. I couldn't see myself ever trusting you. Once upon a time, I couldn't stay mad at you. I would get over whatever you did, of course after I gave you hell first.

"There comes a point when a person has to say that too much is just too much. Now, I don't have those kinds of problems, so why would I want to even come back to those problems? I didn't take your shit because I was some low self-esteem ass bitch. I know that I'm beautiful, and I know the power of my beauty and brains together. I stayed because I loved you, and I thought you would wake up one day. But, Damien, as you sit here and tell me that you're sorry and asking me to come back to you and shit will be different, I have to tell you the truth. I don't believe you."

"Tavares, you don't know how much I mean the words that are coming out my mouth. I'm ready to do as right by you as I possibly can. All I think about are you and my kids. I think about how stupid I was day in and day out. When I see you with homeboy, that shit makes me mad."

"Damien, why did it take for someone else to be good to me and to love me for you to say you want to wake up? I did everything I was supposed to do as a girlfriend and then some. The fact that you cheated on me and walked all over what we had tells me that you were just greedy and ungrateful. I love you because of our history. I love you because you're the father of my children, but I can't see myself being with you like that ever again."

Damien was crushed because Tavares had stuck to her guns and wasn't giving him any play whatsoever. Ironically, he was proud that she stood up for herself and wasn't allowing him or anyone else to walk all over her. It just hurt that he'd really lost her.

"Damien, you had me. You chose, operative word chose, not to be on your j.o.b. After six years of the bullshit, don't you think I deserve to be happy," Tavares asked rhetorically.

"You do, Apple. You of all people deserve to be happy. You're a good girl. I fucked up, and I gotta take the loss on the chin. I just can't help that I'm lost without you, but I'm moving on," Damien said with disappointment all in his voice and across his face. "On another note, have you decided to have the babies here?" Damien asked, changing the subject.

"Yeah, I want to, but it's just all going to depend on where I am when I go into labor. Which brings me to the fact that Dora wants to be in the room, too."

"WHAT!?" Damien asked, jumping up mad and jealous. "Hell no. That nigga ain't seeing my babies be born. Tell that nigga to make his own babies and watch them be born."

"What the fuck you mean, hell no? I was being kind of like courteous by letting you know. I wasn't asking your permission as to who can look at my pussy while I push my babies out," Tavares said while she gave Damien eyes that read *you must be stupid.*

She was sure to leave out the fact that Dora was insistent they were his kids and in her heart, she wasn't sure whose they were.

"So, you want both of us in there?" Damien asked Tavares like he wasn't getting it.

"Damien, it ain't rocket science. Word it ain't. He's my fucking boyfriend and does everything for me, so why wouldn't I want him there? He loves your kids like you love your kids, so don't be like that."

Damien wasn't feeling Tavares. They were their babies, so why should her boyfriend be a third wheel in the delivery room?

"Whatever, Tavares," Damien said, getting up off the brown leather chair. "I'm out, but here's some dough," Damien said, dropping $2000 on the table.

"What the fuck is that for?" Tavares asked, looking at the money like it was poison.

"For whatever you want it to be," Damien said with a lackadaisical tone. "Take it as reimbursement for the baby furniture. Spend it on you, the kids, your new house, or whatever you want. Do you," he said. "And, by the way, I like the new spot. Your boy got you sitting real pretty. Word is he paid for half of it up front in cash, balling," Damien laughed.

"I don't know what he did," Tavares said with a slight attitude, not liking Damien's sarcasm. "Mind your business."

"Well, it's nice, so tell your man I like how he takes care of my girl real good."

"Get the fuck out, Damien."

Tavares wasn't even mad but good with him for the moment. Damien wanted to wait for the babies to come, but he thought now was the best time to tell Tavares what he had learned. Instead, he went against his better judgment and waited.

Tavares was tired but knew that she needed food in her house if she was going to survive for the rest of the week. She debated going grocery shopping up the street at the local grocery store but decided to drive twenty minutes to Boston to the Super Stop in South Bay Mall. Forty minutes later, she was in Stop and Shop filling her carriage up with anything that she saw herself stuffing in her mouth over the week. Tavares had shrimps, scallops, cookies, cakes, pies, wing-dings, steak, cheeseburgers, hot dogs, and French fries and still had six aisles to go. She headed toward the produce section to grab some grapes when she saw Damien's kids. She looked around and spotted Shaunda with her back to her and the kids.

Tavares walked up on the kids and said, "DJ and Ashaunda."

They jumped because they were stealing grapes and eating them while Shaunda was talking to some dude, flirting and not paying them any attention. She gave the kids hugs, and they got excited about being a brother and sister and started touching Tavares's belly.

Shaunda wrapped her conversation up and turned around, looking for her kids. Seeing them at the other end of the produce section with Tavares, Shaunda headed toward them happy that she'd finally bumped into Tavares. She hadn't seen Tavares since Damien got shot. She knew Tavares had moved on from Dame, and it was an eye-opener for Shaunda. She learned that although Dame took care of their kids financially, it was Tavares who got them, spent time with them, took them places, did things with them, and was the backbone for everything Damien did.

Shaunda had heard that Tavares was pregnant by Damien and was happy for her, despite all their drama over the years. Shit was what it was and their kids were going to be siblings, so they might as well let shit go. Shaunda's theory was that babies' mothers had to stick together.

"Hi, Tavares," Shaunda said very politely, almost knocking Tavares off her feet with all her politeness.

"What's up, Shaunda?"

"I heard that you was pregnant and the kids been asking when they were going to see you, so I'm glad that we bumped into you."

"I know. I've missed them, too. I told them that after I have the babies, I would take them out to spend some time with them. Take my number so they can call me."

Tavares gave her number to Shaunda and was glad that she'd bumped into her. She wouldn't ever like Shaunda for all her childish tactics and stunts she pulled, but she really did miss Damien's kids. Tavares didn't want to miss being a part of their lives just because she and Damien were over.

"Tavares, can I ask you a question?" Shaunda asked with a sneaky tone. "Better yet, I ain't even going to ask you here," she said, knowing that the grocery store wasn't the place to mention what she'd seen and heard through the grapevine. "I'm going to hit you up, if that's cool."

"Yeah," Tavares said because she was curious to hear what Shaunda wanted to ask her.

Her tone and her hesitance were sparking Tavares's curiosity. Especially because she and Shaunda had never been cordial to one another. Tavares finished her shopping and errands and headed home. When she arrived home, she pulled into the neighbor's driveway and knocked on his huge navy blue door.

"Hello there!" the jolly neighbor answered.

"Hi, I'm Tavares, your next-door neighbor. I just moved in, and as you can see, I'm kind of big, pregnant, and ready to bust. So, I was just curious if you had some sons that would like to make a few dollars carrying my bags in?" Tavares asked very sweetly.

"Hecks yeah, my two sons and daughter will carry those groceries in. But, by golly no, you don't have to pay them! They'll help you out," the man said to the woman who he assumed was a single mother since she had no husband to carry her bags. "Olivia, Oliver, and Nicholas!" the man still in his work suit with his glasses hanging on the edge of his pointy white nose yelled happily over his shoulder.

"Thank you so much," Tavares said, waddling to her truck.

She parked in her garage and left the garage door open for the three carrot-top redheads coming over to carry her bags. She sat on the couch and watched the kids carry the bags into the kitchen. They happily put the stuff away and looked carefree.

After all the bags were emptied and everything was put away, Oliver said, "That's it, Miss Tavares."

Tavares stopped them before they could rush back to their house to finish playing their Wii.

"Wait, wait! You guys move fast. I didn't pay you."

Tavares was grateful for their help and had to reward them. Gave each of them $50.00, and they looked at the new neighbor like *call us anytime you want.*

"Thank you."

"No, thank you!" the kids said in unison and headed home to tell their parents about their profits from the cool black lady next door.

Tavares took a bath in her cream-colored circular marble bathtub. After relaxing and washing up, she slipped into her wife beater and Victoria's Secret boy shorts and climbed in bed. She flipped on the TV and realized that she hadn't heard from Dora all day. *That's weird,* Tavares thought to herself. As she was picking up her cell phone to call Dora, she was stopped by an incoming call from an unknown local number.

"Hello?" Tavares said skeptically.

"What's up, Tavares? This is Shaunda."

"Oh ok," Tavares said. "I don't answer numbers that don't have names, but I was dialing out and you caught me off guard. But anyways, what's going on? What did you want to ask me?" Tavares asked, cutting to the chase because she and Shaunda weren't friends.

Shaunda wasn't going to beat around the bush with her since she asked. At first she thought it was funny when she heard it, but when she came to see how things changed with Dame and her kids, she felt like it was foul and fucked up.

"Yo, what's up with your girl and Dame?"

"My girl who?" Tavares asked nastily, not even in the mood for any of Shaunda's drama.

"Your home girl that you be with all the time at the park."

"Jazzy?" Tavares said like Shaunda must have been buggin'. "Ain't shit up with them to my knowledge," Tavares said, feeling insulted at what Shaunda was trying to imply. "Yo, forreal. When I gave you my number today, it wasn't because I wanted or needed any more drama in my life," Tavares said, far from entertaining Shaunda. "If the kids want to call me, cool, no problem. But, you, please don't even waste your time," Tavares said, letting Shaunda know she meant every word out her mouth.

"Tavares, me and you ain't never rocked hard-body, but what the fuck am I going to gain calling you asking or saying some shit like that just for nothing? I know what the fuck I seen and what I hear in the streets. Since you been at school, graduated, and been wherever you been, the streets been talking like your girl been slipping and sliding, dipping and gliding with my baby's father. I asked Dame, and he told me he wasn't fucking with that bitch and that she been on his dick for a minute."

261

Tavares was lying in her bed feeling like just when she thought shit couldn't get any worse it did. Her heart ached. Something told her that Shaunda wasn't lying and that the streets weren't wrong. Shaunda wasn't Tavares's friend, so whatever her purpose was for putting Tavares on, Tavares didn't care. She wasn't about to let Shaunda know that she had stung her and stung her real good.

"Shaunda, you know what? I can't call it, but if that's what they're doing, then more power to them. I'm done with Damien past him being my kids' father. Past that, I have no concerns of what he does or who he does it with even if he chooses to be grimy and do it with my friends. With that said, thanks for the info," Tavares said and hung up the phone.

Tavares's ears were ringing as she looked at the phone in her hand.

She asked herself out loud, "Wait, did Shaunda just tell me that my best friend and the nigga I was with for six years were creeping?"

Tavares was shaking her head still in shock because she knew Shaunda. Shaunda was a drama queen, but what would she gain from telling this lie when Tavares and Damien weren't even together? Tavares didn't know, but she was about to get right to bottom of it. She looked at the clock and was mad that Dora hadn't called, but she would deal with that after she dealt with the bigger issue at hand.

Tavares got dressed in a pair of capri sweatpants, Nike shocks, and a wife beater and was in her truck on the way to Boston. She was steaming mad and crying. The more she tried to stop crying and to not be angry, the more her tears kept coming down. Tavares was flabbergasted. Her heart was beating fast. She was choking on her tears and not really grasping how two people could be so grimy and fucked up.

It was well before 11:00 p.m., which meant that Damien was in the middle of the projects. Tavares was driving 75 mph on the highway. The more she drove and replayed the conversation back, the more she couldn't believe what Shaunda had just said. Tavares tried to fight back the tears, but she couldn't. Just when she tried to believe that Damien wasn't the biggest slimeball walking the earth, he made a fool of her again. Tavares didn't know what to say or think about the fact that one of her best friends had stabbed her in the back like that.

Tavares was in Boston in the projects ready to get to the bottom of what she'd heard. When she arrived in the bricks, Tavares spotted Damien and flared up with even more anger and rage. She was ready to kill him. Tavares walked up on Damien and all his friends, who were in a circle. Everyone was looking at Tavares, whose eyes were bright gray and her cheeks were stained with dried tears. She looked like she'd been bawling. The tears were still coming.

Tavares didn't say anything as she walked up on Damien, pulled her hand back, and slapped the dog shit out of him. Tavares never stopped swinging. He never saw it coming nor did he expect it. Tavares was swinging everywhere with power in every blow that she landed.

"You no good trick dick bitchass motherfucker! HOW dare you be at my house begging for me to come back to your hoe ass but never once let it be known that you were fucking my friend?! Really, Damien? Is that how you're doing

263

it? Now you ain't just fucking every bitch in the street, now you're fucking my friends, you piece of shit ass nigga?"

Tavares was still swinging and caught Damien a few good times before he could catch her hands and restrain her. Everyone just watched as her hurt poured out. No one said anything because they warned Damien about creeping with Tavares's girl. Damien was pleading like his life was on the line, but Tavares wasn't having it.

"I fucking hate you, Damien! Hate you!" she kept repeating.

"Tavares, please calm down," Damien was begging.

"You're a no good, filthy, tricking ass motherfucker who ain't never gonna be blessed. As good as I was to you and you fucked my friend? I hope your dick falls off or you catch AIDS and die, whichever comes first."

Tavares realized how far out of character he'd just brought her and she caught herself.

"I'm a bad bitch, and bad bitches don't cry over buster, no good ass niggaz like you. As far as I'm concerned you're dead to me and my kids, so kick rocks and don't ever fucking call me again. You ain't even worth my tears. In love, you have to take chances. I took a chance with you, and I lost. You've shown me that you couldn't have ever loved me. You don't give a fuck about anyone but yourself. But, you know what? That's fine because you'll never get the chance to teach that trait to my babies," Tavares said, spinning and walking away.

Damien followed behind Tavares trying to explain.

"Tavares, I ain't fucking her. I swear to you I ain't fucking her. I would never do that to you. I swear I wouldn't.

264

I would never let one of your girls have one up on you like that."

Damien didn't know what else to do but lie. He couldn't believe that Jazz's ass had fucking told Tavares about them creeping here and there. He stopped fucking her after blasting her about her lying and making him think that Tavares was pregnant by Dora, so he could lean on her shoulder. She was a slimeball, so Damien used her to his convenience. All he did was let her beg for the dick, and then stuck it down her throat, fucked her, and kept it moving. He hadn't fucked Jazz in months.

Little did Damien know, Jazz didn't tell their dirty little secret. He got careless by riding her around in his car. On a late night, he got slurped not knowing that people had seen him - his babies' mother included.

"Damien, you're a motherfucking liar," Tavares said, turning around and slapping the shit out of him again. "I'll never in life allow you to fucking hurt me again. Know that was it. You hurt any idea of a friendship for the sake of our kids. I want nothing to do with you. Nothing. I fucking hate you and truly wish that you would go fucking drop dead. Oh, and FYI, there's a chance that Abdora is the father of YOUR kids," Tavares said before she turned her back to him.

She blocked his words out, got in her truck, and headed to her next destination. As she sped off, she picked up the phone and speed-dialed Abdora. She let the ringback tone of "American Gangster" by Jay-Z play for about twenty seconds before she hung up. While riding to Mona's house, Tavares's thoughts were running rampantly through her mind.

"Niggaz are really grimy," Tavares said, not believing that the two people who she would have never thought could be so fucked up would stab her in the heart, fuck the back.

Abdora's ringtone began to play and Tavares picked up her phone.

"Where the fuck you been all day?" Tavares asked. "I ain't heard from you all fucking day. What you been doing that had you that fucking busy?" she snapped.

"I was thinking the same shit," Abdora said like he had the same attitude that she had. "So, why you ain't fucking call me all day?" Abdora asked, like he was waiting for an explanation and not entertaining Tavares's questions.

"You might wish that I'm going to justify not calling you, when you didn't call me either."

Tavares sucked her teeth, then brought Abdora up to speed on her day and what she'd learned.

"Tavares, tell me, are you upset about it going down or it being a secret?" Abdora asked, trying to get to the root of the problem.

"Both," Tavares said, keeping it real. "That's my ace, and that's my ex. What business do they have to be running around town creeping? Then, let's not forget the fact that they be smiling in my face like shit's sweet, and they ain't sucking and fucking."

"Fuck them, Tavares. That shit ain't gotta get you down or break you. You just know how they are now."

"To be honest, I'm good, baby."

Tavares checked herself after hearing the voice of the best man ever on the other end of the phone.

"I just gotta speak my piece, then I'm done with it. I swear I wish Damien would just die," Tavares said, meaning it from the bottom of her heart at the moment.

"He can," Abdora said.

"No!" Tavares blurted, remembering who she was talking to. "Where are you?" Tavares asked as she approached Mona's street.

"I'm about to go home and pack a bag, then drive to Boston to give you a hug. You need it, Ma. I can hear it in your voice, so I'm on my way."

"You are not," Tavares laughed. "You're so crazy."

"No, forreal, I am," Abdora said with a serious tone.

"You don't have to do that, babe," Tavares said, truly trying to talk him out of it.

"Yes, I do. You're all worked up and need my arms and my touch. Bryce and my niggaz can hold it down till I get back. I'll be there in the middle of the night when you're asleep. I got my key and the garage opener, so I'm good. You'll wake up with my lips all over you," Dora said real seductively.

"You're so nasty. I'm pulling up to Mona's house. I'll see you later, crazy. I love you."

"Love you, too," Dora said before they hung up.

Ding dong, Mona's bell chimed.

"Who the fuck is that this time of night?" Mona said, looking at the clock that read 10:37 p.m. "Heeello," Mona yelled from her upstairs front deck.

"It's me, Mona," Tavares said, looking up above her.

"I'll send Dayna down to open the door, and I'll meet you in the living room."

Tavares gave Mona's twins hugs and waddled to the living room to get real comfortable.

"Chick, you gonna have to twist up for this," Tavares said.

Mona and Tavares sent the kids upstairs. Mona blew it down as Tavares replayed her day. She was shocked and mad all in one.

"A part of me feels like me and her can never be friends or say anything to one another. The other part of me wants to be like, we're bigger than that. I love her, and nothing will ever change that. I'm still going to love her even if I never talk to her," Tavares said.

"I really just don't even know what to say," Mona said at a loss for words.

"Dame's a no good ass nigga, but her, Mona? That's my chick. Why of all niggaz would she be creeping with Dame?"

"You know what, Tavares? I thought shit was funny but kept it to myself when Jazz kept saying that she was always bumping into Damien and he said this and that. At first, it was like ok, they ran into each other. After the fourth time, it was just like ok, is this bumping into on purpose? She be doing her thing on the low and don't never say no names. I wouldn't have ever thought that it would be with Dame, though. You ain't even going to have to say shit to her. I'm going to blast her ass," Mona said, mad at her friend for betraying one of their own.

"Nah, Mona, I got this. Jazz betrayed me, and I'm going to go see her about it. This personal is between me and her. I can't fuck with her, but I love her and would never turn my back on her if she needed me. We just can't be friends in the process. If she can lay down with Damien and feel no type of way knowing all that we shared, then God bless her. I'm blessed right now and not about to let their ugliness tear me down."

"Tavares, I cannot motherfucking believe her. That's my girl, but niggaz ain't going to just let Jazz ride with that bullshit. She ain't even going to call me when this shit hits this fan. She knows that I'm going to lay her the fuck out," Mona said, hoping and waiting for her friend to call her. "Come on. We go back, Tavares. If she did that shit to you, I believe she'll do it to any of us."

The phone interrupted them. Randee called Mona and heard Tavares in the background.

"What the hell is that bitch doing there this late?"

"Girl, you don't even want to know," Mona said, not even trying to go back to the beginning. "She had a very long day and came over here. But, I'll let her tell you about it," Mona said, passing her cordless phone to Tavares.

"Randee, Randee, Randee," Tavares said.

By the time Tavares was done telling Randee the latest about their team member, Randee said, "Whoa? Is that how we're doing things these days? I thought it was a rule we didn't fuck each other's niggaz, boyfriends, side things, or creep thangs. Any dick that entered your girl was a dick off limits to you, bottom line. But, if we changed that rule, please let me know," Randee said, waiting for Tavares to say they had.

"Man, listen, Randee. I can't call it. That shit got me blown. My girl is fucking my baby's father. She was going to be one of my kids' godmothers."

Tavares was just shaking her head as she felt like her best friend and baby's father had hit her well below the belt.

Mona-Lisa smoked a few more blunts while Tavares talked to Randee and Leslie on the three-way.

"You know what? I'm tired of fucking sitting here talking about this," Tavares said, getting up. "I'm going to Jazz's house."

"No, don't go over there, Tavares," Leslie said. "Just go home, get some rest, and relax."

"Get the fuck out here," Tavares said through the phone to let Leslie know that she was buggin' at the present moment. "I feel like she at least owes it to me to keep it real to my face. I'm outta here," Tavares said, tossing the phone to Mona for her to talk on the three-way with their friends.

Lilly had just failed at another run of looking for Dolonda. She'd been looking for Dolonda hard because she had a few words for her. Holton's newfound baby momma or not, she wasn't welcome back into Holton's life, at least not if Lilly had any say in it. She'd been through the projects and all the known places she could think to find Dolonda, but no one had seen her. Lilly wasn't upset that Holton had a daughter and definitely not that it was Tavares, but the hate she had for Dolonda wouldn't even let her imagine them being cordial.

Holton was having breakfast at one of his favorite spots, McKenna's, when his main side chick rang his phone.

"Good morning, Beautiful," Holton answered.

"Good morning to you, too, Handsome."

"Just sitting having some breakfast. I've been meaning to call you the last few weeks, but things have been simply crazy."

"I thought you'd replaced me or something," Valentina joked.

"Never that," Holton laughed. In his mind, he was thinking *I need you more for business than pleasure so replacing you isn't an option.*

"So, what's been going on up there in Boston?" the fiery Dominican woman asked.

"Nothing much. Business as usual," Holton said, needing to speed this conversation up because his breakfast date would be coming in at any moment. "Speaking of business, have you taken care of the business we discussed with the two men in the robes?"

Holton was asking his federal-employed friend about the monthly payments she sent to two judges.

"Everything is all set. All monthly payments went out along with the two newest team members."

Holton liked Valentina. She was gorgeous and a hell of an asset in the federal realm. Valentina loved Holton and had been patiently waiting ten years for him to leave his wife. They had amazing sex, took exotic trips together, and he was a man of power and the man she wanted. So, she patiently played her position.

"When can I come up to Boston to see you?"

"I was thinking of surprising you and coming down there in a few weeks," Holton said.

Valentina smiled from ear to ear.

"Good. I need to see you. I have this case that's stressing me out, and a dose of you is what the doctor ordered."

Holton saw his newest conquest coming through the door.

"Alright, baby. You make arrangements for all that you want to do, and I'll call you later. My business meeting is about to start."

"Ok. I love you," Valentina said.

"Right back at you, Beautiful," Holton said and hung up to entertain the lawyer he met in traffic some weeks ago.

Dolonda was in Jersey so deep on her grind that she was scaring herself. She was in the sober house being a model resident. She was enrolled in an accelerated Master's program to achieve her Master's in Criminal Justice in as little as one year. Dolonda forgot who she was and how she'd been on her way to the top before she hit the bottom. There was no stopping her now. She was determined to make it to the top from rock bottom.

Dolonda was loving life and enjoying having her life back to herself. People hated on her in the sober house, but she didn't care. It was all a part of life. People were going to hate whether she was doing good or bad. Dolonda looked great, felt great, and wasn't letting anyone get her down. Her cheeks were glowing, and her thick frame was back. She had a body like she was twenty-five, and she was filling her size seven jeans real right. Every day she smiled at her housemates and kept it moving doing what she needed to do to walk across the stage.

Dollar entered the TV room after the nightly house therapy session when a tall, heavy, shaved head butch lesbian who was known for being the house bully decided to try her. Sheila was loud talking to her girlfriend Sandy.

"I don't know why that bitch walks around here acting like she's better than us when she was sucking on a glass dick doing drugs just like everyone in this motherfucker. She ain't shit but a wetback, stuck up bitch."

Dollar looked around, looked over each shoulder, and then said, "If you're referring to me, bitch, say that shit to my face. Furthermore, I ain't acting. I'm fucking better than you low-life, court-mandated, only pretending to want to get clean till the next hit comes along ass hoes."

Sheila wasn't used to people in the house talking back to her, so she had to break fly.

"Look here, bitch. I run this motherfucking house, and you better watch your mouth before you find yourself getting up off the floor."

That was it. Dollar had held her composure long enough with all the shit-talking, snickering, and whispering and made an example of the one who thought she was the toughest. Before Sheila could blink, Dollar was punching her in the face. She'd underestimated Dolonda, who was busting her ass. Before Dollar knew it, she was being grabbed by two of the house staff. Sheila was on the floor bloody holding her mouth that was leaking and two teeth were missing.

Dollar was escorted to the administrative office. Jessica, the house manager, informed Dollar that the house had a zero-tolerance rule for fighting and that fighting was an automatic ejection from the sober house. Dollar wanted to cry because she'd been pushed far enough to take herself off track, but the tears wouldn't fall. She was sticking up for herself, so her pride wouldn't allow her to cry. Jessica really liked Dollar, and she respected that she was about her business and on her grind. She knew Dollar hadn't started whatever transpired even though she'd surely finished it.

"Dolonda, listen. I don't have the authority to make the call of letting you stay. That's something only the house owner can decide. I can tell you that it's rare that she allows a person to stay after breaking one of her top ten rules, but I had Justin call her, and she's going to come in and speak with you."

"Thanks," Dollar said, knowing that she would soon be on her way back to Boston.

Dhara wasn't happy about going into work at 9:00 p.m. It wasn't too often that she went to the sober houses unless it was a problem. She hired fully competent staff to run her sober houses, so she knew it had to be a problem for them to be calling her in. Dhara lived not too far from her sober house, so she was there in twenty minutes flat.

Dolonda was sitting in the office contemplating her next move if she was thrown out of the sober house. Being in an unfamiliar place where she knew no one, she didn't know how she was going to make it, but she was going to have to make it happen. Going back to Boston wasn't an option at the moment, at least not if she was trying to stay clean. Dolonda has too many demons there, and she wasn't ready for the pressure of trying to maintain her sobriety and failing, nor was she trying to face Holton, Damien, or Tavares. At least not yet.

Dolonda was waiting patiently when the door swung open. When the house owner entered her office, she walked past Dolonda and took a seat at her desk before she and Dolonda exchanged looks.

"OH MY GOD!" the house owner yelled. "Dolonda Del Gada, what the hell are you doing here? It's been too many years," she said, still in shock at the woman before her.

Dolonda got up and gave the all-too-familiar face a big hug and a kiss. Dhara and Dolonda had been thick as thieves. Their men had been best friends and kingpins when they were in their prime. They hung together, traveled together, shopped together, ran together, and had even tried coke for the first time together. So, it was ironic that they were together in a sober house at the moment.

"Dolonda, you know I'm not going to throw you out, but your ass can't be in here bringing havoc in my damn house. I know you and how you roll, so I'm gonna need you to fall back, finish your stint here, and leave these women the fuck alone, even if they provoke you."

"I'm good, Dhara. Now that the head puppeteer done got her ass kicked, I highly doubt they'll be fucking with me anymore," Dolonda laughed.

Dhara's cell phone rang and stopped their conversation.

"Hello," Dhara sang into the phone.

"What's up, mommy?"

"Nothing much, at the sober house handling some business."

"I need your car."

"Yeah, no problem. Come get it. What's going on that you need my car?" Abdora's mother asked.

"Nothing, forreal. Tavares just learned that her best friend and that bitch ass nigga of an ex are fucking. So, I'm driving down there. My truck needs an oil change, so I don't want to put it on the highway."

"Ain't that some bullshit?" Dhara barked. "That girl is too sweet for that bullshit. She better cut they asses right the fuck off if she know what's good for her," Dhara yelled at her son.

"Ma, I know. I know, but that's up to her. You ain't gotta yell at me like it's me who needs to cut them off."

"My bad, son. I just hate a dirty, stinking, grimy motherfucker, but you come get my car, I'll be here."

"Everything ok?" Dolonda asked Dhara.

"My son just wants my car to go see his pregnant girlfriend. She's the cutest, fucking sweetest thing you ever want to meet," Dhara said, admiring her son's choice of girlfriend. "She's pretty, smart, down to earth, and the last chick my son will be bringing home, if it's up to me. I can't wait for her to have her babies, so that I can be their NaNa. They ain't my son's kids, but her and my son are pretty serious. So, it seems like he plans to assume the role of daddy number one with their father on the sidelines."

"Oh my goodness!" Dhara shouted. "You'll never guess who was at my son's girlfriend's baby shower. Your old old thang, Holton. Girl, that nigga is still fine as hell. Do you know he tried to get brand new like he didn't remember me? Oh, but it was cool, because I kindly refreshed his memory," Dhara said, rolling her eyes.

"Sadly, the motherfucker didn't even know that he was doing business with his best friend's son. At least not till he saw me and put two and two together.

276

"The crazy thing is my son looks just like my father and Tiago, but he's Tiago in every sense and every way of life. I be looking at my son, *like you are your father's child.*"

"Tiago was the man, girl. I can only imagine how fine and flawless your son is. Damn, so was you and Tiago together when he passed away?"

"We weren't. After I got on that shit, he bounced, but it never stopped him from taking care of our babies. He even looked out for me and tried to help me at my lowest point. I always respected him for that. He even left everything to me when he passed. It was the wake-up call to get my life together for my kids, and eventually how I got into substance abuse counseling and owning the sober houses."

There was a light tap at the door. When Dhara told the visitor to come into her office, a tall, handsome, pretty-eyed man with strong features entered. Dolonda could see that he was a perfect combination of his mother and his father.

"Hi, how are you?" Dora said to the strikingly pretty woman.

Damn, she was a fiend? he asked himself.

After a second glance, the lady put him in the mind of what Tavares would look like at her age. It wasn't their looks that were the same, but their features.

"Dolonda, this is my son Abdora. Abdora, this is an old friend of mine. I knew her before you were even born. We met through your father, and I was telling her how much you're like him."

Dolonda greeted Dhara's handsome green-eyed son and excused herself to go get started on her paper for school. Abdora kicked it with his mother for a minute.

"You'll never guess who she used to mess with," Dhara said, whispering like someone could hear her.

"Who?" Abdora asked, laughing at how his mother transformed when she was gossiping.

"She used to fool with Holton back in the day."

"Ma, get the fuck out of here," Abdora said, shocked as all hell. "Ma, no way."

"Boy, what the hell you mean no way? Me, her, your father, and Holton used to be ripping and running. They were the highest rollers on the east coast. They were trapping hard, rolling big, and we were their girlfriends. One day Holton just stopped bringing her out here, and your father told me to mind my business when I would ask. I don't know how we lost contact, but I haven't seen her in over twenty-five years. That was my girly, though."

"Aiight, crazy. You kick it with your partner about old times. I'm going to lay up with my shorty."

"Take care of my car, too."

"No, you take care of my goddamn car," Dora said, rolling his eyes.

"Boy, don't start nothing, it won't be nothing," Dhara said to her son as he was leaving.

Dolonda came back down to her friend's office after her handsome son left. Dhara and Dolonda spent the next few hours catching up on their past from how they got hooked on crack to the beauty and blessings of being clean and sober. Dolonda wanted to tell Dhara about Holton, their child together, and what really dragged her to New Jersey, but she decided against it. She figured she would spill the beans to her old friend when the time was right.

278

Tavares promised her friends that she would wait until she had the babies to say something to Jazz, but she couldn't do it. She called Jazz time and time again, but she wouldn't answer. Instead of getting on the Mass Pike to go home, Tavares went to Highland Street to Jazz's house. As she approached Jazz's door, she could see that the front door was ajar, so she let herself in. Tavares could hear loud noises and screams.

When she made it upstairs to the second floor, she could hear Jazz screaming and someone yelling, "You no good, cum-guzzling whore! You done fucked my life up!"

Tavares's eyes bulged out of her head when she saw Damien on top of Jazz truly trying to choke the dear life out of her bloody face.

"Damien, get the fuck off of her!" Tavares said, trying to stop him from killing Jazz.

At first, Damien didn't even realize that Tavares was behind him. When he did, he got up and spit on Jazz.

As he stood over Jazz, he said, "I don't know why you over here trying to save this hoe ass bitch, when she forced my dick down her throat. She ain't your friend, Tav."

Tavares didn't need Damien to tell her what she already knew.

"Damien, you're just as much at fault as she is, so why you over here fucking her up?" Tavares questioned.

He shook his head and didn't say anything. He looked at both women, then let himself out thinking that Jazz was lucky that Tavares came because she'd saved her life. Jazz was crying and trying to apologize between sobs. Tavares helped her to the bathroom to clean her face off and let her know in the same breath that their friendship was over.

"Jazz, we ain't friends anymore. As far as I'm concerned, you showed me better than you could tell me that you ain't capable of being a friend to a real bitch like me. I held you up, I held you down, and ain't never did you fucked up. So, you fucking my baby daddy was straight outta pocket!"

"Tavares, I'm sorry. So sorry," Jazz kept sobbing but Tavares wasn't buying what she was selling.

Tavares helped Jazz clean the blood and apply her bandages while she gave her some real talk.

"Jazz, we can never be friends, because I can never trust you. Without trust, there's nothing in a friendship. If you'll fuck Damien and kick me under a bus to do it, there's no telling what else you would do to me. I'm not going to allow you to fuck over me again."

"Please, please, Tavares, forgive me. I'm so sorry. We can fix this. I love you. You're my best friend."

Jazz was crying from a genuine place, realizing that the error of her ways had just bitten her in the ass. She didn't get the nigga, and she lost her best friend. With that said, Tavares left her right there in her bathroom with no intentions of ever speaking to her again.

Tavares made her way home and tried to call Abdora but his phone was going straight to voicemail. After taking a shower and baking then devouring some Tollhouse chocolate chip cookies, Tavares curled up in her king-size bed to do some thinking. She couldn't believe that her best friend had been fucking the guy who was once the love of her life. The thought of it had Tavares feeling hurt and broken. She didn't want Damien, but the level of betrayal broke her heart into a million pieces. She thought about it till she drifted off to sleep.

Three hours later at 75 miles per hour, Abdora was in Natick sliding his key into Tavares's door. When he walked into the new house, he was impressed and could see that it was all Tavares. It was simply decorated but had bold colors that stood out. Hues of red and orange decorated the areas downstairs. Abdora headed upstairs and could hear Tavares sleeping like she was out cold. He didn't bother to wake her since it was 3:00 a.m. Instead, he just undressed, crawled in bed, and cuddled his body around her pregnant frame.

Abdora watched his shorty sleep and toggled with the decision of whether or not to kill Damien. It wouldn't be for the one isolated incident at hand, but for all the hurt he'd caused Tavares overall. Dora was a stand-up nigga and couldn't understand how, as a man, Damien could be so fucked up to a woman as good as Tavares. Dora pondered long and hard about the pros and cons of killing Damien. He didn't want Tavares's twins to be fatherless, if he himself wasn't the father, but he questioned if the kids really needed an example like Damien for a father. Not coming to a conclusion, Dora showered and curled up in bed with the woman he'd fallen madly in love with. He was going to sleep on whether to let Damien live or not.

Dora tried to sleep, but his mind kept drifting to just kill the bitch ass nigga. His heart was soft for Tavares, and he didn't want her to feel the repercussions and heartache. Tavares was the only thing keeping Damien alive. If he had his way, he would have killed him when he shot his man,

Holly Hood. Dora always did things with calculated movements, and this time he was stuck on what to do. Should he listen to his head or follow his heart for the woman he loved?

Two days later, Tavares was in Macy's in downtown Boston when her water broke. She thought that she'd peed on herself before she realized that she didn't have to go to the bathroom.

"Oh my god," Tavares said, calling Abdora, who was out with Holton handling some business. "Oh my god, Abdora! I'm in Macy's in the shoe department, and my water just broke!"

"Well, hang up with me, crazy. Call 9-1-1 for an ambulance."

An ambulance was there in two minutes with New England Medical Center just one block over. Tavares delivered two beautiful, healthy baby boys. They had bright and light eyes. One had thick, curly hair and the other had straight hair. Damien, Doll, Holton, and Abdora along with all Tavares's friends were there when she woke up.

"Dang, but is it a party?" Tavares asked with her head still resting on the pillow.

"Congratulations!" everyone said.

"Thank you," Tavares said, drained and still a little high from the pain medications they'd given her.

Damien was leaning back because he was still in the hot seat. He was just proud that he'd fathered two healthy boys. Abdora was amazed at seeing two babies being pushed out and knew that he'd forever bonded with Tavares on a different level. Abdora was in the chair next to Tavares's bed just smiling at her. After he saw her push those two football heads out her pussy, she was a trooper in his book.

"Aren't my babies the cutest things y'all ever seen?" Tavares asked, so proud at how cute her babies were straight out the womb.

"Yeah, they're adorable," Leslie said. "I can't wait to hold them."

Everyone kicked it with Tavares before they headed down to the nursery to see the babies. They all took turns cooing at the babies in the windows while Tavares lay in the bed too tired to move. She would page the nurse to bring the babies after everyone left.

"How you feel, momma?" Abdora asked.

"I feel fine. I just wish that I would come the hell down off these goddamn drugs. These ain't my type of drugs," Tavares chuckled. "I smoke weed. These are real drugs, and they got me feeling high as a kite."

"Yeah, babe, you need it. I saw what you pushed out," Abdora laughed.

"Naw, this shit is a feeling I don't like, because it feels too good. Makes me see why I don't fuck with pills and shit. Got me feeling like I'm floating," Tavares said with a light chuckle.

Abdora couldn't stop rubbing Tavares's cheek and forehead. They were alone for twenty minutes before everyone returned from the nursery.

"Tavares, we're all going to go," Doll said, giving Tavares a kiss and starting a domino effect with everyone.

"I'll be back tomorrow to see the babies. You get some rest."

"I will," Tavares said, knowing that she couldn't do anything but rest as high as she was.

Thanks to modern technology, Tavares and Abdora were able to DNA test the babies in the hospital the same evening they were born. The results wouldn't be back for four weeks, but they got it out of the way. Tavares wanted to know once and for all, even though Dora was convinced they were his sons.

"Tavares, your gut doesn't lie, and the feeling I got when I held them confirmed they're my sons."

"Well, in four weeks, we'll know. Then, I can break the bad news to Damien, his family, and everyone else."

"Don't worry, Babygirl. God wouldn't let you down and give you a nigga like him for a baby's father while you got a winner like me on your team."

Tavares just rolled her eyes but she was praying Dora was their father.

Jazz was at the nail shop with her friends who were barely talking to her when they rushed to the hospital because Tavares had gone into labor. Jazz felt like trash on the sidewalk not being able to go see Tavares and her baby boys. Tavares had been her friend too long and was too good to her for her to have ruined it for Damien. She headed to the bar to have a drink while her friends were off to the hospital with balloons, flowers, and teddy bears to see Tavares. Jazz never meant to hurt her friend. She let her selfish, jealous ways get to her. She decided to go drink her sorrow away until she couldn't feel anymore and was ready to pass out.

Everyone happily departed, but no one had more excitement than Holton about his new grandsons that only he and Damien knew about. They were beautiful, and they were going inherit everything he had. He would be changing his will no sooner than Tavares had names for them. His grandsons were never going to want or need for anything in life. If they chose to never work or go to college a day in their life, they'd still be all set. Holton had missed out on knowing or raising his daughter, but if she gave him a chance, he wanted to be a grandfather to the boys just as soon as she found out that he was her father.

Abdora stayed at the hospital with Tavares. He only left to go take a shower, but he quickly returned. Visitors came in and out all day long for the three days she was in the hospital. Tavares was more than happy when she made it home. At the hospital, she got no rest between the nurses, doctors, visitors, and having to nurse two babies. Hopefully, it would get better now that she was home. Tavares spent the first month of the babies' lives in Boston with everyone loving all over them. NaNa Dancy, Doll, her friends, and Abdora were the best. She still wasn't speaking to Damien, and he could only see the boys when Doll took them to her house for two hours every day. Tavares was past disgusted and still wanted nothing to do with him.

The babies were finally down for a nap and all Tavares wanted to do was take a shower. She felt icky and her breastfeeding titties were always leaking. She left the door open to the twins' rooms and took a nice, long, steaming hot shower. She heard Abdora on the phone downstairs when she got out the shower. Abdora heard her moving around, so he came upstairs, peeped in on the boys, and made his way to the master suite.

"What's cracking, sexy lady?"

"Nothing, just glad to take a shower. Where are you coming from smelling like you just smoked a pound of weed?" Tavares said jealously because her nose was sensitive to the smell she craved but couldn't have yet due to breastfeeding.

"I was out with Holton and Bryce putting some power moves in motion. After that, I went to get up with my mans and them and ended up blowing a few blunts of some crazy loud."

"Speaking of Holton, I don't know what's up with Lilly. I've been calling her, and it's like she keeps avoiding me. She'll answer, be short with me, and say she'll call me back but never does. Even when I had the babies, I was shocked she didn't come or call. I hope she's ok."

"I'm sure she is, because Holton hasn't mentioned anything. Listen, I have to go to Jersey. It's something important I need to take care of, and I want you and the boys to come."

Tavares didn't mean to be so blunt, but she blurted out, "I don't want to go."

Abdora's sour face repeated what her mouth had just said.

"Don't look like that. When we bought these houses, it was decided that we would live between two places. You want to be here with your peoples, and my businesses are in Jersey, so please play fair. Plus, I don't want to be without you and the boys for an undetermined amount of time."

Tavares knew the deal and what she signed up for, so she sucked it up.

"I'll call everyone tonight to tell them that we're leaving. After they come tomorrow, we can leave tomorrow night."

Abdora kissed her forehead and said, "See, that's why you're my future wife."

Tavares rolled her eyes and went to get her babies, who were up crying.

~Chapter 11~
Buster Jones is NOT the FATHER

"Hello," Tavares answered the phone, sounding overly exhausted.

"What's up, Babygirl? I called to check on you and my lil dudes."

"They're finally out," Tavares said, knowing that they would be up at any moment. "I called you earlier, but you didn't answer," Tavares said, lying on the long chaise and watching the rain coming down.

"I was handling some shit, and you know when I'm handling business, I don't pick up the jack. I just talked to my mother. She wants us to come through tomorrow. She's having some kind of dinner party for an old friend that just moved here. She's actually from Boston. How crazy is that?" Dora said.

"Let me find out I done put Jersey on the map," Tavares joked as she cuddled under the throw blanket. "We can do that."

"We can dress the boys up and show them off," Dora said, loving to show his lil dudes off like they were mini Doras at only two months old.

"You'll be getting them dressed," Tavares said. "They be acting crazy when I dress them, like I ain't their mother or something."

"They just be wanting their father to dress them, that's all," Dora said, making it clear to Tavares.

He loved to throw father comments out there since it was confirmed that he was indeed the father of the twins. They'd been in Jersey since they found out, so they hadn't broken the news to anyone. It was Tavares's plans to do it in the next few weeks.

"Oh please, what do they know about you dressing them at only two months old? I just be buggin' like my babies be really wanting to move and show me that their muscles work as soon as I start to change their clothes."

"It's alright, Boo. Don't sound so sad," Abdora taunted. "Just let me do what I do, and you do what you do," he laughed.

"You got jokes, huh?" Tavares said real cool and low. "It's alright, because from here on out, that's your official job like any other job or business you run, smart ass."

"It ain't shit to me," Dora laughed. "I love every minute that I spend with my sons."

His attachment to them was deeper than Tavares could really understand. Dora handled their sons like they were truly the apples of his eye.

"Make sure you call Damien and Doll to tell them that we'll be going to my mother's and that they're invited."

"I'm very proud of you for not holding your feelings against Damien to keep him from seeing my kids. I hate him, word I do, but I ain't going to keep him from the kids. At least not until I break the news to him that he's not the father," Tavares laughed. "I ain't that type of person. We only been here three weeks, and he acts like it's been forever. I'll call him, though. Did you tell your mother that they'll be coming, too?"

"Come on, Ma, don't ask me crazy questions. Why wouldn't I if I know they're coming in town for the weekend to see the babies? It's a party, so two more people ain't gonna matter."

"Did you call all the people about your scholarships?" Dora questioned, making sure his girl stayed pushing toward her dream and goal.

"Yeah, I did," Tavares said, sighing like she was dead tired. "They said that my advisor and department head already called and explained my situation and got my scholarships pushed back to next semester."

"That's fucking what's up, Babygirl. You can do that shit," Dora said like it was a piece of cake.

"Oh really, Mr. Man? You sound real super sure, but I'm not too convinced. I got strong determination, but with two babies that wake up every three hours looking for a nipple or to be changed, I'm skeptical. Not to mention when I'm tending to them throughout the day. They're an around the clock job. You know, shit. You be up with them just as much as I do. I don't know if I can go to law school with them being so small. I'll need to study on top of study, and to do both seems like trying to get over a mountain right now."

"Tavares, are you forreal, Ma?" Dora asked in real disbelief. "You know goddamn well you can do that shit. I'll hold it down with the babies and get a nanny if we need it. I never saw myself having no nanny. It even sounds likes some real bullshit, but if we need it to get you to law school, then add it to the list of monthly expenses."

"Dora, we're not getting a goddamn nanny. Who the fuck is black and has a nanny? I'm good with the crazy lady from nowhere trying to live here and take care of my babies. I don't know what I'm going to do, but Im'ma work it out," Tavares said like she hadn't figured it out but was working on it.

"Well, Momma, I told you that I got you. We gonna do whatever it takes for you to get through law school. I'm on my way home."

"I'll see you when you get here. I'm about to take a shower and get comfortable before the two spoiled brats wake up."

"Yeah, you do that, and after they lay back out, I'll rub you down real good since you ain't healed and shit."

"Ohh gee, aren't you the best?!" Tavares asked sarcastically. "I love you, bye," Tavares said, hanging up and not even giving Dora a chance to say anything.

Holton had been trying to get to New York for over a month to see Valentina. She was missing him and being a whiny bitch. So, Holton packed his bags and told Lilly he had business for the weekend and would be back Monday. Lilly didn't care because this would give her the chance to get high without lying and sneaking. Finding out that Dolonda and Holton created a baby together had broken her up and dragged her further into addiction. Lilly felt awful that she'd even changed toward Tavares. It wasn't Tavares herself but the whole situation.

Valentina had spent the week getting groomed between her heavy workload, taking care of her elderly father, and listening to her pain-in-the-ass daughter whine over a man she needed to get over. When she saw *My Baby* come across her phone, she grew more excited for a weekend of nonstop fun and sex.

"Hey baby, you landed, I see. Are you on the way to the hotel?"

291

"Yes, I am," Holton said, needing a weekend to relax, and Valentina was always a great time in and out of bed. "What's the plan for tonight?" he inquired.

"I got tickets to a Broadway play then dinner and some steamy sex," Valentina answered.

She really wanted to skip the first two but was gonna be nice.

"I'm starting to think you've been around all these years for my bedroom skills," Holton teased.

"You might be right," Valentina said, getting wet just thinking about being with Holton.

"Alright, I'm going to go to the hotel to jump in the shower and get ready. See you in about an hour," Holton said.

"Yes, you will," Valentina replied before they hung up.

Tavares was happy for her peaceful twenty minutes to herself as she got in the shower. She stripped her clothes and powered on the built-in baby monitor that Dora had installed. She was ready to relax for a little while. Standing in the shower letting the water run through her hair and down her now thicker frame, Tavares felt like she'd really died and gone to heaven. Her kids had a weird thing going. They would never sleep at the same time. One would go to sleep and the other would wake right up. It was rare that they were sleep at the same time for more than two hours. They would stay up together all you wanted, but sleeping at the same time wasn't happening. For them to be asleep at the same time was a Godsend and Tavares was taking advantage of it.

Tavares washed her hair twice and showered slowly, enjoying every drop of water all over her body. *Whhaa whhhhaaa.* Tavares heard one of the babies crying just as she was rinsing off for the final time.

"Fuck," Tavares said as she rushed out the shower. Tavares was throwing her robe on her still dripping wet body when she heard Dora.

"Ahh, what's all the noise, little man? I got you. You ain't gots to wild out like that. Mommy's taking a bath, but Daddy got you. What, you need a bottle or something or your butt changed? All you gots to do is holla. You ain't gots to holler literally, little man."

Tavares was just shaking her head as she listened to Dora talking to the baby like the baby knew what the hell he was talking about. That was the last thing Tavares heard as she went to her room to get ready for an evening with her babies wide awake and wanting her and Dora to hold them. Tavares walked down the hall into her oldest son's room that was connected in the middle with huge French doors to his brother's room. Jeremiah was in his crib sleeping peacefully. Elijah was in Abdora's hands, quiet, and just smiling as big as he wanted to be.

"Goodness, Elijah, can you please not hurt your face?" Tavares asked her tiny son as she smiled and cooed at him.

"He can't help it. He knows my touch."

"Whatever," Tavares said. "You and Elijah just don't wake my son up with all y'all laughing and cooing."

"You're the one who came in here with all the noise. Uhh lil man, tell her."

Dora had a natural love and affection for kids, and it showed when he held and talked to the babies.

"Abdora, you and your pet can keep it moving. You only like him because he got green eyes. You're not slick," Tavares said, chuckling and shaming Abdora as she shook her head.

"Don't no one have no fucking pets," Abdora said, knowing that he was guilty as charged. "I be rocking hard with both of my dudes. You be the one all loved up, cradling your little turquoise blue-eyed, light-bright baby."

"Shut the hell up," Tavares said, knowing that she wasn't guilty.

She had no favorites. She just cuddled her blue-eyed baby boy because Abdora was always on Elijah.

"Yo, the boys are going to be spoiled as hell if we keep holding them the way we do," Tavares said, knowing that she wasn't even trying to set herself up.

Abdora just sucked his teeth and went on with the baby like he hadn't even entertained the words coming out of Tavares's mouth. Tavares looked at Abdora holding her baby that was between a honey and caramel color. Elijah and his brother had looks that resembled babies that descended from Hawaii. Elijah's cheeks were all that could be with his tiny chin and forehead poking out. He had a head full of jet-black hair that was bone straight and lying down slick. If he wasn't smiling big, his lips were always puckered like he was mad with his eyes squinting. He was just too mean, and he was the screamer. His eyes just looked clear and sea green when he was crying and hollering to get attention.

Tavares went over to Jeremiah's room and looked in the crib at her olive-colored baby who resembled a pure Indian and had a head full of jet-black hair that was thick and curly. Tavares knew they were going to have lots of hair

294

based on the amount they had at just two months old. Jeremiah had strong facial features. Tavares knew these babies were hers because she birthed them, but they resembled neither her nor Abdora.

The babies only had their parents' eyes. They were a beautiful combination of adorable and too much cute for one baby. Tavares looked at her baby and couldn't help thinking of his cuteness. When he was awake, his turquoise, ocean-colored eyes were breathtaking. Tavares couldn't believe that her babies were identical, but one was lighter and the other was a little richer in color. The color of their eyes, the texture of their hair, and the tone of their skin were their only physical differences.

Tavares walked back into Elijah's room where Dora was still holding and talking to him about the facts of life like he could really understand.

"Dora, would you lay that boy down? If you hold him, he's going to get attached. Didn't I just tell you that? What, you didn't hear me or something?" Tavares asked, knowing for sure that he wasn't paying her any attention.

"I heard that bullshit. I just wasn't entertaining it. Why the fuck can't I hold them and kick it with them? I'm sure that when they get older they'll appreciate their pops holding them and talking to them. How about you go do something, and let me bond with my lil homie?"

Tavares knew she was wasting her breath and didn't even bother. She needed to go prepare some bottles, so she did as Abdora suggested and went to do something besides fuss at him. Tavares was in the kitchen amazed at what her Friday nights had become. She was putting the last breast-pumped bottle in the refrigerator when the house phone rang. She grabbed the phone just as it was about to stop ringing.

"Hello?"

"Hey, mommy," Leslie cooed.

"What's up, Les?"

"Nothing, I just called to see what you're up to."

"I was sitting here making bottles. Jeremiah's asleep, and Elijah's in his favorite place."

"In Dora's hands," Leslie said, already knowing.

"You know it," Tavares laughed.

"So, what's going on with you?" Leslie asked.

"Nothing. Damien and Doll are coming down this weekend."

"Are they?" Leslie said.

"Yeah, they're coming tomorrow and staying till Sunday."

"I haven't put the Acura you gave me on the highway yet, so me, Randee, and Mona-Lisa should come down there."

"Awww, that would be so what's up!" Tavares said, getting real excited. "You guys need to see in person how big the boys have gotten."

"I was looking at the pictures you texted like *what is Tavares feeding them*," Leslie laughed. "They're just so cute, chubby, and bright-eyed, Tavares."

"Thanks. I love my little papa and dada. I can't wait to tell Abdora that you guys are going to come out, too. Dhara is having a little dinner party at her crib, so that will definitely work. Awww, you just called and made my night, Leslie."

"Well, we can pack the kids up and bring them, so why not make it a weekend road trip? And, you said we could stay with y'all, so you can't beat it. I can't wait to see y'all's new house."

Tavares just sucked her teeth, and said, "Girllll, it's just ridiculously big. I told Abdora we didn't need all this space, but you know you can't tell him nothing. He thinks he's a star, but he just isn't in the industry. First of all, we have a waterfall in the house and an elevator for the three floors. There are ten bedrooms, six bathrooms, a meeting room, which is for lounging and hanging out, a play room for kids, a formal living room that's just for show, a library, a game room with every game system and a wall full of games with three pool tables, a movie theater, a sauna, a gym, basketball court, tennis court, two pools, a baby pool for kids, and just way too much free space to party in," Tavares laughed.

"Goddamn, Bitch. Let me find out Dora done bought you paradise. You ain't never gotta leave the house when you out there," Leslie said, excited to see it.

"Yeah, you could definitely say that," Tavares said unenthusiastically.

"Damn, why you sound so down about it?"

"I like it, don't get me wrong. I love it to pieces, but it's just way too big and way too much space for my taste. Like real talk, Leslie. We're fucking black and my boyfriend doesn't sell no records or play no sports, but we could be on MTV Cribs! That's a problem, bitch! I wanted something with the same amenities but smaller and more homely. We ain't got an army living with us. We don't need all this damn space. Abdora doesn't even like people, so who the hell is going to be over here enough to be filling all the empty bedrooms?"

"Well shit, if you want me and Tay to come move in, just say the word, and I'll be packing up the U-Haul faster than you know," Leslie said, only half joking.

"Girl, y'all are more than welcome to come vacation. I don't know about moving in. Dora might not be feeling that," Tavares said in a tone that implied rejection. "But, I was thinking about inviting everyone out for New Year's Eve. I'm not too sure just yet. It's still up in the air depending on what we decide to do to bring the ball in. Girl, I got my baby monitor on and can hear Dora trying to tend to both babies, let me get off this phone. But, I can't wait to see y'all tomorrow. Call me when y'all get on the highway."

Tavares exchanged goodbyes and headed upstairs with two bottles to do what she and Dora spent most nights doing, feeding, holding, and playing with the babies. She walked into Elijah's room to find Abdora with one baby in each arm, pacing the floor and holding a real conversation with them.

"You two dudes are going to be lil princes. Your mother tried to give you a buster for a father, but your dad is a king and a Boss, so y'all are good."

"I hate to break up this little shindig, but they need to eat. Give Elijah to me and take one of these bottles," Tavares said, extending her arms. They each took a seat in their rocking chairs to feed the babies. They shot the shit about everyone coming down and how it was going to be like a mini reunion.

"Are you going to keep it cordial with Damien even though you don't like him?" Tavares asked, knowing that

298

Abdora hated Damien just as much as, if not more than, she did.

"It's not even that I don't like him. I think he's a buster. Only a nigga who's trying to dig deep to be a slimeball would push up on his chick's girl. I can't respect that shit that he did. On the strength of this being my last time having to see or deal with him, I'm going to be nicer than you know. If it were up to me, I would lay him down, but I don't want you feeling no kind of way."

"Aren't you just so sweet, allowing people to have their lives and whatnot?" Tavares said like she was impressed but really being sarcastic.

"So, how do you think Damien is gonna take it when he finds out he isn't the father?" Dora asked.

"Hell if I know, and I really don't care. It's not like I was sleeping with mad different people. I was with him. He fucked up. I moved on and you lucked out with me as your children's mother."

"I think the luck is the other way around. You was tryna pin my kids on a buster. Thank God I knew better," Abdora said, rolling his eyes.

"Damien is gonna be pissed, but I have no sympathy for him," Tavares said. "Karma is a motherfucker, and the disappointment he feels will be the best revenge for all the shit he did to me."

"Ole spiteful ass," laughed Dora.

He was just glad that soon enough Damien would be out of their lives.

Damien was packing his car up to go see his sons and was glad that everyone was going to Dhara's house. The atmosphere would be laidback, and Damien wouldn't have to feel uneasy around Tavares and her man. Tavares had completely cut him off with the exception of seeing his kids, so things were awkward between them lately. He just wanted to see his kids, so he was going to deal with Tavares and her sour attitude, no matter what. Damien picked up his mother, loaded her bags, and hit the Mass Pike toward New Jersey.

Leslie was getting her daughter dressed when the phone rang. Seeing the name on the caller ID made her hesitant about picking up, but she did anyway.

"Hello?"

"What's up, Leslie?" the sad voice asked on the other end.

"Shit, getting Tay dressed."

"Where y'all going?"

"Me, Mona-Lisa, and Randee are taking the kids and going to see Apple and the boys."

"Oh, that's nice," Jazz said, feeling left out and fucked up at what things had come to.

No one had cut her off, but she couldn't tell based on how distant they were. Jazz didn't have Tavares, her other girls, or Damien, which cosigned that she had made biggest mistake of her life by having anything to do with Damien.

"Jazz, you know me. I'm running late as hell, so let me get off this phone. I'll call you sometime next week," Leslie said, trying to direct her daughter, pack, and talk on the phone.

"Ok, y'all have fun, and tell Apple I said hello and congratulations on her sons," Jazz said, hanging up feeling like trash.

Abdora was in the twins' bathroom bathing them when he heard Tavares paging him over the intercom. Dora pushed the button to the master bedroom.

"What's up, crazy? I got my hands in the water, so either make it fast or bring your ass."

"I'm coming," Tavares said, putting the phone back in the cradle.

"Your hair's nice."

"Thanks, it took me forever to do it," Tavares said, running her fingers through her hair that was damn near to her ass thanks to her pregnancy.

"I came to ask you what you're wearing. I got all the clothes laid out, but you didn't tell me what you wanted ironed."

"Don't matter. Just pick something."

Tavares kissed her babies and headed to lay Abdora's clothes out. It was a laidback day, so no one, Dora included, was getting all decked out. Tavares grabbed a plaid shirt, puffy vest, jeans, and Timbs for him and headed to wrap her hair before she showered and got dressed. The ringing house phone interrupted her as Tavares tried to wrap her hair. She walked from her vanity and picked up the phone.

"Hello," Tavares said with an attitude.

"Hey, Boo, What the hell is your problem?" Randee asked.

"Oh nothing. I was wrapping my goddamn hair when you decided that you wanted to call."

"I was just calling to tell you that we left. Me and Leslie are in her car and Mona-Lisa is behind us. We should be there in about three hours. Do you want us to come to your house or are we meeting you at Dhara's house?"

"It seems to take us forever to get out the door with the boys, so we should be ready by the time y'all get close. Y'all can meet us here and we can all leave together. Damien called and said he caught a flat, so he'll probably get there around the same time, too. I don't even want his stinking ass at my house, so he and Doll are going to meet us at Dhara's."

There was a chime at the door three hours and twenty minutes later. Dora's voice came through in Tavares's bedroom telling her to get the door because he was putting the kids in their car seats. Tavares opened the front door and found her friends with their kids. After big hugs, Randee, Mona-Lisa, Leslie, and their kids stopped in the meeting room to see the babies. They toured the house and Tavares's friends decided that they never wanted to leave.

"Damn, boo, Dora truly is your knight in shining armor," Mona said, truly glad that happiness had found its way to Tavares's life.

"Since I have y'all all here, I have a secret to share with y'all."

Everyone got quiet because Tavares looked so serious.

"Even though I spent my whole pregnancy saying the boys were Damien's, I wasn't too sure. Actually, Dora wasn't convinced. So, when they were born, we had them DNA tested, and Dora is indeed their father."

"Shut the fuck up," Randee said.

"Yessssssssss!" Mona-Lisa said, really excited now.

"Well goddamn, goddamn," Leslie said.

"I know, y'all. Trust me, if Dora wasn't so adamant, I wouldn't have ever second-guessed Dame being the father."

"Wait, if he's not the father, why should he and Doll still be coming out here?"

"Oh, they don't know yet," Tavares said nonchalantly. "Only me, Dora, and y'all know. I found out while I was here and didn't want to break the news to him over the phone. On my next trip to Boston, I'm going to happily be the bearer of bad news."

Randee knew her friend all too well and laughed. Tavares was gonna take pride in hurting Dame one good time for the hundred times he'd hurt her.

The girls chitchatted for a few before Abdora said, "Ok, enough gossiping. Let's go."

They loaded up the cars ready to go to Dhara's for a night of fun and partying.

~Chapter 12~
When the Past Meets the Present

On the way to Dhara's, Abdora's phone interrupted his conversation with Tavares.

"What up, Holton?"

"Ain't shit, youngin'. I was over here in New York City and was calling to see if you wanted to come meet me for dinner and to have a few drinks."

"Awww, Holton. I wish I could, but I'm on my way to my mother's house. She's having a dinner party. But, if you'd like, you're more than welcome to join us."

"Nah, I don't want to crash on your family fun. I'm just gonna hang out over here in New York, take care of my business, and shoot the shit with my friend."

"Holton, you know it ain't even that type of party. So, cut the shit. Tavares got the boys out, and her friends are here from Boston. Bitch ass nigga Dame is here with his family. It's like a party, so stop bullshitting and come have a drink with your boy."

Holton loved Abdora because he was only in his mid-twenties, but he carried himself and conducted business like he was forty or fifty.

"Aiight, youngin," Holton chuckled, having changed his mind when he heard that his grandsons were going to be there.

When the crew arrived at Dhara's, the party was in full swing. Dhara never threw anything small even when she tried to. Cars were in her driveway and on the street in front of her neighbors' houses. They were also on the sidewalk and anywhere else cars could fit.

"Damn, it's only 6 o'clock," Tavares said, looking at her phone. "Your mother plays no games getting it cracking up here in the 'burbs."

When they made it in the house, Tavares and Abdora were mobbed for the babies.

"Oh my god, is this a stick up for my kids?" Tavares asked as she and Abdora were being crowded around.

Everyone was saying the same thing, "Let me hold the baby first."

"Everyone, back the fuck up!" Dhara yelled, walking to the front of the crowd. "Ain't no goddamn body holding my grandbabies before me. Ain't that right?" Dhara said politely, picking Elijah up from his car seat and kissing Jeremiah.

Meemaw grabbed Jeremiah and went in the kitchen to hog him up. Dhara's sisters, friends, and nieces were mad, but she didn't care. Randee, Mona-Lisa, and Leslie's kids were gone no sooner than they came through the door and saw all the other kids running around doing their own thing.

"Ok, this is what I'm talking about," Leslie said. "Bring your kids out with you and ain't got to even worry about them."

"Ooook," Mona-Lisa said. "My girls came through the door and went straight to the backyard like they been here before."

Tavares and her three friends went to the kitchen and kicked it with Dhara and her friends while they made plates.

"There's way too much food to choose from," Tavares said.

There was macaroni and cheese, potato salad, tuna salad, bbq chicken, fried chicken, steak tips, two hams, two roasts, bbq ribs, Spanish rice and beans, collard greens, and more pies and cakes than anyone's sweet tooth was going to be able to take.

"Dang, I want a little of everything," Tavares said, feeling like a true big girl.

"Dhara, if I can ask, why are you having a random party on this beautiful November weekend right before Thanksgiving?" Randee asked as she stuffed a tender piece of steak into her mouth.

"You're a nut," Dhara said, pointing her naughty girl finger at Randee. "It's for my girlfriend who hasn't arrived yet. She was at school doing a group project, and they ran over. She's on her way now. She's an old friend who's getting her life right and back on track after a very long time. She's been clean six months. Now she's in school getting her master's, so I thought it would be nice to have a small turned large party for her."

Abdora walked in accompanied by Holton and Bryce and his new chocolate girlfriend that seemed nice but a little off. She looked like a beautiful chocolate Barbie doll, but she was always buggin' about nothing. Everyone exchanged greetings before Abdora crept on Meemaw and scooped Jeremiah out her hands.

"Boy, if you don't give me back the baby, I'll kick your fucking ass all up and down this kitchen. Play with me if you want to," Meemaw said, truly mad.

"Catch me first, Meemaw," Dora said, laughing and moving to the other side of the kitchen with the baby cradled in his arms. "Nah, for real, Meemaw. Im'ma change, feed, and burp him, then you can have him back. I promise. I don't want you throwing none of your old school jabs on me," Abdora laughed. "Tavares, get Elijah and the bottles, please," Dora asked as he played with Jeremiah.

"Can I hold him?" Holton asked, looking at the baby who, unknown to everyone in the room, was the spitting image of him when he was a baby minus the blue eyes. As Abdora passed the baby to Holton, Holton felt his heart sink and knew that he needed to be a part of their lives to make up what he missed in his daughter's life.

"Hey, Dhara. Let's trade," Holton said five minutes later.

While everyone was in the mix, Tavares and Abdora were together at the stove warming up their bottles and looking extremely happy. Holton looked at his other grandson who looked like his twin. He had a spin of silky on him with his straight hair.

Holton was all into the baby when Tavares said, "Holton, I gotta steal him for a little while."

"Oh, here you go," Holton said, passing the baby but not wanting to let go.

Tavares and Abdora checked on their guests, who were good, and headed upstairs to tend to their double bundles of wet and hungry joy. After being gone forty-five minutes, Tavares and Abdora returned to see that Doll and Damien had arrived. They were in the den chillin' with NaNa Dancy.

"Oh my God, NaNa. What are you doing here?" Tavares said, giving NaNa Dancy a huge hug and kiss.

"Girl, please. I know you didn't think that they were going to come see my great-grandbabies and leave me at home. After I heard that they had a flat, I made them get it fixed and turn around to come get me," Dancy said, meaning business. "Let me hold that baby," Dancy said, putting her arms out.

Passing Elijah to NaNa Dancy was the last thing Tavares remembered. The next thing she knew, she was looking around and wondering why she was in the bed while everyone was looking at her like she was crazy.

"My head is rocking. What happened?" Tavares asked her friends.

Abdora and Doll were looking at her, not really knowing what to say.

"Hello? Someone say something," Tavares said, feeling awkward.

"You passed out," Leslie said.

"I did what?" Tavares said, confused.

"Momma, what's the last thing you remember?" Abdora said, being the one to take control of the situation.

"I remember giving Elijah to NaNa Dancy. Where are my babies now?"

"NaNa Dancy and Meemaw have them," Abdora said.

Then, Tavares had a flashback: *Dhara came in the front door and said, "Everyone, the guest of honor is here. Meet my friend Dolonda."*

Tavares turned around to see that it was her mother, who she hadn't seen in eleven years.

"Oh my fucking goodness!" Tavares screamed with her eyes bulging out her head. "I saw my fucking mother. I saw my fucking mother," she kept repeating. "Where is she now?" Tavares asked as she was trying to get up.

"Calm down, Babygirl. Just calm down," Abdora said, sitting on the bed next to Tavares so that she wouldn't try to get up.

"Hell fucking no, Abdora. I remember now. I saw my fucking bitch of a mother come in the door like shit was all hunky dory. Where the fuck is my mother?" Tavares asked no one in particular.

Damien, Dhara, Dolonda, and Holton were in the kitchen discussing what Dhara was the only one in the dark about. Having ended the party due to the nature of the madness, Dhara wanted the truth and nothing but the truth. Dhara was blown away when she learned that Holton and Dolonda had reared a baby together who was the girlfriend of her son, who had no clue Holton was her father and hadn't seen Dolonda in over ten years.

Dhara was holding her head in utter shock. She hurt for Tavares more than anything.

"Dolonda, why you didn't tell me that you had a daughter?" was the first thing that Dhara asked.

"I wanted to, but I was still battling with failing as a mother and Holton finding out about her."

"Holton, all these years and you didn't know about Tavares?" Dhara questioned, so confused about the crazy connection everyone had.

"Nah, not until about the time she graduated."

"Holton, I'm sorry," Dolonda said. "Dhara, Holton finding out was how I even ended up at a sober house in Jersey. Holton wanted me to tell Tavares that he was her father and that I'd never told him about her. Instead of doing that, I bounced. I know it was wrong, but I did what I felt I needed to do."

"But, why did you never tell him?" Dhara asked, unable to understand.

"I told him I was getting an abortion."

Dhara's eyes got big.

"You did what, Dolonda?"

"I just never told him that I changed my mind, since he was marrying Lilly and having a baby. I had Tavares and was a single mom holding it down, but I was totally broken inside as a woman after Holton just turned his back on me and my baby. For years, I masked the pain, but eventually it got the best of me. I let a friend convince me that crack was better than our party drug, coke. I tried crack. Which is when I met Damien. I had it under control for a while, then it got bad, and I lost my daughter. I gave up on life from that day forward," Dolonda said, feeling awful.

"Damien, let's go check on Tavares and give these two some time to talk this out, because it's going to be an even bigger mess when Tavares comes down," Dhara advised.

"Dolonda, I'm trying to be your friend. This is going to be crazy for all of us, so I think we should support each other. Seeing you clean makes me think about old times. That day at your house fucked me up, because I hadn't seen you in all those years. This is the Dolonda I know. I look at you and see the times that were fun-filled and living life to the fullest. We laughed, traveled, ate well, lived good, and never had a bad time between us. There were many after you, a lot of one-night stands, even being married to Lilly all these years, but none of them stopped me from thinking about you."

Dolonda was giving Holton *fuck you* eyes.

"You're trying to be slick. You're trying to push up on me and talk to me like you used to do. You know what makes me tick and turns me on, so you're trying to use that to your advantage. Chemistry wasn't ever our problem, so I already know what's good. Those times are long over between us, Holton. You can save your slickness and worry about working this out with your daughter. All you want to do is get your dick wet and then go home to your wife. You got me twisted. I'm not that little young girl no more. You married Lilly, so you belong to Lilly," Dolonda said, rolling her eyes.

Damien and Dhara made their way upstairs and found everyone trying to control and console a hysterical Tavares. Tears were falling and she was sobbing uncontrollably and hyperventilating. Abdora was holding her and rocking her while everyone else fought back their tears from seeing Tavares in so much evident pain. No one knew what to say. What could they really say to console Tavares after seeing her mother for the first time in over a decade? Tavares cried and cried until she couldn't cry anymore.

"You look good as hell, Dolonda."

"Motherfucker, please."

"Damn, baby, don't be like that. I see that attitude still ain't changed. I'm trying to be sincere. This ain't about no pussy. I'm more than sorry about everything you been through. Especially for the drugs and you losing Tavares. It wasn't on purpose. I had no choice. I did what I thought was right. I was sticking by my woman, who was already pregnant. She was going to leave if I decided to fuck with you. So, when you said you were going to have an abortion, I thought it had all worked out. But, trust me, if I'd known that I fucking had a daughter out here, I would have found

311

you. I'm emotional just like you are. I'm finding out I have a daughter who turned twenty-two three weeks ago. What, you think a nigga ain't got feelings, Dolonda? Well, shit, I do. Just because I don't wear them on my shoulder doesn't mean that I don't have feelings. I have so many emotions that it's crazy. But, most of all, I feel like I'm blessed. I look at her and am more amazed each time."

"I'm not trying to hear you. I'm not even going to allow you to come into my life and play with me. You ain't got a chance in hell with me, Holton. I loved you too hard for you to do what you did to me. That shit broke me beyond words, as you saw when you came to my house. I ain't based the fuck out no more, and I ain't taking no shit."

"Dolonda, don't be like that. I love you. I swear I do. Over the years, I thought about you. All I heard was that you was out there getting high. But I swear I never knew that you had a baby. Now, we're older, I'm trying to do this here."

"Never, Holton," Dolonda said, holding her tears back with everything in her. "Now, because you know that we got a daughter together, you want something to do with me like we can be a happy family or something. Hell fucking no," Dolonda said in her thick accent while rolling her neck and eyes.

"Dolonda, I loved you from back then. Why won't you let me get a clean slate? It's been twenty-two years."

"I wouldn't care if it was thirty years. I wouldn't want to be your friend or start fresh with you. I bet Lilly wouldn't like you trying to befriend me."

"Lilly can keep hitting her crack pipe," Holton said, not even trying to hear about Lilly, whom he was tired of.

312

"Oh shit," Dolonda said, with her eyes popping out her head. "You know that Lilly gets high?" Dolonda asked. "Do you know how hard Lilly dips and dodges for you to not find out that she been smoking all these years?"

"What the fuck do I look like, some sort of fucking idiot, Dolonda? I knew that Lilly got high, but she does such a good job at concealing it that I just let her do her, and I live my life. She started after my son died, so in a way, even though I don't condone that shit, I know why she fell to it. I guess we all lost someone," Holton said with a long sigh.

No one knew what to say to Tavares. Every time she calmed down enough to breathe, she would bawl all over again. As soon as she saw her mother smiling with Dhara, her eyes went to running.

Rubbing her back and softly whispering, "You gotta relax," Mona-Lisa tried to soothe what she had no clue about. "It's been a very, very long time since you've seen your mother. Before you go down there to say whatever you may say, I just want you to get you together first."

Tavares didn't know what to say, how to feel, or how in the hell she'd just seen her mother after eleven years, but she was definitely ready to have her peace. Doll and Dhara were trying to mother her, and her friends were trying to show concern while Damien and Dora said nothing at all.

"I promise I'm ok. I've been waiting a long time for this day, so I just want to go hear what she has to say for herself to justify abandoning me eleven years ago."

Tavares came down the hall and saw Meemaw and NaNa Dancy in the upstairs den with her sons and all the children having a good ole time. They were talking, singing, and dancing with the babies in their arms while the other kids danced around them. It was like they weren't concerned about the madness going on around them. They were in their own world with their great-grandsons and having a ball with all the children. Tavares peeped in and kissed her babies before assuring Meemaw and NaNa Dancy that she was ready to face her mother.

Finding her mother in the kitchen with Holton made Tavares want to cry all over again, but she held back.

"Holton, do you mind if I talk to Dolonda?"

"I think he should stay."

Tavares looked at Dolonda and snapped, "Stay for what? This shit is between me and you. Not me, you, and spectators."

Tavares never saw Abdora standing outside the door.

"Holton doesn't have a damn thing to do with me and you."

"Tavares, Holton is your father."

Tavares's mouth fell open and she looked from her mother to her father and couldn't get words to flow from her mouth. She was waiting to wake up from this bad dream that felt all too real.

"Holton's my father?"

Dolonda said nothing.

"Dolonda, my whole life, you said my father bounced on you. So how did I go from no father to Lilly's husband being my father? You gotta tell me something, because that is just plain insane," Tavares said with her eyes welling up. "Holton, what the fuck is she talking about?" Tavares asked with her eyes fixed on her mother.

Holton tried to explain but was cut short. Dolonda explained their past and how things ended. Tavares couldn't help but cry and cry. Both of her parents wanted to move toward her and throw their arms around her, but they were afraid to move. Abdora had no sympathy or liking for the lady who was Tavares's mother. She chose to get high and to keep Holton from his daughter. Dora felt he was a man of logic. He felt like just because she couldn't have Holton, she said she was having an abortion, kept the baby, and never told him. Then, she blamed him for her using crack. Dora wasn't buying what she was selling. He wasn't into the sympathy card and wasn't feeling her whatsoever, even if she was Tavares's mother.

After fifteen minutes, Tavares pulled herself together with her parents just watching her.

"Holton, I have to please ask you to leave. Before today, I had no clue of your existence in my life, and my mother is the first issue that I have to deal with. I can't fault you for not knowing about me, but today I can't take on a mother and father."

Holton left without another word. This was for Dolonda to mend, and he hoped that she did just that.

Dolonda began to apologize in Spanish. Tavares listened to her mother speak to her in Spanish, and she felt like a kid all over again. Few people even knew that Tavares could speak fluent Spanish. Dolonda was saying she was sorry and that she never meant for things to turn out how they did. Dolonda cried and cried and told her daughter how much she loved her. And, even though life had rained on them for so many years, she wanted her daughter to please forgive her.

Sadness was filled with anger as Tavares listened to her mother beg her for forgiveness.

315

"You got a better motherfucking chance of seeing Jesus. I saw good days and bad days thinking about you and wondering where you were and if you were ok or even alive, and you been putting a motherfucking pipe to your mouth. Now you want me, ME, to forgive you?" Tavares asked, laying her hand on her chest and jerking her neck back, wondering if this lady was crazy.

"Oh, Dolonda Del Gada, you got me totally fucked up. I'm not her. I'm grown and a mother of my own kids. Everything I learned was by trial and error on my own. I don't go for bullshit, and what you're talking is just that. You had eleven long years to get your shit right to be a mother and come try to find me. I don't need a mother. I got a second mother who showed me the way in life. You gave me life and started out, but you bailed and that ain't a mother. Sorry," Tavares said with drained, unsympathetic eyes.

Dolonda looked at her daughter and saw so much of herself. Her daughter was everything she was and more before she hit that pipe. Tavares had her fire, bounce, and attitude.

"Tavares, I can only ask for your forgiveness and pray that one day, you'll come around. I won't force you to do anything that you don't want to do. I'm very sorry for ever even touching crack and allowing it to steal my motherhood. You ain't got to beat me down, because I beat myself down every day. But, if I wallow there and on my mistakes, I'll never be picked up enough to stay clean. Right now, I'm clean for me. In the past, I would try to get clean, then I would think of you, and it would be over. I would relapse from the hurt, pain, and guilt.

"I told myself that if I ever came face to face and you chose, keyword *chose*, to be a part of my life, I would be clean. So, I'm clean and doing what I got to do for me. I love you, and I'm sorry for every horrible thing in your life that you endured that I wasn't there to protect you from."

Tavares couldn't do anything but look at her mother, the person who had left her eleven years ago and hadn't once tried to find her. She didn't know if forgiveness was in the cards.

"Dolonda, I would never wish bad on you, but I'm not sure if I can do this mother/daughter thing with you. Maybe one day I'll get there, but it ain't today, and it isn't going to be in the near future. I wish you the best, and I hope you keep your sobriety and have many blessings. As a mother of two beautiful babies, I'm hurt even more now. So, like I said, I can't see myself forgiving you anytime soon."

Tavares felt the tears coming and knew that was all that she could take. Dolonda was left standing in the kitchen with tears coming down her face. Tavares went upstairs and asked her friends to take her home.

"Abdora, please bring the babies home. Damien and Doll, I think it would be best if y'all took NaNa Dancy and went home tonight. I'm in no shape to entertain," Tavares said, looking like her soul had been ripped out of her body.

"We understand," Damien said, knowing that Tavares was going to fall hard when she found out that he knew about Dollar and Holton.

"Tavares, I'm so sorry," Damien said. "I wanted to tell you when Holton came to me."

An awkward silence filled the hallway of Dhara's house.

"What the fuck do you mean you wanted to tell me? You knew?"

Tavares thought she couldn't hate Damien any more than she already did, but at that moment, she realized it was possible.

"You're so fucked up. You KNEW Holton was my father and said nothing?"

"Tavares, it was crazy how I found out and even crazier that I've been selling to your mother all these years and didn't know she was your mother."

Tavares screamed and gasped for air. Everyone came running. Tavares's friends and Dora couldn't figure out what had just transpired, but Tavares's scream sent them running.

When they approached the soon-to-be crime scene, Tavares was punching Damien, screaming, "I hate you! I fucking hate you! How could you know all this and not say anything all these months? You know what? That's why you aren't the twins' father, and I'm so fucking glad."

Damien heard that and wanted to fight Tavares back. Abdora picked Tavares up and carried her away while she was still screaming how much she hated Damien. Leslie and Randee escorted Damien and his family to their car. Everyone knew the evening was a chain of messy events, so no one said anything. Tavares and her girls hit the highway toward her house.

"Tavares, are you alright?" Mona-Lisa asked.

"I don't know, Mona. I really don't," Tavares said as her eyes welled up with tears.

Tavares tried to fight what was out of her control. "Tavares, you gonna be alright, Boo."

"Eleven years, Mona? I raised myself. She can't just pop back like hey, I'm clean so shit's sweet. And, all this time that bitch ass Damien was her dealer and never thought to put two and two together? I hate them both, fuck that," Tavares said, getting mad.

It was an emotional ride to the house. When they got home, Tavares and her friends headed to the meeting room. They were twisting up their third blunt when they heard the door open and knew that Abdora was home. Tavares went to assist with bringing her sons into the house. While Tavares was on the elevator with Abdora, he couldn't help but notice the withdrawn look on her face.

"Ma, listen. I know this shit is crazy, but you can handle it. I got your back, so you're good."

Tavares tried to crack a smile for his effort, but she didn't feel like this was something that she could handle.

"Abdora, I love you. Love you dearly. You're too sweet, and I hope you're right. Are you good with the boys? Im'ma go kick it with the ladies, make sure they're good, then I'll come join you."

"Yeah, go do you, Momma. I got this."

Tavares did as she told Abdora she would. She smoked three more blunts with their friends, told them they were welcome to anything in her house, checked in on the babies, and found her way to her bed. She stripped all her clothes and climbed in the bed. Tavares snuggled under Abdora and cried as he held her tightly. Abdora wished he could do anything - anything at all to ease her pain. But, the tears that Tavares was releasing were from a broken heart and nothing but time was going to fix it. Abdora simply held her and let her cry until she finally fell asleep.

Randee, Mona-Lisa, and Leslie put their kids to bed and took a tour of Tavares and Abdora's mansion.

"I need Abdora not to be balling so hard outta control," Randee said as they went from floor to floor checking out all the grand amenities.

"So, ladies, do y'all want to go to the spa or to the movie theater?" Mona-Lisa asked.

"Girl, we can go to a movie anytime. I'm going to take advantage of that sauna and hot tub," Leslie said.

"I know that's right," Mona-Lisa said, high-fiving her girl.

The ladies had nothing but time on their hands, so they turned on a movie in the theater that was fully equipped with a concession stand and all.

"Grab me some popcorn and a Pepsi," Randee said to Mona-Lisa as she checked out all the newest movies.

Leslie grabbed some Milk Duds and a Sprite. When the movie ended, they went to the Jacuzzi and maxed and relaxed. The ladies enjoyed themselves in Tavares's mini paradise while she was hopefully being comforted by Abdora.

"I can't believe Tavares came face to face with her mother," Leslie said, still in shock about what had transpired earlier.

"Actually, I don't know what's crazier. Her seeing Dolonda or that Holton is her father? Girl, that shit was just straight crazzzy," Mona-Lisa cosigned.

"I feel bad for Tavares," Randee said. "She's been motherless for so long and hides the pain of not having her mom, and now she gotta deal with this hard pill. Ladies, it's going to be hard for her, so she's going to need us more than ever."

"Randee, you ain't never lied," Mona-Lisa said. "I felt so bad and just didn't know what to say to console her."

"Tavares is good at consoling everyone else, so it was crazy to see her on the hurting end," Leslie said, hurting for her best friend.

Tavares's friends loved her, so although she thought she wouldn't get through it, they were determined to make sure she did.

~Chapter 13~
When a Ton of Bricks Comes Down On You

Dolonda was on her grind harder than ever after her run-in with her daughter. She was broken and hurt to pieces but wasn't trying to fall backwards, so she just pushed harder toward her goals. Dolonda was leaving school when her cell phone started vibrating in her bookbag. She answered the restricted phone call with a friendly *hello.*

"Hey there, Beautiful."

Dolonda stopped in her tracks on the sidewalk.

"Holton, why are you calling me? I thought I told you a few weeks ago that I wanted no parts of you," Dolonda said, aggravated at the sound of Holton on her line.

"Dolonda, you really ain't trying to be my friend? Damn, we're two different people now. Why can't we be friends? I just want to take you to lunch. You're the mother of my child," Holton slid in real smoothly.

"Holton, I don't have time for this bullshit. I'm not going to lunch or anywhere else with you," Dolonda said, pressing end on her phone.

Holton was left in his office looking at the phone in disbelief that Dolonda had hung up on him. Placing the phone in the cradle, Holton leaned back and let it really set in that he'd gotten hung up on. Holton had been thinking about Dolonda since they let the cat out of the bag to Tavares. He couldn't deny the fact that Dolonda had always had a soft spot with him, and seeing her clean made him forget that he had a wife at home. She was still bad, and it amazed Holton that she still had the body of a twenty-five-year-old. Her pale face and blushing rosy red cheeks had Holton unable to fight his temptation to get her.

Holton got up from his desk, walked to the window, and chuckled out loud and said, "Dolonda, still want a nigga."

Holton knew Dolonda all too well. She was cussing him to fight her true feelings. It was cool for the moment, because Holton knew that he could and would wear her down in the end.

Tavares was unable to really eat, sleep, or think for weeks. Seeing Dolonda after so long brought a lot back for Tavares that she wasn't ready for. It had taken her someplace that she wasn't trying to stay. Tavares felt like she didn't have her guard up and a ton of bricks came tumbling down on her heart and head. She was weak, hurt, and sad. At night, when she thought she was the only one awake, she would cry silently. In the night, Tavares would be crying in her sleep and wake Abdora up. Abdora would think to wake her up, but instead held her tightly as he watched her tears clearly streaming down her closed eyes. Her pain was running deep, and it was clear Tavares was broken. Her only saving grace were her boys, who motivated her. Every day Tavares would get up and have fun taking care of and playing with the boys, but when it was her time, she was all hurt and tears.

"What's good?" Abdora said, giving his friend, mentor, and girlfriend's father dap as he sat in the booth at Legal Seafood in the South Shore Mall.

The atmosphere was quiet and laidback during the middle of the day, and Abdora was glad for the conversation he had in mind.

"Holton, yo, I really don't know what to do about my girl. She's fucked up about you and her moms. She always said she wouldn't know how she would react if she ever found her mother, but I never expected this. You know I'm a good dude with morals and values. I love the fuck out of your daughter, and I just want to see her happy. Right now, she ain't happy, and I know that's because her shopping account is way too full," Abdora said, wishing that Tavares would get up and go shopping. "Shopping usually makes her feel better about absolutely anything but this. This is a first, and it got me feeling like this ain't fixable."

"You gotta put your foot down, youngster. You gotta make her get up out the bed. As long as she lies there and wallows and is sad and depressed, she's going to stay like that. She got her plate full right now. Just be there for her. But, first, get her ass up out that bed and back on the grind in life. She'll get through and come around in time, but right now she needs that motivation, and you gotta be it."

Abdora had lunch and two drinks with Holton before he hit the highway to Tavares's house. Holton headed home to face some serious music. He was ready to tell his wife about the fact that he and Dolonda shared a daughter together. He knew that Lilly wasn't going to take it easy, but he knew he owed it to her to tell her.

Holton arrived home and pulled into his garage ready to face the music. He went to the second floor of his oversized home and found Lilly in the den relaxing and watching TV.

"I need to talk to you," Holton said.

Lilly was surprised because Holton had been distant and had little to say to her these days.

"What's up?" Lilly asked as she powered the 72-inch flat screen television off.

After taking a long, deep breath, Holton said, "I need to tell you something, but I want you to know that I haven't known all along. I found out earlier this year but didn't know how to tell you."

"What, that you and Dolonda are Tavares's parents?" Lilly asked with tears trickling down her face.

Holton's eyes damn near fell out of his head.

"Lilly, I'm so sorry."

"Holton, I've known just as long as you have, but what I'm crushed about is that you never said anything to me."

"Lilly, I didn't know how to."

"So, Dolonda wins again. I go visit my son's grave twice a week and here she is with your only living child on this earth."

"Lilly, don't make this about you and Dolonda. This is about Tavares and the fact that she's my daughter and grew up without a mother or a father."

"I adore Tavares, and I'm sorry for that. I guess now you think that me and Dolonda are going to magically be in the same room getting along. It's not gonna fucking happen. And, if I dare hear about you and Dolonda talking, communicating, associating, or any of the above, it's going to be a problem," Lilly said with fire in her eyes.

Holton didn't know what to say because from Lilly's last sentence, it was clear that deep down she knew Holton loved Dolonda. Lilly was done with the conversation. She got up, left Holton on the couch. She went to her room to get dressed and left without saying a word to her husband.

Abdora made it to the house just before eight o'clock. The house was dark with all the lights out. The boys were asleep and Tavares was curled up under the covers knocked out with her TV watching her. Tavares's sleep was light these days. When she heard footsteps, she turned over to see Abdora sitting on the bench that was positioned at the end of the bed.

"I'm glad you're up, Momma. We need to talk," Abdora said, taking his black high-top Prada sneakers off. "Yo, Momma, I love you more than you'll ever know. Trust me, you drive me crazy and get on my nerves, but I love your crazy, spicy, sexy ass! I need my partner in crime back. You know, the one who be talking shit, cracking jokes, and bubbly all over the place. I can't and ain't gonna look at you hurt another day.

"I don't know what the hell we gotta do to get you through this, but we, operative word, *we*, are going to get you through it. I don't care if I gotta get you the best therapy that money can buy. Your problems are my problems, and when pain is your problem, that's definitely my problem. We gotta fix that problem and fix it quick, fast, and in a hurry," Abdora said with a no-nonsense attitude.

Tavares broke down and cried like she really needed to. In the middle of their bedroom, Abdora put his arms around Tavares and held her tight. Abdora couldn't understand what it felt like to get a double whammy like she had, but if her tears told her pain, Tavares's heart was shattered when you looked at her. Tavares cried till she couldn't cry anymore. When she was done, she fought hard to express what she really didn't know how to express verbally. Tavares's heart was aching in a literal sense, was the easiest way to sum it up.

"Abdora, my world feels totally discombobulated. Like, I want to be happy that my mother's back, and I have these beautiful babies that she can be a grandmother to. Then, it's like, oh hell no, fuck her. She left me. She never ever came because she was getting high, so naw, she don't get a pass. Then, she hits me with Holton being my father. What the fuck and how the fuck is all that I can even say to that. Like, Holton is my father. I was homeless, and my father was playing house and home with a crackhead. That set me straight financially once I started hustling. Come on, this is like all too much for my being.

"I want to know how Lilly feels knowing that I'm the baby that she told my moms to get rid of. Abdora, I be trying to convince myself that it's no big deal. Your mother is back, and you got a father. Then, it hits me, and I'm like, *HELLO, BITCH, you're twenty-two and haven't seen your mother in eleven years*, and *your mother picked Holton to be your father that day*, even though he confirmed her story."

"Calm down, Tavares. I don't know how you feel, but trust me, I got your back. We're going to find someone ASAP for you to talk to so you can slowly work on dealing with your moms and Holton. You can't forever say you don't want to be bothered with them. Y'all lost out on a lot of years, but be grateful and blessed for the future," Abdora said, trying to convince Tavares that she should allow her parents into her life.

327

"Dora, I don't know about that," Tavares said, continuously shaking her head in disagreement.

"Alright," Dora said, not pushing the issue. "For now, we're going to get you a therapist, then we'll go from there. Tomorrow, I want you to go shopping."

"What?" Tavares said, knowing that shit had to really be crazy now. "When do you ever force me to shop?" Tavares asked slowly.

"I need to know that you're back and in full effect, so go spend twenty stacks, and I'll know we're all good."

Tavares couldn't do anything but laugh nonstop, because she only heard those words in her dreams. The following day, she got up and dressed her children before she dropped them off at Doll's house while she went to the mall to do as Abdora had advised. She bought everything that she thought was cute for her, her sons, and Abdora. As she was leaving the mall, Tavares realized that was just what she needed. Tavares stopped at The Picture Palace before grabbing the boys, to pick up the pictures they'd taken a week earlier. They looked like night and day with their colors, but identical and beautiful in their looks. Tavares was just curious who her poor babies looked like.

By the time Tavares got home and brought her children into the house along with half of the mall she'd purchased, she was beyond exhausted. She felt like she'd officially worked out. When she was done bathing her sons, feeding them, and laying them down to sleep, Tavares made her way downstairs to the bags waiting for her to carry them upstairs. Looking at the massive amount of bags, Tavares decided that she'd done her part by carrying them in from the car. Abdora was going to have to do his part and carry them upstairs.

Tavares sat in the kitchen at the island and sorted the pictures before putting them in envelopes to mail out the following day. Abdora came in with pretty pink roses in his hand.

"Awww, those are so pretty," Tavares said.

"What the fuck is all that?" Abdora asked, spotting the massive amount of bags that were spread from the kitchen clear across the room into the living room.

"What you think it is?" Tavares asked, snatching the flowers to put them in a vase and water.

"Tavares, did you really spend twenty stacks?" Abdora asked, knowing the answer to his own question.

"Naww," Tavares smiled. "I only spent eighteen and a half."

"Whooptie fuckin doo," Abdora laughed. "You're crazy, but umm... who's carrying those bags upstairs? You buy, you carry," Dora mimicked in a Korean accent.

"Ohh no," Tavares said, putting the vase down on the counter and turning around. "I carried those bags in the house, and I didn't just buy myself stuff. So, you can carry them damn bags."

"I know, and I will," Abdora laughed, just liking to get Tavares all worked up over nothing.

He thought it was cute when she was calling herself going off.

"Come on, girl, stop playing, you know that Im'ma carry those bags. I just like to give you a hard time."

"Abdora, I swear you're too much. Ohh, and I found this black therapist online. I can do face-to-face sessions with her when I'm here and phone sessions if we're in Jersey. I emailed her early this morning. When I got home, I saw that she'd emailed me back. I gotta call her tomorrow to give her some info and to make my first appointment."

"I'm proud of you," Abdora said, leaning down and kissing Tavares's forehead.

"Thanks, but I just need to not go insane because that's what I'm feeling like right now."

"Ma, I ain't going to let you go insane on my watch. I love your little sex kitten ass too much."

Abdora's phone chimed and he said, "Hold up, Babygirl. What's up, Holton?"

Tavares's whole body tensed at the sound of his name. She still hadn't seen or spoken to Holton since the day at Dhara's house.

"We at the house, just chillin'. The boys are asleep and me and Tavares were just kickin it. Yeah, she's right here, hold on."

Abdora gave apologetic eyes as he passed the phone.

"He asked for you," Abdora whispered.

"Hello?" Tavares said dryly as she cut her eyes at Abdora like they were sharp daggers.

"Hi, Tavares. How are you?"

"I'm good, thanks. I was waiting for you to call, but it's been three weeks and you ain't got around to it, so I thought I would give you a call."

"Hmmmm, is that right?" Tavares said, giving the vibe that he'd wasted his time.

"Yeah, I just want to see you and talk to you in person. I promise that I'll leave you alone, if you'll just see me in person."

"Holton, I don't know about that."

"I'm not trying to start trouble or open wounds. I just want the opportunity to know you and my grandsons."

Tavares didn't know what she had against getting to know Holton, but she just wasn't interested.

"I just want to be your friend and get to know you. I would like to be part of the children's lives as our relationship grows. Tavares, trust me, if I'd ever known that you was out there, I would have found you and been there for you. This ain't a game, and the words that I'm telling you are real.

"I'm mad at your mother, just as you are, but for whatever reason, she feels like she did what she had to. I can't and won't speak for her or her actions. I just know that I got a daughter and two beautiful grandsons that I'm trying to have as a part of my life. Nothing more, nothing less."

Tavares listened but still wasn't convinced that she needed or wanted to be a part of Holton's life.

"Holton, how about this?" Tavares said, a fan of compromise. "I'll come see you in person, and it'll be win, lose, or draw. Either I walk away a part of your life or you leave me and my babies alone for the time being."

"That's fair," Holton said to his daughter, who drove a hard bargain just as he did. "You just call me and tell me when and where, and I'll be there."

Tavares hung up the phone and said to Abdora, "You're on pussy restriction for that one."

"Oh, fuck that. What the fuck you mean? Shit, I just got my pussy back, and now you want to put a nigga on restriction? Oh hell fucking no," Abdora said, pulling Tavares's hair.

"Yes, sir. Because of you, the saga continues. If you didn't pass me the phone, I wouldn't be going to see Holton in person."

Tavares was really mad, and she was just giving Abdora a dose of his own medicine. Abdora started running his fingers through her hair as he stood towering over her from behind.

"Would you stop playing in my hair before you put me to sleep right here?"

Abdora bent forward, pulling Tavares's hair to one side. As he began kissing her neck, Tavares jumped up off the stool.

"Ohh no. You trying to hit where you know I'll feel it, and I'm not fooling with you," Tavares laughed. "I'll see what I can do for you after you carry the bags upstairs," she said, winking her eye and walking out of the kitchen and upstairs to shower.

Abdora had a shot to prepare for the task ahead of him. After carrying the bags upstairs in only five trips, Abdora was feeling the downside of telling Tavares to go crazy at the mall. However, he knew for sure that after all those bags, he was about to slice and dice Tavares's ass real good. He was ready to take a shower and climb between the sheets with his shorty, whose pussy seemed to have gotten better since she gave birth. Abdora wasn't trying to make a baby, but as good as Tavares's cat was, it was hard to pull out, so a baby was bound to come. Abdora wanted another baby anyway, so he didn't mind if they got caught slippin'.

Abdora walked into the room and looked at the empty bed. He spotted Tavares on the balcony that overlooked the front of the house. She was wearing a Victoria's Secret hoodie and sweatpants with her hair pulled up in a ponytail. She was watching the stars and smoking a blunt. Tavares looked real at peace and in the zone, so Abdora didn't disturb her. Instead, he took a shower, checked on Elijah and Jeremiah, who were knocked out, and twisted up three more blunts before hitting the balcony to join Tavares.

"Damn, momma, what you doing, just staring into the sky?"

"Yeah, I was thinking and just wishing that I could be as far away as those stars are to Earth. Today was a good day. I didn't cry even once. The more I just try to take all this shit in, I'm just like *wow, why me?* Just when life was getting good, another roadblock falls in my way. I'm just tired of bullshit."

"Baby, bullshit is a part of life. You gotta deal with it, and just do it moving. And, this is something that you'll get through."

"I know. I just wish it was sooner and not later. I'm gonna hit that therapist lady up, then I'll get at Holton in the next week or so," Tavares said, picking up one of the blunts to spark it. "Abdora, you do know that I can handle the boys if you need to go to Jersey, right?"

"I know, momma. You make it very clear that you can take care of both boys all by yourself, but breathe easy. Shit's good in Brick City, so you got me here until you're ready to go back to Jersey. Plus, I couldn't leave until next week even if I wanted to. Holton got some big meeting going down this weekend coming up.

"I talked to my moms today and she misses the boys. She said to tell you that she misses you, too, and that she got you in her prayers. She wants to come out here if we ain't back in the bricks in the next week or so. I told her I would holler at you and get back to her."

"I don't need your mother and Meemaw with an APB out on me and their son, so we'll go back before they make it here. I just want to see this therapist chick, holler at Holton, see my friends, and we can go back next weekend."

Shaunda was at home, needing to go out, and decided that even though it was a Wednesday, she was going to call Tavares to see if she could bring the kids out to her house. Shaunda wasted no time when Tavares said it was no problem and gave her directions to her house. *Oh, I'm loving this being cool with Tavares thing*, Shaunda thought as she was getting her kids dressed.

"Mommy, where we going?" Ashaunda asked like a grown woman rather than the seven-year-old like she was.

"You're going to see your brothers and Tavares," Shaunda said and watched her kids get excited as their faces lit up like Christmas. "I'm going to come back and pick y'all up on Friday."

The kids were dancing like they'd just hit the lottery or something. Shaunda and her kids were out the door and at Tavares's beautiful house on the hill forty-five minutes later.

Shaunda knew she needed a glimpse at the inside when she saw the big house. She got the kids out of the car and walked up the stairs to the front door that was over ten feet tall. Shaunda wasn't expecting a man that was nothing but pure gorgeousness to greet her.

"Hi, I'm Shaunda. This is DJ and Ashaunda. We're looking for Tavares."

"Oh, she's in the kitchen. Come in."

Shaunda's eyes roamed as she walked through the front door. She got a glimpse of the dining room and the stairs that led to the top level. Shaunda was impressed as she admired the brown and tan lounging room and the huge room that was split into a huge kitchen and living room.

"Hi, Tavares!" the kids screamed as they rushed her with hugs and kisses.

"Goodness, but who missed me?" Tavares said, hugging and tickling them.

Damien and Shaunda's kids loved Tavares.

"Thank you so much, Tavares," Shaunda said.

"Oh, you're welcome. The circus is here, and now they give me a reason to take the boys."

"I love your house, especially the hardwood floors. You can tell these ain't no cheap floors. Oh, shoot. I didn't even see the yard, but I know it's huge, as big as this house is. You did a nice ass job with the decorating, too. I like how all the colors flow."

"Thanks," Tavares said, knowing that was the only reason Shaunda came in.

"Let me see these beautiful Hawaiian chunky butt, light-eyed babies," Shaunda said while getting on the floor where they were trying to move and roll over. "Oh my God, Tavares. They're fragging to dieee for. Wherever did you get these precious babies? Are you sure these are Damien's kids?" Shaunda said and busted out laughing.

Tavares wasn't laughing as she replied, "No, they aren't, Shaunda. They're Dora's, and I'm 99.9% sure of it."

Shaunda read between the lines and was a little shocked because she was playing, but she just took the info in and kept it moving.

"Y'all want some ice cream sundaes?" Abdora asked the kids.

"Yeah!" they replied at the same time.

"Come on then," Abdora said to the kids, who were drawn to him no sooner than he said *ice cream*. "Tavares got all kinds of ice cream, sprinkles, gummy bears, strawberries, M&Ms, caramel, hot fudge, and whipped cream."

"Tavares, you're good, girl. You got two beautiful babies and my kids for the next two days. You have a ball. I'm about to hit the highway. Thanks again."

"You're welcome. Just call me Friday, and I'll drive them in, because I'm going to go get my hair done. I'll get Ashaunda's hair done and DJ a haircut before I drop them off."

"Alright," Shaunda replied and she was gone, ready to party and get dicked down Wednesday and Thursday nights with her kids gone.

Tavares and Abdora spent the evening playing video games with the kids and taking turns tending to the babies. DJ and Ashaunda were in seventh heaven with all the junk food and fun around them. After a long evening of fun, everyone made it to bed with a long day ahead of them.

Abdora and Tavares got up the next morning, cooked breakfast, dressed all four kids, and together they headed to the circus at the Fleet Center.

"I'm not sure the babies are going to sit through the circus, but we're gonna see," Tavares said.

"They might sleep, but then again their nosey eyed asses might be up alert trying to see what the hell is going on," Abdora laughed.

They arrived at the circus. Tavares and Abdora had the babies in their matching Gucci carriers. Each of them carried a matching baby bag and a bigger kid on their arm. To their surprise, the boys were awake and enjoying all the animals in the show like they understood what they were watching. Tavares and Abdora couldn't believe they'd spent $1000 on what seemed like nothing at the circus, but it didn't matter since the kids were happy. The circus was raping people's wallets with their prices. Slushes in souvenir mugs were $20. Pictures were $20 apiece. They had toys that ranged from $15 to $40. The kids left happier than they'd been in a while.

"We gotta drop the babies off to hang with these kids," Tavares said as they walked toward the parking garage. "Let me call Doll."

Doll answered her cell like she was at a party.

"Ma, where are you and what is all that noise?"

"Oh girl, I'm downtown. I'm in Macy's. They were having this retarded sale, so I came down here and got me some comforters, pots and pans, shoes, and earrings. Girl, I only paid $200 for everything I bought, and it should have been like $600."

"Ma, you're crazy. I need you to do me a favor. I just took the babies, DJ, and Ashaunda to the circus. Can you watch the babies for me, so that Abdora and I can take the kids out? The babies ain't ready for their speed," Tavares laughed.

"Yeah, you got it. I'm about to leave from downtown right now. Meet me at my house in twenty minutes. I'm about to get in a cab, because I got too many bags for the train."

"Alright," Tavares said, hanging up and letting Abdora know that they were good.

Tavares found it ironic that they were spending time with Damien's kids while he was Lord knows where, doing Lord knows what, but if Abdora didn't mind, then she didn't either. Tavares was ready to fun the kids out, so that when they went to get the babies and got home, they would be ready to bathe and hit the beds. Her plan worked after bowling at Boston Bowl for two hours and running around the arcade for an hour. The kids cashed their tickets in from the games for prizes and were ready to get the twins.

"Did y'all have fun?" Abdora asked, knowing that they did because even he had fun.

"Yeah, y'all are mad fun," DJ said. "I can't wait to tell my mother all the fun we had today."

"I wish my mother and father would take us places like you do, Tavares," Ashaunda said, rolling her eyes and snapping her neck.

"Little girl, you're too grown," Tavares said, trying to not laugh as she was blown away by Ashaunda's tone, as usual.

When they picked the boys up from Doll's house, the kids went inside to say hello to their NaNa, and hurried back to the car, as if they weren't trying to get left.

"Doll, thank you so much."

"Girl, please! You ain't gotta thank me for watching my grandbabies. They don't cry or nothing. I was like wow, this is too easy. All they want to do is laugh and play. That must be what you do with their butts at home. They're too sweet and too precious. As a matter of fact, why don't you bring them back tomorrow with all their contraptions? I'll keep

338

them for the weekend, so you and Abdora can have some time to yourself."

"That sounds like a plan!" Tavares said ecstatically.

Friday morning came, and Tavares was going crazy, getting four kids dressed. Abdora had to go into Boston to pick his friends up from the airport, so Tavares was flying solo. After getting the bigger kids dressed, she dressed the babies, packed their bags to go to Doll's house, and headed to get dressed. Three hours later, Tavares had her car packed up, glad that her mommy of four duty was over. She dropped her babies off to Doll, kissed them goodbye, and headed to the hair salon. After DJ endured two long hours at the hair salon, she took him to Mattapan's Finest to get a haircut. The kids had more than a good time and couldn't stop kissing Tavares enough when she dropped them off. Tavares was childfree and ready to go hang out for the first time since she had her sons.

~Chapter 14~
Not the Average Relationship

Abdora arrived to the house to see that Tavares's car was in the garage. He walked in expecting a house full of kids, but it was the complete opposite. The house was spotless and as quiet as a ghost town. He went upstairs and found Tavares slipping on her thigh-high red leather boots that laced up the back and matched the sexy off-the-shoulder sweater she had laying across the bed.

"Those jeans are very complimenting to your backside. Where you going looking all sexy and it ain't with me?"

"To meet my father," Tavares said with no enthusiasm.

Abdora's eyes popped out of his head. He was speechless for almost thirty seconds. Tavares was stubborn, so he didn't think she was going to come around.

"That's what's up, momma. Where y'all meeting at?"

"I'm meeting him at Margianno's for dinner, then I'm going around the corner to the Roxy to meet the girls. You and your boys are more than welcome to meet us there."

"Sounds like a plan. So how you feel about going to meet Holton?"

"I don't want to go, but I know it's something that I need to do. Im'ma just get it over with because I know if I don't, I'll just keep putting it off. Truthfully, I know I'm angry at the wrong person, but I still feel some kind of way about not having a father in my life."

"Well, Babygirl, I'm proud of you, very proud of you. And, you look gorgeous."

"Thanks."

"Go in there and with an open mind. I can't speak for what kind of father Holton is, but I can say that he's a stand-up man of values, principles, and morals. I can truly say that outside of my father, he's the only man that I have ever looked up to."

Tavares listened and took it all into mind as she prepped herself to go talk to her father after twenty-two years, which she really had no desire to do. Tavares was dressed, sprayed on her Gucci Envy perfume, glossed her lips with some Mac Glass, and kissed Abdora goodbye on her way out the door.

Tavares valet parked her car at Margianno's and walked into the authentic Italian restaurant with major confidence. The lobby was packed with people waiting to be seated. She made it through the crowd and greeted the hostess with a friendly smile.

"Hello, I'm here for an 8:00 p.m. reservation. It's under Holton Montiago."

The hostess perked up when she heard that name and said, "Follow me."

Tavares had to smirk at the two dozen red roses in a pretty red vase in the center of the table. *I guess someone informed Holton of my favorite flowers*, Tavares thought as she took a seat.

"Mr. Montiago is downstairs. He said to inform him when you got here, so he should be up shortly."

Tavares waited patiently for Holton and checked her Facebook to kill time. The waiter came with bread.

"Hello there, beautiful lady. Would you like a drink?"

"Yes, a Patrón margarita with a sugar rim, please."

As the waiter left, Holton approached and took a seat across from his daughter.

"Hello, Tavares," Holton greeted his daughter as he kissed her cheek. "I've been looking forward to this all day. You know usually I have people on edge about meeting with me, but you've had me on pins and needles all day about seeing you."

"Why is that?" Tavares asked, trying to keep her attitude under lock and key.

"This isn't a meeting that takes places every day. You're my grown twenty-two-year-old daughter who I don't know, but I'm anxious to know."

"I can feel that, because I've been the same way all day as well. Holton, can we skip the small talk, because I have some things that I really need to get off my chest?"

"Well, shoot mija, because I see you're like me with the no bullshit and dancing around things."

"I did some thinking and some real soul-searching, and I had to dig deep to realize that this situation isn't your fault. Dolonda told you that she aborted me. You had no knowledge of me, so really how can I be mad at you? I'm not against getting to know you, but you need to allow me to process and come to terms with the fact that I have a father.

"For so long, I wondered what made you turn your back on me. I wondered why didn't you want me and what it would have been like if I had you in my life. Now that I have you here with open arms, it's a little overwhelming for me."

"Tavares, I can't apologize enough. If I'd known you were out there, I swear I would have come for you. We've missed your whole life, and while we can't recoup lost time, we can start from this day forward. I want to be your father,

342

your friend, and be a hell of a grandfather to my grandsons. We can do things at your pace and at your will. I'm just thankful for the chance to make up for lost time.

"If it's okay with you, I would like to have a father/daughter date once a month. That would give us time to build, get to know one another, and enjoy our new relationship."

Tavares was good with that and the tears in her eyes cosigned it.

"Can I just tell you that I want to punch Lilly in the face and stomp a hole in her? I'm extra pissed now that I know that it was my Dolonda she made you turn your back on, and that I'm the child she spoke about making you pick between."

Holton was thrown for a loop and his confused face asked the question before his mouth did.

"How do I know Lilly for us to have had that kind of conversation, you're wondering? I've known Lilly a long time, even before Damien brought me to her birthday party. Lilly has been buying crack from me for years. How ironic that my stepmother was my best customer. You didn't take care of me, but indirectly you did with Lilly having such a heavy habit."

Tavares had to laugh at the irony. Holton was in shock. He wasn't stunned to hear that Lilly smoked crack, because he'd known for years, although Lilly thought he was clueless. He was stunned because Lilly had a relationship all this time with his daughter they never knew about. Holton had to admit that Tavares was a mean combination of him and Dolonda.

"No, don't beat Lilly."

"I really want to, and the bad part is that I have mad love for Lilly. We don't have the typical dealer and buyer relationship. I mean, I fuck with Lilly and got mad love for her in my heart, but she played a dangerous game using a baby as a pawn. And, when she talked about Dolonda and the baby you turned on, it was like she found that shit cool. I promise if I beat the fuck out of her, me and her can be okay."

"No, mija, don't do it. I should have been man enough to not let her use my son as a bargaining tool. The bad part is that I truly, truly loved, and still do love, your mom."

Tavares's body tightened at the word *mom*.

"I pride my whole life on loyalty. I had been with Lilly, loved her, and just felt I owed it to her to stay and be a family. In reality, I wanted to be with Dolonda. Our love and relationship was just something different."

"Dolonda must hold what y'all had in the same regard, because even with you not being around, she never spoke ill of you. Never. The only thing she ever said about you was that you were a good man who made a bad decision."

"I have to agree with her on that," Holton said. "Have you spoken to her since Jersey?"

"No, and I have no desire to," Tavares said frankly.

"Tavares, I could never take up for or defend Londie for what she did by leaving you, but I will say that drugs are powerful. You know this since you're in the streets. They take ahold of you, and you become someone different. The Londie I knew would have never left you, or used drugs for that matter. Never. So, in a way, I feel responsible because I think my poor choice drove her to the edge. She loved me with no conditions, and I shattered her and broke her. She tried a coping method in her innocence and never knew it would steal her as a woman or mother. Forgiving her won't be easy, but I hope in time you'll try."

"I doubt it," Tavares said nonchalantly.

Having dinner and making small talk made Tavares happy that she'd made the decision to reach out to her father. She learned that she actually was a lot like Holton with their personalities, favorite foods, and interests in traveling, reading, and being loyal to a fault. Tavares departed dinner glad that she was going to give her father a chance.

Holton watched as Tavares got into her car and felt like he was given the best blessing that God could give him. He had received a daughter and two grandsons all in one. Tavares didn't know it, but the following Monday morning he would be going to see his trust lawyer to take everything out of Lilly's name and put it in Tavares's name. If anything happened to him, she and his grandsons would be set for life. Holton made a phone call to kill time while he waited for the valet to return with his new 2011 Jaguar.

"Hello," the depressed voice answered.

"Damn, it's the holiday season. Is that how you really feel?"

"Holton, what in the hell do you want?"

"I wanted to call you to say that I think that you're beautiful, and that I can't wait to see you."

Dolonda tried to suppress a smile but failed because it felt good to be complimented.

"I really called to tell you that I had dinner with Tavares, and it went great. She's receptive to us building a relationship. I feel like I just hit the lottery."

Dolonda was happy to hear that after robbing them of twenty-two years together.

"So, how about you come see me and we celebrate?"

"Holton, I keep telling you that I'm not messing with you. Why can't you get it through your thick skull?"

"Well, you ain't gotta mess with me. Just fly here and have lunch with me tomorrow."

Dolonda looked at the phone, because she knew for sure that Holton had lost his mind.

"Holton Montiago, why in the fuck would I do such a thing? Not only do I not like you, but I don't want to have to bust your wife's ass if she catches wind that we're having lunch."

"Listen, you let me worry about her, and you worry about packing your bag and getting to the airport to see me. There's an 11:50 p.m. flight from Newark International. Be on that flight, and I'll be waiting for you at Logan when you land."

"You know what? Im'ma call your bluff. Just maybe if I come tell you to kick rocks face to face, you'll get it," Dolonda said with major attitude.

She slammed the phone down but was happy inside to be going to see the only man she ever loved. She quickly packed a bag and asked herself why she was getting on that plane going to see Holton. She'd stood her ground for two months and wouldn't have anything to do with him. She wasn't sure why she had this time, but she was doing it. After a quick shower, Dolonda threw on some black jeans, charcoal gray booties, and a black and gray wrap sweater, and called a cab. While waiting on her flight, her thoughts were going a mile a minute about returning to Boston after so many months.

It was too early to go to the club, so Tavares made her way to Leslie's house to smoke a blunt before they headed out.

"I bet this bitch ain't even dressed," Tavares said to herself as she pulled up to Leslie's house and got out to ring the doorbell.

Tavares was left with her mouth hanging open when Leslie answered the door.

"OMG, am I dreaming or some shit?"

Leslie started laughing and replied, "What the hell you talking about?"

"I can't believe you're dressed."

"Oh, bitch, shut up. I thought I was riding with Mona-Lisa and I didn't want to hear her mouth. So, I started getting dressed early," Leslie laughed.

They got super high off some loud and kicked it about Jazz.

"Yo, Jazz be calling all the time asking about you and the boys."

"That's nice."

"Tavares, don't be like that. Don't you think you should at least talk to her? If y'all were two men, you would give each other dap and keep it moving. A bitch wouldn't be able to come in between y'all."

"Well, thank God I got a pussy and not a dick, some sense and ain't a fool. Leslie, that's my bitch, and I got mad love for her, but I got nothing for her. NOTHING!" Tavares yelled. "She was FUCKING my man of six years, swallowing his babies, and being a straight slimeball. I'm all set. If you stab me once, you'll stab me twice. I'm good on that shit."

"I feel you, Apple. I'm just saying that she sounds so sad that I kinda feel bad for her. Life's just so short, and God forbid something happened to one of y'all and this is how things were left. Not to mention, it's like we kinda ousted her from the crew."

"Well, that's on y'all. I never asked or told y'all to stop speaking to her or fucking with her for what she did to me."

They rolled out with another blunt for the car ride. The Roxy was cracking when they got downtown and the traffic was crazy.

"Damn, it ain't gonna be nowhere to park," Leslie said, looking up and down the streets.

"Bitch, I'm parking in the garage," Tavares said, turning left into the parking garage across the street from the club. By the time the ladies made it to the door, they spotted the rest of the group coming toward them.

"Damn, that was perfect timing," Randee said when they got up on them. "We was gonna park in here, too, but it be too crazy when you trying to leave the club."

"And, I started to park down the street in the lot where you are, but I didn't want to be stumbling too far when we come out drunk," Tavares replied.

When they approached the line that was too long, Tavares told her girls to wait right there while she walked to the front. She whispered something in the bouncer's ear that made him crack a smile, open the rope, and step aside. Tavares waved for her girls to come on. They all looked at each other skeptically.

"Oh, bitch, you gotta tell me what in the hell you just said to that man," Randee quizzed before they were even out of his earshot.

"I told him that my father is Holton Montiago and he said that we're to be taken care of all night."

"Damnnnnn, so I guess being his daughter has good perks already?" Mona-Lisa joked.

"I didn't even know this was going to be a perk. I told him that I was meeting y'all here, and he said to give that message to the 300-pound high-yellow, blue-eyed motherfucker at the door. So, that's what I did! Apparently a good friend of Holton's owns this place. Holton said we would be good for the night, so let's get it poppin'!"

The girls were greeted by a strikingly handsome olive-colored man in a sharply tailored black suit as they approached the top of the stairs.

"Hello, my name is Quinten, and I'll be taking care of you tonight."

Tavares looked at the man and said, "We don't need to be taken care of. We just didn't want to stand in that line."

"Well, Miss Montiago..."

"It's Del Gada," Tavares corrected.

"Well, Miss Del Gada, your father is a very important man around here, and as long as you're here, you'll be taken care of. There's a VIP section upstairs waiting for you ladies. Just tell your bartender what you ladies drink, and we'll stock your private bar."

"Thanks!" the ladies said in unison, looking at Tavares like she was crazy for not wanting the star treatment.

"My pleasure, ladies. If you need me, just have your bartender call me."

"Bitch, is you crazy?" Mona-Lisa asked.

"Okay!" Leslie cosigned.

"I just don't need the extra stiff treatment."

"Well, bitch, if daddy dearest wants another child, tell him I'm all in," Randee said with a serious face and tone.

The Roxy was huge. It was two levels and could easily hold about fifteen hundred people. The dance floor was on the first floor along with three bars, three bathrooms, and a huge stage at the front of the club where DJ Roxbury was playing all the hottest tracks. At each of the four corners of the club was a set of stairs that led to the second floor that was allotted for VIPs. The space was broken down into multiple VIP sections. Each section had comfy couches and chairs with a bar in the center of every section. Tavares and her girls had been given one of the few VIP sections that were three times the size of the normal ones and had their own bartender and bar.

The ladies were having a great time partying like rockstars, sipping Patrón, dancing, and watching the crowd below them getting it in. The club was shoulder to shoulder and filled to capacity. Tavares was in her own groove dropping it like it was hot when she felt someone behind her. She turned around to go the fuck off and realized that it was Abdora.

"You was about to catch a bad one," Tavares said, kissing his lips instead.

"I know, but I couldn't resist getting up on all that ass."

Abdora greeted Tavares's crew and then asked, "How y'all come up on this VIP section, because I know y'all didn't drop five stacks on it."

They all looked at Abdora like he was crazy when he told them the price.

"Get the fuck outta here," Mona-Lisa said. "That's not what they want for this shit."

"Yes, the fuck they do," Abdora said. "I just copped one for us, but shit, had I known y'all had one, I would have kept my dough."

"We didn't pay for this shit," Tavares informed him. "This was compliments of Holton. He said to tell them to take care of us, and this is what they gave us."

"Shitttt, I ain't even mad at y'all," Dora said, laughing.

Tavares, Randee, Mona-Lisa, and Leslie were having a good time with Abdora, Maniac, Bryce, Nas, and Buddah. They spent the night drinking, smoking, and talking shit.

"Yo, I gotta go to the bathroom," Leslie said, really not wanting to go downstairs in the thick crowd.

"Come on, I'll go with you," Randee said.

They made their way downstairs and waited in line at the closest bathroom. While standing in line, the ladies couldn't help but overhear the conversation between the chicks standing in front of them.

"So, how are things with you and Damien?"

"They're straight, but the nigga still won't let me stay the night at his crib that him and that stinking bitch was living in. And, the nigga sure don't pay like he weigh. He looks out here and there, but he ain't tricking no major dough," the chick said, laughing.

Leslie nudged Randee, and Randee just gave her a look that let her know they were hearing the same shit. By the time the ladies used the restroom and washed their hands, the gold-digger came out to a conversation between Randee and Leslie. They were standing at the sink purposely taking their time so the gold-digger could hear them.

"Only bum bitches hate on the next chick. I hate nothing more than a gold-digging bitch with a shovel on her back," Randee said, cutting her eyes through the mirror for the chick to see.

"Who you telling?" Leslie said. "Bitches so busy fucking for gifts that they can't get off their backs and get their own."

The chick didn't know if they were talking about her, but she suspected they were. She just dropped her head in guilt as she waited for them to finish at the sink.

"But, hey you know what they say," Randee chuckled. "Karma is a bitch, and what goes around comes around."

"Can you believe that bitch?" Leslie asked in disbelief as they exited the bathroom.

"Hell yeah, I can. Just be glad that it wasn't Tavares who heard her conversation, because security would be throwing us out right now," Leslie laughed, knowing her best friend very well.

The ladies pushed the nonsense they overheard out of their minds and headed back upstairs to finish having a good time. When they returned to the VIP booth, they noticed that Tavares and Abdora had disappeared.

"Where are the lovebirds?" Randee asked.

"They went to hit the dance floor," Mona-Lisa screamed over the music.

Abdora and Tavares returned forty-five minutes later to their friends having a good time without them. They were half drunk, still taking shots, and dancing.

It was nearing 2:00 a.m., so Abdora kissed Tavares and said, "We'll meet y'all outside."

Tavares already knew what it was. They had to go get their girlfriends just in case anything popped off. The ladies made their way downstairs where the general population was exiting. There were stairs to the left and the right that met at the bottom of the staircase. The ladies exited to the right. They were kicking it on the stairs when Tavares looked across to the other stairway and couldn't believe her eyes.

"What? What's wrong?" Mona-Lisa asked, trying to see what Tavares saw.

Everyone saw what she was looking at, and they knew it was about to get ugly.

"Oh shit," Mona-Lisa said. "Tavares, that shit ain't about nothing. You're here with your man, and he's here with that bitch. Who gives a fuck?"

"Oh no, bitch, it's about something, alright. That's the bitch he got caught in my house with."

As they neared the bottom of the steps, Damien spotted Tavares and her girls and knew it was about to get nasty.

Tavares yelled across the stairs, "Oh, that's how you doing it, Damien? Bringing trash bag bitches to the club like they more than jump-offs, I heard that!"

Randee laughed, Leslie gasped, and Mona-Lisa just shook her head. The chick saw Tavares and was nervous from their last encounter but decided to play tough since she had Damien on her side.

"Don't be mad because he stepped his game up and don't want you."

"Bitch, he stepped his game down. You was a jump-off that he upgraded to his main PART-TIME bitch, because we both know you ain't wifey material, you punk bitch. Get your life, bitch!"

Everyone on the stairs was soaking up the yelling session.

"And, furthermore, bitch, you ain't got a prize. You got a trash bag nigga just like yourself. But, don't worry, because that nigga can't and won't save you once we get outside."

The chick contemplated if Tavares was telling the truth. She decided that Tavares was wrong, so she kept flipping off at the mouth.

"Damn, what, you mad 'cause he stopped cheating himself and treated himself? You can keep hating that I got your man, because he ain't going nowhere."

"Oh boo, he ain't my man, but I'm glad you're gangster for the public. When we get outside, Im'ma show them how you're all mouth like that night I busted your ass and kicked you down the stairs into the street naked. And, I dare them three mutt-faced bitches with you to jump in," Tavares laughed and said no more.

"Yo, Tavares, there's a time and place for everything, and this ain't it," Mona-Lisa tried to reason. "Abdora isn't going to be feeling you at the club fighting over Damien."

"Mona, I don't give a fuck about what you say, what Dora says, or anyone says. I'm fucking that bitch up when I get outside. This ain't about Dame. I've moved on, and I'm very happy with the man I upgraded to. She wanna play gangster, so Im'ma show her not to let her mouth write a check that her ass can't cash."

"Hollaaaaa," Randee said and burst out into laughter.

She knew Tavares meant business, so she started taking off her jewelry and pulling her hair up in a ponytail. Mona-Lisa and Leslie followed suit.

Holton and Dolonda were at the Copley Marriott in a suite catching up and reminiscing about old times. Holton's phone was blowing up. Every time he saw *wifey* come across the screen, he just rolled his eyes and went back to conversing with Dolonda.

"I think you should call Tavares while you're here."

"I want to, Holton, but I think I need to wait for her to reach out to me. I'm glad that you two sat down and all went well, but I'm not sure she's going to be as receptive to me."

"Well, you won't know unless you try."

"You're right, but I just don't know. I love my baby. I love her to pieces, and I did her wrong, dead ass wrong. So, if she doesn't forgive me or come around, I have no one to blame but myself."

"I think she'll come around. She just needed some time and space to process everything. She can't change the past, but I can't see her wanting to miss out on the future."

"We'll see. So what you going to do about your wife that keeps calling you?"

"Exactly what I been doing, ignoring her. She don't want shit."

Dolonda burst into laughter at Holton's *fuck her* tone.

"I love Lilly, but seeing you and chasing you for the last few months has taught me that I'm not in love with her. I'm getting older, and I want to spend my life in love, not just with someone because I feel obligated to them."

"Are you trying to say that you're in love with me?" Dolonda joked.

"Come on, Dolonda. Cut the shit. You already know I'm in love with you. Been in love with you since the moment I laid eyes on you over twenty years ago."

"Holton, I'm not convinced. You always had the gift of gab, so it sounds good," Dolonda chuckled.

"I'm gonna go take a shower and wash my hair. I'll be back."

"Good, because I wanna taste you. Oops, I mean smell you smelling all good," Holton said with a slick look and wink of the eye.

Dolonda didn't entertain Holton. She made her way to the bathroom to take a long, hot shower to help get her thoughts together.

Leaving the club was crunker than the inside of the club. Niggaz were plotting on chicks to take home for the night. Chicks were peeping the men, trying to see who was who and who had what, so they could figure out who they could get at. Other guys were in the cut, lurking on their enemies. The Humboldt Street Raiders were watching the pretty niggaz from Heath Street bag chick after chick.

"These niggaz are so worried about pussy that they don't even know we on them," Kevin Day and Landell Jackson both laughed.

"That's how I like it," D White added. "Im'ma lay one of these niggaz down for my little homie, York."

London, Wally, and Jackson were collecting number after number. Just when Tavares and her girls came out of the club ready for war, they stepped in their path.

"Damn, ladies, slow down. Y'all looking like y'all gonna hurt someone."

"Something like that," Randee said, looking around for the punk bitch who was lucky enough to make it out of the club before they did.

"Where the fuck this bitch get missing to that fast?" Tavares asked no one in particular as she was burning up inside.

"Damn, Babygirl. Don't get all dirty fucking a bitch up," London laughed, but he was feeling Tavares's fire and could tell that she was 'bout it.

"There that bitch go," Mona-Lisa said, pointing down the block.

The enemy was standing around like she thought it was a game. Tavares was about to show her just how real shit was. The fellas followed, wanting to see the drama.

"Damien, so you fucking with this trick bitch!? First, I catch you in my house with her, now you got the nerve to be parading her in public?"

"Come on, Tavares. Go on with that dumb shit. Me and you ain't together, so it don't matter who the fuck I'm out with."

Abdora stood across the street and watched everything unfold. His mans went to make a move, seeing the argument between Tavares and Damien.

Dora said, "Wait. Let's see how this plays out, because this may be his last day breathing."

"Damien, you're right. You can fuck whatever hoe bitch you want to," Tavares laughed, then turned her attention to Damien's chick. "Talk that shit now, bitch," Tavares said while poking Talesha in the forehead.

"Bitch, you the one that's so gangster. Do what you do."

That's exactly what Tavares did. She commenced to whooping Talesha's ass. She punched her in the face and slammed her to the ground.

Her girls went to jump in, and Randee said, "Im'ma eat every last one of you bitches alive, if you dare think about it."

Damien tried to stop the fight, but his niggaz from Heath Street said, "Nah, nigga. Let shorty get her shit off."

Damien still tried to break it up, but it was no stopping Tavares. She was on the ground fucking Talesha up and punching her in the face. Out of nowhere, Kevin, Landell, and Dwight came through the crowd letting off shots at their enemies without even caring about the stray bullets that were flying. Abdora and his mans whipped out and started running across the streets when they heard the shots in the vicinity of where Tavares and her girls were.

Humboldt was shooting at Heath Street, Heath Street was shooting back, and Dora and his boys were shooting at everyone. It was nothing but chaos with bullets flying and people running for cover. Leslie was under a car praying that her friends were okay. Mona-Lisa was between two cars asking God to please spare her friends. Randee was running with the mass of people. Tavares was caught in the cross-fire and lay out on the ground bleeding massively from her chest. She tried to move, but she began going into shock as she lay looking at Damien bleeding from his mouth, choking on his own blood. That was all Tavares remembered before she passed out.

Dora saw about fifteen or twenty people laid out on the ground when the shots stopped. He heard police sirens and told his mans to take the guns and get missing.

"I gotta find Tavares," Dora said with a bad feeling.

People who had ducked for cover were now standing around looking at the blood bath. Dora went through the crowd and stopped when he saw Tavares's friends lying around her screaming and sobbing. He almost panicked seeing Tavares laid out on the pavement and not breathing, but he caught himself. He scooped her limp body up and ran a block down the street to the Tufts Medical Center emergency room.

"I need a doctor! I need a doctor!" Abdora screamed.

An emergency team came running with a stretcher and took Tavares's lifeless body. By the time the police and the ambulance arrived on the crime scene, there was a count of seventeen people shot. Four were dead and thirteen were wounded. Some were going to make it and some weren't. Tavares's friends were hysterical in the waiting room of Tufts Medical Center. There were about fifty more people waiting to hear about their loved ones. Most of them were screaming, sobbing, and crying.

Tavares had taken three hits to the chest. Two of the three bullets were inches from her heart. Dora was trying to be the calm one, but he didn't know what he was going to do if Tavares didn't make it. Mona-Lisa realized that someone was going to have to be strong, so she calmed herself down.

"I'm gonna go call Doll. Damien got hit too, so shit's really about to be crazy," she as she dialed Doll's number.

Mona-Lisa didn't want to be the bearer of bad news, but she did what she had to do. After Doll screamed for ten minutes, she said she would call Rollo and get her mother to get the twins, then she would be on her way. Doll thought she was in a bad dream but realized it was a harsh reality that both Damien and Tavares had been shot.

Dora couldn't take all the madness in the waiting room. He went to call his boys and Holton. He knew that when Holton found out, the city was going to be in for a bad one. He didn't know who the niggaz were that were shooting, but he highly doubted that they would be living to talk about it once Holton found out. Dora dialed Holton's number time after time but got no answer.

"Holton, your phone is blowing up," Dolonda said, half asleep.

"Fuck Lilly," Holton said, not even opening his eyes as he was snuggled tightly with Dolonda.

The phone was going off time after time.

After the tenth time, Dolonda sat up and said, "Answer that shit, or it's going out the fucking window."

Holton rolled over, slid out of bed, and retrieved his phone from his pocket. Seeing so many missed calls from Abdora made him wake up completely.

"Something ain't right. It's Abdora calling me."

Dolonda sat up and said, "Well, hurry up and call him back. Something could be wrong with our daughter or grandkids."

Holton hit send on his phone and rang Abdora back.

Before Dora could say *hello*, Holton asked, "What's wrong?"

"Tavares and Damien have been shot. I don't know about Damien, but Tavares's condition ain't looking too good. The bullets are too close to her heart."

Holton froze and dropped the phone. He couldn't think, breathe, or move. Dolonda knew it was something serious based on Holton's reaction. She scooted out of bed and picked up the phone while Holton fell in the chair and started crying.

"Abdora, this is Dolonda."

Abdora was shocked but didn't have time to question the two of them being together.

"Yo, if y'all are in Boston, get to Tufts Medical Center now," Dora said and hung the phone up.

~Chapter 15~
When Tragedy Strikes

Dora placed calls to his mother, his boys, and his grandmother to inform them of what had happened to Tavares. Abdora's mother was going to be on the first flight out. Meemaw told Abdora she was gonna pray for Tavares and to call her with every update. Dora had his mans on the mission of finding out what stupid crash dummy ass niggaz started shooting in the crowd. Them niggaz had signed their own death certificates. Doll made it to Tufts Medical Center to learn that Damien was in a coma with a strong possibility that he wasn't going to make it. He was shot in the chest, head, and neck. Damien was holding on, but barely. Doll broke down and had a panic attack.

Dolonda and Holton came in the hospital. When Abdora and Tavares's friends saw them together, they were all asking the same question in their heads, *what the fuck are they doing together?* Holton gave Abdora dap and asked if there were any updates.

"Not as of yet. We're just waiting right now."

Dolonda greeted Tavares's friends as she read their minds with the skeptical responses they gave her.

"What happened?" Dolonda asked.

The ladies began to fill her and Holton in, but Holton's phone kept going off. Lilly was still blowing his phone up, since she hadn't seen him all day, and he hadn't come home. Holton finally answered.

"What the fuck do you want?"

"Holton, why are you speaking to me like that? I was worried about you."

"I'm fine. I'm at the emergency room. Tavares and Damien have been shot."

"Oh my God! Nooooooo!" Lilly yelled. "Well, where are you so I can come?"

"You don't need to come," Holton said, looking at Dolonda, knowing that it would be another bloodbath, and hung up.

Lilly didn't want Holton to be alone at a time like this, so she called around until she found out where Tavares was. Within twenty minutes, she was on the highway headed to Boston to be by her husband's side. What was usually a forty-minute ride, Lilly made in twenty minutes by doing 100 miles per hour all the way from Taunton to Boston. She left her car double-parked in the street and rushed through the emergency room door. She almost passed out when she entered the waiting room and saw Holton with his arms around a sobbing Dolonda. Lilly blacked out.

"You no good motherfucker!"

Everyone looked around to see who she was talking to. Tavares's friends knew that if her mother was anything like her, it was about to get ugly.

"Is this why you couldn't answer my calls? You been shacked up with this no good, home-wrecking bitch."

Dolonda hopped up to fuck Lilly up, but Holton and Abdora restrained her.

"Lilly, I'm warning you. This ain't the time nor the place," Dolonda said, not wanting to kill Lilly tonight.

"Fuck you, you cum-guzzling whore. You still trying to get my fucking husband after twenty-something years!"

Everyone watched Dolonda's face go from pale to fire-engine red and knew it was about to be ugly.

"Bitch, I'll mop you all up and down this motherfucking hospital if you dare disrespect the fact that my fucking daughter is lying in a hospital bed fighting for her life!"

Doll tried to pull the old familiar face out of the waiting room, but she wouldn't budge.

"Bitch, fuck you, and fuck Holton!"

At that, Holton was fed up. He let Dolonda go and grabbed Lilly by her hair while he dragged her out of the waiting room kicking and screaming with everyone looking and respecting his gangster.

"Listen here, you crack-smoking, maggot ass bitch. I will kill you if you don't get the fuck outta here disrespecting my daughter and her mother, who might lose a child tonight."

Lilly began to cry. Not only had Holton threatened her life and meant it, but he even threw her habit in her face.

"So you fucking Dolonda now?"

"Yo Lilly, let's cut the dumb shit and this charade. You forced me to turn my back on Dolonda once, and I won't do it again. She's the mother of my child, and I'm going to stand by her through this."

"Answer my fucking question. ARE YOU FUCKING HER?"

"Am I fucking her? No. Would I like to fuck her? Yes."

Lilly just screamed and sobbed, "Holton, you can't leave me for Dolonda!"

"Lilly, you want to smoke crack. For a long time, I tried to understand, but I can't do it anymore."

"Holton, if you leave me, I'll tell the police all about your business."

Holton almost got mad. Instead, he caught himself and chuckled while biting down on his lip in anger.

Then, he snarled at Lilly, "I'm going to tell you one more time to get the fuck outta here. If you don't, I'm going to put you in a room next to my daughter. Your little threat means nothing to me, because you'll be dead before you make it to the station."

Lilly had been with Holton long enough to know that he didn't make idle threats, so she did as he said. She sobbed all the way to her car and went to get high yet again. It was the wee hours of the morning and the sun was barely rising when Lilly made it to Orchard Park Projects to get high. She had a monkey on her back and was in desperate need of an escape from all the pain she was feeling. She drove her cocaine-white Benz around until she found an early morning dealer.

After spending $500, Lilly was ready to get high on another level. She proceeded to a smelly, grimy crack house and paid the owner of the house with a 50-rock. She made her way to a corner with a makeshift pipe and went to town getting higher and higher. Several hours passed, and Lilly was still at it. She was feeling like her heart was going to beat through her chest. It was beating rapidly, but she ignored the feeling and loaded her pipe with more crack.

Holton stood outside the hospital and decided to call his mother. He still hadn't shared the news with her or his family about Tavares, having grandkids, or Dolonda, but he needed to talk to his mother. It was 6:00 a.m., therefore he knew she was up starting her Sunday dinner. Holton had to crack a half a smile when she answered in her thick Trinidadian accent.

"Mommy, we need to talk."

"It must be good, boy. You call dis damn time of de mawnin."

Holton took a long sigh before he said, "Mommy, mommy, mommy, I don't even know where to start."

"Well, if you don't damn know, what in de hell you call for?"

"I have a twenty-two-year-old daughter who's been shot, and she's fighting for her life."

"God Lawd, Father God, save her Lawd. Save my grandbaby."

"Her mother is the woman I loved way back when Lilly got pregnant."

"Hmmm...that spic gal."

Holton laughed, "Yes, mommy, the Dominican girl. And, I just told Lilly that it's over."

"Well, tank ya, Jesus. Tank ya. About damn time now. I never thought you would get smart and leave that messy ass gal. It sounds like you got it together to me. So, what you need mommy to say? Mommy taught you well. When in doubt, you pray and give it to God."

"You not gonna ask about your granddaughter?" Holton asked, seeking approval from his mother as he'd done his whole life.

"Nope. I'm gonna come see her when she's ready for visitors. She's twenty-two. That tells me you didn't know, because you mommy and daddy no raise no deadbeat piece of shit fadders and mudders. If you love her mother, be with her mother and treat her good. You always say you love that gal and if times had been different you would have picked her. Now you have a second chance to do it. I help you pack Lilly's damn shit and put her de hell out."

"Mommy, I love you."

"I love you more, Holton. And, you call me and tell me about my granddaughter. Wait, what the poor chile name?"

"Tavares."

"Awww, I like that. Well, you pray, and I'm going to pray as well for my new granddaughter. Call me and keep me posted."

Holton did as his mother said and prayed.

He asked God, "How did my life get here? I gained a daughter and grandkids, and I'm rekindling with the love of my life. I just told Lilly it's over, and now my Babygirl is fighting for her life. GOD, please don't take her. Please. We have so much time to make up for. I just want to enjoy it, her, and my grandkids. I'm begging you to please watch over her and protect her through this."

Holton wasn't religious, but he was spiritual. When the situation called for him to do the right thing, he did it. He concluded that was why God was always good to him. He finished his prayers and made his way back inside. Tavares's friends and Dolonda were in a corner chitchatting when he returned. They were keeping her spirits up by telling her all about Tavares. Doll's eyes looked like she was a million miles away. She snapped out of her daydream when she heard Holton come back. Before Holton could fully enter the emergency room, she approached him.

"Can we talk for a moment?"

"For what, Doll?"

"Where did your wife go?"

"I don't know where my soon-to-be ex-wife went. If you're concerned, let me give you her number since y'all are old pals and all."

Doll caught the subliminal cheap shot.

"You know what, Holton? My son is fighting for his life just like your daughter is, so miss me with your bullshit, please and thanks."

"*You* sparked this conversation with *me*," Holton snarled.

Before the conversation could go south, a few doctors came in and began to call the names of a few patients. When Tavares Del Gada was called, Dolonda, Abdora, Holton, Doll, and all her friends sprang to their feet and surrounded him in a matter of seconds. They'd been waiting for what seemed like an eternity, and they were tired of pacing the floors waiting to hear that she was out of the woods. The doctor was hesitant about the words that were about to come out of his mouth.

"Hi, I'm Dr. Grooper. It was a very unfortunate situation that took place tonight. Tavares came in with some very life-threatening injuries. With all of you being here, I can tell that Miss Del Gada is very loved. My team has worked and worked. Her first surgery was a success but her second wasn't. It's with my most heartfelt sympathy that I have to tell you that Miss Del Gada didn't make it. We did everything that we could."

He made it no further with his conversation before everyone started screaming, bawling, and crying uncontrollably. No one was prepared for those words, but he had indeed said them. *Tavares didn't make it.* Abdora punched a hole in a wall. Dolonda was weak and uncontrollably yelling and crying with Holton holding her up. Tavares's friends were hugging and consoling each other, and Doll was speechless. They weren't ready to say goodbye to Tavares just yet, but the sad news the doctor had just given them left them no choice. It was time to be strong and come together to lay her to rest.